CONQUEST

CONQUEST

JEREMY FOX

Matador
9 Priory Business Park,
Wistow Road, Kibworth Beauchamp,
Leicestershire. LE8 0RX
Tel: 0116 279 2299
Email: books@troubador.co.uk
Web: www.troubador.co.uk/matador
Twitter: @matadorbooks

ISBN 978 1800463 837

British Library Cataloguing in Publication Data.
A catalogue record for this book is available from the British Library.

Printed and bound in Great Britain by 4edge Limited
Typeset in 11pt Sabon by Troubador Publishing Ltd, Leicester, UK

Matador is an imprint of Troubador Publishing Ltd

When one considers how many ... facts – habits, beliefs –
we take for granted in thinking or saying anything at all,
how many notions, ethical, political, social, personal, go
to the making of the outlook of a single person, however
simple and unreflective, in any given environment, we
begin to realise how very small a part of the total our
sciences – not merely natural sciences, which work by
generalising at a high level of abstraction, but the human,
"impressionistic" studies, the methods of the novelists,
of the writers of memoirs, of students of human affairs
from every angle – are able to take in.

Isaiah Berlin: The Sense of Reality, 1953

As for the gods, it seemed to be the same thing whether
one worshipped them or not, when one saw the good and
the bad dying indiscriminately.

Thucydides: History of the Peloponnesian War
(circa 415 BCE)

PROLOGUE
MEXICO, TENOCHTITLAN – 1563

Alva Tlacuilotl

How often have I hesitated to begin this history! What could be the value of unearthing memories the gods have buried, of rooting in the ashes of extinguished fires, of recalling a past that has long since fled? Could an old man's faltering powers hope to reconstruct the landscape through which he must travel to retrace his steps? Where are the ways, the footprints? Others have trampled them; rains have washed over them; dust has settled in their hollows; they are shaped like mud by every last encounter.

I have wondered too about the form and language in which I should set this down. Nature should lead me to the pictures and signs of home, but home is no more, and if I were to write in our way, who in the generations to come would understand me? Since Zumárraga, their high priest, condemned our books to the flames, we must no longer write them. He's dead at last, thanks be to the lord in whose name he spoke, but our works like our gods have fallen to the earth as ash, and whoever mourns their passing may find themselves stoking the fire with their flesh.

So I resort to the conquerors' tongue, though it be forked like a lizard's and delivers lies as readily as truth. And I am conscious of the poor resources at my command, for I have found there few devices able to bear the images dwelling in my thoughts. Therefore, I ask whoever comes upon these lines to remember that I grew up in a place that henceforth can exist only as legend, and to accept that I can offer here no more than the thin scratchings that the poorest of creatures make as they pass through life.

They say that once the first pages are complete, a book seizes hold of its author like a serpent its prey. Let me hope it is so, for these words have seemed like a slow crawl towards death. How often have I taken up the pen only to lay it down again, lost in a phrase, discouraged by the size of the task I have set myself, even distracted by a triviality: the recollection of a duty overlooked, a call of nature – the latter being a detail I wouldn't trouble you with were I not struck even as I write with how the simplest act can bear a purpose beyond itself. When Father Hernández isn't looking, a corner of the churchyard serves where the pitaya spreads out against the wall. Countless times I've peed in that spot. I see it as a reminder that defeat is not capitulation. Were this not so, perhaps I would lack courage to set out on this journey. For are not writing and peeing both gestures of defiance?

Every stone in that wall, in our church, and in the priest's house next door came from the temple of Mixcoatl, god of the hunt, who was the guardian of this place. I watched the temple being torn down. Matter of fact I participated in the desecration since I was what they call a deputy foreman in the demolition squad, an honour bestowed by the overseer because he thought I could get others to do his bidding. My job was to supervise the smashing of our idols, and to make sure that blocks stained with sacrificial blood were broken up and scattered so that no one could re-use them.

I cheated, ordering the men to smash as little as possible and to conceal blood-stained stones beneath clean ones before taking them to the construction site. Unbeknown to our masters, the church of San Idelfonso carries marks of sacrifice in its very fabric. No doubt the Christian god would have punished me if he'd known. Though maybe he does know (they say he sees everything) but considers I've already been punished enough, at least in this world. More likely I don't merit his attention given that I'm only a simple retainer, servant to a parish priest; a decline to be sure from my old status, though not the worst job, nor the worst fate when you remember what all of us have been through in our time. If this is my tariff, I pay it without complaint.

Before the defeat, we were the slave-owners. No shame in that for either party. Only prisoners of war became slaves, and families who sold themselves to liquidate their debts. Emperor Itzcoatl's mother was a slave. So too my grandmother, who was a flower of her time by all accounts. She served Emperor Axayácatl in ways that beautiful women are apt to do. Hence my own mother was born in the palace and lived among the nobility until Axayácatl passed on; after which we were set up in a fine house and garden overlooking the lake, just by the Tacuba Causeway, a privileged spot that the old emperor bestowed on our family in recognition of my grandmother's services. Maybe that's why, when Moctezuma Xocoyotzin came to the throne, he chose my mother to suckle his daughter Tecuichpo. Noble families whose wives lacked milk usually chose wet-nurses on account of their health and good looks, but with Tecuichpo…Well, let's just say there may have also been a family connection.

Tecuichpo.

Even today, in my old age, I hardly can think on that name without tears. I suppose I loved her from the moment I saw her – as a sister at first, and then gradually as something more.

That something could never have been a good idea, for the daughters of monarchs are instruments of power and must go where policy demands. Looking back, I can see that our story could only follow a twisted path. We travelled blindly, unable to imagine even in our nightmares the destination to which it led.

I remember her arriving as a newborn, carried by a palace servant in a tiny cradle. Measured in Christian years, I must have been around seven or eight at the time. As soon as the servant had left, my mother clapped our distinguished guest onto one breast and my sister Xochitl, who had also just come into the world, onto the other. That's how I pictured them both in the first months, drinking from those soft swollen mounds that in my childish mind I saw as twin *zapotes* brimming with juice.

Tecuichpo was married shortly after birth to Atlixcatzin, a court favourite whom the emperor had marked out as his successor. But Atlixcatzin died in mysterious circumstances (there were suspicions, never clarified, that he had fallen out of favour and been murdered). That was doubtless why Tecuichpo didn't return to Atlixcatzin's home after weaning but stayed with us until the onset of womanhood, at which time it was no longer seemly for her to dwell in the company of unmarried men like my brother and me.

How well we lived in those "Tecuichpo years"! Never did we want for the necessities of life, even after my father – bless his memory – surrendered his life in battle to Kurikaweri, god of our enemies the Purépecha. Deliveries came daily, courtesy of the palace, not just essentials, but costly delicacies like chocolate, *zacualzapotl*, *necuazcatl* and *huitlacoche*.[1] A princess had to have everything of the best.

"The gods smile on our home," mother liked to say, hastily adding, as if to reassure them of our humility, that "We must share our good fortune." And she'd at once make up a basket of maize and *tamales* to give away to the poor.

Yes, the gods smiled, at least until the day Moctezuma invited

---

1   Custard apples, ant honey and corn truffle.

x

the Spaniards into our city. Then they ceased smiling and bowed their heads.

Some say the emperor behaved as he did because he saw further and understood the limitations of action. Could he have known of our coming defeat, have seen it in the heavens? Or was he a weak, vacillating shame on our people and on the memory of all we have loved and lost? Did we not, in the end, hurl stones at him and call him a Spanish dog? How could we, the strongest nation on earth, have delivered our fate into the hands of such a man? Should the blame be ours? Time was when we the people elected our leaders, choosing them for their wisdom and bravery. Little by little, without notice or ceremony, we lost our way. Leaders became kings, kings became emperors, and thereafter power remained with them and their families. Moctezuma ruled not by election but by right of blood. Given a vote, would we not have made a better choice? Doubts will never leave those of us who bear the scars of history in our hearts.

Be that as it may, what we were is long gone and gone so absolutely that we who remain from the old days know in the deepest reaches of our soul – I use the Christian term for want of a better – that there will be no return. No words can record the pain such knowledge inflicts. Nor, in truth, can I bring myself to accept the finality of the sentence passed upon us. Something must and will endure. That thought alone drives me to this history which is mine and may one day be our people's if Quetzalcóatl so wills. But I must begin with place and time. For these have endured thus far in memory and if I fail to record them now, they will be gone forever.

ONE

TENOCHTITLAN – 1563

Alva

"We never know how important people are until they've left us," my mother used to say. We understood this as a mild reprimand, a warning – ironic as it turned out – that in the natural order of things, she would pass onto the next life before her children, and only then would we fully appreciate her. She never said more on the subject, and I doubt whether any of us gave it much thought. Only as dusk falls on my time among the living do I see how much I owe what I have become to others: to her of course, but also to those who, by love or example, have rescued me from my stupidities, and from despair.

Such a one was my brother, Atzahuatl. My survival to these advanced years I owe as much to him as to anyone, though whether he placed a curse on me or a grace, I hardly dare to ask. Called to the gods at an early age, he escaped the disgraces a long life has forced upon me.

1510–1520

We bore little resemblance to each other, my brother and I. A decade my senior, he stood a head and more taller than me even when I was fully grown. Broad-shouldered, with hands as generous as platters and feet that preceded him into a room, he resembled an oversize sculpture, solid, difficult to move but with an inner fire that smoked from time to time, like the volcano Popocatépetl. By contrast, I reached no more than medium height in my prime, and though blessed with quickness of limb and mind, could not compete with him in strength of arm or, I think, in generosity of spirit. You may perceive from this description that I loved and admired him.

By tradition, Atza would have followed our father's profession as a potter and tool-maker. But he determined to better himself and, with mother's help and a little push from the palace, got accepted as an importer and trader in the Tlatelolco market, a closed shop if ever there was one, normally impossible for an outsider to penetrate because it was controlled by a group of families – *Pochtecas* – who kept to themselves and jealously guarded their rights.

Atza specialized in clothing and would travel far afield in search of good cloth and clever designs. I always looked forward to his return from these business trips because he would come loaded with gifts for the family and with stories of his encounters with the Maya, the Zapotec, the Huichol, the Tarahumara who spoke different languages and worshipped different gods. Sometimes he would come nursing wounds as well, for traders routinely had to fight off highway thieves and handle encounters with hostile cities. Once, he returned on a stretcher carried by a couple of soldiers who'd found him on a wayside. He'd got into trouble in Oaxaca over a deal and suffered a horrible beating at the hands of some local merchants who had left him to die.

In more than one respect, I envied Atza. People said he took after our late father, which I suppose gave him a sense of lineage and identity. No one made such suggestion about me. Instead, gossip bestowed me with a variety of other fathers: a soldier billeted in our house shortly before my birth, a slave from Cholula who later won his freedom and returned home, our neighbourhood priest with whom I apparently shared features, even the emperor because my mother had known him as a little girl! My mother smarted under the innuendo, but refused to budge from the official story – which was that Atzahuatl and I shared the same father and that it would always be so.

To tell the truth, I too have harboured doubts about my mother's version. Rumours of her extra-marital activities circulated too freely for me to be able to dismiss them out of hand. Like my grandmother, she had been considered a great beauty. Pretenders were to be expected, and my father was often called up for army duty which meant prolonged absences from home. Once, when I was a youngster, he was away from *Atemoztli* to the end of *Teotleco* – nine months in the Christian calendar.

Having no wish to see my mother shamed, I hid my misgivings from her. Perhaps because of this, I began hiding other things too, at first my thoughts, then my activities. By my fifteenth birthday, I had fallen in with a group of roughnecks who had taken over a couple of streets in the Azcapotzalco district. I took up gambling, thinking myself a dab hand at *patolli*.[1] At the Telpochcalli where I was supposedly undergoing military training, I began skipping classes. More than once fellow students found me lying drunk in the street, and had to sneak me back into the barracks.

Punishments came my way: lashings, confinements, even threats of turning me over to slavers, or worse to the temple of Xipe Totec for flaying and sacrifice. My behaviour leaked out to the neighbourhood and served to confirm the gossip about my origins. People asserted that my father could not possibly have

---

1   Board game played for stakes.

sired so feckless a creature as myself, and therefore my mother had, indeed, betrayed him. Even this renewed slur on her failed to shake me. As if to challenge the muckrakers, I took ever greater risks both with her reputation and my future. One of the gang leaders, an immigrant from Tetellan who had relations with fellow criminals outside the city, introduced me to *tlapatl*.[2] I became a slave to the sensations it produced. Zolin – the gangster – never lacked supplies but pretended otherwise. That way he held me and others too on a line. Deprived of the drug, I would become desperate, ready to do whatever he demanded in return for a dose. It shames me to admit that I took to thieving to finance my habit.

No thief lasted long in the capital. Sooner or later I would have been found out, judged and sacrificed. Such was the fate of Zolin himself. Two years after the events described here, he was found guilty of corrupting our youth, and sentenced to render his heart at the feast of Panquetzaliztli.[3]

Atza was already well established in the Tlatelolco market by the time I fell into Zolin's clutches. Traders hear everything sooner or later, and before too long news of my dissoluteness reached his ears. One day, having verified that I was not in class at the Telpochcalli, he made inquiries, and after a search found me at Zolin's hide-away in Azcapotzalco. Grabbing me by the hair, he dragged me into the open and thrashed me until I lost consciousness. Then he picked me up and carried me home.

By the time we arrived, I had recovered my wits enough to feel the pain of the beating and the shame of being paraded through the streets over Atza's shoulder. Worse followed. Tecuichpo, the person I would least have wanted to see my humiliation, happened to be visiting my mother. From the floor where Atza dropped me, I found myself gazing up through swollen slits into Tecuichpo's dark eyes which glistened with tears. My nose bled;

---

2   *Datura* – hallucinogenic flower.
3   Fifteenth month of the Aztec calendar celebrated in honour of the god Huizilopochtli.

4

my ribs and testicles ached from the blows and kicks my brother had aimed at my vulnerable parts. Yet no hurt could compare with that of finding myself slumped in such a contemptible state at the feet of the emperor's daughter. I heard my mother apologize to Tecuichpo for my condition in phrases that only fear could inspire. A word from Tecuichpo to the emperor, a mere hint that his daughter had been stained by contact with so disreputable a figure as myself could have ended not just my own life but that of the whole family. Moctezuma was known both for his spite and his piety – a combination that rendered him ever eager to seek candidates for sacrifice. Our family relationship with Tecuichpo did us honour, protected us from enemies and hunger, but left us exposed as a servant is exposed to a master's wrath.

Despite her tender years (she was barely twelve years old), Tecuichpo grasped our predicament and cast it aside. Calling her servants – who waited outside the family compound but who had witnessed my arrival – she swore them to secrecy and promised each a reward in return for forgetting what they had seen.

Then with gentle, inspiring firmness, she assured us that her tongue would never betray a family she so loved and honoured, that our mother was her mother also, and so on. She spoke simply and beautifully. My mother wept, Tecuichpo followed suit, and my sister Xochitl needed no invitation to join the lamentation. Even Atza seemed moved, for I saw the set of his jaw relax. He pulled me to my feet and after extracting assurances from me, heard by all, that I would mend my ways, re-admitted me to the family circle from which, as the senior male following my father's death, he could have cast me out.

Over dinner, a splendid one because Tecuichpo had sent for supplies from the palace, we learned the purpose of her visit. She had come to announce her engagement to her uncle Cuitláhuac: a political marriage ordered by her father probably to ensure that she could not become a tool of diplomacy and thereby fall into the clutches of a noble he did not like.

5

There would be no marriage or children at least until Tecuichpo had completed her journey to womanhood. Still, here was an emotional beating to add to the physical one my brother had administered. Tecuichpo was again to be another man's bride; so young, so soon removed from any possible intimacy with commoners. She had returned to the palace not half a year before, torn from us as my mother quietly lamented. Now, just as had happened at her birth, she had become an object to be gifted like a jewel or a fine cloak. So it is with creatures born into the households of great men. They become whatever is demanded of them, harnessing even their innermost thoughts to the imperatives of power.

Whatever each of us felt about Tecuichpo's betrothal to Cuitláhuac, etiquette obliged us to express joy at her good fortune, to celebrate her golden future, to wish her many children. Royal soothsayers had already set the date for the wedding – 10 Quauhtli 13 Toxcatl in the year 7 Tecpatl (1512) – an especially lucky combination. How wonderful that the gods would smile on the occasion!

I had the impression that all this ritualistic congratulation embarrassed Tecuichpo, that she had no interest in wedding an uncle however distinguished, still less bear the children of so close a relative. Everyone knew that Tlazolteotl, goddess of love, frowned on such marriages. Maybe there would be no consummation. Cuitláhuac already possessed several wives. What need could he have of his little niece apart from another signal of his brother's favour? How would she, so young, summon the affection of a wife for a man more than thrice her age?

In any case, as soon as politeness allowed, Tecuichpo steered the conversation away from the issue of nuptials. Nor did she refer to her new life in the palace, except to say that she missed us all, and that no matter what befell her in the future we would always be her family.

As we ate, Tecuichpo kept glancing at me across the space

that separated us, not with contempt as I might have feared, but with an expression that fluctuated between affection, sympathy for my bruises, and something else that I sensed but hardly dared interpret still less name. Her glances met mine; traces of a smile parted her lips. Atza also noticed but thought she was mocking me and took care to let me know. He wasn't ready to overlook my disgrace. Several times during the meal he found means to dig an elbow into my sore ribs as if to remind me of his warning: that next time he caught me among thieves and drunkards, he would kill me himself so as to spare our mother and sister the shame of seeing me condemned in public.

Still, neither Atza's threats nor my own disgrace could dampen the warmth of the moment. Xochitl and Tecuichpo, happy to be in each other's company, were too excited for that, their shrill voices and laughter drowning more melancholy thoughts. As the meal came to an end, Mother asked them to sing for us in honour of the occasion – as they used to do when Tecuichpo lived with us. Here is what they sang, while Atza and I clapped the rhythm and we all joined in the chorus.

Iz catqui tla yetetl
toxochio
Ayhuaye
ihuan tocuic
quipolohua telel
ah in totlaocol in
Ohuaya Ohuaya
Yya tocnihuan
Aya
xon ahuiyacan
ah mochipa tlalticpac
zan cen on quizaz
in icniuhyotli
Ohuaya Ohuaya

Dear reader, you will never hear the music of those voices. As for the beauty of the words, I can offer only the vaguest shadow:

May the flowers
bloom and multiply
Aya, aya
And sweep away
Our weariness and grief
Ohuaya Ohuaya

Oh my loved ones
Be joyful
Aya
True we are not long upon this earth
But friendship
Triumphs over all.
Ohuaya Ohuaya

Afterwards, we escorted Tecuichpo as far as the palace, parting from her with many entreaties to repeat her visit, and sadly conscious that once married she would join Cuitláhuac's household in the city of Ixtapalapa on the lakeshore, and we would see much less of her, or perhaps not see her at all. Then we each went our separate ways: Atza to his quarters near the market, Xochitl and my mother to visit friends who lived in the Itztacalco district.

For myself, despite orders from Atza to return directly home, I felt a need to walk, to be alone, to be silent within myself as we used to say in the old days. As soon as my brother was out of sight, I opted to take the long route via the shore line. I will take you with me, not to recount the thoughts with which I wrestled on that day, for these are unimportant and the large part you may imagine for yourself, but to paint for you a little of what lay before my eyes – and which alas you will never have a chance to see.

My route took me past the public entrance to Moctezuma's palace (Tecuichpo had entered through a side portal reserved for the nobility). As ever it thronged with people hurrying back and forth: officials and diplomats on affairs of state, palace servants on errands, merchants delivering goods, petitioners with gifts, priests on business of the gods, foreigners bringing tribute from distant parts. On each side of the entrance, soldiers stood on guard verifying the identity of anyone of low rank or whom they didn't recognize. Several more marched in opposite directions round the perimeter wall. Beggars loitered nearby, accosting anyone wearing a half-decent cloak. Gaggles of sightseers dawdled in hope of spotting someone of consequence, a general, a high official, maybe even the emperor himself. As I passed by, keeping my distance so as not to become entangled with the throng, a bare-chested man in a loincloth caught my eye as he sprinted alongside the palace wall. A fleeing slave. His owner, wielding a sword, and shouting for people to get out of the way, careered past me in pursuit. But he was already too late. Ever in sympathy with the underdog, the crowd parted to let the slave through, then closed ranks against his master. Reaching the palace entrance, the slave found his way barred by the palace guards, but a word of explanation or pleading persuaded them to let him through. Once across the threshold, he turned round to thank the guards and the onlookers for their help – this time as a free man, for such was our custom. Onlookers applauded the slave's triumph, while the owner walked away, resigned to the loss of his property.

The scene reminded me that my own bruised body and battered sentiments didn't amount to much and that chance or ill-luck could inflict worse fates than the one so far reserved to me. If I needed a further reminder, I could find it in the building adjacent to the palace, where the Spaniards are now building a church – our great temple with its skull rack of those whose blood had nobly fortified the gods. Prisoners of war thought it a privilege to die there, for it signified a gift to mankind without which the gods would destroy the world and all its creatures. By the time I became a man, the tradition was losing its force at least in the capital. Instead of admiring the sacrificial ceremony, many saw it more as an object of repression, an instrument of fear wielded by our leaders to ensure compliance with their wishes. Under Moctezuma's reign, prisoners of war weren't the only ones liable for sacrifice. Anyone who displeased the emperor would like as not end up on the rack. It had become a punishment of choice, a means of terrorizing the people, of making us bow our heads and give way to the whims of our rulers. Mind you, so far as I can see, the Spaniards are no different. They too have their torturers and executioners.

As followers of Quetzalcóatl, our family had never believed in shedding human blood. That's why we kept away from the downtown area: it made us uneasy. So instead of proceeding across the great square, with its ugly reminders of oppression, I turned right alongside the palace compound and then right again, towards the north side of the lakeshore.

My way led to a promontory overlooking the causeway that ran across the lake to the town of Tepeyac whose grand temple, rivalling our own in height, stood out against the surrounding hills. From this spot, you could also make out the smaller temples of Tenayuca and Atzacualco further along the mainland shore. Tonatiuh the Sun, on his descent towards the horizon, was casting splashes of pink on the surface of the water. Inshore, directly below me, farmers were canoeing home after a day's work in the *chinampas*,[4] their craft laden with produce for the next day's market. A couple of fishing canoes, out late in the day, were drifting slowly in, their raised nets hanging in the air on each side like giant wings. Further east, in that broader part of the lake we called Texcoco, a dozen war canoes in formation were practising their skills. Beyond, looking down on us from their place in heaven, the white-peaked mountain gods Popocatépetl

---

4   Floating gardens.

and Ixtaccíhuatl stood wreathed in crimson, the former smoking a little, though quietly and in peace.

Surrounded by these towns and temples and by so much activity and order, I saw how kindly fate had ministered to those of us who lived here. We stood at the centre of the universe. All nations feared us. Many paid us tribute. Our grandeur, the richness of our life, the beauty of our landscape, the splendour of our island home, everything testified to our good fortune, to the power of our gods over all other gods.

With their help, we had become a proud and accomplished people. Our great city of Tenochtitlan, the other cities that fringed the shores of the mainland, the canoes on the water, the *chinampas* that supplied our food, our armies that had subdued neighbouring peoples and made them our vassals, our buildings and jewellery, and weapons, and paintings, our songs and dances, all these were achievements of our nation. By our labour, we had conquered nature. Our doctors had learned to cure sickness with herbs and plants. We knew how to net fish from the lake, to snare the jaguar and the coyote, to breed turkeys and *escuintles,*[5] to grow maize and *zapotes* so that hunger might never again scourge us as it had our ancestors.

Such thoughts helped me see that by beating me, my brother had forced on me a lesson I might otherwise not have learned. He had shown me how wretched I had become. What use could our people have for a man who spent his days in idleness and debauchery? Atzahuatl, my beloved brother, I owed that question to your correction. Staring through the slits of bruised and swollen eyes I grasped, thanks to your stern teaching, how much the well-being of the whole depended on each one of us, and I promised myself that I would henceforth seek to know where my duty lay in the life of our people, and to perform that duty no matter what challenges fate might bring.

How far I kept my vow, you who read these lines may judge.

---

5   Hairless dog.

TWO

MEXICO CITY – SEPTEMBER 2010

James

Hotel Rendón is still cheap – more so even than when I stayed there as a newcomer to the city all those years ago. Its raw concrete architecture was fashionable then, and the façade, regularly soaped and watered, showed barely a streak of the urban grime that now exposes its decline. Originally a bed and breakfast for travelling salesmen and middling executives, its clientele has widened to include backpackers, teachers on modest salaries, people unsure whether they can afford the rates and who check their purse each day before stepping into the street.

So far as I can see, neither the inside nor the outside has been refurbished since my last stay. Walls and floors have acquired cracks that no one has thought to mend, tables in the restaurant are chipped at the edges and scarred by burns, and chairs creak with the weariness of years. The hotel has come down in the world, as I have.

I wake at dawn to the roar of traffic from the street. On a table next to the window, an electric kettle, a miniature coffee filter and a basket stocked with air-sealed bags of ground coffee, sugar and sweet cookies. I fill the kettle from the faucet in the bathroom and return it to the table assuming there will be an electrical supply somewhere in the vicinity. There isn't. On my hands and knees, I explore the perimeter of the room and at length find a socket behind the headboard. Heaving the bed a foot or so away from the wall, I plug in the kettle. Sparks. An odour of burning plastic. I unplug and return the bed and the kettle to their place, inexplicably happy at the failure.

In the hotel restaurant, I order a Mexican breakfast of *chilaquiles* – spicy and cheerful like the waiter who serves them and who resembles for all the world his counterpart of thirty years before, as if waiting table were not a job but an essence, a breed identifiable by black moustache, protruding girth, brisk efficiency, and unflagging enthusiasm. *Que le ofrecemos? Hay chilaquiles bien picosos. Muy buenos*, cheerfully challenging my taste buds and my resistance to a dawn assault of hot peppers.

"Fuel for the day," he assures me.

Afterwards, as I pay the bill, he asks if I enjoyed my meal.

My lips throb and the roof of my mouth is on fire. "Delicious."

"Ah, señor, you have Mexican blood in your veins."

At the front desk a receptionist wishes me *Buenos días*, takes my key and offers to get me a taxi.

"Thanks, but I prefer to walk."

"The city is beautiful in the morning. If it weren't for the noise. We Mexicans have made such a mess of things."

"At least it's not dangerous."

"Oh no, señor, nowadays it's very dangerous. One of the most dangerous places on earth. Do be careful."

My route takes me through the Colonia Cuauhtémoc, down Río Lerma to Río Tiber and then across Reforma at the Angel roundabout.

13

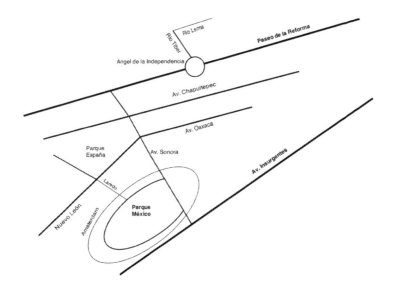

Reaching Nuevo León – where the traffic runs heavy and fast, with drivers racing the lights and each other – I turn into the residential side street of Laredo and across Amsterdam into the Parque México. This little park of twenty acres is dense with vegetation. Tall Oyamel firs, cedars, cypresses and palms tower over gardens of squat green shrubs and hedging. Jacaranda are in flower, spraying pale lavender confetti among the evergreens. It is just as I remember: the open-air theatre, the art deco fountain nymph, the blue clock tower ringed by little fountains, the duck pond with its odour of stagnation and excrement; sights and smells that carry me back to when I last walked here with Olivia on my arm.

Was it Olivia? Perhaps it was someone else. My memory plays tricks, jumbles recollections, juxtaposes disparate events. How easily we change one passion for another to make our history run more smoothly, less soiled with guilt, and so betray the feelings we once thought eternal, whispering to new lovers and to ourselves promises we have made before and that by their very repetition we have failed to keep.

Despite the early hour, the park is vibrant with activity. Young men and women in tracksuits jog round the periphery, an eye on each other. A middle-aged group practises Tai Chi in the amphitheatre. On the western edge, in a paved area where pathways converge, two men in jeans and T-shirts train dogs in the delicacy of manners required of pets domiciled in the affluent environs of the park. A scraggy street vendor in a baseball cap and carrying a tray of cigarettes, lighters and chewing gum is beginning his patrol. Early rays of sunshine slant through the trees, dappling the shrubs and flowers with patches of particoloured light. Car horns blare distantly, too faint to disturb but distinct enough to underscore the tranquillity. On the far side, I cross Amsterdam again – it circumscribes the park roughly on the oval route of the old hippodrome – and at length come to Insurgentes street, which slices through the city from north to south, reputedly the longest urban thoroughfare in the Americas. Suddenly, fumes and din: pedestrians scurrying, cars bumper to bumper, students and workers pouring on and off the metro-buses that course up and down the central aisle. On one corner a middle-aged man selling beakers of fresh orange juice from a rudimentary stand feverishly works his press. Opposite, at another stand arrayed with bowls of green and red sauces, a woman cooks *tacos* and *quesadillas* on a hot plate. Next to her, a newspaper vendor, then a doughnut stall. This is an area of shop assistants, office clerks, impecunious students, waiters, hairdressers, salesmen and women.

Executives don't eat breakfast from a taco stand on Insurgentes. The air-conditioned elegance of Sanborns on the east side of the street, however, will do fine. There, women in peasant costume attend who, in the dark beauty of their skin, in gesture, in the sing-song timbre of their voices resemble the people in the street in a way they do not resemble those they serve.

How can I explain? The middle classes could hail from a dozen different countries. They do not look unequivocally Mexican, I do not, the president doesn't, Olivia. We could pass for what you will, but the street vendors of Insurgentes and their morning clientele can only be Mexican – descendants of those who paddled canoes through the waters of Texcoco, survivors of the dark night of Tenochca and of Tlatelolco, of August 13, 1521, and October 2, 1968.

On the newsstand, a headline catches my eye: *Nuevo Masacre en Tijuana; índice de ejecuciones en aumento.*[6] Execution index? Yes, in large letters: "Over 5,000 assassinations to date this year… drug war escalates…traffickers fight each other for territory and fight police and army for the right to trade".

6   Another Massacre in Tijuana; execution index on the increase.

16

Gentle people of sanguinary history...

Violence permeates all my early recollections. In the seventies, no one spoke of drug wars, yet nothing outside a state of war could have prepared me for my first encounters. Everywhere I looked, every sensation undermined the picturesque fantasy I had entertained from afar of the world that awaited me.

Some of that violence I learned to absorb or to shrug off: cars honking at each other; the ear-splitting roar of buses with their silencers removed; the smog that made the eyes water and dissolved the middle distance into a discoloured haze; the unforgiving brightness and heat of the sun through thin air. Other violence could not be so readily absorbed: women sitting on street corners with a newborn at the breast and a palm raised in supplication; children at traffic lights hawking chewing gum or plastic dolls; old men eager to park the car for a peso – less than one twelfth of a dollar; young men ready to wash it for two; sword-swallowers and flame-spewers at the road side; whistle-blowing traffic cops – *mordelones* – on the prowl for a bribe; dust-bowl slums where human scavengers picked over the spoils of stolen goods and gleanings from city garbage dumps – the unfathomable poverty of the many, the inconceivable wealth of who? Who were the people that lived in the shuttered mansions of Lomas de Chapultepec and Pedregal de San Ángel, that glided by in chauffeur-driven limousines? Casual murders: the film star with the pistol who left a bar one night with joy in his heart, fired twice into the sky and once into a passer-by just for the hell of it and who afterwards paid a fine to a judge and walked free. The only way to summon a waiter in a restaurant, by whistling or hissing as you might call a dog or chase away a cat.

Olivia had asked to meet me in a place not frequented by her friends.

"I want you to myself for an hour or two," she had said on the telephone. "The International Bookstore is still there, did you see? Grown old like me."

Yes, it is still there, its window display heavy with works on engineering, medicine and forensic science. I think of all the books that have been and will ever be published, Borges's Library of Babel, repository of everything there is to know and not to know, sense and anti-sense in infinite proportions so that we cannot even begin to grasp what it contains or how much of it we might and can't conceive. I think it possible – likely even – that of the several thousand volumes on the shelves of the International Bookstore, I have not read a single one. By its vastness the infinite mocks us, revealing only so much as to make us believe in its existence and in our own incapacity.

At the kerbside, a middle-aged woman in peasant dress sits beside a tiny griddle making tortillas. She slaps the dough between her hands until it is round and thin, then sets it gently on the griddle, unleashing a succulent odour of corn and ancient pasture.

Olivia steps from a four-by-four parked a hundred metres down the street and walks towards me. She is wearing a loose linen skirt, grey with red highlights in the form of petals, and a shapeless red jacket over a cream blouse. Her clothes flap and billow, like washing on a line. I figure it must be her because she is smiling at me. Women don't do that any more. Then she is holding my hand, leaning towards me, her cheek angled to receive my kiss. She is oddly taller than I expected, her face and lips fuller, rounder, more relaxed, and her body rounder also, rounded by years, by children, by domestic life and by a sense of having let go of something, a discipline that was once part of the energy of youth and its joy.

"You haven't changed."

"Nor you."

THREE

TENOCHTITLAN – 1512–1516

Alva

A few days later, Atza took me back to school – not to the Telpochcalli where students could get away with a bit on the side – but to the Calmecac where the strictest discipline prevailed. No drugs, no women, no leisure. Most of the Calmecac students were aristocrats training for the priesthood or for officer rank in the army or the emperor's service. A few were sons of merchants whose parents had money and influence. Atza already belonged to the latter, his prosperity opening doors that otherwise yielded solely to rank.

He marched me in himself, aired my past misdemeanours with the superintendent and received assurances that they would "turn me round", a disagreeable phrase reminiscent of the vocabulary my father would use in shaping pots. I had no wish to be shaped, yet I was now glimpsing what most of my contemporaries (those on the right side of the law at any rate) had already grasped: to achieve a happy and successful life, you toed the line and bowed to custom even when it wasn't as old or well set as the elite tried to pretend. Common people didn't make the laws or the customs; priests and aristocrats shared that task between them, with the emperor having the final say.

Anyway, if you valued your life, you didn't try to flee the Calmecac. Five years I spent in that miserable hole, training to be an officer (I was "unsuited" to the priesthood): up at dawn, a run and a scrub before breakfast, days and moons in the classroom, forced marches, mock battles, fatigues and humiliations. Plus, no one graduated from the Calmecac without a spell on some lowly activity through which we would come to understand the nobility of work and our own insignificance.

Some students required more abasement than others. My reputation spoke for itself so I was sent to shovel shit for a muck-merchant, a malodorous occupation and one for which I was well suited according to Calcatzín the head trainer. I won't trouble you with more about Calcatzín except to tell you that he was a spiteful son of a bitch, cheerful only when inflicting misery on his charges.

Shit-shovelling was as physically demanding as it was mentally numbing. You were allocated a district and then went from street to street collecting ordure which you loaded onto canoes for conveyance to the manure market. When a farmer or gardener bought a load, you paddled it over to their patch and helped them to spread it.

As it turned out, good fortune came to me in this unlikely setting. Another student from the Calmecac had been assigned the same fatigue and in time he was to become my dearest friend. Unlike myself, Tlacotl – Tlaco to you and me – was blue-blooded, scion of a family that had produced several generations of brilliant military officers. Though the same age, we had barely spoken to each other at school. I was transparently of a lower caste than him, cruder in language, ruder in dress, and generally undistinguished. No reason for him to notice me.

Our new detail, however, reduced us to the same social level. From the day we were thrown together, he acted warmly towards me, welcoming me with good humour to an occupation into which he had preceded me by only a handful of days.

I asked him why he'd been chosen for such a degrading exercise.

"They think I'm too arrogant. So I'm being pulled down to size."

At first, I was guarded with him, watchful for the slightest condescension, the least sign that he wished to put me in my place. His appearance hardly helped. Tall, slender, with patrician features, deep-set, slightly crossed eyes, and a mop of black hair that refused to be tamed, he qualified as very handsome according to the canon of the time. These physical qualities allied to a natural shyness with strangers made him appear stiff-lipped and aloof, though in reality he was neither. Both his parents had died when he was still a child and he had grown up at the palace, well cared for in respect of his physical needs but lacking the warmth of family life. I think this made him a little reserved in unfamiliar company. More than anything else, his voice betrayed his gentle nature, for it was deep-toned, slow-moving and richly armed with humour and expressions of goodwill. Until the catastrophe overtook us, I never heard him utter a sharp or bitter word.

On my first day at work, he came to pick me up at the Calmecac.

"Our esteemed Calcatzín thinks shit-shovelling is a punishment," he said. "He's wrong. It's a privilege. Manurers are Mexica just like us. Our brothers and sisters. We have only to learn from them."

When we reached our destination, a scruffy part of town I had never seen before, Tlaco took me by the arm. "Before you meet the boss, I should tell you that he calls himself Huecuitlatl[7] because he's been here so long. You'll like him."

7   Old shit.

"I can't call him that."

Tlaco's eyes shone with good humour. "Everybody knows him as Huehue[8]. He adds the shit himself."

Huehue – small, with a hunched back, a spindle frame on grasshopper legs, massive arms designed for a man twice his size – offered me barely a glance at our first meeting before informing me that anybody who had worked as long as him in the shit business ended up reeking of the product.

"After a time, it won't wash out," he warned. "Spend too long here and you could end up smelling like me." I must have looked startled because he added, "You'll be all right as long as you do as you're told. Takes years to be a real Huecuitlatl."

His gruffness and snappy speech gave an impression of permanent anger as if a snake lived inside him. And to be sure, I think his lowly status had lodged a trace of bitterness in him, which he fought off with sharp wit and sudden gestures of kindness.

He'd been a labourer of one kind or another since childhood, forced to fend for himself when his parents rejected him on realizing that he would not grow into the striking son of whom they dreamed. So much, at least, we understood from the occasional reference he made to his past.

Huehue's physical toughness belied his diminutive stature. His stamina for work seemed to us prodigious. Tlaco and I prided ourselves on our fitness but Huehue could outdo us both. He was no mean hand at business either, for he hinted several times that the Calmecac paid him tidily for taking us on.

"I'm contracted to toughen you lads up," he told us with a wink. "But the pair of you look to me beyond rescue, so what's the point? Just make sure the teachers think I'm working you half to death. That way they'll be happy and I'll get paid."

Sometimes, in the afternoons, he would order us to stop work early so that he could invite us to his home. He lived alone in a hut on a tiny island west of Tenochtitlan. On the city side,

---

8   Old man.

chinampas came to within a canoe length of his little beach, but on the other side he looked across the lake directly at the frosty peak of Xinantécatl, which hovers in the air and seemed to me in those days like a god watching over us from his place in heaven.

Huehue turned out to possess every luxury permitted to a commoner: multicoloured mats on the floor, walls lined with fine textiles, a garden arrayed in amaranth, yucca and may flowers which we call *izote* and *cacaloxochitl*. He also grew tomatoes, avocados and *zapotes*, and he had corn delivered by canoe every day from the market. For as long as we worked for him, we ate royally. Tlaco once offered to pay for our share of the food, implying that it was unseemly for someone of his noble background to be living on Huehue's generosity, but Huehue brushed him aside.

"I have everything I need," he said, "except perhaps a good woman. And neither of you look right for the part."

Tlaco grinned shyly. Students brought up in the Calmecac were forbidden so much as to look on a woman until they'd completed their studies. My own experience scarcely exceeded Tlaco's, for while in theory the Telpochcalli permitted some intermingling of the sexes, only prostitutes readily offered themselves to young men outside marriage, and in return for their favours you had to give presents of a kind that lay beyond a youngster's modest means. I had had one fumbling effort with an older woman – a wriggling, squirming affair that had ended when my excitement got the better of me prematurely and her enthusiasm flagged in response.

Out of courtesy, Tlaco and I would not have ventured to mention the subject of female company in our conversations with Huehue, but the latter's casual admission of need – however off-hand – lowered the barrier.

"Surely a woman's not so hard to find," I said.

"So you're the expert?"

"Well, no. But…"

23

He spat on the ground. "What would a woman want with a shit-shoveller apart from *quachtli*[9] and cocoa beans?" He gave me one of his angry looks and then chuckled. "Mind you, if that's what it takes…"

Tlaco's and my lack of sexual experience must have been all too obvious, and at times I got the impression Huehue liked playing on our unworldliness. "Spend your time beating your meat," he would taunt us. "No way for young soldiers to behave."

Tlaco's refined upbringing had not prepared him for Huehue's earthiness. "We don't mention such matters so as not to inflame our senses," he replied. "Leaders require discipline. We must conquer ourselves so as to be able to command others."

Such stark Calmecac philosophy seemed to me even then hopelessly at odds with our nature. For myself, it had the opposite effect to the one intended, evoking sensuous thoughts rather than suppressing them. Whatever is desirable becomes more so when it seems unattainable, is it not so? The more our teachers emphasized the need for purity, the more lust invaded my thoughts as floods invade the land during the rains.

Later, Tlaco and I confessed to each other that Huehue's assessment of our lonely pleasures hit the mark. Tlaco expressed and felt more shame than I, however. Abstinence had become in his mind, as in that of many of his social class, a sign of manhood, as if you could only be a man by not acting as one. I pointed this out to him, but he said, "Don't mock me, Alva," and begged me not to mention the subject again. How easily he became upset, not so much at his intense desire to see a woman but at his difficulty in hiding it from view!

On this question, as perhaps on no other, Calmecac and Christian teachings seem strikingly similar. Both affect to despise whoever indulges in the act of coupling; both consign licence and debauchery (for so they call the gift of sexual bliss) to the lower specimens of humanity who are supposedly too undisciplined to

---

9   Cloaks.

24

refrain from pleasure. Yet I wonder if those despised, pleasure-loving creatures will not one day emerge triumphant, overrunning the world with their own kind, while the abstainers diminish and fade away for lack of procreation. Common sense seems to desert those who rise above the mass of humankind. The higher they climb, the greater their fear that the horde will follow them up the mountain demanding to share the joys and powers gifted only to the few who live close to the gods. Masters will suffer no servants to come among them, and all the energy they once directed to reaching the top, they then spend on preserving things as they are. So they live in sterility and die alone.

Our period of labour with Huehue lasted until the emperor ordered preparations for a new campaign against the Tlaxcalans, the oldest of our enemies.

Tlaco and I, soon to graduate, were called up as reserves. Though we weren't expected to do any serious fighting, we could hardly contain our excitement. Young men imagine no other outcome to war than victory, and the Tlaxcalans had never been a match for our armies. This would be fun.

The aim of the war was not to conquer, still less to kill in battle, but to capture prisoners for sacrifice to the gods. Tradition held that our prosperity and strength rested on keeping the gods well supplied with human flesh and that failure to meet their needs would bring disaster on our people. Hence why death on the sacrificial stone was supposed to confer honour even on an enemy prisoner. Better by far to be consumed by a divine being than left to rot on the battlefield.

I give you the official line, the one maintained by the priests and the government. Did the rest of us believe it? Most tried not to pose the question, even to our own thoughts. Dissent wasn't an option. You kept quiet and hoped to get through life without troubling the authorities. If you went to war, you tried above all to avoid capture, because what our priests did to prisoners of war, enemy priests did to us.

25

Happy as we were to leave the manure business, we felt sad to be parting from Huehue and told him so.

"Dog shit," he countered. "What do lads like you want around here anyway? You're made for better things." As if to dispel the gloomy light he cast on himself, he added, "Besides, you're no fucking good at the job."

We were sitting cross-legged in his hut. He had prepared a treat for us of chocolate sweetened with honey, and as we sipped the delicious liquid, he casually asked Tlaco if he would collect some *zapotes* from the garden, a request he would normally make of me as the social junior.

When Tlaco was out of earshot, he said in a conspiratorial tone, "As this is our last day, I thought you two might like to celebrate." His sharp eyes bored into mine.

"Celebrate?"

"You playing stupid?" He accompanied the question with a leer whose meaning no one could mistake.

I nodded with what I hoped was suitable sobriety though my pulse was racing. "What about Tlaco? He's committed to the rules."

Huehue made a show of spitting. "A soldier needs to get laid before going into battle. If he is to risk his life, it must be as a man."

We discussed how to overcome Tlaco's commitment to celibacy and in the end decided not to tell him what we were about but to say instead that we were going to visit some of Huehue's friends. Huehue reckoned that once Tlaco had brushed up against a girl or two, he would forget all about the Calmecac.

We bathed and changed our clothes, and at dusk set out in Huehue's clean canoe – the one he kept free of shit – paddling north-east towards the mainland. By the time we landed on the outskirts of Texcoco night had closed in, but a row of beacons was burning on the shore and by their flickering light we could make out several streets lined with small houses leading inland from the water's edge. Tlaco, already suspicious, wondered where we were going, but Huehue ignored the question and ordered us to follow him.

He led us up one street, turned into another, then into a third and a fourth each a little narrower and darker than its predecessor, until we emerged into a square bordered by tall acacias. In the centre, a log grate smouldered over a fire sending a sweet scent of *copal*[10] into the air. At the far end, just visible in the dim glow, a huddle of young women sat cross-legged on mats. Hammocks were suspended between the trees, some occupied by couples.

An older woman, heavily painted, greeted each of us with an embrace before exchanging a whispered word or two with Huehue. Evidently they came to an agreement, because the woman led us to some vacant mats.

"Since you are newcomers," she said to Tlaco and myself, "I give you a special welcome. Here we treat every guest as an emperor, and with even more discretion. When you cross the threshold of our little community, you lose your name. No one knows who you are, nor who you will become when you leave. We care only for your pleasure."

No sooner had she melted away than a girl approached with a bowl of rolled tortillas and fruit which she set on the ground before us.

Huehue sat down and I followed suit.

Tlaco remained on his feet. "This is a whore house."

"A house of entertainment," Huehue corrected. "The most refined in Texcoco."

Tlaco appealed to me. "It's against our principles."

I had rehearsed a collection of what I thought to be unassailable arguments against those principles, but had failed to add Tlaco's unease to the picture. We were already fond of each other, no doubt about it, but our friendship was yet fresh and I had no idea whether it would weigh more with him than

_____
10 Incense.

27

adherence to the discipline to which he had been committed since childhood. If not, then he might see it as his duty to condemn me for trying to lead him astray. Conscious of his seniority, I chose the safer course of holding my peace.

"You know I'm right," Tlaco persisted, interpreting my silence as shame.

Huehue came to the rescue. "You don't have to screw the girls here."

"We're not going to."

"You're allowed to watch the show, surely?"

Tlaco muttered that watching entertainment probably wasn't against the rules.

"So sit down then," said Huehue. "Relax, eat some fruit. There'll be dancing, music."

As if on cue, a group of musicians began to play. Several of the girls stood and began dancing.

Tlaco still hesitated.

"Come on," I urged. "It's Huehue's parting gift to us. Don't refuse him this pleasure."

Yes, my words reeked of dishonesty, but they achieved their effect. Tlaco softened. His aristocratic status inclined him to gentleness with social subordinates whom, in any case, he considered to be in no way inferior to himself; and besides, he'd grown fond of Huehue. He sat down.

Huehue winked at me. "Try this." He offered a rolled tortilla to Tlaco.

"What's in it?"

"Dressed mushrooms. Speciality of the house."

We each ate one. They tasted of earth, only partly masked by a sweet chocolate sauce. I heard myself telling Huehue that they couldn't have been washed, my voice sounding distant as if carried from afar on a breeze. The scene began to change as if it had a life of its own. Undulating shadows of the dancers drifted across the square through a haze cast by the central fire.

Hammocks began to sway from side to side – even those that were unoccupied. Women with painted lips floated in the air towards us, singing.

I glanced at Tlaco. He was staring at one of the women. She was tall, slim, wearing a red and white *huipil*[11], and her hair flowed and bobbed as she walked like a cluster of reeds in a stream.

"Anyone you fancy?" Huehue asked, addressing both of us.

The girl approached Tlaco, offering her hand.

"I can't," he said.

"What do you think of our guest?" Huehue asked her.

"He's…" She made a show of shyly searching for a word and, after a pause, of finding one adequate to her feelings and purpose. "…beautiful!"

Smiling, she directed her reply to Huehue but her gaze to Tlaco. She was standing close to him now, bending towards him, her nipple almost touching his lips through the cloth. He grasped her hand and stood up, brushing her body with his arm. A residue of resistance made him turn away for an instant but the girl pulled him gently back towards her.

"It's okay," I said. "Nobody will know."

The girl slipped his hand round her waist and together they disappeared into the darkness. Moments later, a second girl approached, and I too allowed myself to be spirited away. As we passed by one of the occupied hammocks, half-hidden in shadow, I heard a gasp that could only have been of pleasure and that served to inflame an already simmering desire. My girl took me behind the square, down a side alley and into a small garden where a bed of matting and soft grasses had been laid out under an awning. Letting go of my hand, she slipped out of her robe and stood up close to me so that I could sense her nakedness. I had never before felt the body of a young woman, firm yet so soft against the roughness of my fingers, that I feared to hurt her

---

11 Tradition tunic.

until she placed her hand over mine and guided it against her, whispering as she did so that she thrilled at my touch. Oh yes, she had learned the tricks of her trade as well as the finest actor, and yet she bore her knowledge lightly and made me believe she gave herself with joy.

"To a satisfied woman you may always return," she told me. And when her cry preceded mine, I believed I had cast off the raiments of childhood and become a man. If she faked her delight, her performance convinced and I was content to take the act for the deed.

When we reconvened in the square, both girls clinging to our arms, I asked Tlaco how he felt. He could hardly speak, and when he managed to stammer a few words, they were of gratitude. He kept thanking me for persuading him to it, and Huehue for leading us on; and as for the girl, we had to stop him declaring himself to her. She knew who he was – I suppose secrets are few in such places – and could have ruined him had she a mind to do so, or alternatively forced bribes from him in exchange for her silence. But she was good-hearted and seemed only protective of him. In the days that followed, he showered her with gifts and later found her a good man, oversaw the marriage and arranged their accommodation.

"About those rules?" Huehue said.

"Maybe after all they're not so important as living," Tlaco replied, adding, in an echo of Huehue's remark to me, "Now I can go into battle and die, if I must, as a man."

On the way back to Tenochtitlan, we sang to givers of joy and of life:

She who brings happiness
Offers up her body to delight
She stands erect, sways
Seduces with her dress,
And with the beauty of her form.

30

Like a flower she stands proud,
Quivering, restless
Her heart ever fugitive
And palpitating
Her hands beckoning
Her eyes provoking
Her gaze wandering.
She is ever laughing
For laughter walks with her
As she unveils her loveliness.

Back on land, we did our best to thank Huehue for releasing us from our virginity, but as usual he would hear nothing in praise of himself. He made just one request.

"Don't forget me, lads? You never know when you might need a Huecuitlatl."

We were still giggling as we climbed over the Calmecac wall that night – bearing in our hearts and senses Huehue's humour, traces of the crazy mushrooms we had eaten, and the heady afterglow of love.

FOUR

MEXICO CITY – 1970S

James

I n those days, I knew the Tlalpan highway as well any in the world, because I travelled it every day of my working week.

Along its length it changes identity as if to accommodate the evolving history of the neighbourhoods through which it runs. It begins in the great central square, the *Zócalo*, pulsating nucleus of the old nation, as a simple urban street lined with buildings dusted by time and the shifting pulses of prosperity and decline. Here it is known as Pino Suarez after a vice president who lost his life at the hands of a murderous general and thus became a national hero like so many whose end comes prematurely on the anvil of another man's ambition.

But the name detains us but briefly, for as we thread our way south through crowds of shoppers, street vendors and tourists, it widens, turning into San Antonio Abad, the Egyptian monk, revered ascetic of the Coptics (sunlight on white sand, plainsong echoing from the dark stone of an ancient church, the measured pace of priests in white robes), and is suddenly choking with the fumes of traffic. We cross more names: Fray Servando Teresa de Mier, hero of the fight for independence from Spain; Chimalpopoca, third king of the Mexica-Tenochca the Aztecs; Fernando de Alva Ixlilxochitl, the historian through whose veins ran the mingled blood of heavenly victory and defeat, the old kingdom of Huizilopochtli, and the new kingdom of Spain and the Church of Rome. All the glorious dead reduced to city streets, their origin and story lost in time, their legacy a line among thousands on the map of one of the untidiest, most richly dense and tangled urbanities on earth.

San Antonio Abad is a highway already and a highway it remains when a few blocks further on it emerges as Calzada de Tlalpan. Though cars and trucks and buses rumble endlessly along its double lanes, and a smart overland metro speeds back and forth along its central aisle, in this guise, beneath the tarmac and the steel rails, it bears the outline tracing of its past: the ancient causeway that ran straight and true from the island city of Tenochtitlan across the lake to the town on the shore just east of the village of Coyoacán, the causeway along which Cortés led his little band of Conquistadors towards the largest and most beautiful city any of them had ever seen.

Lake Texcoco is no more, the *calzada* an urban thoroughfare thick with grime and diesel fumes, the old wooded slopes of the shore now draped in a multi-layered sprawl of human settlement, part of the untidy commingling of loved and unloved neighbourhoods that make up the impossible, labyrinthine abundance of the metropolis.

Sometimes I drove to the college along the Calzada de Tlalpan, but mostly I took the metro, less because it spared me a daily encounter with rush-hour traffic than because, for the half-hour or so of the journey, I travelled as one with the "people": the toilers who passed under the radar of the middle classes but on whose labours they and the city depended, the brick-layers and carpenters, maids and street-cleaners, shop assistants and gardeners, garbage collectors, tailors and cobblers; peasants, newly arrived from the southern sierra or the dust plains of Durango and San Luis Potosí, their features scarred and scorched by the earth that nurtured them; school kids in flabby uniforms and sneakers; students in T-shirts and baseball caps; and the interminable hawkers who passed through the carriages with sweets, peanuts, cigarettes and chewing gum; all darker skinned than I, and with a high-pitched lilt in their voices that spoke of ancient deference but also an unremitting and defiant cheerfulness. Over the hiss of the wheels on the track and the rattle of the carriage, I could listen to their conversation, soak up unfamiliar expressions, and learn to laugh when they laughed and to know why. Singers would step aboard, often blind or with twisted limbs, a cash bag on one shoulder and perhaps a tambourine or a small drum on the other, and we would hear strains from an old country of tears and yearning and inconsolable melancholy – S*olamente una vez, amé en la vida*…Only once did I give my heart…

Olivia and I first met on the metro, or rather on the platform at General Anaya station, where we found ourselves standing next to each other among a gathering of workers on their way home.

She said something in English I didn't grasp, though the impact of her voice stays with me, a gentle Mexican lilt with a trace of Manhattan learned maybe at an American school or more likely at the movies. Later, several months later, she confessed in her own language that she had introduced herself with a lie.

"A lie?"

"I told you I had been hired to interpret for a visiting American professor."

"That wasn't true?"

"I lied about travelling by metro. I had a car."

Spotting me on my way to the station, she had decided on the spur of the moment to *ligar* me. So she parked her car and followed me on foot.

"Why didn't you just offer me a ride?"

"You might have been a rapist."

Ligar means to pick someone up, but it also means to bind, and sometimes I wonder if that's not the true sense: to tie someone down, to enslave them. Even now, in the twilight, I can never think on her in a different light: the image of those dark eyes, the black cascade of hair resting on her shoulders, the graceful form, the voice, deeper and more mature than her years, that sang to me and gave meaning to thoughts too poignant, funny and captivating for me ever to feel entirely free again.

FIVE

TENOCHTITLAN – 1517

Alva

At school we learned that our greatness as a nation rested on feats of arms. And we should guard against ever settling into a state of peace because it could lead to decadence and exposure to attack. Always the army was engaged somewhere, if not on full-scale expeditions against hostile nations, then on disciplining unruly cities, quelling revolts and discouraging rebellion.

A war with Tlaxcala was the second of two fought that year. First came an assault on a miserable Totonaca city which ended swiftly with few spoils and little glory. Tlaxcalans were a different matter. Though in my lifetime we had never lost so much as a skirmish against them, nor had we been able wholly to conquer them. They were numerous, well organized and difficult to subdue. We might have considered living side by side with them, but for reasons never communicated to common folk, the emperor and his high command preferred to keep them as enemies. They thereby stoked a fire of hatred towards us that would, in the end, consume both our peoples.

Our group of new Calmecac graduates, too inexperienced for the front line, went as reservists and were expected to fight only in case of emergency. Against the Tlaxcalans, the main battle took place as anticipated, lasting for most of the day, providing a workout for our soldiers, and ending at sundown when the Tlaxcalan army turned and fled in disarray. The action took place at a distance from where we had been told to wait in reserve, so we saw nothing of it beyond a cloud of dust on the horizon. Only when our soldiers returned, tired but singing happily and with an impressive haul of prisoners in tow, did we learn how the day had gone. We cheered them as duty demanded, but with longing in our hearts for the day when we too would be able to boast of hard-earned victories and honours won in the field.

Many of the prisoners were sacrificed the following month at the feast of Xipe Totec, the flayer, bringer of birth and death. Because we had been present at the action, our group of novices was expected to attend even though we had taken no part in the fighting.

None of us could claim a capture, nor any military experience, so we were ordered to stand at the back with the least distinguished soldiers. I would have been happier if they had placed us in the next town. Many of my companions surely felt the same though dared not say so.

I'll describe the scene, but before doing so I offer a few words of explanation.

According to our custom, prisoners of war became food for the gods, and if we didn't sacrifice them, we'd have to choose the same number of victims from our own ranks. When you consider that any of us could just as easily end up in the gods' larder on the emperor's say so, the whole business seemed pretty crazy to me even at the time. It looks crazier now in the light of all we have lost. What kind of gods were they that required so much feeding?

If they were so powerful, why couldn't they feed themselves? And if we fed them so well and with so much effort, how come they failed to protect us from the Spaniards? Take my word for it, this whole sacrifice business was hatched up by the elite not just to keep our enemies afraid, but to make sure the rest of us knew our place and didn't harbour ideas above our station.

Now that we belong to the Spanish empire, everybody finds sacrifice hard to stomach. Christians think it's evil because at some time in the past, their god told them to do away with the practice. Or, to be more accurate, they decided to make it symbolic instead of real. By eating the bread and drinking the wine of their lord – his flesh and blood – the faithful join themselves to him without having to kill anyone. Or something like that. I don't claim to grasp exactly how it works. According to Father Hernández, Christians aren't supposed to kill people, but I've seen them do plenty of that in my lifetime.

The ceremony of Xipe Totec took place at the great pyramid, home to the priests of Huizilopochtli and Tlaloc whose twin shrines towered over our capital. All our armed forces were massed before the temple with as many of the citizenry as could find a place to stand. So many were we that no one could count our numbers. One of our poets described such gatherings as a dark sea on which floated the spirit of our people.

Distinguished military personnel – finest flower of the army – lined the one hundred and thirteen steps of the pyramid. First the jaguar and eagle warriors, great soldiers and commanders of men who bore on their shoulders the weight of defending the honour of our nation. Below them, the regular officers, followed by the soldiers who had fought on the last campaign. In the forefront, at ground level, sat the *pipiltin*[12], senior officers of state, the bureaucrats, military governors, *tlatoani*[13], regional officials from the colonies, and the senior administrative staff.

---

12 Nobles.
13 Chiefs.

Next came divisions of the regular army with their commanders, and finally the untried soldiers like ourselves and the common citizens.

High up, at the top of the steps, priests in black robes manned the terraces before the twin temples, forming a semi-circle round the *cuauhxicalli*[14] where one of their number would place each victim's heart before offering it to the god. Above all humanity, on a dais between the temples, sat the emperor with his deputy, the *cihuacoatl*, and members of the inner cabinet with crowns of eagle and quetzal feathers, and embroidered cloaks the colour of a thousand flowers.

Pressed together at the back, with unnumbered heads bobbing in front of us, we novices turned a wait that seemed interminable into an excuse for banter, mostly about assholes – literal and figurative – and off-the-wall sex, the usual nonsense of young men with overloaded desires and inadequate means of relieving them. Against the distinctive chatter of our immediate circle, the rumble of countless other conversations made a noisy accompaniment.

At long last, Moctezuma cast his imperial gaze over us, the *tlacatecatl*[15] raised an arm clad in golden eagle feathers, and a hush descended over the square, sweeping from front to back like a gust of air rippling across the lake. Now we could hear the drumbeats of the royal orchestra and the strains of flutes marking the dance of Xipe Totec.

Shuffling in time to the rhythm, each captor side by side with his prisoner came into view as they climbed the stairs to where the priests awaited them. Reaching the top, the first pair stepped forward and the captor formally handed his prisoner to the *tolpitzin*[16] saying, "As a father I hand my son to the earth, to the sun and to the god from whence he came." The phrase

---

14 Eagle bowl.
15 Head of the army.
16 Priest in charge of the sacrifice.

was repeated by callers positioned around the perimeter of the square to allow everyone to follow, though the same words tumbled into each other from different quarters and came muddily to the ear. Not that it mattered because we learned the words at the Calmecac together with their meaning: that the father symbolically offered what he most loved – his son – so that the world would continue to flourish. Except that it wasn't his son he offered, but his prisoner who took his son's place. Not so different from the lamb taking the place of Abraham's son as the Christians teach. All gods seems to hunger for blood, and we are made to feed them as best we can.

So the prisoner lay down on the sacrificial stone and the priest raised his dagger, which in those days was made of black stone we call obsidian, the sharpest known to us before the Spaniards brought us steel. He plunged the dagger into the prisoner's chest and cut out his heart which he held up for all to see before casting it into the *cuauhxicalli* before the emperor. At a signal from the priests, the crowd emitted a sigh that echoed round the square. Then, as soon as the sound faded, came the next prisoner and the next; fifty-two in all, fifty-two sighs, with the priests taking turns to wield the knife, and each body thrown down to the butchers who waited below so that they could flay them before cutting them up. Afterwards, the drums began to beat again, and the priests, splattered with blood, danced the dance of Xipe Totec.

How did we novices receive the ceremony? From where we stood, we could barely make out what was happening. A few craned their necks. Most of us looked at each other or at the ground, preferring to avoid the spectacle rather than stare at it. For myself, I hoped I would never have to get any closer than this to such a ceremony. Vain hope as it turned out because not long afterwards, I found myself mounting those same steps with a son of my own.

When the time came to disperse, the gaiety of the multitude had long since drained away like water through sand and I for one was left with an awareness of my own helplessness before the demands of those who ruled over us, who sanctioned our life and took it away again according to needs or compulsions known only to themselves.

At the Calmecac, we learned how honourable it was to render one's life to a god. Teachers entertained us with stories of captured heroes who refused to accept offers of pardon but insisted on having their hearts cut out. Given what has befallen our nation, I wonder if our leaders' love of sacrifice didn't weaken us in the end by making enemies of all our neighbours, even those who became part of the empire. Not that this was the only reason they looked upon us with fear and hatred. We also forced our trade on them, set the rates of exchange and the medium, exacted tribute, stole their most beautiful women, kept them in ceaseless anxiety about our next demand for prisoners or the date of our next assault. Who would not feel hatred for a people that inflicted so much tribulation?

I don't need persuading that our nation's behaviour was foolish and unpleasant. But commoners like me didn't make the rules, and if we stepped out of line, we risked the sacrificial knife ourselves. All of us lived under stress in one way or another just as we do now.

My own initiation into the true meaning of conflict came soon enough, on the day I first fought in earnest as a soldier with my courage on the line and, so I thought, my future.

SIX

MEXICO CITY – 1970S

James

On her way to my apartment, Olivia bought flowers from a street vendor.

"Your place needs brightening up," she said when I opened the door to find her wielding an extravagant bouquet.

She arranged each flower in a kitchen jug, changing her mind several times about the order and distribution. Carrying the jug into the living-room, she essayed the sideboard and bookcase before settling for the coffee table in front of the sofa.

"The whole apartment's a bit dull."

"Took what I could find."

"Is that what you always do? I imagined you'd be more discriminating."

"What flowers are these?"

"We call them *cempasúchitl*. They're Mexican."

You wore a black overall open at the neck, a hint of lace beneath, and a silver pendant nested in the hollow between your breasts. Your hair tumbled in untidy dark waves onto your shoulders.

Love came easily without persuasion or guile.

What hunger you made in me, Olivia, not for simple satisfaction. No. Hunger to hear your conversation, your songs, your tales of daily life, your confessions, your cries of pleasure; hunger for your skin, for the moulding of your body to mine and mine to yours, for the touching of our thoughts. Hunger for the generous obscenities that grew between us that neither decency nor shame could still or silence.

You gave no quarter to my ignorance. I had come like an intruder into your world, knowing nothing beyond the simplistic prejudices of my anglophone world. And so you generated another hunger in me, to know your land, your culture, to reach into the rhythms of your language, to see colours and hear sounds of whose existence I was scarcely conscious, to become...yes... Mexican even, though such a thing was by definition impossible, and the hunger could never be satisfied.

You told me about the Conquest, the Revolution, the Burning Plains, the Labyrinth of Solitude. You said I needed to know about the scarred tissue on which the city was built. And about Tlatelolco.

"Tlatelolco?"

"Where Mexico met her last defeat. A patch of earth soaked in blood."

Little by little she told me what she knew, over lunch, over coffee. In the aftermath of love. And I learned that *cempasúchitl* were flowers of the dead.

SEVEN

MEXICO CITY – 1970S (1968)

Olivia

My parents still don't know I was involved in the student strikes. Some of my friends are still in jail. Beto, one of the dearest to me, gave his life. I'd known Beto since childhood, because I went to primary school with his sister, Marina. He was crazy, passionate about everything. A socialist, of course, or Marxist or something. He used to talk about Marx all the time, and other left-wing people. I don't remember all the names; Gramsci was one and there was another – the one who killed his wife. He was so full of ideas and he seemed to have read everything, to know everything that mattered. Mostly we didn't follow what he was talking about, but he carried us with him because he was so sincere and he made us think we could change the world. All my girlfriends were a bit in love with him. Me too. Not that I dared do anything about it. I felt like a little girl beside him and was sure that's how he saw me. As his kid sister's friend. Too immature to bother with.

He was only twenty-two but had nearly finished his degree already. I was still in pre-university – *prepa*.

When the protests began, Beto was in the thick of the action. On the day the police raided the offices of the Communist Party, he had just left the building. He stood outside with the crowd while they trashed the offices and arrested his friends. Then they rounded up a few foreigners with long hair and accused them of being, I don't know, anarchists, hippies, infiltrators who were poisoning the minds of Mexico's youth. All nonsense, but that was how it started. Students reacted by going on strike. Just a few at first, but the idea overtook us like a storm. Suddenly there were thousands and then hundreds of thousands refusing to show up at classes and protesting in the streets, not about what happened to the Communist Party but about years of government repression, corruption, lack of freedom and democracy. I hadn't really thought about any of this before. My girlfriends were the same. Middle-class girls didn't do politics. We were never rich, but we've always lived well. I said this to Beto once, then wished I hadn't. *Me puso como camote.* He was furious. Told me if I wanted to live a decent life, I'd need a social conscience. Hadn't I noticed that most of the people were poverty-stricken, that the worst insult you could throw at someone was to call them a *pinche indio* – a fucking Indian?

"We're all fucking Indians," he would say – I can hear him now with his lovely warm voice. "I'm a fucking Indian, you're a fucking Indian. *Vivamos los pinches nacos, hijos que somos de la madre patria*"[17]

I don't remember our school making a decision to join the strike. It just sort of happened. Not that we mattered because ours was a religious college in San Ángel – a bit conservative and snotty. Downtown is where the strike took hold, particularly in *prepa 1*, which had one of the oldest and most beautiful of our colonial buildings. The army came with a bazooka and blew the door down. Can you imagine an army firing into a school? Not a

---

17 Long live us fucking Indians – children of the mother country.

foreign army but our very own, the one that's supposed to protect the people. It was an original baroque door, part of our national heritage. Beto said the door was unimportant. What we should never forget were the bodies lying on the ground. Soldiers went in with bayonets. Beto showed me a photograph. You could see the blood, and shoes and books scattered on the tiles, with Orozco's mural in the background looking down on the destruction as if it were part of a single tale of pain and suffering – the violent heritage of our nation. Newspapers only showed pictures of the door, of course, and blamed the whole thing on the students and foreign agitators. Agitators! They were teenagers, like me.

A day or so later, the Interior Minister Luis Echeverría appeared on television. "We've taken measures," he said, "to safeguard the independence of our universities from those whose vile aim is to hinder the progress of the Mexican Revolution. Few countries in the world enjoy the liberties that prevail in Mexico…"

Something like that anyway. What a joke. He was minister of the interior then. Now he's become president. A reward for murder. I shouldn't say that but it's what I think.

His speech made everyone angry because he was hiding the truth. He refused to apologize for what the army had done, so students responded by putting up barricades. The polytechnic and the university vied with each other to prove which of them was the more revolutionary. Peasants joined with the students and then the workers' unions joined too. What started as a student rebellion became a mass protest.

The authorities ordered the army into the university, which was against the law because universities are supposed to be independent and protected from political interference.

They arrested whoever they could find on campus. One girl, frightened that the soldiers might rape or shoot her, hid in a women's washroom. Out of delicacy, the soldiers didn't check in there, but they didn't leave either. They just hung around, sitting on tanks and jeeps, standing to attention when an officer went by, but otherwise idle, smoking, cracking jokes. She could see them out of the washroom window. Two weeks she spent there, with no food, drinking water out of the toilet. Eventually, a cleaner forced the door and found her collapsed on the floor. Everything was getting out of hand by then. The university and the polytechnic were closed. So too the *prepas*. Many no longer knew why they were protesting. I wasn't sure myself. But the movement had developed a life of its own and couldn't be stopped.

I didn't see much of Beto during those days because he was so busy, but he left some pamphlets with Marina and then we sort of *pues agarramos la onda* – got the message. The students made six demands. I don't remember all of them. One was about political prisoners and another about the penal code. We had a horrible law about "social dissolution" that allowed the government to jail anyone they didn't like. That couldn't happen in Europe or the States, could it?

47

Some intellectuals took the army occupation of the university as a sign that the government was afraid and that we had it on the run. Posters appeared on walls. Buses and trains were painted overnight with slogans against the outrage. It became personal. Anti-government pamphlets called President Díaz Ordaz the ugliest head of state in the nation's history.

He gave a speech that everybody remembers because it has a name: *la mano tendida* – the extended hand. I know it almost by heart: "*Let us hope that circumstances do not force us to take measures we would prefer to avoid. But let there also be no illusion. If we have to take such measures, we will do so. Whatever they may be. Order must be restored. I say to the students, to the strikers, to those of you who are bringing chaos and violence to our streets, you have a choice. I offer you peace. I hold out my hand to you in friendship. Will you grasp that hand, or leave it hanging in the air?*"

No one understood the threat. More demonstrations followed. In the *Zócalo*, before the balcony of the national palace, a crowd chanted: *Sal al balcón, chango hocicón, sal bocicón*[18]. And somewhere in the bowels of that building or maybe in the official residence at Los Pinos, the snout flared, the muzzle curled, the voice growled that the nation's youth was turning to filth and had to be cleansed like scum from the surface of a lake. They're not my words – I read them somewhere – but they're exactly right. They say the insults stung the pride of a man accustomed to deference and self-conscious about his appearance. He must have been worried too about the country's international image. Mexico was to host the Olympics that year. What would the foreigners think? The Americans? Students marched with tape over their mouths to signal the silencing of the people's voice, and the press sent photographs round the world.

Then came the protest meeting in Tlatelolco.

---

18 Come out onto the balcony, monkey snout, horse mouth.

EIGHT

TENOCHTITLAN – 1517–1518

Alva

Tlaco and I received our insignia as imperial soldiers the day
Moctezuma declared war on Quetzalan. The town – finest
in the land for quetzal feathers – had refused to send the
usual tribute, and knowing we would not let this pass had made
an alliance with the Totonacas to rebel against our rule. For good
measure, they had attacked our traders, stolen their merchandise,
and then sacrificed them to their gods. Or so we were told. I don't
vouch for either story. I asked Atza about the robberies thinking he
was sure to have picked up the story but he'd heard nothing, even
though one of his friends at the market was a supplier of feathers
to the army high command. As for rebellions, Tlaco – who knew
the score well enough from listening to palace gossip – said that
for sure it was a trumped-up charge because the Quetzalans were
like us while the Totonacas spoke a different language and had
been kicked out of the region by Emperor Ahuizotl long before
our time. The government was always ready with a story to suit

its purposes, one of which was war. I used to wonder what was in it for them. Now I understand. Leaders declared war not to benefit the people but to keep control. Conflict kept the rest of us obedient: we had to support our country, follow orders, risk our lives for the cause and so on; and we didn't dare protest for fear of being branded a traitor. To the emperor and his commanders went the spoils of victory: tribute, reparations, enslavement of the defeated, captured women. Ordinary soldiers never saw much in the way of reward. Maybe we got an acknowledgement from the high command, promotion to a higher rank, a pay rise if fortune smiled on us. Mostly we were happy enough to survive and get back to our families in one piece without having disgraced ourselves on the battlefield. Terror in the end is what ruled everyone, patriot and enemy alike: the awful terror of the knife, the hunger of the gods.

You should know, by the way, that I express thoughts here that could not be voiced in the old days, not even to Tlaco whose great-grandfather, the Deputy Emperor Tlacaelel, was said to have originated the policy of keeping order through oppression and sacrifice.

Both of us were real soldiers now, and this time we would be going to war. We were happy enough about it. Nervous too, though not about risking our lives. Youth assigns death to others, to the elderly, the defeated, the weak, those who have no stomach for the world. What we feared was failing to show courage in the heat of battle. Would we falter on sight of the enemy – or at the moment of cutting into flesh with our blades? All our training, the mock engagements we had fought with each other, the days and nights spent on mountain slopes in bad weather, the numbing lectures and harangues of our teachers, our "free" ride on the expedition against the Tlaxcalans, even the shit-shovelling with Huehue were designed to make us ready for combat. Yet nothing quite prepares a soldier for the real thing, for defending his own life, for capturing the life of another.

Quetzalan nestled in the eastern highlands, a good ten days' march for the army, dawn to dusk days of tramping through mountain passes and bare plateaux, days of sweat and dust under a scorching sun and nights spent shivering beneath a cold moon.

For the first part of the trek, we passed through the territories of subject peoples. They fed us dutifully and gave us nightly shelter, but already I felt we were among enemies, for their courtesies were strained and their eyes glittered with repressed contempt. And who could blame them? I had never seen hatred before, but I knew it in the manners of these conquered peoples whose role it was to satisfy our needs at their own expense.

I remember wondering what might befall us if these subjects were ever one day to find allies powerful enough to challenge us.

"Did you feel their disdain?" I asked Tlaco.

"Don't mean a thing," he answered, mimicking Huehue's loose speech, "because they have no guts."

"Suppose they joined together? Called in the Purépecha?"

"The Purépecha wouldn't risk a war with us. Besides, they're too far away."

Some things you could never get Tlaco to take seriously, and one was the idea of our defeat. I guess it was the complacency of being a member of the aristocracy. Top dogs rarely look down, even to urinate.

Once we had crossed the fertile lands of Cuauhnahuac, we found ourselves in a plain of sandy grey earth where no one lived and nothing grew except sad-looking *biznagas* and *pitayas* with drooping spines and skin scarred by drought. Here there was no succour, no food or water except what we and our porters could carry for ourselves, no shelter from the blazing sunlight or from the chill of the desert night. By day, our tramping feet raised clouds of dust that clogged our eyes, our nostrils, our throats, soaked up the sweat on our foreheads and in our armpits, raised a maddening thirst in us that we could quench only when General Palintzin ordered a halt.

Palintzin was a good deal older than any of us, with more than a few grey hairs, and he had little of the dignified bearing or the patrician features that were the norm for his rank. His wiry frame and gnarled features, made more unprepossessing by facial scars and a partially severed left ear, reminded me of Huehue. Both shared a compelling ugliness that might have caused aversion but instead commanded attention, and in Palintzin's case, respect of a kind a soldier will only give to a leader who has won honour in the field. He resembled Huehue also in being a man of the people, son – according to gossip – of a Tlatelolco street trader and a prostitute from Texcoco. Whatever his origins, he had worked his way up on merit. His skill as a swordsman was legendary and he had distinguished himself both as a fighter in his own right and as an officer. He made eagle warrior, our highest rank, through courage, skill and intelligence. Though the men joked about his odd appearance, they loved him, and admired him too for his energy, of which he seemed to have more than any of us youngsters. At the end of a day's hard slog through that vile desert, he would still have time to visit and chat with us as we sat or lay in exhausted groups on the bare ground. At dawn he would rise as fresh as if he had spent the night in Moctezuma's palace, and while we were still rubbing the sleep from our eyes, he would be busy issuing instructions for the day ahead. As the sun rose above the horizon, he would assemble the men for a pep talk which always ended with a prayer to Huizilopochtli for our success, and an oath of fidelity to our great emperor recited in the solemn tones of a man given over to the cause of his nation and its imperial mission. Unlike some of us, Palintzin harboured no doubts about his duties. His commitment was total, his allegiance absolute. Had he been less acute, I might be tempted to liken his faithfulness to that of a domestic pet, a *xoloitzquintle*[19] perhaps, whose fragile frame and squirrel face offered a canine

---

19 Hairless dog.

version of the general's modest stature. But Palintzin's brilliance in command and bravery in battle closed the door to mockery, qualities confirmed both by his countless victories and by the admiring tales of his daring that soldiers brought back from the front. His one weakness – I call it so in hindsight – was for royalty. That he worshipped Moctezuma might be understood as the allegiance expected of a military leader, but mention any of the wives or uncles or ancestors of the monarch – or of any past monarch for that matter – and Palintzin's voice would soften, his lips tremble, and his first words would be a prayer for the health of the emperor and his family. Under the spell of such feeling, he could not but single out Tlaco for special attention and, despite my friend's youth and inexperience, seek his advice.

"Should we rest here for a while?" he would ask, addressing my friend as Tlacotzin, the formal suffix accorded to noted warriors and officials of rank. And Tlaco would gravely signal assent as if the fate of the nation hung on his answer.

"It's embarrassing," Tlaco confessed to me. "He offered me deputy command of the expedition."

"Such are the rewards of lineage."

"I'm not qualified."

"True."

"I'm serious."

"What do you expect? You'll get a command one day. That is if you don't get killed."

"Fuck off!"

I made as if to obey, but he stopped me at once.

"Wait." The laughter in his eyes faded. "You know I'm not a soldier. I pray the gods will give me some other task than that of leading men to war."

"Huehue will give you a job if you ask him nicely."

"Asshole."

"Deputy commander, sir."

53

Palintzin must have seen well enough that Tlaco lacked the qualities of a first-class officer. To allow the scion of a distinguished family to fail, however, was unthinkable and so the general kept him close, armed him with the sharpest weapons, ensured that he came to no harm and praised him for acts of courage that Tlaco told me were wholly fictitious.

"I have to play the game," Tlaco said. "So as not to embarrass the general. In his eyes I'm a symbol of our nation. He would die of shame if anything happened to me on his watch. He keeps warning me that the Quetzalans are a treacherous lot, and that I should always be on my guard and never wander out of his sight."

On the eve of battle, Palintzin made a speech to the army. He told us that many Quetzalans didn't live in the main city but in villages built on lush hillsides and in valleys rich in vegetation, most of which were hidden from view beneath canopies of trees and tall bushes. They lived well. They had abundant corn and animals to hunt, and forest pools laden with fish. Their weapons were the equal of ours and in war they lacked neither bravery nor cunning. A worthy enemy, he concluded, though of course no match for our army.

Our final approach proved difficult since much of the terrain was uneven and thickly forested. Strips of level ground cleared for cultivation were the only possible places for full engagement. With so much cover, the enemy could easily surround us or, in retreat, melt into the forest. Palintzin decided it was too risky for us to go straight in, so when the time came for a full assault, he ordered half the army to position itself out of sight just forward of our overnight encampment, while the rest were to advance, engage for a short while and then quickly retreat. The ploy worked. Thinking they had won an easy victory, the Quetzalans gave chase and ran straight into our ambush. Before the sun had begun his final descent, we had their temple on fire and their surrender assured.

Never a good soldier, luck saved me from shame on this first outing.

I was among the contingent chosen as bait. Palintzin had selected the place where we were to re-enter the forest and had ordered a path to be cleared behind the first line of trees into which we could run safely and from where those lying in wait could launch their attack on our pursuers. When the moment came to turn and run, however, I was seized with a terror of being captured and taken prisoner for sacrifice. Panicking, I ran blindly, hearing only the whoops of the Quetzalans behind me and scarcely aware of what the others were doing or even of the direction in which I was heading. As a result, I entered the forest in the wrong place, tripped over the root of a tree and fell into a thicket. Apart from a few scratches, I was uninjured and soon back on my feet, only to realize that my sword had slipped out of my hand. After a search, I spotted it at the bottom of a gully overgrown with brambles. With the help of a branch torn from a sapling and by lying full length on the ground, I managed to coax it towards me until it was near enough to retrieve, but the manoeuvre took time and all the while I could hear the cries of men and the clash of weapons close by.

The encounter sounded violent, at least to my raw ears. While duty called me to the defence of my comrades, I was also conscious that to show up at the end unwearied by battle would bring disgrace. I had to get back to the fray. But which way should I go? The noises seemed to be coming from different parts of the forest and offered no clue as to the whereabouts of friend or foe. In my confusion, I hurried first one way, then another, the main thought in my head being to avoid falling into enemy hands.

Exhaustion alone might have brought me to a halt had I not stumbled, at full tilt, into an enemy soldier. Neither of us had seen the other. He fell backwards, striking his head on the trunk of a tree, and I clattered on top of him, his body cushioning my fall. This time, I held onto my sword and I was back on my feet at once, ready to defend myself. Less fortunate than I, the soldier remained on the ground. Blood was trickling from his head and for a few moments he lay motionless, though the heaving of his chest told me he still lived. By the time he had recovered enough to be aware of his surroundings, I had him disarmed and in my power. When I asked him how he had become separated from his troops, he said that he had caught sight of me through the undergrowth and was rushing to challenge me when I had unexpectedly changed direction and run into him. At the time of our clash, we had been no more than twenty paces away from the main body of the Quetzalan force.

A glance at his insignia told me that my prisoner was no ordinary soldier. His name was Macuiltzin. An officer of high rank in the Quetzalan military, he had taken part in many battles, and had even participated in expeditions with our army – as an obligatory ally. In a straight fight he would have polished me off without trouble, but on the day of our encounter the gods deserted him and gifted the outcome to me.

My anxiety ceased. With so distinguished a prisoner in my possession, I could wait out the rest of the battle before going in search of our troops. So intoxicated was I by my success that I could now imagine no other outcome to the day than our outright victory, and so to my good fortune it proved. At length the din of battle faded, giving way to a tell-tale crackle of flames that I knew could only be confirmation that we had captured the Quetzalan temple. I could now head for the town in the direction of the fire, knowing that our troops would be in possession of the square. On emerging from the forest with Macuiltzin in tow, I was greeted at first with astonishment, then with the cheers accorded to a hero. I had risen in the morning as a novice, and by the day's end had emerged a warrior. Henceforth, my skill and valour would never be questioned.

After congratulating me in person, General Palintzin announced that he was promoting me at once to the rank of junior officer of the jaguar class. Far too young and inexperienced to deserve the honour, I had the pleasure of being paraded before the assembled troops with my prisoner, though not without quiet embarrassment, for I knew how undeserving I was of such esteem and how much more noble, strong and dignified was the prisoner I now displayed to the world as my "son".

Later, in quiet conversation with Tlaco, I confessed what had happened.

"And to think," he said, "I might have had to look up to you!"

"What if Macuiltzin reveals the truth?"

"He won't say a thing. Honour demands that he show you respect. Besides, no one of his rank wants to be captured by a common soldier."

"But where does justice belong in all this? If honour comes without merit, then so can disgrace."

"The gods bestowed honour on me by birth and on you by fortune. Macuiltzin, though abandoned by fate, holds fast to his own honour and will die nobly. What more can we ask of life?"

Following the victory, we spent several days resting while Palintzin negotiated with the defeated Quetzalans. Tribute included cloaks, feathers, bales of fine cloth, sixty-three prisoners of war for the emperor's larder and a clutch of young women. Future deliveries would be according to agreed terms whose details Palintzin did not disclose to us, though I got the gist later from Tlaco who had accompanied the general in the negotiations.

"An amazing man," Tlaco said, as he recalled the clever thinking and the skill with which Palintzin had steered a course between overburdening the Quetzalans with demands that might induce them to rebel again, and satisfying the emperor that the spoils were sufficiently punitive and compensatory.

Time taken over the negotiations afforded me the opportunity to talk with Macuiltzin. Ten years older than myself, his bearing and manner were those of someone accustomed to command,

and when he spoke, I listened with no less deference than if he were an officer of our own side. Both of us understood, without saying as much, that in allowing him to fall into my hands, the gods, ever mysterious in their ways, had reversed the natural order of things.

A prisoner of Macuiltzin's rank was free to walk around the camp as he wished, and wherever he wandered, our men treated him with respect. As I got to know him, all my misgivings about feeding captives to the gods resurfaced. Why, I wondered, should so fine a man be lost to the world? What would happen if, instead of marching with us back to Tenochtitlan, he took advantage of his freedom of movement to escape? On the day before our departure, I ventured to ask him. He answered that no man could avoid his fate. To shrink from an encounter with the gods could only bring shame on him and thereby preclude a dignified return to his people. He might have continued to survive among us, but only as something less than he had been, a coward clinging to this life for fear of the next.

"I go to my destiny with open arms," he said. "There is no other way."

The march home took longer than the outward journey. Our prisoners could only sustain a measured pace since they bore heavy loads of tribute on their backs as well as food for us to consume on the way. Whenever we reached a town, a contingent of local girls were summoned, whose pliancy stirred our common soldiers to forget the weariness of marching and to spend their last energies in warm embrace – pleasures denied for reasons of discipline to those of officer rank, among whom Tlaco and I were both now numbered. And thus we entered the capital in triumph, both Tlaco and myself enhanced in reputation and rank for reasons neither of us deserved.

A few days after my return, Tecuichpo paid us a visit. Ours was the only ordinary home which she could enter without attracting comment. I was alone, still recovering from the fatigue of the expedition. We strolled together in the garden. She had heard of my military success and said she was proud of me. I tried to disillusion her with an honest account, but she took the attempt for modesty and answered only with words of admiration for a " true hero". She allowed me to take her hand in mine and by various signs and touches and circumlocutions such as we used for courtship in the old days, I ventured to declare my devotion. Of course, as the emperor's daughter and a royal bride, she could not reply. But her silence and the smile that played on her lips told me that she was not displeased. More I could neither do nor expect. I suppose most of us live so, with barriers that can't be crossed. It was thus in my early life, and so it is now. Only the master has changed, and the god I'm supposed to worship.

NINE

MEXICO CITY – 1970S (1968)

Olivia

No one could ever forget October 2nd, 1968. The students organized a public meeting at the Plaza de la Tres Culturas in Tlatelolco, where all our history gathers in a single place: apartment blocks and high-rise towers, the colonial Church of Santiago Tlatelolco, ruins of the ancient Temple of Ehécatl Quetzalcóatl.

Beto invited me. Said I was the only one of his kid sister's group who cared about what was happening. I'd supported the strike at my *prepa*, and I'd even spoken a few words at a school meeting, though I was far too shy to create an impression. I took it as an adventure, like skipping class. But Marina was in the midst of a row with Beto at the time and so were his parents – all about his radicalism and the danger he faced of ruining his career. So I came into the picture because "unlike his sister", I was going in the right direction. Marina was so angry with me when she found out. How could I betray her? Said her brother was leading me astray.

Beto came for me early in the morning. I told my parents we were going out for breakfast with friends. They liked Beto and knew I was safe with him. We went to somebody's home in Tlatelolco, in one of the apartment blocks – the Edificio Chihuahua. Everybody there knew Beto and embraced him and then embraced me because I was with him and because we were all one. They served *pan de pueblo* (sweet bread) and coffee, and there was much laughter and talk of how Mexico was going to open up at last and become a truly free country. I didn't say much, just listened. They were so full of vitality – and everything they said seemed right and honest and noble. I'd never given politics much thought, but it was common knowledge we had a horrible, corrupt government. Even my father used to say so. He still does. Though he also says you can't change the world, only adapt to it, that Mexico isn't like the United States, that democracy can't work in a country with so many poor people because they're not educated enough to know what to think, and so on. Of course I couldn't agree with him about that. We were a different generation. We felt we could change everything. Including ourselves. I was wearing new jeans, very tight and pretty, and was feeling grown up, excited. I wanted Beto to notice me. I even wondered if I would lose my virginity that day, become a complete woman, like the other women in the room. They seemed so self-confident. I was just a young girl beside them, yet they treated me as one of their own, called me *compañera* which was a way of saying that we were all equal because in the New World there were no distinctions of class and it didn't matter whether you were single or married because you owned your own body and could sleep with whoever you wanted. Not that we *would* sleep with just anyone, but we wanted the right. Everything was mixed up in my mind. It didn't make sense and yet it did.

The meeting would begin in late afternoon, so we had all day to prepare. Since Beto had his own things to do, I went with one of the girls – Rosario – to distribute leaflets. Rosario was tiny, very dark skinned, wearing a beautiful *huipil* which she told me was made by the Huichol people from Nayarit. *Padrísimo.*

I thought distributing leaflets would be fun, but once outside we saw soldiers and police arriving in the plaza. Rosario said not to worry because they wouldn't do anything, but I wasn't so sure and when we reached the nearest street, I suggested we split up to cover more territory. As soon as Rosario was out of sight, I left my leaflets in a doorway and went to Sanborns on Madero for coffee. After that I wandered round the shops until it was time to return. Beto had arranged to meet me outside the entrance to the church. By that time, there were people crowding into the area, thousands, and I started to feel uneasy, especially because there were so many policemen. If Beto hadn't been on time, I probably would have gone home. There he was though, waiting for me, and he gave me a hug and kissed me on the cheek. On a balcony of the Chihuahua building, they had set up microphones and loudspeakers and were testing them. Beto had been expecting to make a speech, though with many others anxious to say their piece, they asked him to step down. I remember him saying it wasn't an ego trip and the message was what mattered, not the speaker.

Soldiers had arrived and taken up position round the periphery, but when I mentioned to Beto that we were surrounded, he just nodded in his funny way, with his head on one side, which made him look stiff and much older, and said they wouldn't do us any harm. We spotted little knots of men wearing white bands on their arms or wrists, some of them on rooftops and walls, others mingling with the people. I asked Beto who they were, but he just shrugged his shoulders. A few minutes later the speeches began.

Beto took me by the hand and we moved forward until we stood close enough for a clear view of the speakers. I couldn't forget that the police and soldiers were watching, but Beto seemed so sure of himself that he gave me confidence. Looking round, I saw we were not just students but workers, *campesinos,* teachers wearing badges with the name of their school or college, nurses in uniform, even some middle-class people who looked as if they'd just come from the office. Above us, onlookers were leaning out of the windows of their apartments waving flags and shouting or cheering, although their voices couldn't really be heard down below. A few were throwing flowers, and the thought struck me that they were showering us with solidarity, a sense of belonging, of being Mexican and equal. We weren't equal materially, of course, but at that moment I think we felt as one, and that the world was returning to how we thought of it as children, before we knew about cruelty and injustice.

When the speeches began, I snuck closer to Beto and held onto his arm because I was afraid of losing him in the crowd. I was so proud to be with him. Part of me was pretending to be his girlfriend and half hoping that afterwards he would take me to his apartment and that I wouldn't be able to resist him. What the speeches were about I don't remember. Not a word. In any case, they hadn't been going on for long when a helicopter appeared above where we stood. The noise distracted our attention from the speech. We looked up at the sky and saw green lights shining above our heads, like fireworks. They looked beautiful, a celebration. We heard firecrackers which I felt sure were part of the show, except that the crowd began to sway, carrying us forward then backward like a wave. One of the people on the balcony grabbed a microphone and told us to remain calm, but several of the men with the white bands appeared and started beating him and smashing the loudspeakers. Then I saw a line of soldiers on a low wall aiming rifles. They were shooting. The firecrackers were bullets. I heard screams; I must have been screaming myself. People were scattering now, running into each other. Someone knocked me over but Beto helped me to my feet and we hurried one way and then another. There seemed to be no way out. I fell again over a woman lying on the ground. She was covered in blood; I wanted to stop but Beto pulled me, and a man behind me picked the woman up and carried her away on his shoulder.

Over the firing and the helicopter, you could hear cries and calls for help or for friends or loved ones, or a lost purse or bag or shoe – as if everything had the same value. Everyone was panicking, running blindly, trampling over anyone in their way. We made for the church, but the doors were locked and people were banging on them and begging the priests to let them in. We turned round and dashed somewhere else, hesitated, turned again. Impossible to tell where the shots were coming from; everywhere seemed just as dangerous and frightening. We reached one of the ramparts reconstructed from the ruins of the Aztec temple. Beto pushed me over and I fell into a trench on the other side. Seconds later he dropped beside me. How long we crouched there I don't know. It seemed like an age. Others came over the rampart, some falling on top of us. And the gunfire went on and on and on as if it had become the background noise of the world so that if you wanted to live you would have to suffer it, like traffic. Someone shouted that it wasn't safe to stay put because the soldiers were advancing. Several began to crawl along the trench. I asked Beto what we should do, but he didn't answer, so I shook his shoulder and still he didn't move. I shouted in his ear that we had to get away. Nothing. He said nothing. When I put my hand on his back, I felt something sticky but the light had all but faded and we were in shadow anyway so I couldn't see what it was. I shouted again and shouted and told him not to be stubborn and to answer me even if I was a stupid little girl who didn't understand. Nothing. He lay still. I put my face against his and it was cold, colder than the air. At first I didn't react or even feel anything. My brain refused the message, sent it away. You can't feel something truly unless you know what your feeling is about. Do you know what I mean? There was a space between that sensation of cold on my cheek and my understanding. I shook him and shook him again, and punched him and shouted at him. Finally, I begged him in the

64

name of God to answer me because I was frightened and needed him.

Rain began to fall, and as I felt the drops on my face, it dawned on me what might have happened, dawned slowly, slowly for me but maybe only a few minutes to the world. Then inside I too became cold, clear-headed, and I saw my mind hovering somewhere over my body, looking on and giving instructions. I took the shoulder bag Beto had been carrying and put the strap over my head. I don't know why I did that. Perhaps it was so as not to leave him behind, to take him with me. Rain was pouring now, like it does in season, and I thought it would drown the gunfire, silence it in some way. But it didn't. The firing went on in bursts, voices were shouting orders, sirens were blaring.

I could smell burning and smoke which made no sense because fire and water don't mix, and it made me think or maybe hope I was in a nightmare and soon would wake up to find myself in bed at home. I bent close to Beto again to see if the rain had revived him. My stomach heaved. I had to get out of there, to get help for him, because maybe if I could get him to hospital, the doctors could bring him back. But while the shooting was going on, I didn't dare move; so I waited and waited, with the rain soaking me and the fear running through me like a current, until the firing at last died down and then I raised my head over the rampart.

It was dark but I could see flames coming out of the Edificio Chihuahua, and there were flashlights. Some people were moving about and I could make out a line of figures with their hands in the air and soldiers aiming guns at them. Ducking down again, I felt my way along the trench and was shocked to find it empty. The others must have crept away. I felt so alone. I crawled to the corner – it was only a few metres – and tried to pick out shapes from nearby shadows, to recognize something or someone.

The rain had stopped. No one seemed close enough to notice me. But which way to turn? I hadn't been to Tlatelolco since my father took me when I was a little girl, and all I knew was that I was somewhere near Reforma. Without thinking, I stood up and at once a soldier appeared out of nowhere. He was carrying a rifle and a flashlight, and in the second it took him to reach me, I saw the glint of a bayonet. For some reason, I imagined that there was blood on it. Perhaps I saw blood, or a stain on the blade, or it might have been just water from the rain. I don't know. Instinct took over I think. Before he could say anything or bring the blade closer, I spoke to him. I told him I was only 17, that my cousin had brought me here to watch. I pointed to where Beto was lying. My cousin. The soldier shone his light on Beto's face and after a moment shook his head. "I'm sorry, señorita." I asked him if he was going to kill me too, a young girl who could be his sister, or his girlfriend. "No," he said, "nothing like that." "I just want to go home," I told him. Couldn't he show me the way? And he did. He escorted me past all the soldiers and police. One of the officers stopped us and asked the soldier what he was doing, and he answered that I was his cousin. I took his arm as if he were a familiar, and the officer nodded us past. We reached Lázaro Cárdenas street and then the soldier said simply, "Get out of here, señorita, and thank God you met me."

"What about my cousin?"

He asked me for Beto's name and I made one up. Antonio Moreno. "I'll look after him," the soldier said.

He was a peasant from the north. I could tell by his accent. A simple man, good-hearted in his own way. Yet when I look back, I see the rifle and the bayonet. He saved me, but he might also have been the one who killed Beto. In the street, I ran all the way to the Alameda not daring to stop until I felt sure no soldier or policeman was pursuing me. Once there, I looked around and everything had returned to normal. Traffic flowed, headlights glistened on the wet road, people walked in the street, the cafés and restaurants were busy, just as if nothing had occurred. How could it be that a few blocks away the army was busy killing students? How could Beto be lying there alone with no one knowing or caring about him?

We never found out what they did with him. His body disappeared.

Not long afterwards, the Olympics began. A triumph for Mexico. The whole nation was proud, not least Luis Echeverría, the hand behind the Tlatelolco massacre, the president in waiting.

TEN

TENOCHTITLAN — 1518

Alva

Important prisoners could only be sacrificed at major festivals. Macuiltzin was assessed as one such and was thereby reserved for the feast of Huizilopochtli; a special honour for me, however undeserved and unwanted. Public acclaim is a two-edged sword because a reputation is not something you can escape. People expect things of you: the poor expect help, the army outstanding courage, the neighbours generous gifts, while relatives proudly shower you with abilities you don't possess. Worst of all, the government demands that you carry on as you have started, and you end up with responsibilities you never asked for, also challenges you may not be able to meet and which may bring only shame and disgrace.

Tlaco came to see me a couple of days before the ceremony to check that the "hero" was ready for the public arena. He made a point of praising me in front of the family – to their delight (my mother's especially) and my discomfort. I called him outside on the pretext of needing to discuss a military matter, and as soon as we were alone, begged him to spare me the praise which I neither deserved nor enjoyed.

He looked at me with an expression of hurt. "Your mother is so proud of you."

"I'd be happier if you could take my place at the ceremony."

"You crazy?"

"For me it will be torture. Whereas for you, it's your kind of thing. Everybody knows who you are. They will nod their heads and say being a great soldier runs in the family."

Nonsense as we both knew because a substitution under the watchful gaze of Palintzin could never succeed, and to attempt it would have dishonoured us both.

Instead, Tlaco offered to accompany me at least as far as the temple and to seek permission – which he felt sure to obtain – to mount the steps as my "second", seeing that this was to be my first delivery of sustenance to the sun and patron of our people.

While we were in discussion, my sister Xochitl, prettily dressed and wearing make-up, came out to announce with a flutter of her eyelashes that she was off to the market, at which Tlaco discovered a need to go there too. That was the moment I realized something was going on between them. It caused a shadow to flit over our friendship, like a wisp of cloud over water. Don't get me wrong. I understood Tlaco well enough. Since our little trip with Huehue, I had had passionate thoughts of my own, lustful ones too in which Tecuichpo, my princess, often figured. In dreams, however, we can leap barriers too high for the waking world. No one needed to tell me that an emperor's daughter could never become my wife. I wondered if Xochitl perceived how remote was the prospect of marriage to Tlaco. The emperor would surely not allow it. A man of Tlaco's rank, once free of the Calmecac, could keep mistresses to his heart's content, but marriage was a different matter. Would my sister be happy as Tlaco's concubine rather than his wife? It seemed to me obvious that she would not.

In those days I thought myself infinitely wise and knowledgeable about the motivations of people and what made them happy. How firmly we walk when young and light-headed! Only with age do we tread warily, burdened by experience and fearful with each step that the earth might give way beneath us.

I grasped Tlaco by the forearm. "What about our discussion?"

"If you two are so busy…" said Xochitl, keeping a respectful distance but tapping her foot coquettishly.

"Of course we're busy," I said.

"Not too busy," Tlaco said, looking hard at my sister, and then turning to me, he added in a whisper, "For me it is both a pleasure and an honour to escort the sister of a hero."

"What do you mean?"

"Just a thought."

And with that he and Xochitl left, walking side by side and very close together.

The day of the ceremony arrived and, true to his word, Tlaco appeared at dawn to collect me. Both of us were dressed in military uniform, myself as a junior jaguar warrior and Tlaco in the full regalia of a deputy general, a rank confirmed by Palintzin on our return from the Quetzalan war.

Xochitl and my mother were fussing about me, making sure I was presentable. Not that they approved of the occasion. To lead a captive to his execution ran counter to everything she and my father had taught us as children. Both were Toltecas, followers of Quetzalcóatl, god of all creation, whose priests insisted always on our obligation to love life and to respect life in others. Ritual killing was abhorrent to my parents and so it became to my brother and me. Though no one dared speak openly against the practice, among ourselves we were never slow to do so, and even on this august occasion, my mother bridled a little.

"If you ask me, the gods should feed themselves," she muttered as she prepared breakfast that morning. "Why do they need us to do it for them?" And so on, until Tlaco arrived, whereupon she hid her opinions, made him welcome, and pretended to an enthusiasm for the occasion that Tlaco knew (I had forewarned him) was entirely false. Xochitl had no need to simulate enthusiasm, though it was not the forthcoming ceremony that excited her but the presence of Tlaco in his splendid attire.

After looking me over and suggesting some modifications to my uniform – a fold here, a feather there – Tlaco pronounced himself satisfied. We left to collect my prisoner.

Macuiltzin was waiting for us at the entrance to the prisoners' palace. How strange the word palace must seem to whoever reads these words. When the Spaniards imprison a man, they throw him into a rat-infested dungeon, stretch him on the rack, feed him with scraps fit only for the vermin with whom he shares his lodging, and so humiliate him that he no longer feels worthy of a place either here on earth or among the gods, and thus in his degraded state yearns neither for life nor death.

No prisoner of the Mexica, however mean his status, ever received such treatment, not even a thief or a murderer, let alone a soldier in defeat. A hero like Macuiltzin merited the treatment of a prince. No one would think it needful to watch over him, still less to lock him up.

He embraced us both when we came up to him, and on the way to the temple he walked with a firm step, chatting calmly, as if he were happy to pass through the door from this life to the next. It was I who was nervous, and upset too – that I should be the one to lead such a figure to the underworld against the teaching of my faith.

We reached the temple precinct to find it already thronging with people. Tlaco, who had witnessed these events close up since childhood, led the way to the prisoners' compound which stood to one side of the great temple. Who can say how many prisoners were to be sacrificed that day? They seemed to me uncountable, like the stars, most with their heads bowed, many of them weeping and imploring their god for mercy, for not all faced their destiny with Macuiltzin's equanimity or believed like him that they would spend the afterlife in glory as companions of the Sun.

We settled down to wait. Nothing would happen until the emperor arrived, and he would appear only at his pleasure. For a while we chatted, until the wailing of prisoners and the day's growing heat took their toll on our spirits and stilled our tongues. Then we stood quietly, speaking only the occasional word, each of us drawn into ourselves. My own mood (I can't speak for my companions) darkened as the ordeal edged closer, and felt all the more sombre in contrast to the gaiety of the spectators massed before the temple and who were amusing themselves with banter, or gambling, or formed circles to watch the antics of jugglers and dancers, while hawkers and good-time girls weaved among them offering the enticements of their trade.

At last Moctezuma came into view. He was dressed not like the others in all the finery of rank, but in a plain robe whose very simplicity proclaimed that he lived on a higher and more godlike plain than his subjects and had no need of the fripperies on which mere mortals relied as manifestations of power or standing. He was taller than most men, too, and for this reason if no other looked down on those to whom he spoke.

Two rows of troops formed a passageway of honour between Moctezuma's palace and the temple pyramid. Preceded by guards and followed by an entourage of ministers and generals, Palintzin among them, Moctezuma walked with measured pace to the temple and mounted the one hundred and thirteen steps until he stood before the twin shrines of Tlaloc and Huizilopochtli. After acknowledging the gods, he turned to face the people. Horns sounded and drums began beating out a slow rhythm. Several priests appeared from within Huizilopochtli's temple, hair unkempt, black garments ragged and stained with blood – so unlike the rest of us that they seemed another kind of creature, neither human nor beast but something in between, nearer to the underworld and to death.

Down below, a messenger appeared with instructions to begin the ascent of the captives. Tlaco had told me that Moctezuma would remain only for the highest-ranking victims because he lacked patience to tarry the whole day in the heat while lesser men were fed to a god already half-sated with the choicest flesh. As soon as he grew bored, he would have himself called away on urgent business.

Being one of only a handful of top-rank prisoners, Macuiltzin was among the first to be selected for the ceremony, and I soon found myself leading him up the stairs with Tlaco by my side. We mounted slowly, every step, every breath measured by drumbeats, so as to eliminate all appearances of effort. At the top, we bowed to the emperor without looking at him, for it was forbidden to gaze directly on a god. We bowed also to the officials and generals who stood on either side of the emperor, Palintzin among them. Then Macuiltzin and I embraced, clasping each other body to body, and I remember my reluctance to let him go and a stupid hope entering my mind that if I held him long and hard enough, I would be able to feed him with more life than the priests could take away. I thought how easily my stumbling victory over him – this great personal success that brought me honour in the eyes of the people – could just as easily lead me in a few years' time up a similar flight of stairs with roles reversed.

I suppose the gods care little to know who is the victor and who the vanquished. But I can't deny that I cared. Even though I admired Macuiltzin and wished him well, I would not willingly have exchanged my life for his. Surely, no one could go into battle if they did not place a higher value on themselves than on the enemy. Now that he and I were no longer at war but stood clasped in each other's arms, my strongest feeling was of guilt for delivering him to the unkind fate that awaited him. I saw no glory in such an end, nor dignity in the foul air emanating from the priests who alone among our people rarely if ever seemed to wash, nor spirituality in the cloud of flies that hovered in anticipation of the sacred banquet.

Macuiltzin could not share my distaste. Of course not. Like our nobility, he believed he was going to join the gods. Capture and sacrifice were triumphs born of defeat. Had our fortunes been reversed, he would have led me to my end without regret.

I said farewell to him, and he told me he was happy and loved me as his father. Still I clung to him until Tlaco gently pulled me away. Afterwards, he told me a few moments more of dithering would have been enough to hasten my own deliverance to Huizilopochtli as punishment for disturbing the rhythm of the ceremony.

As soon as I stepped back, four priests seized Macuiltzin by his limbs and laid him across the sacrificial stone. What emotions ran through me then: nervousness, disgust, terror! I glanced at Macuiltzin and saw his eyes open, serene, sure of himself. A fifth priest approached, wielding a knife sharpened and polished so that it glinted in the sunlight. He raised the blade over Macuiltzin, alert for the emperor's signal. I stood to attention on the other side. The emperor rose and looked down over the great square and the people that filled it, the troops standing in a line directly below, and behind them the citizens massed together and spilling into the side streets. The drums fell silent. As we waited, my knees started to wobble and I felt myself urinating in little spurts. Had it not been for Tlaco's support, I believe I would have disgraced myself still further by falling, but he pulled me upright and squeezed my arm so tightly that the pain brought me back to the moment and to a sense of my own dignity. Fortunately, the emperor was still gazing out at the crowd and saw nothing of my disarray. Had he done so, he would have seen me as a traitor, a man whose fear displayed a disbelief in our people and contempt of his own sacred person.

Resuming his seat, he gave a sign to the *tlacatecatl*, who then raised an eagle arm and held it aloft for a moment before bringing it sharply down. The knife flashed in the sunlight and plunged into Macuiltzin's chest. Blood gushed into the air, I felt thick droplets spatter me, and in a blink, the heart appeared still beating in the priest's hand. He brandished it for all to see before placing it in the eagle bowl, while Macuiltzin's body, pooled in blood and already invaded by flies, quivered and jerked and shuddered where it lay.

Tlaco nudged me forward and I took the heart from the bowl as I had been taught, together with a cup of blood that a second priest had collected. Still with my eyes averted, I offered both to Moctezuma. Palintzin came forward as my general to accept the offerings on the emperor's behalf. Then the bearers picked up the body and swung it back and forth a couple of times before hurling it down the steps. There, another team of bearers carried it to one side where a butcher waited for me to join him before severing the limbs and quartering the torso on my behalf. What happened to the pieces? In theory, I was to take a leg home to eat and thereby join Huizilopochtli in a sacred feast, but in reality I had only to touch the leg and mutter what the Christians might call a blessing, for no one truly expected me to make off with it. I left its disposal together with the rest of the body to the butcher's assistants. They worked happily, chatting and cracking jokes, commenting on the quality of the meat as if the corpse before them were not that of a man but an animal or a fish being dressed for a palace feast. Before long, Macuiltzin lay stacked aside in pieces and another body was yielding to the knife.

I made my way out of the precinct alone, Tlaco's high rank obliging him to stay until the emperor's departure. My clothes were sticking to me and the smell of Macuiltzin's blood on them made me feel sick. I decided there and then to do my best to find a different career from that of a soldier. Shovelling shit, if it came to that, seemed a preferable way of life.

ELEVEN

MEXICO – 1971

James

How little I knew in those days. But before I could learn, I had to dispense with the certainties dragged like a suitcase of old books from my country into this unknown one. For a time I clung to those volumes because they seemed like landmarks of stability on a shifting horizon. When they began to disintegrate under that unfamiliar sun, I still held onto them, finding it hard to relinquish the idea that somewhere within their brittle pages I might discover stable artefacts of wisdom: ideas and convictions valid everywhere and for all time. Years went by before I could accept the contingency of what passes in our minds for knowledge, for love, for sympathy.

I had heard of the student unrest in Mexico long before Olivia told me about Tlatelolco, but until then had thought it a remote offshoot of more important happenings. Nineteen sixty-eight was the year for such protests, and those in the Old World and in North America were closer to home. And who could forget the riots in Paris led by their hybrid leader, Daniel Cohn-Bendit, and the chant that his fellow students unleashed in his defence: "We're all German Jews" with its reminder of the Holocaust? How I envied the influence of French students, the fear they inspired in the body politic, their familiarity with rebellion. Richard Nixon took the White House in sixty-eight, too; the burnt ochre clouds of Vietnam hovered over our lives, and on May 4, 1970 – just a few months before my arrival in Mexico – the Ohio National Guard poured live rounds into students at Kent State University.

Remember the sweat on Nixon's face, the shadow on the jaw, the oblique gaze, and the gravelly, inflected drawl of his sidekick Henry Kissinger, the sinking sensation of inhabiting a universe too large and complex to grasp, and of being irrelevant, a pawn among countless others in a game played by men who neither knew nor cared if we existed? Threads such as these were sewn into the canvas of our thoughts.

For participants in the game, Mexico figured merely as a backcloth to the Olympiad, an exotic setting in which competing nations could beat their breasts in public, and where foreigners could go native in mariachi hats, particoloured serapes, and *huaraches*.[20] Politics did not happen in Mexico, nor matters of import to the wider world.

---

20 Traditional sandals.

TWELVE

TENOCHTITLAN – 1518

Alva

After the sacrifice, I had intended to go directly home, but my footsteps carried me down to the lake, to a tiny patch of beach sandwiched between overhanging rocks and hidden by vegetation from the path that ran along the top. I used to go there from time to time to be alone. Sometimes I would recite poetry, or gaze out across the water to the town of Texcoco opposite, or at night to contemplate the stars and the great shining orb of Coyolxauhqui[21], and wonder what I was doing there, what could be the purpose of being a creature of no account, so insignificant that my journey through this world would soon be forgotten as if I had never lived. Who, among us, would history remember? Moctezuma? Perhaps Nezahualcoyotl, King of Texcoco, not for his royalty but because he was the greatest poet in our language? The rest of us would pass like birds across the sky, leaving no sign that we were ever here.

---

21 Goddess of the moon.

The sun was halfway to the horizon now, the hottest part of the day. Its rays blazed off the surface of the water so that my eyes couldn't linger there. I took off my clothes and adornments and dropped them into a shallow at the water's edge. One by one I washed them, pounded them against the rock as I had seen the women do, rinsed and pounded them again until every trace of the blood had disappeared. Then I laid them out to dry over the hot stone before plunging into the water and scrubbing myself with fine earth from the beach. And I felt the poetry of cleaning and its healing quality. Afterwards, I lay down, closed my eyes and bathed in the warmth of the sun, and in my thoughts, I begged Quetzalcóatl's forgiveness for my part in the death of a good man.

Tlaco found me as I was dressing. He had left the ceremony at the same time as the emperor who, as expected, had soon tired of the monotonous repetition of sacrifice. Not finding me at home and knowing I would not allow myself to be seen in public splattered with blood, he had guessed where to find me. His arrival irritated me, though I wasn't sure why.

"You did well," he said.

"Bullshit."

"By the way, I bumped into Tecuichpo on my way out and she told me how proud she was to see you on high."

"Please don't bring her into it," I said. "We were brought up together. I know what she feels about sacrifice."

He looked at me, startled. "You have no right to claim knowledge of a princess."

"Don't worry. I know my place."

"Just be careful."

On hearing that warning, I knew for certain that something had occurred between Tecuichpo and myself, something wonderful and forbidden that needed no words, no confession, not even a meeting, and that Tlaco knew too.

We were silent while I finished dressing, and then Tlaco said, so softly that it might have been to himself rather than to me: "Your sister and I…"

With a gesture, I stopped him from continuing.

I didn't want to know if they were already lovers. None of my business. Besides, Tlaco wasn't seeking my permission for anything. He was choosing that moment to confirm, through his passion for Xochitl, that he was binding himself to our family. Whatever occurred between Tecuichpo and myself, he could henceforth never be the one to reveal it. This I understood. And yet my irritation still threatened to break out, and so as not to offend him, I excused myself and wandered off. Only later did it dawn on me that envy lay behind my bad behaviour. He could love my sister freely with no peril to himself. Whereas I courted danger even by thinking on Tecuichpo. I feared the strength of my desire for her and its capacity to betray me.

Later I questioned Xochitl just to be sure of her feelings for Tlaco. I would not have made her an object of exchange for his silence.

Were they already lovers?

She didn't have to answer me for Atza was the head of the family, and she reminded me of the fact before offering a kind of answer. "We have pleasured without joining."

An unspoken custom among us before marriage.

"But if he asks me," she added, "I will say yes. Didn't our father always say that life was uncertain and that we should never refuse happiness when it stands before us?"

"You know that a man like Tlaco will have other wives too, or concubines?"

"I will care for them as I care for him."

I had never been close to my sister Xochitl, but her simple, honest replies moved me, maybe because they seemed so much purer than anything I might express about Tecuichpo, whose place in my thoughts came always accompanied by guilt.

All that was long ago. When I look back, it seems as if

the past was bathed in the glow and scent of all the flowers of Xochimilco. Not that it lasted long. Ours was the last generation to live in a world framed by our own thoughts and customs, so that whatever befell us seemed familiar and according to what it should be. The only outsiders in our lives were the ones we had invented for ourselves: the gods who ruled over us, and the lesser nations over whom we ruled.

Until an alien broke in, as a crow breaks into the nest of other birds.

THIRTEEN

MEXICO – 1971

James

Olivia introduced me to Pepe Osnaya. He was the son of María del Carmen, one of several maids or *muchachas* who cleaned, cooked, served and laundered at Olivia's home.

Muchachas often came from afar, places of which few in the city had heard, villages hidden among the sierras, a day's journey on foot from the nearest highway. They would leave home speculatively, despatched by poverty and dreams of betterment, leaving behind the elderly, the young, siblings, maybe husbands as well, clinging to a promise that they would reunite as soon as funds allowed. En route, the *muchachas* as likely as not would spend a night or two at the roadside, waiting for local buses that would take them by stages – several buses and days later – to the fabled capital in the valley. Countless men and women had made that trip over the centuries, even before the Conquest when the Aztecs ruled these lands, and before them the Toltecas, and –

who knows? – other peoples forgotten or destroyed by time and the flames of vanished conquerors. Tenochtitlan was a place of eternal pilgrimage, of eternal hope, closer than anywhere else to the glittering empire of the gods and to their terrible anger.

We met in the family home, to where Pepe had returned on his release from jail. It stood on a patch of waste ground at the foot of a rocky hillock west of the ring road – the *Periférico*.

"I've never been anywhere near here," Olivia said.

"Nervous?"

"These places can be dangerous."

Pepe had given us directions, but it was hard to find because it lacked the dignity of an address. The final kilometres were via a rutted track that weaved drunkenly between clusters of tiny breeze-block houses with polythene windows and corrugated tin roofs. Children played in the dust beside the track, and outside every dwelling women were stirring in earthenware pots, hanging out linen to dry, sweeping the entrance to their home with straw brooms, tending little gardens. All stopped to stare as we bounced by. Pepe spotted our approach and waved us towards his home. When we came to a halt, he opened the passenger door for Olivia, helped her out and kissed her on the cheek. He was dark, skinny with a pencil moustache, and shining black hair. We shook hands.

"Welcome."

Ten metres from where we stood, a giant flame tree blazed under the midday sun.

"My grandmother says that tree is a gift from God," Pepe said.

Beneath its boughs, an elderly woman dressed in a clean but faded *huipil* sat in an upright chair before a table on which two pots were steaming on gas rings. She rose in greeting, stout, white-haired, her face soft, full-featured, criss-crossed with lines and crevices.

"My grandmother, Rosa," said Pepe.

Olivia embraced her. "*Doña Rosa, encantada.*"

Disengaging from Olivia, Doña Rosa offered me her hand palm down as if to place it in my safekeeping.

"*Encantado de conocerla, señora.*"

She reached up to embrace me.

"You are friends of Pepe. Friendship is the most beautiful thing..."

"We love Pepe," Olivia said.

"Our house is yours and bids you welcome."

The ritual of welcome with which Moctezuma had greeted Cortés.

Doña Rosa ladled coffee from one of the pots into earthenware mugs, unleashing a mingled odour of earth, cinnamon and raw sugar.

"Your hair's growing back, Pepito," said Olivia. "He used to have hair down to his shoulders, hippy style. Isn't that so, señora?"

Doña Rosa sighed. "*Dios mio. Dios mio.*"

"*Me chingaron,*"[22] said Pepe. "My hair grows. But inside my head..."

"Fetch chairs for our guests," said Doña Rosa, glaring at Pepe with feigned indignation.

Pepe disappeared into the house.

"He's not the same since he came out of jail," Doña Rosa said in a low voice. "What are we coming to in this country when they treat our youngsters like gangsters? Pepe never harmed anyone in his life. God alone knows what they did to him in there. Don't tell him I said so, will you?"

I followed Pepe as far as the threshold and peered inside. My eyes took a moment to adjust to the gloom after the harsh light outside. A single room, bare concrete floor, beds ranged alongside the walls, a small square window opposite the door. Extending

---

22 "They screwed me."

84

from corner to corner on each wall were two shelves laden with cardboard boxes and plastic supermarket bags. Each shelf had hooks fixed at intervals into its edge from which shirts, pants and dresses were suspended on wire hangers. A flimsy screen in two hinged sections stood in one corner, while another corner was piled with pans, bowls and cooking utensils. Pepe handed me an upright chair and carried two himself: office stacking chairs with chrome frames and plastic seats. We placed them at the table in the shade of the flame tree and sat down with Doña Rosa.

"Now I can listen to all your gossip," she laughed, her body shaking.

Pepe turned to me. "As you see, we are not well off."

"We don't complain," said Doña Rosa, softly contradicting. "We have life, enough to eat and nobody is sick. We should thank the Lord. You don't remember how things were before."

"We come from Guerrero," said Pepe. "From the *campo*. There was nothing for us there. My father worked a piece of land on the *ejido*." He glanced at Olivia. "*Explícale que es un ejido*."[23]

"Common land owned collectively by the peasants," Olivia said.

"We were poor," said Doña Rosa, "but we survived. Until a policeman came. A chief of some kind. He took the land for himself."

"Illegally?"

"The whole *ejido* protested, but soldiers came – or gangsters – and killed three of our men, including Emiliano, Pepe's father. They killed my darling son."

Doña Rosa dabbed her eyes with a kitchen towel. A blowfly and a wasp began fighting, buzzing furiously, bumping against the pot and the tabletop, clinging to each other in frenetic, unyielding battle. I wondered why they were fighting when they had so much unoccupied air around them and – with all the cooking in the vicinity – an abundance of food.

---

23 "Tell him what an *ejido* is."

From where we sat, the view gave onto untidy clusters of homes, thinning as they rose to the brow of a hillside in the middle distance beyond which a high peak reared sharp and silvery into the blue haze of the sky. Olivia followed my gaze.

"That's El Ajusco."

"We had nothing to live on after my father died," Pepe said. "Poverty brought us to Mexico City."

"Your mother came first," said Doña Rosa. "What tears we shed thinking we might never see her again. She was here alone for over a year. Then I came to join her. And at last Uncle Chucho brought Pepe and Graciela."

"Graciela's my cousin," said Pepe.

The battle of the insects ended suddenly, the fly dropping directly onto the table beside the coffee pot, where it lay on its back inert, while the wasp hovered for a moment, before settling on a corner of the table. Pepe, seated nearest, swatted it from the table to the ground and crushed it with his foot. Doña Rosa closed her eyes.

"Such is life," she murmured.

"We all had to work," Pepe said. "I was in primary school when I got my first job packing boxes in a soap factory. No way I was going to do that all my life. Though I had no idea what I could do, not even in my dreams, until they started building a new factory next to where I worked. One day I saw a man walking about the building site with drawings which he kept unfolding and showing to the men who were with him. He seemed to be in charge, so before he left, I went over and asked him what he was doing. He looked down at me and I thought he was going to tell me to get lost. Instead he took me to a café, treated me to a sandwich and drink, and explained all about this job. He was a gringo, a structural engineer. He designed factories and roads and bridges, made calculations and so on. Never saw him again. Probably went back to *Gringolandia*. He was okay though, that son of a…" Glancing at his grandmother, Pepe checked

86

the epithet. "Anyway, I knew what I wanted to be. An engineer. Seemed a crazy ambition. How was I to get to the Polytechnic? Where would the money come from? We didn't have contacts, nobody who could help. I felt like I was always looking up – to the priest, to school teachers, to people who lived in proper houses. When I glanced down, there seemed to be nobody; everybody who lived in the world was closer to god than us."

Doña Rosa opened her eyes with a start. "*Dios mio*, how can you say such a thing? Closer to God than your own family!"

"No, *abuela*,"[24] Pepe answered gently. "I was saying how it seemed to a little boy."

"What little boy?"

"A boy at school. Years ago when I was in primary."

"Bring him here. I'll teach him a thing or two. Far from God! Our family? The cheek of it."

"He died, *abuela*."

"Well then," said Doña Rosa, "may God keep him safe in heaven. We mustn't abuse the departed."

"Politics didn't interest me," Pepe said. "When you're hungry, worried about food for the family, there's no room in your head for much else. I saw how my uncle lived. He's a plumber. Still goes down to the *Zócalo* and sits in front of the cathedral – you know where they all go, carpenters, electricians – waiting for a job. He's good, really skilled, but sometimes when he's finished a job they refuse to pay him, or find a pretext to pay him half. I saw how they used to treat my mother when she went to people's houses to wash their clothes. Sometimes, instead of paying her, they gave her leftovers from their last meal."

"That never happened in our house," Olivia said.

"We were five years here before my mother found a job with your family."

Olivia sighed. "*Ay Carmencita.*"

"The Polytechnic accepted me in the end," Pepe continued.

---

24 Grandmother.

"Wasn't easy but I kept at it, failing exams and then passing them, failing then passing. Took me twice as long as most students because I was working all the time. So once I got in, I kept my head down and left politics to the others. Don't think I didn't have a conscience. Nobody needed to tell me anything about injustice, or that our politicians were corrupt and couldn't care less about the people. But I thought if I screwed up, they'd kicked me out of the poly and my life would end. When the police started jailing *compañeros*, however, something came over me, a kind of anger that maybe I'd carried with me all the time but couldn't let out. I saw that the student leaders weren't trying to deceive anyone. They were honourable; they had courage, ideals. They opened my eyes and made me think we could change things, make a better country for all our people."

"Do you still think this way?" I asked.

Pepe looked at me, surprised. I had said nothing until this moment. He glanced at Olivia and then back at me.

Doña Rosa lifted the lid on the larger of the two pots. "Time to eat."

Removing the coffee pot from the other ring, she replaced it with an iron griddle – a *comal*. From a bowl on the table, she took ready-made corn tortillas, reheated them on the *comal* and placed them in a tortilla basket, covering them with a cloth to keep them warm.

"*Platos y cubiertos, Pepe, por favor, despiértate que ya está la comida.*"

Pepe fetched plates, forks and spoons from the house. The plates were brown earthenware splashed with green glaze. Doña Rosa ladled steaming black beans onto each one and handed them round.

In the middle of the table, beside the tortilla basket, were dishes of shredded lettuce and a bowl of red sauce.

"*Que aprovechen,*" said Doña Rosa.

"*Gracias*, Doña Rosa."

We each took a tortilla, coaxed beans into the centre from the side of our plates, topped the filling with lettuce and a teaspoon of sauce, and rolled it up. Tortillas and beans, the staple of all Mexico, the butt of peasant humour, the piquant irresistible flavour of survival.

"*Qué tal los frijoles?*"

"Delicious, señora. You are a wonderful cook," Olivia said.

From an urn under the tree, Pepe ladled out *agua de jamaica*[25] into beakers and handed them round. I wanted to repeat my question about whether he still thought the country would change but sensed he had avoided the question. I asked him instead what he intended to do now that he was free again.

"I have to make up for lost time," he said. "I learned in jail that what the country needs most is educated people. I have to finish my degree if I want to make a difference."

"No more politics?"

"Not for the moment."

"Not ever," said Doña Rosa. "Not while I'm still alive. It's too dangerous."

"They tortured him in jail," Olivia said as we drove away. "I saw him when he came out. Like a skeleton. No hair, cuts and bruises everywhere, a big scar on the side of his head. He won't speak about what happened. I heard they told some of the students that if they ever talked about their experiences, the police would come back and cut their balls off. Can you imagine?"

I shook my head.

"*Ay! si con sólo una gota de poesía o de amor pudiéramos aplacar la ira del mundo.*"

"What's that?"

"It's a line of Neruda's. 'If only a drop of poetry or love could appease the anger of the world.'"

---

25 Hibiscus tea.

FOURTEEN

TENOCHTITLAN – 1519

Alva

Turned out Tlaco was smitten. Not long after my brotherly quizzing of Xochitl, he sent word that he would be making a formal visit to our home. We guessed what that meant, but to remove any possible doubt as to his purpose, he made sure to tell me "in confidence" that he had obtained permission from the palace to wed a hero's sister.

On the appointed day, he showed up smartly dressed with a servant in tow carrying gifts. Uncles and aunts came for the ceremony, friends too, including Tecuichpo, without whom no family occasion could ever be complete. Our mother was beside herself with happiness. Xochitl looked appropriately fetching. Everyone was wreathed in smiles.

Atza, as the male elder, amused the party by pretending to give Tlaco a hard time, questioning his credentials and his family background, and doubting, tongue in cheek, whether his prospects were sufficiently promising to maintain my sister and her children in the lifestyle they had a right to expect. Too excited to catch the humour, Tlaco answered every question so seriously and at such length that before long, Atza took pity both on him and his listeners, embraced him, told him how pleased we all were with his choice, and invited the happy couple to live with us – as was the custom – though everyone knew that Tlaco already owned a house a couple of blocks away, a family inheritance.

As for me, I could not have been happier for them, though my feelings were inevitably tinged with a wistfulness that I could only express through sidelong glances at Tecuichpo. Once or twice she caught me looking at her and sent a smile in return that made my heart leap with foolish hope.

We toasted the couple with *yolixpa*[26] – well fermented – and my mother and aunts served a feast of *guajalote* with *mole*, *mextlapique and huitlacoche*[27] all garnished with *tecuitlatl*[28] and guacamole. And for dessert, we ate black *zapote* and *tetzapotl*[29] and drank chocolate and more *yolixpa* so that we all became a little tipsy as the evening drew on.

I made sure to sit next to Tecuichpo round the fire and as darkness fell – along with my inhibitions – I ventured gently and unobtrusively to caress her. She pretended to pay no attention but I felt her tremble and her reaction set me aflame. Oh, how I wanted to seize her then! I could not do that, but I wondered madly if my hand might find its way to a more intimate place, and mentally I willed her to shift her weight just enough to allow me licence so that at least she would know the strength of my longing and, perhaps, if luck found in my favour, I would know hers. Even now, as an old man, I look back on that moment with embarrassment yet with pleasure too, savouring the recollection of our innocence and the urgency of young love. What is more

---

26   An alcoholic drink made with herbs and honey.
27   Turkey with sauce, tamales of salamander, and corn truffle.
28   Spirulina.
29   Black sapote and mamey.

beautiful than to know a woman's desire, lovelier by far than anything I could imagine for myself?

I never found out if she would have acquiesced, for a messenger arrived summoning her back to the palace. His name was Yaomahuitl and we knew him for a gossip. He wore the knowing expression of the conspirator, and always spoke softly and "in confidence", drawing his listener aside to whisper tittle-tattle into their ear as if he were passing stolen goods.

As ever he had something to impart. Usually, his secrets went no further than repetition of titbits he'd picked up in the market or in the corridors of the palace, nonsense about courtships and family rows. This time, however, he revealed something so startling that we knew at once it must contain an element of truth. He said that gods had arrived on the eastern shores of the empire. They had journeyed – so he said – over the sea in huge floating houses, and on land they travelled on the backs of mighty deer that foamed at the mouth. The story seemed too fantastic for a pedestrian scandalmonger like Yaomahuitl to have invented.

"Who told you this?" Tlaco demanded.

"Couldn't say, could I." He bowed to Tecuichpo. "A man like me, trusted in the highest circles, must guard his sources."

Tlaco tried again. "How do you know these creatures are gods?"

Yaomahuitl looked round the room at our faces flickering in the light of the fire. "Stands to reason. What else could they be?"

FIFTEEN

CULIACÁN, SINALOA – 1971

James

The college sent me to give a week of lectures in Culiacán, capital of the state of Sinaloa, a steamy coastal city famous for its hospitality, the beauty of its women, its criminal underworld, and the corruption of public officials. I was chosen as the youngest member of faculty and the one least likely to be missed should I get into trouble. Besides, no one else wanted the job.

Teachers from all over the state were bussed in to a downtown theatre, and I spent the week imparting knowledge I barely held and wisdom I could not with honesty claim to possess. Arriving back at my hotel on the final afternoon, I found a note of thanks for my efforts from the mayor, and an invitation to a farewell dinner with himself and the local minister of education. A car would pick me up at seven-thirty.

At the appointed time, three black limousines drew up in front of the hotel. A uniformed chauffeur verified my identity before ushering me into the middle car, where I found myself seated in the rear alongside my host while the minister rode in front. We drove to a nearby restaurant, a low, whitewashed building with a wide lawn fringed by flame trees and acacias where a long table had been furnished to receive us. The mayor took the seat at the head of the table with the minister and myself on either side. Occupants from the other two vehicles took the remaining places. All of these were men in their mid-thirties dressed in identical dark suits.

Night had fallen, but the air was warm and heavy with moisture. Sprigs of jasmine in slender vases had been placed along the centre line of the table, their sweet scent vying with coarser odours of singed garlic and peppers drifting from the kitchen.

"This is the best restaurant in Culiacán," the minister assured me.

"Some say El Norteño is better," said the mayor.

The minister leaned towards me.

"His cousin owns the Norteño. My brother-in-law owns this place."

Minister and mayor might themselves have been brothers. Both were heavily built with thick black hair and sideburns and wore white guayaberas over dark pants. Only their moustaches differed: the minister's pencil thin, the mayor's florid like Emiliano Zapata's.

After we had sat down and toasted the Republic with a shot of tequila, the minister gave a speech thanking me for my help in bringing education to the state. My contribution would not be forgotten. I would always be made welcome should I ever wish to return.

Over a dinner of ceviche and grilled snapper with garlic, my hosts lectured me on the delights of their state: the beaches and seafood, the fertility of the soil, and the women who were irresistible to any man worthy of the name.

"Sinaloa," said the mayor, "produces more Miss Mexicos than all the other states put together." He appealed to the bodyguards. "Isn't that so, muchachos?"

"*Sí, señor.*"

After dinner, we returned to the limousines and drove out of town. Night closed in on us as we left the street lights behind, becoming black and impenetrable beyond the narrow beams of the headlamps. For half an hour we drove in silence, my one question about where we were heading evoking a chuckle and a comment that I would "soon see for myself". I began to wonder if I had unwittingly given offence, committed an unpardonable breach of etiquette that demanded retribution of a kind from which there could be no redemption.

We branched off the paved road onto a gravel track, loose stones crackling against the car's undercarriage. My hosts became animated, talked of the pleasures that awaited me – their guest – at journey's end. Ten minutes later, lights appeared in the distance. I took them to be those of a village or a small town, an impression seemingly confirmed as we drew closer and could see the outline of buildings. On entering the first street, however, it became apparent that the structures on each side were neither shops nor houses but bars, one after the other, the exterior of each illuminated by hundreds of coloured bulbs flashing the name of the establishment and the delights to be savoured within: neon images of women kicking their legs into the air and winking with an incandescent eye. Under the minister's direction, we drove by the first bars and rounded several corners until we came to the one of his choice, a long single-storey building decorated to resemble a log cabin of the old American West but with a vast illuminated headboard of a woman riding a bronco and making vigorous thrusts of the hips while her head reared back in pleasure.

Inside, a rectangular room was furnished with round tables mostly unoccupied and, at the far end, a bar with shelves stocked with liquor and beer bottles. Along the near-side wall, as far as the entrance, a line of young women in miniskirts and high heels sat cross-legged. A waitress led us to a pair of tables in the centre of the room. The minister ordered refreshments for the party – cans of beer, bottles of tequila, salt, wedges of lemon and a plate of delicacies. He waited until the order had been delivered and we had consumed a round of drinks before turning to me.

"Which one would you like?"

I looked at him, puzzled.

"Feel free." He gestured towards the line of women. "Anyone that takes your fancy is yours."

Seeing me hesitate, my neighbour at the table leaned towards me and spoke in a whisper. "You must accept. The minister will take it as an insult if you do not."

"Our professor is shy," the mayor said.

"Then I'll choose the girl," returned the minister. He looked directly at me and I nodded assent.

Casting an eye over the line of girls, he selected one and beckoned her with a jerk of the head. At once, the girl stood up, approached our table and stood before the minister. She was around five feet tall, slim, delicate, with pale brown skin and a cascade of black hair.

The minister surveyed her from head to foot before turning to me. "Beautiful is she not?"

"Very beautiful."

"We have a special guest with us tonight," said the minister, addressing the girl and pointing me out at the same time. "I want you to show him some true Sinaloan hospitality."

She walked over to where I sat and stood at my shoulder.

"Do you like him?" the minister asked.

"He's very handsome," said the girl with a show of admiration.

"How handsome?"

"One of the most handsome I ever saw."

"More handsome than a Mexican?" the mayor grunted.

"I thought he *was* Mexican."

"He's a foreigner."

"Well he's every bit as handsome as a Mexican."

The mayor nodded.

"What are you going to do for our special guest?" the minister inquired.

"Whatever he desires, señor."

"Then you'll entertain him for pleasure."

"I'd be willing to pay him." she said.

The minister laughed, and the table followed suit. She had sensed that this was a powerful man who was not to be crossed.

"What luck he has," the mayor said.

The girl brushed a breast against my shoulder. "Come." She took my hand and led me in the direction of the bar at the far end of the room. I was aware at once of being an object of interest, as if I were moving in a pool of light. We continued behind the bar and along a narrow corridor lined with doors, one of which the girl opened with a key. Inside was a narrow room with barely space enough for a double bed pushed against the wall and a sink with a red towel suspended beneath on a rail. The room smelled of humidity and carbolic soap. I sat on the bed, and the girl sat beside me, her body pressed against mine. At that moment I could not have produced an erection to save my life.

"I'm not in the mood," I apologized. "It's not your fault. You're beautiful. I'm...too tired."

My excuse sounded implausible even to my own ears for the young are seldom too tired for love. Nor was there an absence of chemistry, for I found her attractive and sensual. Perhaps I felt sorry for her, for her delicacy, for the dreariness of the bar, for the barter that made of this lovely girl a bauble on a market stall, one of twenty or thirty distinguishable from each other only by perfections and imperfections of face and form, and the individual lusts of clients. "Compassion," Norman Mailer once remarked, "dulls the appetite."

"Not to worry," the girl said. "Happens from time to time. I'll get some coffee."

She left, returning a few minutes later with a pot of coffee, two mugs, and a plate of cookies.

"If you change your mind," she said, "you can have me later."

She wanted to talk, and I wanted to listen.

She told me she was twenty-two and had grown up in a squatter neighbourhood on the edge of town. Except for a communal water supply from a single faucet, there were no services of the kind we expect in a city: no electricity, no transportation; an open ditch that ran a few metres behind the shack served as a sewer. Her father died after a fight in a bar with someone who was carrying a gun and turned out to be an off-duty police officer. Her mother did her best to feed and clothe three children, but there was no money and one day she walked out and never came back.

I asked how she got into the...business and she told me that the nightclub owner had spotted her in the street and given her food and shelter in return for providing comfort to customers. She was fourteen years old.

"I'm not supposed to do this work," she said. "Because God doesn't approve. Father Joseph knows all about it. I go to confession. He's such a good man. Are you a Catholic? Well it doesn't matter. Father Joseph says everyone is a child of God. He says he understands me and that God will forgive me because it's my work and I have mouths to feed."

"You have children?"

"Three girls and a boy."

"Four?"

She nodded.

"You won't have any more?"

"I don't know."

"Don't you use contraceptives?"

She looked shocked. "I couldn't. Father Joseph says

contraceptives are made by the Devil. If God wants to give me more children, He will."

An hour later we emerged hand in hand, walking the gauntlet to where our hosts sat – noisy now with the effect of drink. One of them spotted our approach and pointed us out to the others. They turned towards us, eyes on the girl. As we reached the table, she snuggled close to me.

"Well," the minister asked her. "How was he?"

Swaying in his chair, the mayor glared at us with dull suspicion.

"Fantastic," said the girl. "He pleasured me twice."

"We must congratulate our guest," the minister said. "Our women are not so easy to please."

He looked at the girl for confirmation.

"*Sí, señor*, we can be difficult. But sometimes we are conquered."

The mayor eyed the girl with drunken malevolence. "How come you like being screwed by foreigners? Why don't you consume local produce? Eh? Tell me that?" He turned towards me. "We don't allow strangers near our women. Didn't anybody tell you?"

He half rose from his chair, knocking a tequila bottle over and spilling the contents across the table.

"We cut their balls off…"

The minister stood up and pushed the mayor back into his chair. "*Cálmate*, Durán. *El licenciado* is our guest, and we gave him the girl."

A waitress mopped up the spilled liquor and brought a replacement bottle. The minister ordered one of the bodyguards to pour everyone a drink – including the señorita. He raised his glass.

"To our guest and to the beauty of Mexican women."

The mayor tossed back the drink, his eyes bloodshot. "They're all fucking whores."

"Don't take it personally, señorita," the minister said to the girl. "He doesn't mean it."

I had a hundred-dollar bill in my back pocket, and while another round was being poured, I slid my arm round the girl and slipped it into her palm. Her hand left mine momentarily while she secreted the note. My fingers settled against her hip and through the thin material of her skirt, I could feel the outline of her underwear. Desire flashed at me, free from the pity I had felt earlier but free also from any possibility of fulfilment and of subsequent remorse. We had made a silent pact. She had defended my status, for no other reason than sympathy, and I had done what little I could to put bread on her table and into the mouths of her children. At that moment lust seemed to me more like a homage than an impulse to use her beauty for my own ends, and more pleasurable than a ten-second spasm in a humid box room.

I still dream sometimes of meeting her again, though if she lives she is old now, like me, and we would not recognize each other. I never knew her name nor gave her mine.

SIXTEEN

TENOCHTITLAN – 1519

Alva

Shortly after Xochitl's betrothal to Tlaco, my regiment left for a month of exercises: marches across the valley and through the passes to Cuauhnahuac and back again, there and back, there and back in the insufferable heat of the dry season with mock battles against each other for entertainment. Tlaco, called to a higher station, was spared the fatigue. He had been nominated to the emperor's advisory committee on war and peace – an elevation that placed him almost on the same level as Palintzin. Only then did I grasp the extent to which Tlaco's birth had blessed him with privilege. Here was the explanation of why the general had given him such special treatment when we fought the Quetzalans.

Because my own status had also changed following Macuiltzin's capture, it fell to me to marshal the columns, keep them in line when we were marching, set up battle orders and observe the mock clashes so that I could afterwards correct

101

mistakes. What did I know about such things? For my pains, I received only a sense of loneliness, distance from the troops I commanded and no less distance from my superior officer, an older man whose name I forget but whose condescending attitude towards me I remember well. My recollection of that miserable military workout – my last – was that I spoke to no one except to issue an order or to acknowledge one. By the end, I was longing for company, anxious of course to see Tecuichpo who had not ceased to trouble my dreams, and curious to hear more about the mysterious travellers who had landed on our eastern shore. I knew the troops were talking about these strangers, but they clammed up for fear of a reprimand whenever they thought me close enough to hear them. They can't have known more than I did, but still I would have much preferred their chatter to my own solitary musings.

The day after my return home, I made for the market, knowing that Atza would have picked up the latest news. I found him at his stall, deep in discussion with a gathering of shoppers and merchants.

By then everyone had heard about the strangers on the coast; the subject was on every tongue. I joined the group and listened. One speaker maintained that the strangers were gods, another that they were enemies bent on conquest, a third that they were merely travellers and came as friends, while a fourth was sure that Lord Quetzalcóatl and his retinue had returned to live once more among the people.

Seeing Atza hotly engaged, I wandered off to see what was happening elsewhere. All over the market I found similar discussion, people arguing with each other, joining one crowd then moving to another in search of fresh detail or to repeat an opinion they had already heard elsewhere.

Back at my brother's stall, I hung around until, at length, he spotted me; at which point, he introduced me as his little brother the brave soldier, a young hero of our people. The pride in his tone ran over my embarrassment for he had never expressed himself that way before. Could I after all be a hero? For a few moments I basked in the crowd's applause. That is until my brother returned to the subject in hand, the strangers, in a way suggesting that his brief acknowledgement of me had been no more than a distraction from more serious issues. Speaking in his deep, resonant boom that brooked no competition (he was reputed to have the loudest voice in the market), he embarked on his own interpretation of the news, and was in full flow when one of his bosom pals showed up.

Teudile was the closest I ever got before the disaster to being acquainted with a conman. There weren't many of them around in those days, not in the capital at any rate – the least penalty for a deceiver being a life sentence as the victim's slave. Not that Teudile had ever been convicted. He was too shrewd to risk direct confrontation with the law. Rather, he skirted trouble by making a living and building a reputation where the law could not reach. Information was his trade, though "informing" might be a better description. He was everybody's messenger, selling the truth when he possessed enough of it of value, but more often peddling rumour, betrayals of confidence, innuendo and gossip his clients dared not ignore because the price of doing so might be much higher than the price Teudile charged for revealing what he knew. What he traded on were the weaknesses of those who paid him. And when his revelations proved untrue, his response was always that a god had undergone a change of mind, as gods were wont to do.

Much of his success in our city he owed to being not one of us. Some said that he was Mayan, others that he came from the north. He told my brother that he was from Cuetlaxtlan – a region that had had more than its share of clashes with the empire and whose main city we had destroyed some thirty years before. What is certain is that he spoke our language with a foreign accent and with less than perfect accuracy – stressing

103

words in the wrong place and sometimes falling into simple grammatical errors. His appearance, too, seemed to us a little odd. The careless way he dressed, his waddling gait reminiscent of a duck, his large hooked nose ever poised to pry into the affairs of others, his angular frame and the colour of his skin much paler than ours all gave him a mysterious air of otherness, and of being privy to knowledge that could not be uncovered without him.

He spent much of his life travelling from place to place delivering what he knew to whomever would pay for it and picking up scuttlebutt that he could sell elsewhere. Atza used to say that there were no goods in all the world so valuable as the ones Teudile traded. And it was true that he made a handsome living, since many of his customers were chiefs and high officials, including Moctezuma himself.

When Teudile arrived that day at my brother's stall in the market, he had just been released from the palace where he had spent the previous ten days detained at the emperor's pleasure.

"Here is the man who can tell us what's going on," Atza proclaimed, beckoning his friend forward. Teudile needed no prompting. Facing the little audience, he embarked on a lengthy account of his recent journey to the coast, his encounters with various chieftains, narrow escapes from thieves and so on. Naturally he had met with the strangers, and as everyone could see, had lived to tell the tale. On his return to the city, he had performed his duty by going straight to the palace. There he had been ushered at once into the emperor's presence.

Having aroused our interest, Teudile paused. We urged him to continue, but he surveyed our eager faces, tapped his nose with his forefinger, cocked his head on one side and then on the other. He could not reveal details of his report to the emperor, still less how the latter had replied. It was more than his life was worth.

Despite repeated urgings from the crowd, he refused to say anything more but he whispered that he would tell my brother and I all that he had seen in private, over dinner that evening.

We dined at Atza's house where Teudile usually stayed when in town. Typically, he made us wait until the meal had been cleared away and we were sipping chocolate before he returned to the subject we were so eager to hear. Food, he insisted, should never be allowed to compete with matters of great weight. His technique of securing attention could hardly be bettered. By the time he was ready to speak, both my brother and I were ready either to enter his service or to strangle him.

"You know me," he began at last, "I wouldn't trouble the emperor with trifles. Wouldn't dare. On the other hand, I wasn't coming with ordinary news, was I? I mean, I'm one of the few people in the world who has seen these creatures up close. Dined with them. No kidding. They invited me. Frightened I was at first because I thought I might end up on their table myself. Turns out they don't hold with eating people. Their food isn't like ours though. They eat white stuff with almost everything. Bread – that's what they call it. Not bad."

"Are they gods or people?" Atza asked.

"On balance, I'd say they're people. Only…"

"Go on."

"They're different. They have fair skin as if the sun had burned away their colour. Maybe that's why they cover themselves with clothes, leaving only their faces and hands exposed. Most of the men have hair growing on their faces, but I saw two women and several boys among them whose faces are smooth. I asked them how they reached our shore, and they pointed to three big houses on the water and told me they'd floated across the sea in them. Now they've set up on the coast and are living on the land. They have big deer they call horses that snort and foam at the mouth, and fierce dogs that bark, snarl at strangers and are easily roused to anger. Their weapons are fearsome. Strapped to their sides, they carry long swords of shining metal harder than anything we know. Worst of all, they have reeds that make loud bangs and kill at a distance. The biggest ones sit on the ground and throw heavy stones that destroy everything in their way. I saw a demonstration. With one bang they knocked over a palm tree as if it were a sapling. On the coast, everyone is terrified of them: all submit, and if they do not, they are killed or worse, tortured. They insist they are not gods but worship a god of their own who they say is the only one. Before meals they bow their heads while one of their priests chants a prayer. If they were gods, they wouldn't bow their heads, would they? Their chief has a woman with him, one like us, who translates for him. Her name is Malinali. She is Mayan but she speaks our language.[30] One of their soldiers speaks Mayan so the two of them serve as translators. She translates from Mexican to Mayan and he translates from Mayan to their language. It's a bit slow."

Now that I write this down, I see how confused we were. It took us a long time even to learn the chief's name: Cortés. Malintzín we called him at first – husband of Malinali. At the time, it didn't seem to matter. It was as if all the important truths we already knew, because truth was power and no people were more powerful than the Mexica.

"Why have they come?" I asked.

"They want to meet the emperor."

"You told him that?"

Teudile nodded.

"What did he say?"

"He went nuts. 'They're gods. Gods,' he kept saying. Walking back and forth, and muttering to himself. I told him 'They're not gods; they're just men, almost like us.' When his back was turned, I snatched glances at him. He was trembling like a leaf, and in front of me, too, a nobody. 'What should I do?' he said. He wasn't asking me, of course. He was asking the air, the gods. 'Maybe the strangers want presents,' he said. 'Send them gold, Lord,' I said, 'that's what they asked for. Gold.' 'If that's what

---

30 Nahuatl.

they want, we'll send it,' he said. 'Gold and jewels and the best food and blankets. Anything they need. Perhaps then they'll go back home.' 'Well, Lord Emperor,' I said, 'they seem very keen to meet you personally.' Stupid of me. I should have kept my mouth shut. 'Meet me?' he said. 'What are you talking about? I don't want them here. Meet me, you say? Who am I? What am I? What do they want of me? Are the gods coming for me? Am I to meet my father? Why are you standing there?' On and on he went with questions, though I don't think he took any more notice of my answers. Anyway, at one point, he caught me staring at him. I probably looked astonished. It wasn't that I meant to insult him, don't get me wrong. I know my place. I just couldn't believe what I was hearing. Here was the greatest emperor in the world behaving, well between us…This is between us, isn't it ?…Behaving, like a. No, I daren't say it…Scared out of his wits. Anyway, he was walking away from me talking to the air when he suddenly spun round and saw me looking straight at him. That was it. Just as quickly, he remembered who I was and who he was and he gave orders to detain me."

"How did you get out?"

"He wants me to go back with presents and messages. Only a few of us have ever met these strangers. He thinks since I survived the first encounter, I can probably handle another one."

"He's sending you alone, with gifts? He trusts you with them? A man of your reputation," said Atza.

Teudile grinned. "More or less. A couple of bearers will come with me and three warriors – rank and file, of course. When he called me back into his presence, he spoke kindly like a father. Can you imagine? I'm to tell the locals on the coast to keep the strangers well supplied with food and anything else they need. Gifts and food. 'Make them feel good,' he said. 'And if they don't want the food…' The emperor thought for a moment. 'If they prefer to eat people…' The idea seemed to please him because he brightened up. 'Well then,' he says to me, 'allow yourself to be eaten with good grace and I promise to look after your wives and children.' As if he knows whether I'm married or how many kids I have. I mean, even I don't know that. Not that it matters. He's happy to send me because I'm disposable. He probably doesn't think I'll survive a second time."

We drank a round of *pulque*, the sixth or seventh of the evening. My head was buzzing.

At some point, Teudile admitted he hadn't told Moctezuma everything. "I couldn't, in the state he was in."

"So?"

"These strangers, Spaniards they call themselves, are persuading people to stop sending tribute to us and to join them instead."

"They're preparing to make war on us?"

"Wouldn't be surprised."

After a pause, Atza said. "Take care of yourself on this trip, won't you?"

"I'm already on a second life," Teudile replied. "Know how many people the emperor has had sacrificed over this? Anybody he consults who tells him something he doesn't like goes to the gods. If you ask me, we're in deep trouble."

SEVENTEEN

TENOCHTITLAN – 1519

Alva

Nothing stayed secret for long in our city. Within a few days, Teudile's interview with Moctezuma had found its way down every street and alley, along every canal and across the water into the towns and villages on the shore. Some reacted with terror to match the emperor's; others took little notice or dismissed the story as chit-chat; while the wits for which our city was famous busied themselves inventing jokes, many of them at Moctezuma's expense. How wonderfully brave we are when the enemy is distant and our rulers out of earshot. Not one of us but would have shat himself if we thought the emperor or any of his officers could put a name to the jokes or the jokes to a name.

When the strangers began to march inland though, the general mood coalesced first to apprehension and later to fury when reports reached us that they were pressuring subject nations to rebel and slaughtering those who refused. Perhaps anger is a natural reaction when threats become so grave that no alternative remains but to meet them head on. Indignation overcomes fear, and thoughts of flight give way to determination to look death in the face. To my last breath I will carry the knowledge that my own survival to the age of white hair is nothing but a defeat and that my finer duty would have been to pass beyond this earth in the company of those nobler souls who fell in defence of our way of life. Time has taught me that survival is not the same as living.

Anyway, the gossip about Moctezuma ran rife, and though I've no doubt the authorities heard it, there wasn't much they could do. A few people were arrested for rowdiness and disturbing the peace (euphemisms for insulting the emperor, which was a crime so serious as to be unthinkable, indeed so unimaginable that there was no law to prohibit it), but in the end they were sentenced to no more than a few days of hard labour.

Chances are Moctezuma had no time or patience for trivia, being too busy dealing with his own fears and the demands of leadership. What he foresaw, perhaps more clearly than anyone else, was the prospect of an enemy invasion on a scale that no emperor before him had encountered.

He called a meeting of top advisers. Some of the most important were absent on missions to other parts of the empire which may have been why Tlaco received a summons at so young an age, although his pedigree and the reputation he owed to Palintzin made him an obvious candidate for the honour. To my astonishment, on the second day of deliberations, I also received a message to attend the palace. The emperor had expressed a desire to know the opinion of a young hero. Given that I'd spent the previous afternoon in the market with a group of Atza's friends sniggering at the emperor's expense, my first thought was relief that at least I was not being arrested.

When the emperor sent for you, you didn't hang around. He'd been known to sacrifice people who kept him waiting. So I washed, put on fresh clothes and hurried to the palace.

Only at the entrance did I slow down. Never before had I passed into the inner sanctum of this huge building which ran the full length of one side of the central square. A soldier on guard pointed me in the right direction, though he also warned me that I would need further guidance as I went on because the palace was "a bit complicated".

Following his instructions, I entered to find myself in a courtyard from which various corridors led to different parts of the interior. People were hurrying to and fro, emerging from one corridor and plunging into another in a constant stream. We Mexica were a smiling people, but here everyone looked solemn. Crossing the courtyard, I entered a series of rooms linked by passageways with a soldier on guard in each one. With their guidance, I found my way to Moctezuma's outer chambers where I was instructed to wait. So I waited. And waited. From time to time, a fellow citizen would arrive, summoned like myself at the emperor's pleasure. At midday, refreshments appeared which we shared with the duty guard. In return he favoured us with the observation that it was common for people to wait in vain for a summons into the imperial presence, but then he lapsed into silence after reminding us that conversation in the emperor's antechambers was forbidden. By now we were around twenty, standing quietly, strangers to each other, wrapped in our own thoughts. Only one of us was called that day, and no one on the next. We ate where we were and slept in an adjacent room. On the third day, several got the nod but I was not among them. My turn came on the fifth day. An attendant led me through yet another maze of corridors, the last of which opened into a large hall at the far end of which sat the emperor on a dais with his council below him to his left and right. The attendant positioned me just inside the entrance, indicating by a gesture that I was to go no further. I spotted Tlaco among the counsellors, sitting at a distance from the emperor, as befitted his youthfulness.

111

He nodded in my direction. Palintzin was there too, further up the hierarchy. Of the others, I recognized Itzquauhtzin, governor of Tlatelolco and, flanking the emperor, his brother Cuitláhuac and cousin Cuauhtémoc, the latter no more than my age but the finest-looking warrior I ever saw – tall, muscular, with an expression of innocent nobility of the kind that inspires men to be better than themselves, and women too you can be sure of that, for they loved and respected him and I believe gave themselves to him with no less ardour than men fought and died for him in battle.

More waiting followed. Messengers had arrived with news that the strangers were moving inland, voicing opposition to our way of life, trumpeting the virtues of their god and destroying idols of the local gods. According to one report, they had made an alliance with the Totonacas in Cempoalla, though whether this signified hostile intentions towards us no one could say. This was the subject of debate when I entered the imperial hall. Opinion was divided. Moctezuma, speaking in that strange high-pitched whine that resembled – so we were told – the speech of the gods, wondered if these strangers really were either divine themselves or messengers of a great deity, and if so then his responsibility was to welcome them as equals to himself. Better to seek their favour than to risk offending them with coldness. He should send them more gifts and invite them to visit, for our home was also theirs. And so on. Everyone murmured agreement as was our custom, though without obvious enthusiasm.

Cuitláhuac ventured the reply that others did not dare. "Lord, I think it would be unwise to invite someone into your house who might put you out of it."

"Do you contradict your Lord?" Moctezuma asked.

"My concern is to protect him."

More murmurs, stronger this time.

"And you?" The whine shot like an arrow in my direction. All eyes followed it. "What do you think?"

I had anticipated this question and had my reply at the ready. "Lord, I am but a soldier and my duty follows my one desire which is to be as a shield to my sovereign Lord."

"Very good," came the reply. "But what do you think we should do?"

"Friends are better than enemies. Therefore, since we don't know the newcomers, we should try to make friends of them, and whether they are men or gods we can thus do no harm to ourselves."

My reply had only one objective: to find a way of agreeing with the emperor without seeming slavish, for both contradiction and emulation were known to irritate him. Of course, I knew that Teudile had been instructed to return to the strangers with gifts, so I had no need to puzzle things out: the emperor was already following his own advice and leaning towards appeasement.

What did I really think? Nothing. I'd listened to Teudile but as a child listens to a storyteller, hearing the tale as if it belonged to an imaginary realm where endings are joyful and lull you to sleep with a smile. Here, standing at the foot of the mountain at whose summit great men decide whether lesser ones are to live or die, I could answer only as I had been taught, in the way and with the words that would best gratify the most powerful of my listeners.

So I sided with Moctezuma against some of his counsellors, including his own brother who could barely hide his displeasure. Nature had not favoured Cuitláhuac with a graceful stature. Unlike the emperor, he was short and squat, with clumsy features, a heavy aquiline nose, thick eyebrows and protruding lips. But if he lacked physical presence he made up for it with a piercing and brilliant mind. Also I knew him to be honourable, not least because, though betrothed to Tecuichpo and with the rights of a future husband, he had left her alone or rather continued to act as her uncle and protector. I do not think, in the end, that he was angry with me, for he understood my dilemma and that my words were dictated by self-preservation. He was, to put it bluntly, pissed off with his brother.

"You see how it pays to consult from time to time with young heroes," said the emperor, "especially those who are freshly home from war."

An audible exhalation. The emperor had made his decision. Tlaco, especially, looked relieved.

"I have sent gifts to the strangers," Moctezuma continued. "Perhaps, our generosity will satisfy them and they will proceed no further. If they do come to our house, we must welcome them as guests, even if we would not have it so."

I was dismissed from the royal presence and ordered to remain in the antechamber in case the emperor asked for me again. This time, however, my sojourn was brief for the meeting soon broke up.

Tlaco and I walked home together. He told me that it was probably the longest meeting the emperor had ever held and that few of those who had preceded me into the meeting room had survived his questions. Failure to please, he reminded me, would at best have meant jail and at worst execution.

"I was fortunate to hear the emperor's own opinion before he asked for mine."

"So you lied?"

"Not exactly. How should I know what we should do?"

"But what do you think?"

I hesitated.

"Just between ourselves of course."

"I think Cuitláhuac was probably right."

Tlaco nodded but said nothing. We walked on for a while in silence. Then I asked if I had said something wrong.

"No," Tlaco said.

That night, I tossed and turned, unable to sleep. Usually when danger looms or I feel the world press in on me, or the heavens threaten, longing for a woman takes hold. This night was no

114

exception. My thoughts conjured the image of Tecuichpo. I took her, naked, in my arms, felt the gentle swell of her breasts against me, savoured the smell of her, ran my hands along the soft curves of her body and, at length, buried my strength in the place where a man finds happiness, and there spent my force. Though the act may seem sterile in the recounting, it was never so in my mind. It was a communion with her as well as with myself: the young woman I knew, the only way I thought I could know her, or know myself in her.

EIGHTEEN

MEXICO CITY – 1970s

James

Nothing tore at the fabric of the cosy world I inhabited more than my encounter with poverty and inequality. Beggars on street corners, jobless tradesmen waiting in the *Zócalo* for someone to hire them, the endless availability of labour for petty services, the flimsy homes sprawled over barren hillsides where the *paracaidistas* – squatters from the countryside – lived.

One day, on my way to a meeting, I made a wrong turn and ended up driving along a twisting road that turned out to be the old road from Mexico City to Toluca.[31] For a kilometre, there were houses and small stores on each side, but these then gave way on my right to a wire fence lined on the inside with dense brushwood, and on my left by a crude wooden railing high enough to obscure whatever lay on the far side. I drove slowly, looking for an entrance where I could turn the car round. At length, a

---

31   The provincial capital of the state of Mexico.

dumper truck emerged from a gap in the railing. I turned into the same spot and found myself staring through the windscreen into a deep valley framed on the far side by a sheer cliff face. A wide, rutted track led in a series of curves to the valley floor where a line of similar trucks were unloading their contents. A stomach-heaving stench of household waste rose from the depths, revealing that this was a city garbage dump. Between the piles of refuse and on the flattened summit of the largest ones were huddles of rudimentary shacks cobbled together from bits of corrugated iron, hoardings, old tarpaulins and cardboard boxes. I tried to count the number of dwellings, but they were too many – stretching as far as the eye could see along the valley at odd angles like a cubist collage.

As the trucks disgorged their contents, inhabitants of this strange inferno – men, women, children – rummaged through each fresh pile, while groups of others waited for the next consignment or the one after.

The clatter of trucks arriving and leaving, the clouds of dust thrown up from the track, the steepness of the valley, the relentless digging, searching, and sifting, resembled a perverse industrial process, a gigantic human machine operated by a labour force of slaves in a terrible, ceaseless drudgery. Here was a Dantesque inferno from a deep circle of hell.

A group of men had gathered at the top of the track, some drinking from liquor bottles, a few carrying stones in their hands. One wielded a broken bottle by the neck and was waving its jagged edge in my direction. I turned the car round. As I did so, a rock cracked into the passenger door; a second one slammed into the windscreen, crazing it in concentric circles from the point of contact. A third grazed my jaw – I hadn't thought to close the side window – and I heard the men's cries as they advanced towards me:

"Anything that comes here we take apart…"

"Strangers."

"Assholes."

"Faggots."

"We fuck them first."

An instant later, I was through and out into the open road. Out but not away, for I could never forget that town built on city garbage, the countless souls living on and from trash, the children – above all the children – not consigned to hell for their misdeeds as Dante would have it, but born there in innocence under an indifferent sky, in sight of god and a careless world.

Not long afterwards, I found myself in odd juxtaposition to that hellish place.

NINETEEN

TENOCHTITLAN – 1519

Alva

'd been told not to breathe a word to anyone about Moctezuma's conference.

Tlaco reiterated the warning. "The emperor doesn't want to cause alarm. That's the official explanation anyway."

"And the unofficial?"

"My guess? He doesn't want people to know he's trying to bribe the strangers to go away. If you ask me, he's scared to death."

"You don't like him, do you?"

"You're the only man beneath the sun who'd dare ask me that." He glared at me, then burst out laughing. "What do you think?"

I made no reply and we let it drop. Some things couldn't be said. I can say them now, but why bother? When someone has passed on and the circumstances lie buried, why let them rummage around in your thoughts, disturbing your feelings as if they still lived?

Anyway, Moctezuma's precautions were in vain. Everyone knew what was going on, or thought they knew. News arrived thick and fast, most of it alarming and much of it confirmed from different sources as more messengers arrived from outposts of the empire. What we still didn't know was who the strangers were. A few days after the council meeting, we learned for certain that the Totonacas – goaded by the strangers – had rebelled against our rule. The announcement evoked humour rather than alarm. By reputation, Totonacas were the ugliest and laziest people known to humankind. We considered them an inferior people, an opinion I admit to sharing. Their chief, Tlacochcalcatl (we called him Fatso), didn't help. I had never seen him in the flesh but everyone knew roughly what he looked like from caricatures daubed on the Totonaca pyramid in Azcapotzalco (it stood in one of the back streets, near a dung pile), and from descriptions by traders. Not only was he the fattest leader in the empire, but he was also the most venal and corrupt. Stupid too by all accounts. A buffoon that only idiots like the Totonacas would tolerate. Though maybe with hindsight, a foolish leader is preferable when you think on the mess the clever ones make.

Not that rebellions generally gave much cause for concern. Every year there were several, and hardly a moon passed when we were not quelling an uprising somewhere and bringing a foreign leader to heel. Soon, however, it became clear that this was no ordinary insurgency: the strangers who instigated it imprisoned two of our tax collectors and then went on to smash all the idols in the local temples, while that grubby obesity, Tlacochcalcatl, happily looked on. Well, in truth, we weren't sure the fat chief had been happy about the destruction, but rumour had it that he accepted whatever the newcomers chose to do. None of us had any doubt as to why. He was a coward and feared to confront them. Instead, he looked on as they sacked a nearby garrison – one of ours. It was lightly guarded and by all accounts the battle was over almost before it had begun.

Lightly guarded? Nothing more was usually required to keep order. The mere sight of a Mexican soldier was enough to put fear into the Totonacas, and clashes with them were always brief. Something unusual was going on.

Tlaco, Atza and I saw Teudile off on his journey. He had anticipated travelling with no more than a couple of bearers and maybe a soldier or two. Instead, his retinue consisted of five soldiers and thirteen slaves, the latter laden with the emperor's gifts. We prayed to Yacatecuhtli, god of travellers, for his safe return but in truth none of us felt any anxiety for him, only curiosity and a certain excitement. We were eager to hear more of the strangers, and urged him to complete his mission quickly so that he could hurry back with more news.

How trite our enthusiasm seems now. It was as if we were living in a child's dream where everything imaginable worked to our pleasure, made to order like a set of clothes from a tailor. We knew our fortunes might change should we ever be so foolish as to neglect the gods who had favoured us. At school, we were even taught that one day our civilization would disappear, as others had (for we knew of ruined cities, like Teotihuacan, long since abandoned by a people who had left scant record of themselves). But such a day seemed far distant and would come long after our own generation had passed away.

With no thought in our minds that Teudile might be running any kind of risk on the trip, we spent the night before his departure partying with him and his aides, and as the sun was casting his first rays over the lake, we sent them on their way in high spirits and very drunk.

As it happened, only Teudile survived the trip. The strangers thought the bearers and the soldiers were imperial spies and killed them all, sparing only Teudile so that he might bear witness to their ferocity.

TWENTY

MEXICO – 2010

James

Who could explain such poverty? Where did it come from? Why was it tolerated in a world whose presiding myths demanded belief in progress and the sanctity of human life? European myths in their origin to be sure, but carried westward in small ships and laid down wherever they dropped anchor? Were we not the civilizers who brought enlightenment to the savages of America?

In 1580, three Tupi chieftains from Brazil journeyed to France – the first visitors to that country from the New World. Montaigne, the great essayist, met them in Paris and asked for their impressions of what they had seen. "They expressed astonishment," he wrote, "that a select handful of us were fabulously rich while so many of our people were poverty-stricken and starving, and they wondered why the poor didn't put the wealthy to death or set fire to their houses."

Were our myths delusory, or maybe a convenient cover for

rapaciousness, lying and trampling on the weak? Did we carry injustice to the New World as we carried disease and a lust for gold?

I set down these questions now, but then I lacked the words and maybe the thoughts to express them. I sought out teachers and read their books – Franz Fanon, Paulo Freire, Gustavo Gutierrez, Camilo Torres, sons of different countries, philosophers and priests bonded across continents and seas by indignation at the injustices of capitalism, neo-colonialism and the misery of the people. One of them, Father Camilo Torres, died with God's name on his lips and a weapon in his hands, leaving behind a phrase burned into the conscience of his nation's history: "If Jesus were alive, he would be a guerrilla fighter."

Mexico, too, had its rebellious priest: Bishop Méndez Arceo, a prelate well beloved of the people, but a thorn in the side of the government and the Church of Rome. Hard to believe that only a few years ago, clerics stood at the forefront of dissent. Liberation theology rejected the submission of the poor to the hierarchies of Church, state and market. Instead, it tied ethics to economic and political dignity to the end of labour exploitation, to free education, to equality before both human and divine law, to justice on earth as well as in the afterlife. Simple ideas, but irresistible to the fire of youth, and inspiring in their pursuit of an alternative vision for the future of humanity.

TWENTY-ONE

TENOCHTITLAN – 1563

Alva

I don't know if there has ever been a time without enemies. Priests used to speak of a golden age, when everyone lived in peace, and they'd tell of a future time, too, when the gods will no longer dispute among themselves nor set earthly creatures against each other. But the past of which they speak is so remote that no one remembers it, and that longed-for future so distant as to lie beyond the range of mortal eyes. Our present life resounds with the clamour of war, with cries of triumph and the lamentations of defeat. Perhaps war is the natural form of life on earth. Do the gods move us to violence, fighting through us the battles they would otherwise unleash upon themselves, embittering our days instead of their own with murder, sacrifice, terrible wounds and ugly death?

What provokes these sad thoughts is the moment of my story that begins on the day news reached us that the strangers had made an alliance with Tlaxcala. I'll call them Spaniards and

Spanish from now on because that's what they are – though we didn't know their name at the time.

Tenochtitlan – 1519

Unlike Totonacas, Tlaxcalans were a numerous and disciplined nation and in those days our most settled enemy. We ruled the territory around them, controlled their trade and rationed their consumption of luxury goods like cotton and salt for which they had no local sources. But though they suffered at our hands, we never managed to subdue them. And in response, they took good care after every bout of hostilities to taunt us with their love of liberty.

Now we heard that after a brief trial of strength in which they had thrown an army against the strangers' smaller force, they had bowed their heads and begged to join the enemy. Their famed resilience made the news all the more disturbing.

This was bad enough, but it paled in comparison with what occurred next. Within a few days, an army of a few hundred strangers and many thousands of Tlaxcalans marched on Cholula. A sister city to our own, Cholula was a great cultural and religious centre and only a few days' march from the shores of our lakeland home. The Spanish leader, Cortés, made a show of entering the city in peace and was received courteously and given provisions for himself and his troops. Having enjoyed the town's hospitality, he ordered its destruction, which he brought about by a simple but savage trick. He requested a peaceful meeting with all the Cholulan leaders in the central square, and once they were assembled he put them to the sword. After the initial slaughter, Spaniards and Tlaxcalans alike ran through the streets killing whoever they could find, burning the temples and the greatest houses, smashing idols and pausing only long enough in their bloodlust to rape the young women. Butchery such as this was unheard of in the annals of our people. Until that moment, though wars were frequent and hard to bear, they had their codes of honour and good conduct, among the most sacred of which was that hostilities were forbidden between host and guest. The massacre at Cholula threw everything into confusion. Suddenly, the rules by which we lived and which the known world had always observed were set at nothing. Here were different rules of a more ruthless, savage and implacable god. And we didn't understand them.

From then on there could be no pretence that the Spaniards had peaceful intentions. Anxiety hung over our city like a rain cloud. People began gathering in the streets every day to hear the latest news, to express their fears, and to fret at the lack of direction from the palace. Stories began circulating about government panic. Through Tlaco, who was now a fixture in the inner circle, I learned that Moctezuma was racked with indecision. Instead of steering a course we could all follow, he floated between two shores, on one of which stood outright capitulation and on the other helpless passivity. Rumour had it that he had contemplated flight – leaving his people to face the invaders without him.

TWENTY-TWO

MEXICO CITY – CORPUS CHRISTI, 10 JUNE 1971

James

Hearing that Bishop Méndez Arceo was going to preach downtown at the Church of St Paul the Apostle, I went to hear him. He was controversial, lauded by some as a passionate defender of the poor, criticized by others as a trouble-maker, frowned upon by the Vatican, feared by the elite, pilloried by the media as the "red bishop". Still he enjoyed the love and admiration of his flock who knew him as *el obispo del pueblo* (the people's bishop). He held a place of honour too on student campuses and in the hearts of the many who dreamed of a better world.

The colonial Church of St Paul the Apostle stood on a barren strip north of the city centre surrounded by modest homes, tiny groceries and hardware stores, and *taquerías*. Cushioned between two bare hills, it may once have looked noble and inspiring in the days before urban sprawl had hemmed in the perspective. Now, settled at an oblique angle in response to an earthquake or slippage brought on by the drying of the old lake, its thick stone walls and heavily ornate façade looked as if they were listing into the dusty earth like a stricken vessel on its way to the deep.

A small crowd, half composed of children, waited quietly in the forecourt. I threaded my way past them to the entrance, where a young priest in surplice and cassock greeted me. The church was full but if I didn't mind standing, one more person wouldn't make a difference. Or perhaps I would prefer to wait for the procession.

I asked if Bishop Méndez Arceo had arrived.

"*El Obispo no, señor. No. El Obispo no.*" He spoke softly so as not to intrude on the service taking place inside.

"I heard he was coming to preach a sermon."

"He did come once to see us. Unofficially because…You are not from round here?"

"No."

"The Church authorities didn't send you?"

"I'm a stranger."

"Ah. You are seeking God."

I nodded, thinking perhaps it might be true somewhere in a corner of my thoughts.

"He came once as a humble priest because this isn't his diocese. To show solidarity with the congregation. A lot of people here live poorly. There were disputes with the government over land."

"I came specially to hear him."

"Please stay. Father Armando Rodriguez is leading the ceremony. He is a follower of the bishop. A true revolutionary of the Church. By the grace of God, you will not be disappointed." He motioned me into the building. "Slip round the side. You will be able to see better."

Every seat and bench was occupied. Congregants were pressed together in the aisles and massed ten or twelve deep in the atrium. The women wore sombre shawls over their hair while the men were bare-headed, holding their hats by the brim. I found a vantage point near the entrance on a step leading to a side chapel from where I had a view of the upper part of the altarpiece – a high apse decorated with painted bas-reliefs of the saints, the artwork technically simple, balanced on a tightrope between reverence and kitsch.

Choristers were chanting, their amplified voices filling the church with tinny, distorted sound. Members of the congregation, mainly the women, followed the words silently with movements of their lips:

Pange, lingua, gloriosi
Corporis mysterium…

Sing, my tongue,
The mystery of the glorious body,
And of the precious Blood,
Shed to save the world,
By the King of the nations,
The fruit of a noble womb.

An elderly cleric mounted the pulpit. The young priest I had met at the door tapped me on the shoulder.

"That's Father Rodriguez."

Tall, pale, with a white beard, his appearance offered a contrast with that of his congregation, which was mainly small in stature, swarthy, the men beardless with dark moustaches.

Father Rodriguez gazed down at his flock, expressionless. "Let us take the love of God and understand what it means when His light shines upon us. Let us look at the evil His light exposes: the cult of wealth and power, of unlimited ownership, of inequality. These are the roots of suffering and dissent, the roots of our own Mexican Revolution. Scripture condemns the violence of inequality, condemns the oppression of those who, for centuries – ever since the Conquest – have been robbed of their land, their livelihood, their right to a dignified life. What true Christian can remain silent in the face of all the lies and corruption of our politicians, the ostentations of the rich, the wilful blindness of our intellectuals, the complacency of our media, the inequities of our way of life? True Christians must fight for justice, for the transformation of society and of the Church so that both serve the interests of the people. The word of God is the voice of revolution. The time has come for Christians everywhere to cease acting as counter-revolutionaries and to reject the artificial distinction between faithfulness to God and to mankind."

A respectful silence reigned while Father Rodriguez spoke, but I found it hard to tell how his words were received. Does revolution enter so readily into the hearts of those who might be too downtrodden, too poor, perhaps too pious, to risk their tenuous hold on survival? Would they even have ears for the message, and even if they did, what could they do to implement it? How, in any case, would the authorities permit the expression of such sentiments if there were any chance they might lead to action?

"A new commandment I give unto you," the priest intoned. "That ye love one another as I have loved you. By this shall all men know that ye are my disciples, if ye have love one to another. And now the Lord be with you."

"And with thy spirit," the congregation replied.

Robed assistants prepared the bread and wine of communion, and while the congregation lined up to receive the sacrament, the choir sang.

Panis angelicus
Fit panis hominum
Dat panis coelicus…

Thus Angels' Bread is made
the Bread of humankind today:
the Living Bread from heaven
with fantasies does away:
O wondrous gift indeed!
the poor and lowly may
upon their Lord and Master feed.

"O God," prayed Father Rodriguez, "who in this wonderful sacrament left us a memorial of your passion, grant, we implore you, that we may so venerate the sacred mysteries of your body and blood, as always to be conscious of the fruit of your redemption."

And then quiet in the church save for the shuffling of feet and Father Rodriguez's soft murmuring as he administered the rite, each communicant in turn kneeling for him to press the cup of wine to their lips and place a wafer, the bread and flesh of the Saviour, on their tongue. I leaned forward to see the faces of those who knelt. Veneration, humility, faith in the figure standing over them – the earthly Father – who promised absolution and peace if not in this world then in the next.

I made to leave but the young priest stopped me at the door.

"Will you not stay for the procession? We pass through the neighbourhood with song and prayer. It is very beautiful."

"I am at peace now, Father, and need to be alone."

"Then may God go with you."

TWENTY-THREE

TENOCHTITLAN – 1519

Alva

For as long as I could remember – that is from when I was a child and my father lived – we held a special family meal at least once every moon. We would gather round the hearth and my mother and my aunt Izel would serve a fine meal: *guajalote* with *mole*, *tamales* of *cuitlacoche* and *nopal*,[32] and sweetmeats. Izel, my mother's younger sister, was a tiny bundle of fire, passionate about everything, from the ardour of love to the flavour of a sauce. Never married – they said no man could keep up with her – she bathed delightedly in her reputation as a skilled and generous lover, and though her liaisons with both sexes seem to have been numerous, she aroused no malicious gossip. Everyone loved her, for she was generous, warm hearted, quick to praise and gentle on the rare occasions when she found something to criticize. If she sometimes voiced eccentric views, strange ideas that popped out of her with no forethought, we

---

32   Turkey with sauce, corn fungus tamales, prickly pear cactus leaf.

listened with respect, ignoring the message but taking affectionate pleasure in the messenger.

News of the Cholula massacre came on a family meal day: Miquiztli in our calendar, meaning death.

"Stands to reason," said Izel, seizing on the coincidence. "The gods have made this an unlucky day."

My mother embraced her. "Cholula fell several days ago, dear Izel. It's Miquiztli today."

"But the news came today." Izel looked round for support but found only smiles. "I know you think I talk nonsense."

We turned to Tlaco, always the senior figure when he dined with us. Xochitl was sitting beside him. She was resting her cheek against his shoulder.

"The Spaniards are powerful and treacherous," Tlaco said. He glanced down at Xochitl. "Perhaps this is not the moment to speak of such things. They are military matters."

"These strangers don't just kill soldiers," Izel objected. "They slaughter everybody. There can be no love in them, or honour, or happiness."

"How can you know that?" Atza asked.

"I have my sources."

Rumour had it she was conducting an affair with a senior palace official. Again my mother embraced her.

"Now, now, sister," my aunt responded. "Any more of that and people will get the wrong idea about us. You know my reputation." She made a show of presenting my mother to the assembly. "Isn't my sister gorgeous?"

"Can't do a thing with her," my mother said when our laughter had subsided. "But we really shouldn't joke. These strangers are coming and I fear the worst. Our men will go into battle and many will not return. What will happen to those who are left? What will become of our country? Our way of life? People say it's the end."

"What does the emperor say?" Xochitl asked, gazing up at her husband.

133

"I'm supposed to say that he is resolute, determined and unafraid," Tlaco said.

For a while, no one spoke. Tlaco could not say more without breaching his duty to defend the emperor.

"We'll be okay," said Atza at length. "The world can't do without trade. Even the strangers have to eat and clothe themselves. Sooner or later, they'll turn up at the market. They won't kill traders or their families."

"From what I've heard," Izel said, "they don't bother to trade. They just take what they want."

"And what *do* they want?" I asked.

"Gold," said Tlaco. "According to the reports, they can't live without it."

"What about salt, jewels, cloaks?" Atza asked.

"Only gold truly interests them," said Tlaco. "They melt it down. Nobody knows why."

"Maybe they eat it," said Xochitl.

"One thing in our favour is that they are allied with the Tlaxcalans," I said. "Shows they're not so strong. When have we ever lost a war with that bunch of traitors?"

Similar discussions were taking place all over the city, in people's houses, in the street, while at work. Everyone had an answer, but no one was so sure of theirs as to be incurious about what others knew and felt. What little knowledge was to be had came blended with rumours and half-truths. Our own debate left us no more enlightened.

I remember that evening especially: the brightness of the stars, the moon casting her pale light over the rooftops and temples, the stillness of the air, the quietness of our great city at rest, such a contrast with the storm building just beyond our horizon. Never was there another evening like that one. Our next family gathering was supposed to be on Quiahuitl (rain day). But a few days can be a long time in a person's life. We could not know that we would never again share a family meal in such tranquillity.

134

I went to see Huehue in the hope of gaining comfort from a dose of his earthy scepticism. He greeted me with his usual warning to keep my distance because he carried a foul smell about him and was not suitable company for a national hero – his way of expressing pleasure at seeing me. In turn, I assured him I could smell only the flowers of his garden.

He guessed the purpose of my visit. "You want to know what I think about the rumours, right?"

I nodded.

He filled and lit a couple of pipes, and handed one to me. We smoked in silence for a while.

"Fate will have its way," he said finally. "We just have to face things with courage. What's the worst that can happen?"

"I guess they could defeat us and kill us like they did the Cholulans."

"So we get to dwell with the gods a little sooner than expected. What's so bad about that?"

"You mean it doesn't matter?"

"In our little world, we make much of such things, but in the end they are lost in time and life forgets them." He gave me a crooked smile. "Whatever happens, who will remember an old shit like me?"

"Who will remember any of us?"

"As a hero, you have a better chance of surviving a little longer…"

"So you think they will defeat us?"

"How would I know? The gods don't talk to old shits."

I stayed with him most of the day, and helped him with some manuring until the sun began to go down. Then, after a bath, we went to the market for a meal.

While we ate, our conversation turned to worldly matters. The subject of women cropped up, their beauty, our inability to resist their charms. We worked ourselves up until, without a conscious decision, we ended up paddling across the lake. I had some cacao beans in my bag and insisted that it was my turn to pay. Huehue soon found a favourite and wandered off with her. I looked for the girl who'd so skilfully taken my virginity but she was not available. Another offered her services and I accepted – though with disappointment. I couldn't help reminding myself that for the girls, this was a job: to pleasure a man – any man – and that neither their identity nor mine mattered. That thought became entangled with others – the uncertainty surrounding the strangers, the rumours about the emperor's state of mind, a longing for Tecuichpo whom I hadn't seen for many days, and so on, all contaminating the desire I'd crossed the lake to satisfy. As the girl and I lay naked together, the erection I'd been nursing since dinner vanished. She did her best to help with some intimate massage, but her success in evoking the reaction we both sought proved fleeting, since each time we approached the main event, I lost the impetus. After a couple of repetitions, I abandoned the attempt, taking care to reassure the girl that she was beautiful and desirable, and that the fault was mine.

"Maybe you are not eating properly," she said. She knew of a good doctor…

I thanked her with some additional beans.

Huehue emerged a while later in good humour and evidently well satisfied. He saw at once that my evening had been less successful. I told him I had too much on my mind. We paddled back across the lake without speaking, but once we were on land, I asked him if he sometimes had failures.

"Your problem is you're in love," he answered. "I've never been so lucky."

As I was leaving, he embraced me with a rare show of emotion. "You're the only one who's ever come back to see me."

A day or two later, all divisions of the army were put on high alert. Despite Moctezuma's efforts to delay the Spaniards' progress, they were now a mere day's march from the shores of the lake. Excitement and nervousness rippled through the population. No one knew what to expect. Moctezuma issued an order forbidding non-military personnel from observing their arrival and instructing everyone to go about their business in the normal way. I guess he wanted to give the impression that nothing of significance was taking place. Looking back, I sometimes wonder if he was not off his head. He must have known that the whole city was on tenterhooks. Was his understanding of the people so poor? Did he think we were mere playthings of his imagination, that we would behave as he wanted instead of as we were? Whether he liked it or not, civilians would watch as they usually did when delegations came to the city, sometimes surreptitiously, usually openly and jostling for the best view. No emperor, however godlike, can suppress curiosity. People were not going to miss what many already thought could well be the most exciting spectacle of their lives.

TWENTY-FOUR

MEXICO CITY – CORPUS CHRISTI, 10 JUNE 1971

James

L eaving the Church of St Paul the Apostle, I walked to the nearest thoroughfare then took a taxi to the central square. Bordered by colonial architecture and dominated by the largest cathedral in the Americas, the *Zócalo* remains the nation's symbolic heart, crowded, vibrant, still beating as it did when Moctezuma dwelled there. Twin lines of worshippers were flowing in and out of the cathedral as if by command. Pedlars wandered back and forth draped with hammocks, woven blankets, holding a festival of balloons on strings, bearing trays of sweets, chewing gum, cigarettes, or little mules made of corn leaves and pasta in commemoration of the artisans who on Corpus Christi days of yore came on mules to sell their merchandise. An untidy double row of market stalls stood in front of the national palace stocked with particoloured sarapes from Saltillo, nylon shirts, Bakelite radios, woven baskets, batteries, earthenware pots, shoes, leather belts, straw hats, statuettes of the Virgin Mary, the Virgin of Guadalupe, the Virgin of Santa Rosalia…

Dark-eyed couples drifted, absorbed in each other; families, spotless in holy-day best, strolled in ragged clusters; widows in black crossed themselves before the cathedral or at sight of a cleric; police chatted in twos and threes at corners; beggars wearing an expression of agony or hopelessness extended a hand for human mercy because God's had manifestly faltered.

In the centre, beneath a limp national flag, dancers stomped to the beat of a drum while one of their number circulated with an upturned hat. They wore indigenous costume, tunics adorned with Aztec designs and brilliant headdresses with plastic trimmings shaped and coloured to resemble feathers of the quetzal bird, the green-winged life-giver of sacred beauty.

Crossing to the far side, I bought a soda pop from a pedlar standing with his icebox on the corner of Madero street. How was business, I asked him, and he twisted a hand from side to side.

"Can't complain. On a day like this, a day of peace, we must give thanks for what we have." He looked me up and down. "You're not from here."

"No."

"We are all brothers at heart."

"Yes."

"Any time you need a drink, you will find me here, God willing."

I walked on down Madero, past the Fine Arts Theatre and Alameda Park, crossed Paseo de la Reforma, the city's homegrown version of the Champs-Élysées, and thence to the Monument of the Revolution.

A handful of students were standing under the arch, holding placards.

"Is this a demonstration?"

"The march is on its way."

"What's it about?"

No one answered.

"It's okay," I said. "I don't work for the police."

A tall young man stepped forward. "Freedom. It's about freedom and equality." His tone defensive, challenging, alert for criticism.

I stretched out my hand. "Good luck."

He looked into my eyes, surprised, wondering perhaps if this was a trick but then gave me the benefit of the doubt and enfolded my hand in his. "Thank you."

I crossed a succession of nondescript streets lined with food stores, *taquerías*, workshops, parking lots, tyre dealers and small hotels. Barely a handful of pedestrians, the traffic quiet and slow-moving, respectful perhaps of the day's holy purpose. The dense, eye-searing smog had cleared so that the sun glared from a sky too brilliant for the eyes. At a street café, I sat under an awning nursing a coffee. To my left, at the far end of a line of empty tables, a middle-aged couple nuzzled, as oblivious to oblique curiosity as teenagers in their first awakening of love. The waiter, white-haired, thick-set with a heavy tread, appeared at the doorway. I caught his eye.

"Days like this must be bad for business."

"*Sí, Señor.* For those of us who have to work."

"Is it worth staying open?"

"People have to eat. Shall I bring the menu? Our Enchiladas–"

A sharp crack interrupted his flow, and before he could recommence, several more cracks followed in quick succession. I took them at first to be a car engine backfiring. Except that they came repeatedly, in short bursts, and though I had never heard such sounds before, they could only be gunfire. Excusing himself, the waiter made a sign of the cross and hurried back into the interior. I looked across at the couple hoping to see their reaction, but they had vanished. So too the few pedestrians and the traffic. If the street was quiet before, it was now deserted.

As I rose to leave, a young man ran past me; he was followed seconds later by others – men and women – at first ones and twos, then untidy groups. All were running. One had a crimson patch on his sleeve. More shots, louder. A scream. Voices shouting, urging people to flee. Someone ran into me, knocking me onto a bollard. I lost my footing and as I fell, another body, that of a young woman, tumbled on top of me.

"They're killing us," she shouted. "Run."

We scrambled to our feet, only to be thrown against a wall by the onrush.

"Run, they're killing us," the girl repeated.

Three or four men, I can't say for sure how many, appeared at the far end of the street. They were wearing bandannas and carrying firearms. One of them raised his gun and fired.

A metre from where the girl and I stood was a narrow alley between two low-rise buildings. I darted in, grabbing the girl's arm as I did so and pulling her behind me. Halfway along, a recessed alcove gave onto a doorway into which I bundled her, pushing her firmly against the door with my body while I knocked over her shoulder. She fought me, cried at me to let her go, her arms and fists flailing. I managed to pinion one arm against her side, but with the other she hit me hard on the cheek.

"Let me go."

Another blow.

I put my lips to her ear.

"If you go out there, they'll kill us both."

More shots – a fusillade – close by. Her struggling stopped and I could feel her body next to mine trembling, and the beating of her heart. I did not knock at the door again for fear of being heard.

"Check the alley," a voice shouted in the breathless sing-song of the *Chilango*.[33]

We pressed as tightly as we could into the alcove. A flood of

---

33 Native of (downtown) Mexico City.

wild thoughts flashed through me: that this was the end, that it would be better to run rather than wait there to die, that maybe we could persuade our pursuers to let us go, that our hearts were beating too loudly and would betray us, that God must help us, that He would not, that He did not exist. Footsteps. Two shots in quick succession ricocheted from the brickwork near where we stood. I gasped; my companion, steadier than I at that moment, slapped a hand over my mouth.

"No one there," a voice shouted, the speaker no more than a couple of feet away from where we huddled. A moment later, the noise of sirens and screeching brakes signalled the arrival of police.

"Let's go, the voice shouted," suddenly anxious. "Go, go, go."

I wanted at once to step out but the girl held me back. She pressed her lips to my ear. "You can't trust the police."

How long we stood there, I can't say, only that we didn't dare move until the sirens had faded and the noise of passing traffic in the street outside told us that the danger had passed.

When at length we emerged, the girl at once took off. I ran after her. Back in the street, I called to ask her name. She hesitated, ran back towards me and kissed me on the same cheek that had received her blows.

"*Discúlpame*."[34] She was crying. "I have to find my *compañeros*."

"At least tell me your name."

"Maribel Rivera Martínez. I'll never forget you. Adios."

---

34 "Forgive me."

TWENTY-FIVE

TENOCHTITLAN – 1519

Alva

Like the wind, knowledge travels where it will, impervious to the threats of those who seek to keep it for themselves. Moctezuma's vindictiveness was well known, and danger shadowed anyone who talked about him even if their words and thoughts were innocent. And yet the whole city knew or at any rate suspected that the emperor was losing his grip.

Swearing me to secrecy, Tlaco gave me the low-down. Moctezuma was doing everything he could think of to avoid meeting the Spaniards. One day he would be plotting their defeat, the next he would proclaim them to be gods, sending them food and gifts, and volunteering to be their vassal. He summoned soothsayers, instructing them to tell him who these strangers were and what were their intentions, but if he heard a reply he didn't like, he would send the unhappy respondent to his death. No one knew what to tell him. Even retainers who had worked for him for years trembled in his presence. Only his inner cabinet, members of his family and senior allies felt safe from his bouts of ill humour, fear and spite. These he did not dare touch for they were national figures. Everyone else was food for his madness. Tlaco, who saw much of the emperor's disarray at close range, said you could never tell what he wanted.

In one of his panics, he called a meeting with our closest allies, Totoquihuatzin, King of Tacuba, and Cacama, King of Texcoco. What confusion! None knew what to do. They commiserated with each other and then went their several ways with promises of mutual support, half convinced the battle was lost before it had begun. That evening, Moctezuma was seen wandering about town in tears, pretending to be an ordinary citizen. Eventually, a senior aide persuaded him back to the palace, and his servants received an order on pain of death that no one was to talk about the episode in case it demoralized the people. Fate dictated that when the Spaniards arrived on our shores, an unsteady emperor occupied the throne, someone feared and hated not only by our traditional enemies but increasingly by his own people.

I don't say matters would have been easy for us against the invaders. They had much better weapons – cannon and steel. But they were so few, I reckon we could have picked them off little by little before they took hold. Who knows what we might have achieved under a different leader?

TWENTY-SIX

MEXICO CITY – 11 JUNE 1971

James

"*Hijos de la pinche chingada*,"[35] Pepe said.

We had met by chance in the Gandhi bookstore on Miguel Ángel de Quevedo. He proposed lunch and led me to a tiny restaurant tucked into a side street: half a dozen Formica-top tables, shelves round the walls arrayed with earthenware plates, bowls, and pots decorated with angular patterns like those on the façades of ancient ruins. Doña María presided. Short and stately, she cooked from an open stove at the entrance, served the food, handled the cash, and greeted every customer with a word of welcome.

Comida corrida, people's food: bean soup, tortillas, rice, chicken, egg custard and *café de olla*[36] – all for ten pesos, less than a dollar.

"What language is this?" Doña María demanded as she

---

35 "Fucking sons of bitches."
36 Sweet coffee flavoured with cinnamon.

145

placed steaming bowls of soup before us. "In my restaurant, we keep a civil tongue."

"My apologies, señora," Pepe said. "But who can stay calm after what happened?" He took a newspaper from his shoulder bag and showed her the front page. *Corpus Christi Massacre: Fifty students shot in the street.*

Doña María glanced at the text and the accompanying photograph of a body being fed through the doors of an ambulance while two police officers holding machine guns looked on.

"*Madre de Dios.*"[37] She returned to her stove at the entrance. "I like students," she said loud enough for all the diners to hear. "They're my clients. Why would anyone kill them just because they're young and have ideals?"

Four men in oil-grimed overalls entered and Doña María's smile returned on cue.

"*Buenas tardes, señores.*" She pointed them to a table near the entrance and without asking set steaming bowls of soup before them and a basket of tortillas. "Those poor kids could be my own children," she said.

I asked Pepe if he knew who did the shooting.

"The Falcons. Nobody knows who they are. But one thing's for sure, they couldn't have got away with it without the government's knowledge. This goes right up to the president. He knows all about murdering students."

The president's portrait was also on the front page of the newspaper above a small column headlined by a denial of responsibility for the shootings, his face expressionless, lips pencil thin, eyes hidden behind dark glasses.

"Everything is tainted," Pepe continued, "even the news. A conquered people lives in shadow, hides its nature because the truth is dangerous." He glanced at the book I had just bought

---

37 Mother of God.

which was lying on the table. "*El Laberinto de la Soledad*.[38] Paz says we Mexicans live behind masks, that we don't reveal ourselves even to each other. According to the government, this is a free, democratic country. But what does freedom mean when half the people live in shacks?"

"Maybe you should run for office."

"I'm not sufficiently corrupt. And besides…" He looked at me shyly. "I like men."

---

38   The Labyrinth of Solitude, by Octavio Paz.

TWENTY-SEVEN

TENOCHTITLAN – 1519

Alva

We rose at dawn on the day the Spaniards were due to arrive. My orders were to join the rearguard of Moctezuma's retinue as he went to greet the invaders, and to help marshal the guard of honour.

Yes, I saw the first encounter of worlds made to live as strangers to each other. It took place on the main causeway that ran into the heart of our city from near the town of Coyoacán on the shore. Moctezuma travelled from the palace on a litter borne by four of his counsellors – of whom Tlaco was one. What a sight! The litter was awash with flowers, its uprights studded with jade, its canopy woven of green and crimson quetzal feathers under which Moctezuma reclined like a god at leisure. He wore a cloak embroidered with gold and silver jaguars, sandals encrusted with jewels, a headdress of the same fine feathers as the canopy, and on his lower lip, his nose, his ears, precious stones that sparkled when the sun touched them. Around him in close escort walked the kings and lords: Cuitláhuac, Cuauhtémoc, Totoquihuatzin of Tlacopan, Cacama of Texcoco, Itzquauhtzin of Tlatelolco, all in their ceremonial outfits; and behind them came bearers carrying gifts of cloth, jewels and gold. In the vanguard marched twin columns of soldiers followed by six servants who swept the path clean of dust for the emperor's passage, while two more columns formed the rearguard headed by myself and a fellow junior officer, Xihuitl, under General Palintzin's overall command. From my position, I couldn't see the emperor, though Tlaco told me later that he seemed to be in a kind of trance – not trembling but more as if he'd eaten a dish of *teonanacatl*,[39] his eyes glazed and staring.

Was I nervous? Yes, but not terrified, maybe because I was young and my excitement at the prospect of seeing these strange creatures prevailed over any underlying insecurity. Even if they were gods, I thought, what could they have against me? If I trembled, it was from anticipation of a dizzying confrontation with the unknown. What information we had about these newcomers portrayed them as the equal of any god in capriciousness and cruelty, but then so was Moctezuma, and we had learned to live with him. No one had any idea what this moment had in store for us, but we had all been brought up to accept our fate, whether it was to die of old age in the bosom of our family, or on the sacrificial stone at the edge of a knife.

Acachinanco, half a morning's slow march from the city gates, was the traditional place on the causeway for greeting dignitaries. We arrived to within a spear's throw of our destination before noon and halted there in formation. Canoes full of sightseers were already stationed out in the lake to view the proceedings, heedless of Moctezuma's orders to stay away. Presently, though no one was allowed to speak, a stir flowed through our ranks telling us well enough that the newcomers had been spotted. Palintzin signalled to me to verify what was happening and I

---

39 Flesh of the gods – entheogenic mushrooms.

stepped out of line and looked towards the mainland along the edge of the causeway. In the distance, a procession of what could only be soldiers was moving towards us, a few of whom at the front were riding the big deer. I reported what I had seen to Palintzin and then on his instructions informed my fellow officer, Xihuitl. He and I had met during military exercises, but I didn't know him well. When I walked up to him, he was staring straight ahead with a fixed expression as if determined to press down on his emotions, and he heard my news without flinching or moving his eyes from the middle distance. I glanced behind at the soldiers. Tense but under control, I figured they would remain calm provided we officers kept our heads.

An order came for us to move forward slowly, but we managed no more than a handful of paces before coming to an abrupt halt. There had been no signal, so the troops behind careered into those in front. The resulting confusion added to the tension, and it took time for Xihuitl and I to restore discipline. Palintzin walked down our lines telling the troops they looked splendid and were a credit to the empire. His words soothed us.

After what seemed an eternity, we set off again, this time drawing up just before the towers of Acachinanco Fort, which marked the city's outer defensive line. By craning my neck, I could now make out individual figures among the approaching strangers, notably those astride the animals. Behind the first group who rode four-abreast came a solitary soldier carrying a banner on a pole which he waved back and forth and from side to side so that it floated in the breeze like a giant bird; then a contingent of foot soldiers, some bearing swords that glinted in the sunlight, others equipped with crossbows and arquebuses (though we knew nothing of such weapons at the time); then more horsemen; and finally an army of Tlaxcalans in their unmistakeable red and white cloaks. As these latter came into view, angry murmurs broke out among our troops. The arrival of our traditional enemy along with the strangers could only mean hostility. At the slightest signal from the emperor, we would have been at their throats.

The newcomers halted and, though we could only see the rear of the emperor's litter and the heads of the riders, we assumed the foreign vanguard and our own were now face to face. For a while, nothing much happened. No one within sight or earshot moved or spoke. Ahead, the two vanguards were doubtless running through the greeting rituals. Moctezuma remained motionless in his litter. Overhead, the sun bore down on us. At first, the animals pawed the ground and snorted, but then quietened, subdued perhaps by the midday heat. Flies buzzed round our heads as if we were carrion. We could hear the gentle lapping of the water and the sporadic surfacing of fish in pursuit of insects. Onlookers in the canoes fell silent. Who knows how long we waited before at last the emperor's litter inched forward and we were able to shuffle behind, too hot and thirsty to care any longer about the possibility of conflict, our curiosity dampened by discomfort, tension dissipated for lack of sustenance. Besides, no matter what fears of annihilation had run wild in our thoughts, the strangers had after all not attacked us, or eaten us, or apparently even threatened. And since they had arrived in peace, custom demanded that the emperor should receive them with grace.

One kind of custom anyway. The other kind would have sent them for sacrifice on account of the rebellions they had fomented against our rule.

We stopped again. Ahead, the riders and a forward detachment of foreign soldiers split into two lines and came to attention on each side of the causeway, forming a guard of honour. Between their ranks, a solitary rider advanced. I remember his thick beard, the soft green cap he wore at an angle, his breastplate flashing in the sunlight, his pale skin, and the way he gripped the creature's's reins to keep it in check. He had about him an air of command such as one might expect of a monarch, but though he differed from us in appearance and came mounted on an unfamiliar beast, anyone could see that this was not a god but a man. This, we learned later, was Malintzín – Cortés.

He rode right up to Moctezuma's litter and I saw him look at the emperor directly in a way forbidden to ordinary mortals. He made a gesture with his hand – which I gather was a form of respectful greeting – before dismounting.

What happened next? From our position, we could see no more of the encounter, but according to Tlaco, the emperor stepped out of his carriage, spoke some words of welcome and received a suitable reply. There followed a formal exchange of gifts, precious baubles that leaders use to impress each other. All this took time, as such ceremonies do.

Meanwhile, we were left standing under the sun, hungry, thirsty and some of us – including me – in need of a piss. Palintzin got the message – he was known to have a dodgy bladder himself. After verifying that no one in the emperor's entourage was looking, he made an unambiguous sign with his hand, and an instant later we were at the edge of the causeway with our peckers out in best military order. He commanded us to wait until he was ready. "The general lets go first," he whispered down the line, after which on pain of death we couldn't have held it because we were helpless with laughter. That's the only time I've seen so many dicks in line: sixty-seven hanging out at once and in full view of a bunch of sightseers in canoes. One of the nearest was full of women giggling and pretending not to look. I remember thinking how a single warrior with a sharp sword could destroy all our manhoods with a few quick strokes.

Once we were back in line, Palintzin peeled off a contingent of troops and sent them for water, which they distributed not just to our group but also via a canoe to the Spanish vanguard as well (though not, of course, to the Tlaxcalans who were, in any case, too numerous). A man of the people, Palintzin always saw the human before he ever saw the enemy.

At long length, a message came that the emperor was ready to lead his guests into the city. Now it was our turn to form a guard of honour. The senior lords and counsellors — including Tlaco — passed between us first; then came Moctezuma in his litter with the chief stranger riding alongside, the two of them apparently doing their best to converse. Cortés was wearing necklaces of flowers and jewels that the emperor must have bestowed on him for they were of the finest quality. Close behind rode Cortés's translator, a woman with another stranger, a Spaniard who also seemed to be translating – although from the snatches of his voice that came to me, we knew he didn't speak our language but another one, Mayan. I remember thinking at the time that there can't have been much communication between our leaders and the newcomers. In the end, I reckon both sides understood what they wanted, though our government's grasp of things rested mainly on hope, while the Spaniards heard only the voice of their ambition.

Next came the Spanish soldiers all armed to the teeth and with their weapons at the ready. A few of our officials walked among them, but how exposed they seemed, for none carried weapons, and they looked small and fragile. Two of the strangers were different. Dressed in simple black robes with hoods, they bore no arms, nor any adornment beyond a metal cross suspended from their necks. These turned out to be priests – messengers of the Spanish god. They looked frightened, muttered to themselves as they walked, and drew signs of the cross on their breast over and over as if they were casting spells.

Once the Spaniards had passed through, Palintzin called Xihuitl and myself to him, put his arm round each of our shoulders and shook his head sadly. "Who knows what will come of this?"

I think he was going to say something more, but the Tlaxcalans were almost upon us, and we needed to be on the alert. Instinct inclined us to bar their way and since Moctezuma had given no instructions regarding them, we let only a token number through before closing ranks and separating their main corps from the Spaniards. At a signal from Palintzin, Xihuitl's column turned to face them, and in a moment they were retreating back to Coyoacán on the lakeshore, doubtless shitting themselves with fear at what we might do to them. If we'd had any sense, we'd have wiped the whole lot from the earth, Tlaxcalans and Spaniards alike, there and then. That would have been the moment.

While Xihuitl's column chased the Tlaxcalans off the causeway, Palintzin and I assembled my column into position at the Spanish rear. We set off at a measured pace, re-entering the city to find what seemed to be the entire population massed on the rooftops and pressing each other so tightly in their anxiety to see the procession that some lost their footing and toppled into the street or a canal, who knows with what injuries. Every eye was full of wonder at these odd creatures with their beards and bright hats and breastplates, the beasts they rode on, and their big dogs on leash that sniffed and cocked their legs against trees and the corners of dwellings. None of us had seen the like before, even in our dreams.

For their part, the Spaniards did their best to appear unmoved, but as we proceeded further towards the city centre and they saw our fine buildings, our magnificent temples and great houses, they lost all pretence of cold dignity and looked around with wonder. When they reached the main square, they could hardly constrain their amazement. Years later, one of their priests – I think it was Father Díaz – told me they had thought our city the most beautiful in the world, and I do believe it was, though perhaps the picture in my mind is no more than a figment seen through the smoke and ruin of time. As the poet said:

Nothing made of man can live
Jade will shatter, gold will break,
The finest raiment tatters make
The lord of death does not forgive...

I'd been wondering where Moctezuma planned to host the strangers: whether he would lodge them as guests within the city precincts or demand that they return to quarters on the mainland. For reasons known solely to the gods, he led them to the only house – apart from his own – big enough to accommodate so many: his father Axayácatl's palace, which stood opposite his own, just across the main square. Enormous that building: countless rooms and passages, great halls, and interior gardens, a menagerie, guest apartments, offices, barracks…Moctezuma kept his concubines there and would visit whenever the mood took him, selecting one with whom to lie – or more than one if his vigour so inspired. When they became pregnant, he would marry them off, usually to a man of noble birth, and from time to time, he would send scouts about the city to pick out pretty replacements. Heaven knows how many children he made in this way. Many others lived or worked there too, jewellers, weavers, sculptors, makers of furniture and weapons.

Some areas of the building I cannot speak of for I never saw them. One storeroom – of forbidden entry – reportedly contained the treasures of past monarchs stored in silent testimony to their greatness and guarded day and night by a company of soldiers quartered in an annex at the rear. Also forbidden to the common gaze were the living quarters of Axayácatl, where he ate, slept, held court, and to where Moctezuma would return from time to time, escaping the duties and intrigues of his palace to relive the carefree days of his youth. No doubt these chambers were luxurious, for leaders of the modern world seem to need comfort and ease beyond anything to which the rest of us aspire, rewarding themselves when perhaps their eyes should rather seek out the needy and their hand stretch out not to receive but to give. Our prayers, recited by all those who live well, demand as much:

Oh gods, look kindly on those who lie on the floor of life, the poor, the miserable, those who have no joy in this world and have nothing.

Too often the grand do not do what they ask of the gods, but treat the lowly as the least of beings, worthy only of slavery or sacrifice.

On that fateful day, all personnel were ejected from Axayácatl's palace to make way for the strangers and the strangers' horses and the strangers' dogs; all that is except for the women, who the emperor had apparently decided to give as a gift to his guests in recognition of their natural needs.

As for our column, after seeing the strangers into their lodging, we received orders to guard the entrance overnight, so it was not until the sun was well risen on the following day that we were stood down and I was finally able to get back home. I took Xihuitl with me because he was from the coast and had no family around him.

Weary but still excited by all we had seen, we arrived to find the house full: Tlaco with Xochitl clinging to his arm, my mother and her two sisters Papan and Izel, Papan's husband Zolin, my cousins Cualli and Mazatl, whom I rarely saw because they lived and worked across the lake in Texcoco, and several neighbours. Atza should have been at the market already, but he was there too, as was his pal Teudile who was back in town and – I could hardly help noticing – paying very close attention to my aunt Izel. Everyone clamoured to know about the strangers, what they were really like, their language, their ferocity, would the emperor have them killed? Tlaco held court.

"They're definitely human. No doubt about it," he was saying.

"How can you tell," someone asked.

"For a start, they stink. Have you ever heard of gods who smell like beasts?"

This was true. I had caught a whiff myself as the strangers passed by on the causeway: the pungent, nauseating odour of sweated garments and unwashed bodies.

"They will bring disease on us," my mother said.

How prophetic those words! At the time, I suppose, we took them as an expression of moral superiority; for the truth is, we thought ourselves better than other mortals, chosen by the gods to show lesser beings how to live.

"What I don't understand," said my aunt Izel, "is why the emperor let them in if they're going to make us ill."

This outburst seemed to surprise her for she giggled, covered her face with her hand as if she were a little girl, and slipped behind Teudile. Everyone in the family understood that she was not seeking our attention but Teudile's, and that she would shortly be in his arms.

"The emperor received them with kindness," said Tlaco. "We must trust him. No one can doubt that these men are savages, filthy in their bodies and habits, violent in their customs, cruel in war. They have powerful weapons, better than ours, which means we must be careful and cunning in how we deal with them. They are few in number and we are many, and in the end that means we will defeat them. But the costs may be high and I fear many will fall in the line of duty."

These words reduced us to silence. Tlaco's position as a counsellor gave authority to whatever he told us, and we took it as truth.

"I'm frightened," Xochitl said.

My mother turned to me. "What do you think, my son?"

"The strangers are few," I said, "but they have defeated our allies and won over our enemies. They brought a Tlaxcalan army with them."

A chorus of protests ensued.

"The Tlaxcalans are nothing."

"Bunch of wasters."

"We always defeat them."

This last from my cousins who were librarians and knew nothing of war.

"We did lose to them once," said Xihuitl. He paused just

long enough to be sure of our attention. "Three years ago. The night before the battle, I dreamed we would be annihilated. And I remember marching towards their army the next morning with dread in my soul." He stopped speaking, as if he had nothing further to relate.

"What happened?" we asked.

"What happened?" Xihuitl repeated slowly. "With whom?"

"The Tlaxcalans."

"Ah yes, the Tlaxcalans. They ran away as they always do. We only lost the battle in my dream."

"Your friend is really something," my mother said quietly to me after the laughter had died down. "Is he a brave soldier?"

I nodded.

"Then I will speak with your brother if you do not mind."

Atza readily gave his consent, for our mother had lived a solitary life since our father's death. That night and for more than a few nights thereafter, she shared her bed with Xihuitl and her morning smiles with the world.

Mother was not alone in admiring Xihuitl's humour. He succeeded in lifting all our spirits, even though in our hearts we sensed that with the arrival of the strangers, something hard and malignant had entered our days and would not easily be put out of them.

TWENTY-EIGHT

MEXICO CITY – 1974

James

"I told my father it's a girls only trip to Acapulco."

"He believed you?"

"He needs to believe I'm still a virgin." She ran a hand lightly over my cheek, my chest. "My mum knows. She saw my underwear drying in my bedroom and wanted to know why I hadn't put it with the household washing. When I told her I'm a woman and she shouldn't ask such questions, she dragged me to the doctor's and more or less ordered him to put me on the pill."

We headed west through Chapultepec park, the city's central lung, and then along the residential stretch of Pasco de la Reforma with its lining of elegant mansions.

"I bought new lingerie for our trip. I wanted it to be a surprise but here I am telling you. There's a store in the Zona Rosa that sells clothes from Paris. Well, they're made in Mexico but the designs are French. I want you to find me irresistible. Last night I was so excited. I dreamed we were making love over and over again. That we couldn't stop. I told my cousin Marina that I have multiple orgasms with you and she said it was impossible, that only mature women come more than once. But I do have them, don't I? Last week, I was sitting on the patio of the summer house trying to read that book you gave me, Under the Volcano, but all the time I was thinking of you, day-dreaming about the last time we made love. I was wearing shorts and when my father called me in to lunch, he made me change into something "decent" as he called it because we had guests."

Breathless, your words, Olivia, tumbling into one another; so excited by your own sensuality, your womanhood, your delight in the discovery of love.

And you sang to me: *Dicen que la distancia es el olvido…*" Your voice playful, like a peal of bells.

Out of sight is out of mind they say
But I don't believe a word
Because I will always be a slave
To the caprices of your heart
You made me clarify my thoughts
And chased away my fears and doubts
That night when I held you in my arms.
Now my horizon fills with bitterness
Because your boat must leave these shores
And brave the turbulence of unknown seas
Let it not founder far from home.
When twilight falls
And you tire of wandering
Remember I am waiting for you
Alone and longing for your return.

She leaned over and kissed me lightly on the cheek. "It's called *La Barca* – The Boat."

"Beautiful but sad."

160

"All our songs are sad. They're about despair, about lost love, the end of happiness. We are fatalists. We embrace whatever comes our way, the joys and the sorrows. There's an old saying, *la vida es sueño y los sueños sueños son* (life is a dream, and dreams are only dreams). It's the title of a play by…oh someone we had to study at school…who was it…how could I forget?"

As we climbed out of the valley, the urban sprawl gave way to a landscape of rough meadow interspersed with clumps of pine and outcrops of jagged rock. Beyond, to our left, the flint-hard face of a mountain rose sheer above us, one of several ringing the smog-enshrouded dust-bowl sprawl of the city.

"I need to make love," Olivia said.

"Now?"

"Yes."

I steered off the highway onto a stretch of meadow that flowed into pine trees. At this altitude – some ten thousand feet – the air felt cool even under the fierce sunlight. We walked towards the nearest clump of pines, away from the whine of speeding cars and the roar of buses and battered trucks straining towards the summit of the high pass. As soon as we reached the cover of the trees, we were in each other's arms. Her orgasm came at once, her body shaking, limp in my arms.

We lay in a hollow on a nest of pine needles and soft grass, and joined without undressing, our breathing intermingled with the sighing of the breeze through branches. She seemed to me ineffably beautiful at that moment and I felt a swell of reverence for her and for the gifts of life. I remember telling myself that this, surely, was happiness and that the woman I held in my arms embodied all I would ever know of truth.

Writing this as an older man and from afar, I am tempted to condemn such sentiments as the overblown romanticism of youth. Imaginary critics lean over my shoulder, mocking – sophisticates, arbiters of taste, you know the kind – and I am all too ready to bow down, even before they speak, censoring my

161

thoughts, pressing back the emotions that emerge when the gates of memory spring open. Yet, though they carry suffering as well as joy in their fibre, I would grasp these feelings again if I could but find them.

How transitory they are! As soon as we broke the peace of that moment, exchanging vows with words that magazines, soap operas, pop songs, the poor resources of language itself had already trivialized, the truth faded, leaving behind the shadow of an epiphany that was perhaps after all no more than a figment of imagination.

We lay still. She was weeping quietly, her mascara running in black streaks down her cheeks. I wiped her face with the edge of my sleeve.

"I'm just happy," she said.

Adjusting our dress, we crawled side by side to the rim of a nearby precipice and peered into the void. A crater, three hundred feet in circumference, fell to a pool far below that glinted like a mirror in the sunlight. It heard our whispers and echoed them. Halfway into its depths, a buddleia rooted into a rocky ledge shook violently as a parrot in brilliant red and green plumage erupted from its foliage and glided to join its mate at the water's edge.

"Now I remember the name of the playwright."

"What?"

"The one who wrote *La Vida es Sueño*. His name's Calderón de la Barca."

"Right."

A heavy thud startled us. We spun round to see a man on horseback no more than twenty feet from where we lay. He was sitting motionless in the saddle, broad-brimmed hat low over the forehead, deep-set eyes in shadow, thin black moustache, a holster at the hip with the butt of a pistol hanging from it like a question mark. Olivia stiffened. Doubt and fear ran through me. Wasn't it a man's job to protect a woman? I was unarmed. This was his land. We were trespassers. He was offended. Our licentiousness outraged him. No. It was simpler: he was a bandit and planned to rob us. After which he would let us go. Or he would kill us. Or he would kill me and rape Olivia before dropping us both into the crater. No help was at hand. We were out of sight of the highway, of the law. His face was expressionless, inscrutable. How old was he? Forty, forty-five? We were children beside him. Perhaps that was our only defence.

"*Buenas tardes, señor.*"

The horseman nodded so imperceptibly he might have been acknowledging a thought of his own. Olivia was trembling. I filled the silence.

"The crater is so beautiful. The pool far below, and the vegetation. A parrot just flew down there."

The words were mine, but he ignored them. He was staring at Olivia.

"Is this your property?" I said. "If we are trespassing…"

He interrupted. "The señorita has been crying."

His eyes did not stir from Olivia: her hair flecked with pine needles, her blouse open, exposing the swell of her breasts.

"My tears are of happiness, señor. Because we are newly married and in love and the world is beautiful."

The horseman nodded, touched the horse's flank with his heel and rode off at a gentle trot.

"He could have killed us," Olivia said when we were back on the highway.

"Why would he?"

"To rob us. Steal the car. Who knows? In Mexico it happens because a man doesn't like your looks. Because he feels jealous. Because you are a foreigner with a Mexican woman. Sometimes for the hell of it, for no reason at all."

TWENTY-NINE

TENOCHTITLAN – 1564

Alva

W hat did the Spaniards see in those first days? How could
I or anyone conjure out of mere words the vanished
contents of a universe? The sights that met our eyes
at first light, the landmarks, signposts and routines, so familiar
I barely noticed them, are vanished now as if they were no more
than mist on the surface of a lake. No painting survives to remind
our successors of what was; no chronicle escaped the flames; and
who among us could remake even the shadow of a city built by
a forgotten god? Soon no one will remain who holds in memory
the barest image of our lost inheritance, the grandeur of the
central square with its royal palaces, the sacred temple of the
Sun and Rain, countless temples dotted through the city among
the houses of the people, canals and pathways lined with willow,
cypress and jacaranda, smoke rising from a forest of cooking
fires at dawn and dusk; horns sounding from the lips of priests
at the sun's rising and going down; flowers strung like necklaces

from rooftops; drums beating the rhythms of day and night; the festivals and dances and feasts by which we acknowledged the eternity of heaven, spent the brief energies of life and opened our hearts to the certainty of death?

Oh yes, death was ever our companion; we have always walked towards it willingly, resigned to whatever may be our direction of travel to the afterlife. Hence why the tears of those left behind dry quickly, for they too will pass from this world to another. As the poet sang:

> *How transitory is our life on earth!*
> *Just time enough to meet, converse, befriend*
> *Ere long we needs must bid farewell and so,*
> *Descend into the unknown realm of night.*
> *Therefore, let us seek pleasure and delight...*

Tenochtitlan – 1519

Peace reigned for a while after the Spaniards settled in Axayácatl's palace. For several days they were hardly seen, time enough for the city not perhaps to forget them but to allow them to drift into the background while the daily round of work and ritual resumed their place in our thoughts. When they began to emerge, it was in small groups and always well armed. They walked the streets and the shoreline, visited our gardens and *chinampas*, gazed with admiration at our fine buildings and at the web of paths, causeways, canals and bridges that linked us to each other and to the mainland. Yet they were nervous for they kept glancing round, and two or three of their number marched a few paces behind the others with their weapons at the ready as if expecting an assault – even though neither the rules of hospitality nor of war would allow such a thing.

Moctezuma meanwhile appeared in public with Cortés and some of his officers. He showed the Spaniards our temples, wandered with them through the Tlatelolco market (where Atza had to part with his finest cloaks as "imperial gifts" to the visitors), took them on canoe trips, even went hunting with them in the forests of Amecameca. He seemed to have struck up a friendship with the Spanish leader. At night, the two played games, bestowing their winnings on each other's servants. The emperor was said to be learning their language while two of their priests were learning ours. People began gossiping. Rumour had it that the strangers had cast a spell over the emperor to make him care more for their needs than for ours. He seemed to be neglecting affairs of state. Petitioners and officials alike found themselves having to wait many days for a hearing. Determined ones spent untold nights sleeping in line in a palace antechamber. Decisions all but dried up like a river reduced to hard mud in a summer drought.

Then, without warning, our world changed. How it happened no one knows, nor why. One day news circulated that the emperor had left his own home and gone to live with the strangers. He had gone there on foot, escorted by Cortés and a platoon of Spanish soldiers. Why was he not carried as befitted a god? What had become of his servants? According to an official report from the palace, he had sent them away and had crossed the square unseen. Few believed it. Moctezuma's guards saw him depart for sure. He must have sworn them to secrecy about the manner of his going; though secrets, like rumours, find their way through walls and the denials of those who harbour them.

Why would the emperor behave in such a way? We were all asking the same question. That he should become "a guest" of the strangers in his own city was disquieting enough. Worse was to follow. With all the servants and ministers coming and going, the truth was bound to leak out, though in the end many of us might have preferred not to know. Soon enough, we learned that the emperor dwelled among the Spaniards not as a guest but as a prisoner, his feet secured by metal thongs, his every move guarded by soldiers so that he couldn't even take a shit without Cortés's permission.

We the people, meanwhile, found ourselves with no government, no authority, no order, no means of organizing ourselves or of knowing how to act. Such a sudden transformation lay beyond comprehension. Solely another god could imprison an emperor, though in all our history none had done so. Yet by our own observations, we knew Cortés to be a man. Witnesses had seen him bend a knee to the black-robed priests, and to kneel in prayer with eyes cast towards the sky – acts that surely no god would perform, still less permit a lowly human to observe. But if he was merely a man, from where did he acquire the power to bend our emperor to his will?

THIRTY

MEXICO – 1974

James

"The countryside is dangerous for a woman," Olivia said.

"Don't worry. I won't let you out of my sight."

I had picked out Playa Turquesa on a map because the name was written in tiny six-point and I knew no one who had been there. It would be an adventure. If there was no hotel, we could sleep on the beach, or in the shelter of a cave.

We drove through the green hills of Michoacán, through the colonial splendour of Morelia, the state capital, and then down into the coastal lowlands, until the highway, by then little more than a rutted track, ended in a patch of land dotted with tufts of course grass and cacti. Three cars and a four-by-four stood at odd angles on hillocks of compacted sand. We parked among them and walked over the brow of a dune.

Waves pounded a wide fringe of beach that curved into a hazy distance. Strewn along its length: seaweed in untidy scum lines, scatterings of driftwood, spiny puffer fish lying bloated where the tide had tossed them amid swarms of sandflies. Shoreside, on a broad ledge overlaid with coarse grasses, three ramshackle huts were littered with the detritus of occupation: black garbage bags, towels draped over open doors, a couple of beach balls, and in front of each, a cloth awning held up by sticks thrust into the sand, beneath one of which several figures sat chatting and smoking – the men in shorts, skinny with sun-baked skins, the women bikinied with towels round their heads. One of the men looked up as we approached but offered no encouragement. None of the others showed awareness of our presence.

"Junkies," Olivia said with a shudder. "You said Playa Turquesa was beautiful."

She looked up and down the long expanse of the beach and then turned her gaze inland where the sand gave way to vegetation – entanglements of pitaya and tuna, clumps of fat biznaga, coconut palms.

"There's nowhere to stay."

The sun was sinking, a blood-red disc dipping into a wash of pink, blue and green on the horizon and sending shoreward a beam of evanescent points of roseate light like fireflies dancing on the ripples of the sea.

"I don't like it here."

"I'm sorry."

We headed back the way we had come. On the way to the coast, we had chatted ceaselessly, now neither us spoke. Night closed in, deep and black. As we twisted and turned into the highlands, huge rocks would rear up in our headlights seeming to bar our way, goading me to steer past them into a darkness that might have been the edge of a cliff.

"Can't we go faster?"

"Too dangerous."

"We should have gone to Acapulco."

Close to midnight we reached the town of Uruapan. There we found a cheerless flophouse off the main square, and slept apart on twin bunks, the room bare of decoration and with a doorless washroom smelling of earth and drainage.

Heavy traffic from the street outside woke us just after dawn. We showered in cold water, and dried ourselves on threadbare towels.

"Who stays in hotels like this," Olivia asked the desk clerk as I was paying the bill. He was no more than twenty-five, deferential.

"Commercial representatives mainly. Occasionally, a couple. But it is not our business, señorita."

"I'm not señorita, I'm señora."

"*Disculpe*, señora. You are not wearing a ring so…"

"I'm allergic to gold." She leaned against me, proclaiming possession. "There was no hot water for the shower."

"Everyone complains, señora. But the owner does nothing. He owns the whole block on this side of the square. He's a cousin of the mayor."

"Ah."

"There was another hotel, a better one, but it was closed down on the mayor's orders."

"Ah."

We travelled along back roads, across parched plains, through craggy mountain passes, adobe villages with unpaved streets and drunks swaying in doorways, listless country towns suffocating in dust and heat.

"I thought we would make love all the time," Olivia said. "That's why we came, isn't it? To be lovers? Mostly we're too tired and dirty."

"I never stop wanting you."

"You don't show it."

We argued. At a rural gas station, she got out and began to walk; and then ran back because a group of peasants in straw hats hoeing a field had heard our voices and were staring at her. One of them called to his companions, loud enough for us to

170

hear, that the problem with city men was that they didn't know how to fuck their women properly.

"She needs a good screw. Then she'll be happy…"

Laughter.

"They know what's wrong," she said.

We reached the little town of Tzintzuntzan, ancient capital of the Purépecha. A colonial enclave in the centre harbours the sixteenth-century convent of Santa Ana with its church dedicated to San Francisco, its temple of the Virgin of Solitude, and the *Hospital de los Indios* built to tend the bodily and spiritual needs of the conquered. Decay, crumbling stonework, heavy wooden doorways wormed by centuries of neglect. Within the lichened walls of the enclosure was a luminescent lawn criss-crossed by overgrown pathways and dotted with ancient olive trees, branches soaring from semi-necrotic trunks of impossible girth, all gnarled and wearied out of shape by life.

We walked through the gardens separated by hurt. No one in sight, a silence so deep in the shadow of those time-worn buildings that we might have been strolling through the expiring remnants of the first garden brought to a last exhaustion by millennia of fertility and the noisy peopling of the world.

"How old these trees must be, carrying their branches like grandfathers with their children on their backs."

I took her by the hand, pulled her roughly towards me, lowered my lips to hers.

She twisted out of my grasp. "Don't."

I tried the monastery door and then the doors of the two churches. All were locked. We were standing before the Church of Saint Francis when a priest appeared: bare-headed, a bronze cross embossed with a figure of Christ pendant over a black cassock, leather sandals clip-clopping on the flagstones.

"You can't go in," he apologized. "Everything's in a state of disrepair. We are raising funds to restore the fabric. A contribution would be welcome; there is a box at the main door of the convent. The Church of the Virgin of Solitude will be open at six for a service or confession. It's still in use thanks be to the Lord, though it also needs restoration work. You must be tourists? Newly married? Congratulations. I saw you from afar and you looked so happy. Love is a wonderful thing. A gift from God. Have you seen the ruins of the Purépecha? They're extraordinary. Just a short walk from town. Do go. Plenty of time before the service. Hardly anyone visits them and they are among the finest in the country. The Purépecha were as powerful as the Mexica only no one talks about them. But please, if you can, a small contribution to the repair of this wonderful place…"

I gave the priest a hundred-peso note. He made a show of recoiling, begging me to put it in the box so that he wouldn't have to touch it, but I insisted, and so he slipped it into the sleeve of his cassock before bidding us farewell and clip-clopping away like a noisy shadow.

"A conman like so many priests," Olivia said. "He'd sell the Lord Almighty if the price was right."

The entrance to the ancient capital of the Purépecha was padlocked. Inside the gate, a notice pinned to a post read *Abierto diario de 10 a 5*.[40] Behind the fence, a single-storey brick building with a corrugated roof – and a sign over the door that read *Museo Arqueológico*.

Olivia called out, "*Buuueeeno! Olaaaa!*"

A diminutive figure appeared at the door – white-haired, stooped. He approached the gate slowly supporting his right leg with a stick. "*Muy buenas tardes. A sus órdenes.*"

"Can we see the ruins?"

The man consulted his watch and reflected for a moment as if searching for a reason to refuse. Finding none, he produced a key from his pocket, unlocked the gate and motioned us to pass through. A smile to order.

"We are supposed to be open, but I'm here by myself with all

---

40   Open daily from 10 to 5.

172

the artefacts, the museum, and so forth. I keep the gate locked for safety. Hardly anyone knows we're here. I keep asking the authorities to publicize the site, but you know how it is." He stopped to lock the gate behind us before leading us to the museum. "A whole month since our last visitors. American professors, husband and wife. Charming. One would hope for a little more interest from our compatriots. It's ten pesos each."

I handed him a twenty-peso note. He tore off two slips of paper the size of lottery tickets from a roll, entered the date and time in the space provided and handed them to me. Making a note of the date in a ledger, he said, "See for yourself." He turned the ledger round so that we could see the entries on the page. "Twenty-second of May. That's the entry before yours. Today is the seventeenth of June if I'm not mistaken. Such is the level of culture in this country. Perhaps I shouldn't say this, but those priests down there in town don't exactly help."

"One of them suggested we come here."

"That will be Father Roig. He's the only one who values our history. The rest are stuck in the sixteenth century. They think the Devil spends his vacations here. Would you like me to show you the museum and the ruins? On this occasion, since there's no one else to attend to, I'll include my services in the price of the ticket."

He looked at us sad-eyed. "Dr José Noriega Alvarez at your service. Truth is I'm retired already. Just standing in while the authorities search for a new curator. The old one left suddenly without notice. Nobody knows where he went. My mother was Purépecha, Tarascan as the Spanish called those who lived here, so I'm among my ancestors. I'm a Christian; you can't not be a Christian in these parts, take my word for it, but I can tell you for sure that the gods still dwell here after their own fashion. The villagers know it too despite four hundred years of effort to suppress the old ways. That's why the priests are, let us say, ambiguous in their attitude towards this place. Does it really matter, I ask myself. As the Hindu sage Krishnamurti says, many are the paths to heaven and all gods in the end are manifestations of the one Eternal. Is it not so?"

He led us to a promontory from where we could see a broad expanse of Lake Pátzcuaro sparkling under brilliant sunlight, framed by verdant hills, cornfields and swathes of forest. Beyond, on the horizon, purple mountains danced in the afternoon haze.

Olivia nested her hand in mine. "It's breathtaking."

"*Así es*," Dr Noriega agreed.

Olivia leaned towards me and I caught the scent of her breath, familiar yet elusive.

"Now look behind you," Dr Noriega said with a sweeping movement of his arm. "The city of the Purépecha covered at least five square kilometres, perhaps more."

Directly in front of us, several monumental stone buildings fallen from their original glory but restored enough to suggest what they might once have been: the ceremonial nucleus of a vanished theocracy. Shaped at one end as angular pyramids with wide steps, at the other they curved into semi-cylinders, like the footings of medieval towers. Behind them, grass-covered mounds and indentations sloped downwards to a flat plain of farmland extending as far as the eye could see.

"Here was the ceremonial centre in the most beautiful spot commanding the water," Dr Noriega said. "And these buildings, some people call them pyramids but that hardly does justice to them, don't you agree? They're Yácatas. Nothing like them anywhere else in the world. Forgive me if I say this with a touch of pride."

Dr Noriega produced a large white handkerchief into which he blew his nose, folded over the area that had received the deposit, and used a clean portion to wipe his nostrils with flourishing thoroughness.

"Forty thousand people were living in Tzintzuntzan when the Spaniards came. Strangely few by modern standards I suppose, but numbers are relative, are they not? Our ruins may not offer the intricate reliefs of Hindu temples or the glories of Greek sculpture…" He paused, long enough for us to acknowledge the learning. "…but still we have here, on national soil, evidence of a deep and mysterious past, of a culture as strange and alien to us as if it were Martian and yet as human as we are."

"What became of them," Olivia asked.

"Purépecha civilization faded after the Conquest, and so too the city, for they were one and the same. The people are still here, but we are much reduced." The handkerchief reappeared. "Please excuse…hay fever. Where was I? Yes, the people. *Muy reducidos*, and the old ways forgotten, though perhaps it is just as well." He pointed to a narrow trench cut into the hillside. "Thousands of human bones have been found in that ditch. It's where they threw the bodies of sacrificed victims. Our ancestors were even bloodier than the Mexica if you ask me."

Olivia shuddered. "All those bodies in one place. Didn't it attract rats?"

"No doubt it did," said Dr Noriega with an air of satisfaction as if glad to have struck home with the awfulness of his message. He lowered his voice. "Here the rites of the Purépecha, over there in town, the rites of the conquerors. How many deaths do we assign to each? The ancients killed by sacrifice, the moderns by massacre and pestilence. Does the Lord approve of either? Do we? History is a tale of death and sacrifice, isn't it so?"

At the end of the tour, Dr Noriega bade us farewell, shaking my hand before kissing Olivia's and telling her with a slight bow that she had added enchantment to his declining years. After shutting and locking the gate, he remained standing behind its wire grill like the warden of a detention camp. Our parting wave he neither acknowledged nor seemed to notice for he was staring beyond us at a vision of his own. Such was our last image of him, a patriarch standing watch over the last vestiges of an ancient race.

175

"You should have paid him extra for taking us round the site," Olivia said.

"I didn't want to insult him."

"If you had given him the right amount, he wouldn't have been insulted."

"How much would that be?"

"A hundred pesos. You could have asked me. As it is he'll remember you as a stingy gringo and me as yet another *malinchista*."[41]

---

41 Woman who betrays the nation.

THIRTY-ONE

TENOCHTITLAN – 1519

Alva

Tecuichpo's favourite chaperone came to see me. Eldest daughter of Itzquauhtzin, Patli had reached the ripe years of womanhood without ever marrying. Short and stubby, with a mischievous wit, she was a consummate matchmaker with her own special method of achieving success: she was said to try the manhood of all the men she chose as husbands for her clients.

She delivered her message – that Tecuichpo wanted to see me alone – without elaborating, but the suggestive smile that played on her lips as she spoke made my heart pound with excitement. For Tecuichpo to visit our household bore no special significance, but to arrange a meeting with me alone could only have one meaning – and it signified a death sentence if the emperor or his brother should find out.

"No one will know," Patli said, reading my thoughts.

Not that her assurance made a rack of difference, for in any case no man could refuse the command of a royal princess. I told myself that if I were to die in Tecuichpo's service, my end would, at least, be noble and I would have cause only to rejoice.

Patli told me that the emperor had offered Tecuichpo to Cortés – disregarding her relationship with Cuitláhuac – but the Spanish leader had refused her. Refused Moctezuma's own daughter, one of the most beautiful women in Tenochtitlan! I've wondered about this over the years. The Spaniard can surely not have found her unworthy. His excuse for rejecting her was that she had not been received into his religion and that he was already married. Both objections have always seemed strange. I have seen for myself that Spaniards take several different women for their needs and even exchange them among themselves. As for religion, they seem to trot out their faith only when it suits them, while at other times they disobey their god, committing acts of violence, rape and pillage that are forbidden in their holy book. I conclude that Cortés restrained himself, repressed his own desire (for who would not have desired Tecuichpo as she was then, in the flower of her youth?), because he did not want the obligation of joining Moctezuma's family. Marriage to her would have obliged him to treat her father with a reverence unsuited to his darker purpose. Later, when the emperor had departed this world, Cortés took up the gift for long enough to make a child, before bestowing his princess on one of his fellows.

Patli and I settled on arrangements for the encounter. Tecuichpo and I were to meet at my beach the next day just after sunrise, a time when no one would question her absence.

"You are lucky," Patli said coquettishly. "If it doesn't work out, I'll be ready to console you…"

She hurried away, leaving me in a state of feverish excitement. I slept little that night and was on the promontory overlooking the beach before dawn. There, seated beneath an overhanging rock that gave shelter from prying eyes, I awaited the footsteps that would herald the arrival of what I took to be my destiny. In such a place, the day would normally advance all too quickly, for my mind would be full of the awakening scene before me – the silent gliding of the fishermen, the gentle lapping of the waters barely breaking the stillness, the far shore enshrouded in mist – so that I would scarcely notice the sun's march across heaven. Now I had ears only for the sound of footsteps. and every moment that passed in their absence seemed like the length of a sleepless night.

My vigil ended as the sun touched his first rays to the water. Patli and Tecuichpo duly appeared with a palace servant in tow carrying two baskets of food. I watched them descend the narrow path to the beach before hurrying to join them. I kissed the earth before Tecuichpo as custom demanded – to which she smiled and told me not to be silly – but in a way so warm and intimate that I felt silliness became me and took it as a compliment.

"While you two are engaged," Patli said, "I will be enjoying the view. By the way, the story is that my princess and I have gone to bathe in the lake, while you, young man, are somewhere else."

"What about your servant," I asked.

"Itotia will be rewarded for his silence in a way a young slave can hardly dream of."

He was young and good-looking; the salacious gleam in Patli's eye left no doubt about the reward she had in mind.

"Off you go," she said with a trace of impatience. "You have until midday."

I took one of the baskets from the servant and accompanied Tecuichpo into the larger of two caves set back in the rocks. Or rather she led me, for she clearly knew the way.

The accommodation was not as I expected. A fire lit the interior, casting a flickering light on walls draped with cloaks, and just visible in the depths was a bed with a covering of blankets.

"How come?"

She stopped my questions with a caress so gentle that my hand, my gestures, my own breathing felt clumsy by contrast. In a single deft movement, she untied her robe and let it fall to the ground, and so stood facing me, neither shy nor proud, but as if it were the most natural thing to show the work of nature. I was the shy one, conscious that here was a princess and I, no matter our shared childhood history, a mere commoner. My gaze, deferential, found its focus on the cave floor.

"Look. It's for you."

More out of obedience than licence, I raised my eyes to hers which sparkled in the half-light, and then as if embarking on a voyage they wandered over her young breasts not yet fully rounded, the curve of her hips, her legs slightly apart with her weight on one side so that her form undulated in and out of shadow like drapery across a bed. Her softness made her seem vulnerable, and yet her seeming defencelessness contained within it a strength that rendered her proof against uninvited assault, for it resided not in the outward form of the body but in a kind of knowingness about the world and her place in it, a determination to fit herself to circumstance and bend circumstance to her will. Don't ask me how she acquired this wisdom at so tender an age. For my part, I grasped much of this only in hindsight. All I perceived then, through desire and wonder, was the presence of a mind sharper and more powerful than my own, and one that exceeded mine too both in daring and gentleness.

Stepping towards me, she untied my cloak and I felt her breasts press lightly against me.

"Come."

I put my arms around her with a tumble of emotions, surprised that her form yielded so pliantly to my touch as if I could mould it to whatever shape my fantasy demanded, puzzled by my own contrasting roughness and physical strength, tempted by raw desire to a rough imposition of my will, eager to hear her cry of pain and pleasure in pain, but no less prompted to tenderness, to shield her from the brutality of men, myself included.

We lay down and, oh how I remember my nervousness vying with my excitement for possession of my senses. For a long time, or so it seemed, I ran my hands and my lips over her body, her face, her neck, her hair, leaving only the most intimate part untouched for fear, I suppose, even then of venturing where I should not. At length she guided me there herself, and I discovered – with what astonishment – her desire, abundant in a way unknown with any of Huehue's friends across the lake who used oil to compensate their indifference and histrionics to simulate the sighs of passion.

"Come," she said again.

And yes, I entered her slowly, even then restraining an impulse to dominate and force until her insistence and my own urgency overcame inhibition. And then madness took over, and I knew I would gladly die after this, on the anvil of her father's wrath if need be, and this time, yes, I emptied my being into her and she received me, and I believe I felt the breath of god.

Why do I put this down? Perhaps it is because such moments are rare in our lives, unique in mine, for though I have loved other women, no coupling thereafter could be more than a shadow, a poor one, for the wonder I knew in Tecuichpo's arms. To be sure, I have used words and gestures of affection with other partners. A mere description would reveal nothing different, a simple repetition, the act of love being something all of us have in common. But can words and gestures of love ever be the same a second time? When we reuse them, do they not lose their force and ring false even to ourselves?

"Now I can never be the plaything of my father's politics," she told me. "He can dispose of my body, hand it to the man of his choice, but it is I who own it, and you who keep it safe."

I summarize her words, and the version I set down here may seem cold. But the thoughts she whispered into my ear between caresses in the restful aftermath of love are engraved in my mind in all their beauty. I know them by heart and could not then expose them to another's eye.

"How did you find out about this cave," I asked.

"You told me about it years ago. Besides, you're not the only one who comes here. Patli knows the way like the pattern of her own face."

"Patli?"

She kissed me. "Forget that I told you."

I asked her what would happen if she became pregnant.

"I will not," she answered. "You men are rather simple about these things."

She summoned me to her again, and a third time, and we would have stayed there the day long and into the night had not Patli's anxious call intruded on our idyll. Midday was upon us, and a more prolonged absence could be noticed at the palace. While we bathed and dressed, Patli gave us a lecture on the need for discretion, remarking that even Tlaco – she looked at me sternly – was not to know.

And suddenly they were gone. I watched them climb the steep path, Tecuichpo and Patli arm in arm with Itotia close behind.

"When shall we meet again," I called stupidly after them. Tecuichpo continued on without responding or looking round. I don't know if she heard.

I looked out at the lake shining in the midday sun, and sang for us the song of lovers.

In the place where lovers meet
I call for a woman
I sing out for her
to heaven
And to earth.

yesterday
I wept
and cried
I sought the bower of the god of love
the secret of her power

Tomorrow will I still lament?
What of today?

I am a man,
a soldier made for war,
She the sunlight and the dawn
The shimmering of the night

From where did I spring?
From whence the darkness and the light?
Only from a woman's womb
born of a woman's flower...

Still I seek the god of love
the secret of her power
Will I find her
when I search, maybe
tomorrow or tomorrow?

I am a man,
a soldier made for war
She the sunlight and the dawn
The shimmering of the night

Will I meet my end in war
Will love pour out her last intent?
Surely death cannot be for
The creature of a woman's womb
Born of a woman's flower?

THIRTY-TWO

TENOCHTITLAN – 1564

Alva

Don't get me wrong. I'm not one of those who look upon
the past as a golden age. Much of the beauty of those
times – the splendour of the landscape and our island city,
the temple, the flowers, the ordered bustle of our great market
– was darkened by frequent wars and the bloody tyranny of
rulers. We were not a free people. All of us went in fear of the
emperor's petty whims, his savage temper, his wilfulness. True,
we lived better than other nations, most of which we disdained
and oppressed with war and tribute, but in return we earned their
hatred, turned them into enemies willing to befriend whoever
might help them take revenge.

Nor do I look on my brief moment of joy with Tecuichpo as a
lost paradise, or imagine that if by some miracle fate had allowed
us to marry and live together, I would have been a happier man.
Who knows if in time we would not have tired of each other?
Perhaps I would have become a philanderer or drunkard, or

she…no, she would not have betrayed me, of that I'm sure. But would she not have lived miserably, the brilliant daughter of an emperor reduced to the companionship of a common man?

I don't know if Tecuichpo and I might have forged a better life, only that I knew love with her and that it remains with me, I mean the spirit that will always dwell within her. Happiness, I believe, comes to us only in little bursts and knows only the present. It has no more substance than the mist at dawn that veils the landscape in mystery but flees before the rising sun. So I sing in her name:

Slender flower they call you
For your body is slender
your sash is a tapestry of flowers
You flow like a river as you walk.

THIRTY-THREE

MEXICO – 1974

James

We chose a back-country route that would take us through the fertile plains of the *Bajío*; an extra day to reach the capital but the way would be beautiful and we could spend our last night maybe in Guanajuato or Dolores Hidalgo.

"The revolution was born in Dolores Hidalgo," Olivia said. "José Alfredo Jimenez, too. Our greatest composer of *rancheras*."

"Sing something. One of his."

"No vale nada la vida
La vida no vale nada
Comienza siempre llorando
Y así llorando se acaba."[42]

She stopped singing and kissed me on the cheek. "Where else in the world would a popular song begin with such words? It is

---

42 "Life has no value, it begins in tears, and so in tears it ends."

186

what we feel, that life is cheap, and so we drink each day to the last drop, *hasta no verte Jesus mio*,[43] because we know always that it may be our last."

We drove through a succession of hamlets, fleeting huddles of adobe houses lining the road, at length emerging onto a plateau of fields planted with corn and peppers.

"You're right not to answer," she said. "Just because you've explored my body, doesn't mean you see into my mind or have possession of my heart."

"You're trying to crush."

"I'm just expressing my views."

"Sounds more like flexing your power."

"Mexican women don't have any."

"Except maybe when they are loved?"

A gust of wind buffeted the car and moments later the luminescent sky and the sparkling green crops fell into shadow as if the earth had accelerated and the sun were falling prematurely into night. Twin flashes of lightning lit up the fields, silhouetting the trees and roadside bushes against a jagged backcloth of peaks and ridges. A fusillade of heavy raindrops thudded onto the roof and hood, followed by a low rumble of thunder and then dead calm as if the Erinyes were verifying their target before venting their anger. Then the storm burst over us in a howl of wind and lashing rain and hailstones, and the way ahead, the sky, the fields, the edges of the road dissolved into a curtain of aluminium and lead. Lightning flashes came hard upon each other, though instead of illuminating the landscape, they enclosed us in a grey cocoon shutting out the world beyond. I slowed the car to walking pace. Thunder cracks shook the road, so loud it seemed as if the sky had the earth under bombardment and was bent on reducing whatever stood upon it to rubble.

"Can't we go faster?"

---

43 Literally "until we see you, my Jesus."

"I can't see ahead."

Pause.

"What if lightning strikes us?"

"It won't."

"How can you know that?"

"The tyres."

"What about them?"

"They're rubber."

"So?"

"They resist electric current. Lightning always takes the easiest path to earth."

"You don't know that. You're guessing."

"It's a good guess."

"What if you're wrong?"

"We'll be okay."

"What if the car breaks down now?"

"We'll be okay."

The lumbering bulk of a cow appeared in the headlamps directly in front of us. We skidded to a halt no more than a couple of feet from the animal and watched it plod across the road and out of our frame, as impervious to the danger of our approach as to the weather.

"Get me out of here," Olivia shouted over the din. "I'm sick of this journey. Why did we come this way, into wilderness? What is wilderness to me? I don't belong here."

She was shivering with fear and anger, and I was conscious, too, of my own heart leaping and of our desolation which seemed as pitiless and unresponsive to appeal as the storm.

Night closed in, shutting us still further into the reflected light of the headlamps. We reached another hamlet, a stretch of wall at the roadside, and just beyond, barely visible, a row of low adobe houses. I drew up outside one of them. Through the rain, we could make out a double wooden door and beside it a window with a trickle of light leaking through the shutters. We waited with the engine running, half hoping, half fearful that someone would open up.

"Perhaps we should stay here and sit it out," I suggested.

"The countryside is dangerous. Someone might see us."

"Isn't that what we want?"

"No one will open their door on such a night. Except to wave us away."

I turned the car back onto the highway and we motored on into the darkness. The eye of the storm passed over us, offering a few moments of calm, before the wind buffeted us again from the reverse direction. Neither of us spoke. We drove on and on, winding our way through a land that seemed as endless as it was invisible. Until, as suddenly as it had begun, the rain dwindled, the wind lost its strength and the road ahead reappeared with its central white line clear and glistening as if it had just been painted. For a while, flashes of lightning continued to light up the interior of the car, allowing me to catch glimpses of her. She sat leaning against the passenger door, lips clenched, eyes fixed on the way ahead.

At that moment, I knew I had lost her or, more accurately, lost the illusion of possessing her. I remember it as crossing a threshold of self-knowledge, perceiving for the first time my own inadequacy, a rite of passage we all must undergo as we move from youthful exuberance through those bewildered years we call maturity where victory and happiness can never again seem other than immodest dreams. Yes, I saw that I had failed her, but in what? Failed to abate the storm? Failed to calm her fears and to wrestle down my own? Failed to inspire in her the confidence I lacked in myself? How trivial this all seems compared with the greater cares of the world. Yet nothing seemed to me so significant or so painful as this dawning sense of loss, this abyss into which I seemed to stare with its dark, unforgiving message that I was not loved.

How long did the storm last? At its fiercest perhaps no more than a couple of hours, but as the thunder rumbled off into the distance, it bore something of our innocence with it, and that night, in a grim hotel in the centre of Irapuato (*"no, señor, the only half-decent hotel in this place is, well, only half decent. Tourists don't come here, you see, only salesmen and bosses with their secretaries"*), we slept in twin beds, and over a solemn breakfast the next morning, understood that we wouldn't make it to the birthplace of the revolution and of the greatest songwriter of the Mexican people, but would head straight home by the shortest route.

"Is this it then," I asked her.

She took a sip of coffee, taking her time. "I will always love you."

Always? Always signified something else, betrayed its meaning by promising the impossible. Didn't we know, both of us, don't we all know, that nothing is ever always, and that the word carries – in a hidden recess of meaning – a burden of despair?

"Always is about the end, isn't it? Like the song, Love is Worth Nothing."

"No," she said. "It's life that's worth nothing. Love is something else. Life we can do without, but not love."

THIRTY-FOUR

TENOCHTITLAN – 1519

Alva

The Spaniards made us remove the statues of Huizilopochtli and Tlaloc from the temple shrines. Under guard we carried them down the stairs, smashed each one into small pieces and threw the shards into the lake, while their priests looked on with hands clasped and voices raised in prayer as if they were presiding over a sacred rite. I thank fate I was not one of the work party forced to carry out this desecration but merely observed it as a horrified spectator. When the first statue – that of Tlaloc – descended the steps, such a clamour arose among those who saw what was happening that everyone who heard dropped whatever they were doing and came running. An angry crowd grew in a semi-circle before the temple steps. More than one voice called us to arms and to wipe out these strangers who had entered our land not as guests but as a pestilence, and I believe we would have followed such a call had a commander been available to issue us with arms and direct us into battle. Instead, an imperial official appeared on the temple platform flanked by two Spanish soldiers. Though I stood too distant to identify him, I could clearly see his robes of office. He flung out his arms to call for our attention and despite our collective fury, we at once fell silent – it being unthinkable to disoblige a servant of the emperor.

"Do not be dismayed," he told us. "For Moctezuma himself has ordered our gods to be removed and it is he who has invited the Spanish god to dwell with us. Such are the demands of courtesy to strangers. Therefore, you are to disperse in peace."

Murmurs of astonishment. Was he conveying Moctezuma's views or those of the Spaniards? How could the emperor so suddenly decide to treat our people's gods as trash? We had no way of knowing. Sensing our bewilderment, the official drove home his message, ordering us again to disperse and reminding us of the sanguinary consequences of disobedience. Suddenly, the threat that confronted us came less from the violence of strangers than from the wrath of our ruler. In response, we behaved as we had always done, with deference to authority, and so drifted away, leaving the team of labourers under its Spanish guard to complete its destructive work.

Looking back, I wonder if that official was not telling the truth. Moctezuma may have decided to give the new god a chance in the hope of being freed, seeing as how the old ones had not protected him.

In the days that followed, the Spaniards washed the shrines clean and placed images of their own god there, the Christian one. Well, not the god himself but his son, Jesus, and his mother, Mary, who they say was a virgin. Apparently, the son is more important than his mother, though as far as I can make out, it is Mary who gets most of the honour because they name all baby girls after her, adding a second name to distinguish one from the other: María del Carmen, María Eugenia, María Cristina and so on. Jesus gets plenty of prayers, but far fewer men receive his name and no special distinction attaches to them. I've met poor

Spanish soldiers called Jesus, pageboys, servants. Once I saw a man executed for violating a woman and stealing her purse; his name, too, was Jesus. Go figure. I don't think I'll ever truly get to grips with Christianity.

Nor for that matter with their lust for gold. Whenever they came across a gold ring or a pendant, they did their best to conceal it from each other, or if the discovery was shared, they would fight for the right of possession like wild dogs over a carcass. No amount of the metal satisfied them. After they had emptied the imperial treasury, they looked elsewhere, torturing other leaders to make them reveal what they claimed were our hidden chambers and our mines.

We couldn't work out what they wanted with it. While we used gold to make jewellery, earrings, brooches and bracelets, the Spaniards melted it down into blocks and stored it away. According to one rumour, they used it as food. But you can't eat metal. No, it had some other value for them that for a long time eluded us. Only after living among them did we come to understand that they buy and sell with it, exchanging it for land, animals, food, even people, and that it makes some men rich, others poor, and all men greedy once they have succumbed to its power. But I ask you, how can a life or the beauty of the world be priced as a piece of metal?

Visitors to the city after Moctezuma's imprisonment might not have noticed anything out of the ordinary. The market remained open, fishermen continued to leave before dawn to harvest the waters, farmers carried on cultivating the *chinampas*, the streets were kept clean, the bridges repaired, children attended school, even the priests – though they stayed away from the main temple – did their best to observe the rites.

In reality, however, nothing worked in quite the same way. Petitioners no longer lined up in Moctezuma's palace seeking decisions or redress, for he was not there; and where he now spent his time, confined in his father's palace, no one wished to go, because the Spaniards guarded the entrance and we feared them. Little by little, shortages of food and cloth became apparent. Imports were drying up. Traders, like my brother, hesitated to venture far afield because our people had lost respect beyond our borders, and the hatred others felt for us broke to the surface now that the Spaniards had challenged our power.

An odd story emerged from the palace of Axayácatl during those days, about the emperor and a young Spanish servant called Orteguilla. A beautiful boy by all accounts, slim with a high forehead and close-set eyes such as we hold in high regard. One of the women who took food to him said the emperor spent much time with the boy, gazed at him in fascination, and seemed to love him especially.

Gossip began to circulate that the Spaniards were turning the emperor into a woman with their magic.

THIRTY-FIVE

MEXICO – 1970S

James

On June 27, 1973, the Uruguayan army took control of their country and launched a reign of terror against dissidents. That same year, on September 11, Chile fell under the military jackboot to the applause of prosperous members of the local bourgeoisie and the US State Department. How many died at the hands of the Chilean and Uruguayan military no one knows, but they say the number for Chile alone exceeded thirty thousand.

Many escaped death by slipping across borders to Argentina, Peru or Bolivia, or finding sanctuary in foreign embassies. Where they ended up depended on their status: the least prominent travelling the furthest to Canada or Europe, while elite refugees – intellectuals, artists, politicians, those who had most to fear from the military in their country but expected most from their condition as exiles – settled either closer to home or in the United States.

Many of the intelligentsia found refuge in Mexico where some – the lucky ones with contacts and influence – were shoehorned into well-paid jobs in academic institutions, government agencies and think-tanks.

One such institution was the freshly created Centre for Social Sciences, known since its inception as CENCIAS. The organization's founder and first director was a young economist of Spanish extraction, Carmen Azcárraga, a compact bundle of energy, who persuaded the Mexican government to finance the enterprise and to allow her to spearhead its development. Few Mexicans of note paid attention to this female upstart whose Castilian intonation alienated those not already put off by her gender, a Spanish accent being like a scratch on the old but still painful wound of a colonial past. They would not risk their reputations by joining her organization.

Looking around to see who might staff her new organization, Carmen's eye fell upon the refugee community, the Chileans, Uruguayans and later Argentinians (Argentina's military coup came in 1976), among whom were writers, economists, politicians, renowned in their own land but barely heard of elsewhere.

In Mexico everyone knew about the South American coups d'état, of course, but those southern countries seemed a long way off. In those days, few flights linked Mexico City to the great capitals of the southern continent. Travellers to Buenos Aires, or Santiago de Chile, or Montevideo had to start by heading in the opposite direction, north to Miami or New York or some other city of the United States which then, and perhaps still, occupied the largest place in the physical and intellectual transactions of her southern neighbours. Cargo had to follow a similar circuitous route, there being little trade worthy of note to a shipping line even between the largest Latin American countries. Nor was it possible to drive north–south because of the Darién gap, one hundred miles of swamp and jungle separating Panama and Colombia, an impassable overland barrier between the continents.

And so these newcomers came to Mexico less as brothers than as distant cousins. Although from different nations, they reached

Mexico as comrades, sharing histories of political struggle and defeat that rendered them more at ease with each other than with their hosts. I did not see when I joined CENCIAS – as the lowliest of junior members of the faculty – how deep were their insecurities, how much their need of mutual support bound them together, made them shun the mildest diversity of opinion. Polemic was not for them an intellectual discipline, a means of exploration and discovery, but a form of warfare. They had fled regimes where torture and death were the wages of dissent. A word out of place could have someone flung out of an aircraft at ten thousand feet, or burned alive in a farmer's field. To dispute with men such as these – they were mainly men – was to threaten them, to shake the flimsy structure of their new-found refuge.

Set in the house and grounds of a modest mansion in a middle-class suburb, CENCIAS more resembled a sanatorium than a place of learning. Students came and went quietly. I never heard them laugh or raise their voices. They had already spent years studying Economics or Political Science at places of more or less higher learning, but "they know so little…" Carmen would lament, not without satisfaction, since therein lay the justification for the new venture: "They must start over."

Perhaps this low opinion of their attainments – of which the students were keenly aware – kept them quiet, and maybe they were in awe, too, of the refugees who taught them, several of whom had been ministers of state in their own country, or important politicians, or glittering academics, men accustomed to deference, to commanding the heights of public discourse, to delivering their thoughts from the mountain top in language powered by self-belief and sanctioned by celebrity.

From Monday to Friday, the faculty took lunch at a long table set into a rectangular alcove next to the kitchen. We were no more than a dozen in those days, and sat where we would, Carmen permitting no hierarchy; that is until a newcomer in an ill-fitting suit took possession of the head of the table, after which no one thought to occupy that place again. For five years, Carlos Bustamante had been an important minister of state, but in the last year of the presidential term, he had been put out to grass. Perhaps he had overspent his ministerial budget or, more likely, being by reputation an honest man, had been deemed too principled to participate in the kleptocracy that outgoing presidents operated prior to handing over power to a new administration. So he came to rule over us, perhaps with a special remit to keep an eye on the South Americans in case their revolutionary influence should prove compelling to the students.

Nature had done Bustamante no favours in respect of physique. Squat, pudgy-faced, rotund, he resembled a large toad, and though less noisy than the proprietor of Toad Hall, he shared some of the latter's disdain for lower orders of humanity. At table, he acknowledged only those – a handful – he considered worthy of notice. Not that he was rude or dismissive: he just paid no attention to anyone else. I dined in his company maybe a hundred times, but I don't believe he ever returned my greeting or took the trouble to learn my name. Ironically, the South Americans he did acknowledge gave him little enough in return beyond the formal respect owed to his position. Perhaps his race counted against him. They could all have passed for northern Europeans and some of them seemed to me not wholly free of disdain for their darker-skinned Mexican cousins.

Picture us together at table, Bustamante presiding. On his right, Alfredo Fernández. Formerly a member of the Economic Commission for Latin America, Fernández was on first-name terms with the most celebrated Latin American economists and could often be heard conversing loudly with them on the telephone, long distance to Argentina, Brazil, or further afield. "Celso," he would cry at the top of his voice, "Raúl... Enrique..." – and all who were within earshot knew that at the other end of the line was Celso Furtado...Raúl Prebisch... Enrique Iglesias, figures of such renown that we were in awe of anyone who claimed to know them. Clever, witty, charismatic, Fernández radiated impatient energy, his shock of dark, curly hair taking to the air when he became animated as if struggling to keep up with his thoughts. He never showed himself other than contented with his lot – a heroic refusal, as I thought, to bow to the still unfolding tragedy he had left behind in Chile. Far from dwelling on the brutal regime he had fled, he had refocused his attention and was busily completing a book on the politics of international trade. He had various consultancy jobs, too, and like many of the elite – *cobraba en varios lugares* – picked up a salary in several places. It was almost, I write these words even now with wonder, as if he had arrived in Mexico less out of fear of his life than as a career move.

Next came Fernández's compatriot, Luis Mendoza: tall, slender, with thick black hair and heavy-framed spectacles; a bobber and weaver of fine phrases, adept at avoiding confrontation or, as I learned to my cost, at provoking it when it suited his purpose. Liable to switch without warning between warm enthusiasm, brooding cautiousness and snarling menace, Mendoza had sharpened his political technique on the anvil of student politics before embarking on a career as a professional politician. Starting out in the centre-right Christian Democrat Party, he had been blown leftwards on the political wind that brought Salvador Allende to power and, for his pains, ended up on General Pinochet's "most wanted" list. Less gifted than Fernández, Mendoza hung onto his compatriot's coat-tails whenever the discussion at table required a display of learning, and he was unfailingly quick to make Fernández's opinions his own. I never saw them disagree even about the strength of the coffee. Once I offended him by referring to him as a politician. "I used to be a politician," he snapped. "Now I am an academic," as if by merely saying so, he had assumed a more convenient identity. From the moment we were introduced, I sensed that behind a surface affability lurked a ruthless mind, cold in its calculation of advantage, subtle in its sense of when to advance and when to retreat, determined to have its way.

Of all the exiles at CENCIAS, Pedro Vronsky, a professor of political science, seemed most devastated by the Chilean coup and its aftermath. Committed body and soul to Allende's brand of "democratic communism", he had lost both his country and a cherished ideal of social revolution, a vision of a nation in which no one suffered hunger or lacked access to education and health care. He had had a dream, worked to bring it to life, and instead seen it shattered by gunfire and the distant meddling of Henry Kissinger and the White House. He wore his defeat like a coat, walking about the campus head bowed, face etched with sadness. Often he didn't bother with lunch, but went off somewhere by himself, and whenever he did choose to dine with us, he ate without relish and spoke little. I used to wonder if the struggle to come to terms with his defeat would prove beyond him. He gave an impression of being uncomfortable in the company of his fellow refugees, maybe because the majority seemed content with their new surroundings and easily able to hide their sorrows – if they had them – in a rush of fresh activity, whereas he carried the past like a last possession, heavy, cumbersome but too precious to part with. In 1975, two years after the coup, he produced a book of ferocious polemic – *La Pesadilla Imperialista* (the Imperialist Nightmare) – in which he took the United States to task for fomenting Salvador Allende's overthrow. A sad, angry little book now gathering dust among numberless other volumes on remote, seldom-visited shelves of academic libraries.

One figure enjoyed a reputation among the students for unfathomable intelligence: Dr Samuel Espinosa. When the military forced him to leave his native Uruguay, he was already, at forty, head of a university. Heavy-set and lumbering, he looked much older than his years, weighed down we supposed with the burden of learning, wisdom and conferred authority.

None of us knew him well. Like Vronsky, he was reserved, taciturn even, immersed in his own thoughts, and he disliked the small talk so essential to community of feeling. One might easily spend an hour at table with him without hearing from his lips more than the responses demanded by courtesy.

By contrast, before a class of eager students, Espinosa could talk for hours with barely a glance at his notes or a thought for his awestruck listeners. "Five hours is his record," Carmen once told me delightedly. "Sometimes we have to rescue the students and send them home to recover."

Among the exiles, I made one friend, Pablo Spielman – a Chilean of vast, melancholy bulk who struck me as most ill at ease in CENCIAS's refined, Socratic ambience.

"They all speak with such authority," he told me one day, "forgetting we come from countries where the pool of talent is small. None of us would feel so important if we came from Europe or the United States."

"Where do you fit in," I asked him.

"Me?" He sounded surprised by the thought that he might be sufficiently interesting to evoke a question. "I'm just a minor player with a social conscience. The rarefied atmosphere of this place is not for me. I end up over-eating." His mouth puckered in a half-grin, the nearest I ever saw him to mirth.

On another occasion he told me that although he had supported the government of Salvador Allende and been forced to flee Chile after the coup, he thought of himself simply as one of the people.

"We believed a new age was dawning, of equality and human dignity," he told me. "But most of Allende's people were armchair revolutionaries. I thought the revolution was for real, but I'm not sure they did."

I didn't grasp the meaning of this last sentence until later, though I couldn't fail to notice that he lacked the confident bearing of his fellow exiles. For their part, they treated him less

201

as one of them than as a camp follower who had somehow found his way into the same sanctuary like a stowaway aboard a ship. They tolerated him, acknowledged him in the corridors with a "Pablo!" or a *"buen provecho"*[44] at lunch, but, his rotundity aside, he otherwise came and went unheeded like a truck on the highway. Perhaps that is why he singled me out for companionship – seeing that I too was a stranger.

As the only native English speaker, I had been appointed to translate a couple of books written by members of the faculty, and so received an office of my own not as a privilege but so as to protect others from the disagreeable tapping of my fingers on the typewriter. Pablo got into the habit of popping in to see me. Invariably, he arrived with coffee and doughnuts – consuming most of the latter himself, his desire for nourishment apparently never mollified. His appetite became a joke between us – self-deprecating on his part because he felt his excess weight to be a reflection of what he called "other things". He used to close the door behind him, settle into the wooden armchair in front of my desk, and talk about the beauty of his homeland, and his love of music and literature. Sometimes he would recite a verse or two from a favourite poet – Darío, Martí, Mistral, Neruda. He seemed to believe – not always correctly – that I would understand and that through those poems I would see something of his own experience. He spoke as if I were as familiar with them as he, his egalitarian spirit rendering him incapable of believing himself anyone's superior, even in knowledge of his own culture.

Once he asked if I knew where he could get a copy of Neruda's *España en el Corazón* (Spain in My Heart). I didn't.

"It's about lilies," he said. "And blood in the streets."

---

44 Bon appétit.

THIRTY-SIX

TENOCHTITLAN – 1520

Alva

Put down tales of the emperor's feminization to idle gossip. More important was the news that Cortés had left for the coast with half his soldiers. Some other strangers had arrived – Cortés's enemies – and he had left to do battle with them.

How fervently we hoped he wouldn't return! The soldiers he left behind continued to occupy the palace of Axayácatl, and to act as jailers of our finest, the emperor being merely the first. They had also captured Cacama, King of Texcoco, Itzquauhtzin, the revered old governor of Tlatelolco, Field Marshal Atlixcatzin, and Cuitláhuac himself, who had gone of his own accord to see Moctezuma and ended up a prisoner.

But with half the Spaniards gone, rumours circulated that our army was planning an assault. My own family plied me with questions, thinking that as an officer I would be in on the plans. In fact, I knew nothing. No orders came from on high because there was no one to issue them. Without leaders, we lacked direction; Cuauhtémoc, the emperor's young cousin, might have stepped in but he was still very junior and maybe uncertain of his ability.

I asked Tlaco if he thought we could do anything, but he just shrugged. Perhaps he was too occupied with the pleasures of domestic life, for my sister was engaging much of his time and thoughts. He looked at me with those doleful eyes so warm and noble and with a little too much innocence for the cruelties of war, and I knew the question would garner no response.

Cortés's absence coincided with the Feast of Toxcatl – one of the most important in our calendar. There would be dances and merry-making, culminating in the sacrifice of a fine youth who, for the previous year, had lived in honour as the incarnation of Tezcatlipoca, lord of beauty and war, of magic and the wind. Tended by servants, garlanded with jewels and dressed in fine clothes, he would parade through the city playing music and receiving homage from the people. A moon before the end, four young women became his brides so that he would leave the fruits of his spirit among us. When the time came for him to depart this world, he went covered in glory, but with these words of warning on his lips: "Whoever covets riches ends his life in misery. For no one leaves earth with happiness or wealth." Priests alone witnessed the sacrifice for it took place in secret on the little island of Acaquilpan, and we have only their assurances that Tezcatlipoca did not return in priestly garb as one of them.

A Spaniard called Alvarado, whom Cortés had left in charge during his absence, gave permission for the feast to proceed. Think on that for a moment. Permission! To what depths had the emperor's submissiveness reduced us that we should feel obliged to request a licence from the arrogant foreigner?

We did our best to ignore the humiliation. Preparations for the festival proceeded without incident, and the Spaniards gave no sign of wanting to interfere. On the opening day, Tezcatlipoca appeared in the main square dressed in all his finery. Our best dancers performed for him, warriors did him homage, and young girls fed him the choicest foods. When on the fourth day priests led him away, the drums that had been throbbing day and night fell silent while we stood quietly waiting for the horns to sound from Acaquilpan which was the signal that Tezcatlipoca had commenced his journey to heaven.

How deep the quiet that preceded that signal! Stillness invaded the city. No one moved or spoke. From childhood we had been taught to focus our thoughts at this moment on Tezcatlipoca's words, on the vanity of riches and the evanescence of life. When the horns sounded, they woke us as if from a sleep. Drums once more began to beat, dancers sprung to life, swaying and stamping their feet, and we joined in, chanting our thanks to Tezcatlipoca for his bounty, to Huizilopochtli for his protection, and to Quetzalcóatl for bestowing us with wisdom, learning and knowledge.

Weapons and military display were forbidden at the feast, though junior officers remained on duty to control crowd movement and deal with disturbances. I had been ordered to a plinth outside the emperor's palace from where I could observe a section of the audience over the heads of the performers. So great was the assembly that individuals melted into each other and the whole square became a moving river of light and shadow, radiant with all the colours of the rainbow. Centre stage were the musicians and dancers wearing headdresses of quetzal and turkey feathers – while the most senior counsellors and officials, each in his robe of office, sat above them on the steps of the great temple, solemn in appearance but heady with feasting, the joy of celebration and who knows what more gentle delights savoured in the company of dancers under the shade of night? Moctezuma's absence seemed hardly to matter.

As I write these words, I am reminded that I have never again heard those drumbeats nor felt those rhythms, nor seen that glittering expanse of colour. They have departed from my life and from the land, from the waters, from the heavens, from the eyes and ears of humanity. And nothing will ever bring them back.

Absorbed in the spectacle, I almost forgot that an enemy remained in our core like a worm in fruit, until a disturbance at the edge of the crowd drew my attention. At first I could see only that people were making way for what seemed to be a wedge of intruders coming from a street on the far side of the square. Then I spotted similar disturbances elsewhere. From the entrance to Axayácatl's palace, several Spaniards on horseback rode directly into the people. Flashes of bright metal in the sunlight left no doubt that these were soldiers, and as a group of them came into view from behind the great temple, I saw they were wearing full armour and carrying weapons of war. To appear at so sacred a festival arrayed for battle breached every convention and code of behaviour – so much so that no formal law against it was ever thought necessary. Before any of us could react, a cry rang out from the roof of Axayácatl's palace, the cry of a Spaniard, a single word taken up and repeated by the soldiers in the square, a word in their language whose meaning, though we didn't understand it, soon become clear and has remained ever since scarred in the tenderest flesh of my thoughts: *Muerte! Muerte! Muerte! Death! Death! Death!*

With swords and spears, the Spaniards bludgeoned their way through sections of the crowd until they converged on the open central space where they fell like a pack of wild dogs on the dancers and musicians. Every one of the performers they murdered, splitting heads, severing necks, arms, legs, slitting open stomachs so that entrails spilled onto the ground. One enemy detachment forged a path to the temple and set upon the chiefs and nobles, chasing them up the temple steps, running them through and then hurling them to the ground like food for an avenging god. After butchering the performers, the Spaniards regrouped and stormed the crowd. In their desperation to escape,

206

people at the forefront of danger ran into those behind, whose flight was held up by sheer numbers blocking the exits. Some who died that day fell not to the sword but crushed underfoot in the general panic. Spectators on the periphery who tried to slip away into side streets found their way blocked by more soldiers lying in wait to bar their way. Everywhere blades flashed in the sunlight, jabbed and slashed, plunged into breasts and stomachs, sliced off heads and limbs with single blows. Blood spurted into the air, spattered onto the faces and clothes of the attackers, dripped on the façades of buildings and statues, oozed over the ground, settled in pools between the bodies of the fallen. On and on went the slaughter, the Spaniards wielding their weapons without pause as if their god had made them immune to the fatigues that afflict ordinary mortals. Cries of pain and fear filled the air, a spine-chilling, anguished clamour of stricken voices that has ever since dwelled in my waking thoughts and haunted my dreams.

All this I saw, transfixed with horror so that for a while – how long I can't say – I stood paralysed, unable to take in what was happening or even to comprehend that the same death that was devouring others threatened to hold me too in its jaws.

Murder directly below where I stood brought me to my senses. A Spaniard caught up with a man trying to flee, pressed him against the plinth on which I stood, and ran him through. I watched the sword enter and withdraw, and its victim slump to the ground. Now it would be my turn. The Spaniard had only to look up. He could reach me easily with his weapon. I pictured him sweeping his blade through my legs, my body toppling over, my days passing like the sun into night. Closing my eyes, I braced myself for the journey to the next world. Nothing happened. When I reopened them, moments later, the Spaniard had gone. Fate had turned his eyes elsewhere. I was inexplicably alive.

Looking round, I confirmed what I already knew – that all exits from the square were blocked. My only chance seemed to be through Moctezuma's palace. Ten paces away was a side door used by palace servants. No killing was taking place there, not, at least, at the entrance. If Spaniards were waiting inside, then my life would be over, but staying put was not an option. Jumping down from the plinth, I covered the distance in a few strides.

Inside, no one was about. The clamour and violence beyond the palace walls sounded distant, as if carried from another world. I found myself at the junction of two corridors, one of which ran left and right, the other straight ahead. I turned right so as to avoid the main gateway, aiming to skirt round the interior perimeter and reach an exit in the rear which I figured would offer the best hope of avoiding the enemy. The route turned out to be more straightforward than the one I had followed to the emperor's chambers.

Moctezuma's home was designed to forestall attempts by those unfamiliar with its layout to penetrate its interior at speed. One corridor led to another, then to rooms and more rooms, some with passageways running off at unexpected angles as if to confuse the uninitiated. I came across workshops with hand looms and tools for making jewellery and feather work, a laundry with a patio open to the sun where linen had been set out to dry, an interior garden with fruit trees. Most of the rooms were deserted, but in one or two I stumbled on huddles of people numb with terror who begged me to spare them as if I were an enemy, even though I wore the insignia of an officer. One chamber, hazy with perfume and drapery, harboured twelve or fifteen young women dressed in a way pleasing to an emperor. They shrank from me when I burst in on them – for they were forbidden on pain of death to hold discourse with any man of productive years. I urged all those I met to flee with me, but none chose to do so, and later that day most of them perished. Only the young women would survive. The Spaniards took them for their pleasure.

By trial and error and with directions from an old retainer I encountered in a passageway and who said he was too old and tired to join me in flight, I found my way out of the rear of the palace and onto a footpath that ran alongside one of the canals. My first thought then was to run home. But alone and without weapons, I had no means of defending the family. Nor could I be sure of leading them to safety since I knew not where safety lay.

While I hesitated, a group of our own men emerged from a side street, several of them bleeding from sword-inflicted wounds. Three canoes also came up, paddled by warriors. We fell upon each other in gratitude and sorrow. Though the encounter strengthened our spirits, we were too bewildered and frightened to work out a course of action. Nothing in our training or our way of life had prepared us to confront merciless carnage. War was subject to rules, one of which was that it had to be announced and the enemy put on notice of an intention to attack. To slay unarmed opponents was undignified, a humiliating disgrace, a crime punishable by the gods. Despite cries of fear and pain still audible from the central square, and the pressing need to act, I am ashamed to admit that we dithered. I think we were struggling to grasp that this race of intruders lived and fought by different rules and cared nothing for our ways. What was occurring in the heart of our city and our people could not happen; Tezcatzontecatl – god of drunkenness – must have abused our senses, or perhaps the origin lay with Tezcatlipoca himself, who was also the trickster and sower of strife. Was he discontented with the feast? Had we failed to please him? Perhaps the sacrifice had not been according to his liking. Was this his terrible revenge?

Such was our confusion that we might, like a clump of weeds, have taken root in that stretch of pathway and waited for the Spaniards to come and wipe us out had not a group of fleeing women rounded the corner of the palace to remind us that we were Mexica, that the nation was under attack and that we had a duty to defend it. My own lack of initiative – as an army officer – suddenly seemed shameful.

Remembering that a weapons store stood next to the market temple in Tlatelolco, I ordered our group to proceed there, adopting a tone of authority I neither felt nor deserved. No one needed prompting. Taking the women on board, the canoeists paddled off at once towards the market, while those of us on foot ran in the same direction, threading our way through back streets, crossing a couple of canals, and running as fast as we could along the causeway connecting Tlatelolco with Tenochtitlan.

THIRTY-SEVEN

MEXICO – 1970S

James

"We should publish a journal," Fernández said one day over lunch at CENCIAS. "Something original that represents what we are, a radically new kind of institution." He looked round, inviting suggestions but, as we understood, expecting none. "We'll study the USA," he continued. "What do we really know about that country? Hardly anything beyond a few titbits picked up in American magazines. Yet we are constantly under the US microscope. CIA agents, Pentagon operatives, scholars, journalists, you name them, all keep busy twenty-four-seven watching us and listening to what we do. Round this table, only our esteemed director can say what he ate for breakfast, but I wouldn't be surprised if the Americans have the information. Isn't that so, Doctor Carlos?"

Bustamante answered, unsmiling. "I am hardly important enough to trouble the State Department."

"On the contrary, Doctor."

"You're important to us, Carlos," Carmen said. "That's what matters." She turned to Fernández. "You left us in suspense."

"The United States is the most important influence on our region both politically and economically," Fernández said. "We owe to ourselves and to the continent we share to study that country and to share our understanding of how it operates."

"Brilliant," Mendoza agreed.

"Samuel?" Carmen said, turning to Espinosa.

"The neighbours may not like the noise," Espinosa replied. "On the other hand, they might be flattered."

"You must work up a budget," Bustamante said.

"So you approve, Doctor?" Mendoza asked.

"My job is not to approve but to encourage."

Fernández and Mendoza would form the editorial nucleus. Espinosa declined to join and Vronsky was not asked, though as a political scientist, a fluent linguist, and one of Salvador Allende's former advisers, he knew more about the United States than the rest of us. Why was Vronsky omitted, his name unmentioned, his wisdom ignored? Beneath the shared experience of exile lay individual histories opaque to whoever had not witnessed them, and whose effects showed up only in marginal details, occasional nods or frowns, ripples in a placid surface that hinted at turbulence below. Both Fernández and Vronsky had worked for the socialist cause in Chile and had fled in fear of their lives, but I never saw them converse nor heard either refer to the other in tones of solidarity or affection. Factions prevailed among the exiles, reflecting those that had existed in Chile before the coup. Allende's Popular Unity government had drawn parties of the left together that had been otherwise as antagonistic to each other as to their right-wing opponents.

"Has anyone approached you yet?" Mendoza once asked me.

"Approached me?"

"From MIR or MAPU or the Chilean Communist Party?"[45]

---

45 MIR: Movement of the Revolutionary Left; MAPU: Unified People's Action Movement.

"Why should they?"

"Stay away from them. We are all refugees in this country but while some behave as guests, others come spoiling for a war they already fought at home and lost. They'll aim either to convert you or kill you."

Over a bottle of wine one evening in my apartment, Pablo elaborated. "Politically we Chileans barely tolerate each other," he told me. "Take Mendoza. He's a centrist, a Christian Democrat. In the 1970 elections, he campaigned for his party's candidate, Radomiro Tomic. When Allende won, he changed direction, ran after the train, and just managed to board as it was leaving the station, though as a late-comer he found himself seated in the rear coach. Vronsky on the other hand travelled up front with the president. Result? They don't speak."

"Jealousy?"

"They inhabit different worlds. One dreamed – still dreams – of rebuilding Jerusalem; the other…Who knows what Mendoza wants? He's a politician."

"You don't think much of him."

"I wouldn't say that. He's not brilliant like Vronsky, but he's shrewd and speaks well. Fine phrases don't come from an empty barrel. Allied to ambition, the gift of speech can take you a long way in our beloved region of America. Hunger for success is something he shares with Fernández which is one reason they get along. Another is their ideological ambivalence, their refusal to glue themselves to a party or a political programme. They know how to dodge and weave; they are survivors, and for this I can only admire them."

"What about you, Pablo?"

"Aren't we always a mystery to ourselves?" He paused long enough to refill his glass and savour a swig, holding the wine in his mouth for a few seconds before swallowing. "If I were you," he said at length, "I'd put money on those two surviving longer than me."

213

Less than a month after this conversation, and long before publication of the journal's first edition, Fernández invited me onto the editorial team. My joy at this signal of acceptance – at the prospect also of a steady income – came tempered with self-doubt. I had no sense of personal significance, of deserving a place alongside people whose knowledge and experience far exceeded mine. Nor could I offer any special knowledge of the United States, still less a Latin American perspective of that country. Was Fernández anticipating from me something that lay beyond my capabilities? Was my Spanish good enough to contribute at the level of my colleagues or would I weary them with schoolboy errors and limitations of expression? Fernández brushed away my misgivings.

"Do you take me for a fool?" he said.

"Of course not."

"Then why question my judgement?"

Intimidated, I mumbled my acceptance.

When the editorial team assembled for the first time, I learned that two other members had also joined. One was young Argentinian economist Roberto Balcedo, the other a lawyer and politician called Felipe Ayala.

Sole Mexican of the group, Ayala resembled his compatriots in little other than nationality. Tall and thin with a pale complexion, he moved and spoke not with their nervous vitality and quickness of wit, but with the stately bearing of a seventeenth-century Spanish courtier who might have just emerged from a Velázquez portrait and would be returning at the end of each gathering to his place on a wall of the Prado. In our little meeting room, he would sit with one hand resting languidly on the arm of his chair and the other supporting his chin or tucked inside his double-breasted, a pose from which he would shift only when making an intervention. Then he would place his hands at chest level, touch the tips of his fingers together to emphasize the portentous nature of what he had to say, and begin speaking in slow gravel tones as if his words were the product of centuries of accumulated wisdom. Of all the figures I met in CENCIAS, Ayala was the one who most clearly evinced wealth and privilege – an impression fortified when I dropped off some papers at his house and saw that he lived in a mansion in one of the city's most elegant neighbourhoods. He did not invite me in but stood at the door as if he were guarding his home against an intruder.

Where Ayala was all grace and delicacy, Balcedo, the Argentinian, radiated nervous energy, restlessness, discontent. Like a tectonic plate, he seemed to live on the edge of anger. From the outset, he viewed me with suspicion, kept his distance, avoided my eye. When we were introduced, he refused my hand and offered instead a cursory nod before hurrying off on "urgent business".

A few days later, Juan Pablo and Gerardo, two students to whom I occasionally gave classes, stopped by my office. They told me Balcedo was openly questioning my inclusion in the editorial team on the grounds that my intentions could well be malign, that I might even be a CIA agent (a nervousness about which country might be next on the White House hit list).

My two students were an odd couple: Juan Pablo small in stature and wiry, black mop of hair, shadow moustache, a perpetual frown; Gerardo an untidy giant by his lover's side, plump, slow-moving but armed with rapid-fire speech that belied his ponderous appearance.

Why had they taken the trouble to tell me?

"In Mexico, we don't do xenophobia," Juan Pablo said. "Balcedo is from South America, you are from Europe. Who cares?"

"Under the skin, we're all sons of bitches anyway," Gerardo added.

"Did you personally hear Balcedo say those things about me?"

"Sí, señor," said Gerardo. "In the Gymnasium."

"He means the Mole Café." Juan Pablo grinned.

"But why…"

"We just wanted to let you know – in case you hear something – that Balcedo doesn't represent anybody but himself."

Hostility is a mysterious beast. That its seed germinates and grows in people's hearts no one can deny, but how does it find its way there? Who plants it? What may be its purpose? Self-preservation? Defence of race or culture? Or is it a human neurosis, an illness like cancer that after centuries of effort we haven't yet succeeded in eliminating? So readily do we think ill of others that perhaps we carry the impulse within us from birth as a concealed mark of Cain, the sign and curse of the fratricide. Like the ill-fated farmer, those who become its victims may never learn its cause or origin. Religionists would have it as the dark purpose of an all-seeing God and therefore beyond our understanding, but can solace truly be had from explanations dependent on a life hereafter?

I tried to shrug off the warning. "Balcedo has no reason to hate me. We met for the first time just a few days ago."

"He probably thinks gringos can't be trusted," Juan Pablo said.

"I'm not a gringo."

"You're a native English speaker. To many, it's the same thing."

I did not argue, but I understood even then that years of humiliation lay behind the distrust, at least part of which was rooted in the concept of Manifest Destiny, a US fantasy about that country's right to control the western hemisphere.

For three months, our editorial group met weekly to discuss themes, examine alternative formats, work out budgets. As the end of term approached, Mendoza announced that the first edition was to be published at the beginning of the new academic year and that each of us should return from the summer break with an article ready for inclusion. I was tasked with the editorial – a statement of our aims.

We were excited at the prospect, happy in our companionship, in a shared conviction that we were doing something useful and important. Before parting, we embraced – even Balcedo acknowledged me – and I felt proud to be among such colleagues, honoured by their friendship and their willingness to think of me as one of them.

THIRTY-EIGHT

TENOCHTITLAN – 1520

Alva

At the arsenal, we found Tlaco busy supervising the distribution of spears and knives. His presence there struck me as miraculous. I had seen him in the main square seated among the officials on the steps of the temple and had given him scant chance of survival. We embraced in tears. He told me that just before the enemy assault, he had slipped out to answer a call of nature. On his way back, he had heard the cries of pain and fear, approached close enough to see a flash of Spanish blades, then turned and ran.

I asked him how many other officials had survived.

He handed me a sword and a shield, fixing his eyes on mine as if seeking reassurance he knew neither I nor anyone could offer. "They can't kill us all…"

Once we were armed and armoured, Tlaco put me in charge of our group on the grounds that I was "a distinguished officer" – an assertion that in better times would have been a joke between us. How strange the effect of conferred authority! No sooner had Tlaco spoken than those who stood waiting for instructions were ready to follow me. In our hearts we might question the verities and diktats of leaders, but still we accept the roles assigned to us, swallowing shame if we are honoured without merit, or indignation if unjustly debased. Thus do we receive power as if by right, and bow to its conceits!

I led my makeshift platoon back along the causeway to the city, marching at its head and doing my best to dispel fear by disguising my own. As soon as we reached the outskirts, others began to join us, some carrying weapons, others armed merely with stones or sticks, so that our numbers had swollen to seventy or eighty by the time we reached the Atzacualco district. There we came upon Cuauhtémoc with several hundred well-armed soldiers. By a miracle, he too had evaded death. I at once placed myself and my men under his command, anticipating that he would absorb us into his column. Instead, he hatched a plan to counterattack the Spaniards via a pincer movement. I was to lead my troops slowly towards the main square via the temple of Ehécatl, while he would approach by a longer route via Moyotlan district so as to emerge on the far side of Axayácatl's palace. Once we were within striking distance, we were to keep out of sight and await his signal.

Though Cuauhtémoc was no older than me and had never been to war, I felt relieved to be acting on his orders rather than issuing my own. Leadership sat easily on his shoulders. By the firmness of his voice and bearing, his obvious courage and intelligence, he at once gained our trust, stiffened our courage, made us anxious and proud to serve him. Such are the special qualities required of a true commander.

Having further to travel, Cuauhtémoc set off first with his column, but no sooner had they disappeared than a marauding squad of Spaniards and Tlaxcalans materialized in front us. Evidently they had peeled off from the main massacre so as to hunt for additional victims. They fell on us with wild cries. Fortunately, they were few in number and after a brief though violent skirmish, and with help from civilians who appeared without warning and hurled rocks from the rooftops, we put them to flight. One Spaniard fell right in front of me, and without thinking, I bent down and slit his throat. So it was that I, Alva Tlacuilotl of the Mexica, for the first time added drops of Spanish blood to the river of my people's.

We met up with Cuauhtémoc's column as planned. All day we fought, urged on by our young general whose bravery and energy shone like a beacon that each one of us could see and proudly follow, until as the sun sank into the lake, the enemy retreated into Axayácatl's palace, leaving the square and the slain to us. Then, as dusk settled upon the scene and we who had fought dragged ourselves away wondering at our own survival, women and boys and men too old for war waded through the blood and odour of death and bore away the bodies.

In the days that followed, we fought again and again, attacking the Spaniards whenever they attempted to break out from the palace. Several times, we set fire to the entrance only to see them smother the flames with blankets that had once graced the beds of nobles. Meanwhile, before the city temples, thirstier flames licked at the bodies of the dead, and the smoke of funeral pyres drifted over the houses and the stricken hearts of those we mourned.

One of our difficulties was that we lacked the presence of our emperor. We knew he was inside Axayácatl's palace; we knew he was imprisoned. Not that we any longer believed in him, for he had betrayed the people and shown himself a coward, but it is one thing to despise a leader and another altogether to replace him while he lives.

Under Cuauhtémoc's orders, we mounted a permanent siege round Axayácatl's palace, preventing the delivery of food and water, while at night our musicians beat drums and blew horns so as to deny sleep to those within. Early one morning, Moctezuma appeared on the rooftop side by side with Itzquauhtzin, the old governor of Tlatelolco. We were already massed in front of the palace ready to forestall any attempt by the Spaniards to break out. At sight of the emperor, we lost our bravado for a while, fell silent and hung our heads to avoid causing offence by gazing at him. When he began to speak, we noticed at once that his voice had lost authority. He stumbled over his words, repeated them haltingly as if uncertain that his ears had heard them. His message was simple enough. We should stop fighting, he said, because the Spaniards could not be defeated.

I stood among the crowd of warriors and listened to that speech. And for the first time, I heard dissent; I heard people complain about the corruption of power in high places.

"Is the emperor a fool?" someone cried out. "Have the Spaniards cut off his manhood and turned him into a woman?"

On hearing this insult – it rang out loud and clear – I looked up at Moctezuma for the first time without fear, and saw his face twist into an expression that I can only describe as horror. It was as if he had suddenly understood something even his captivity had not revealed, that his power had ebbed away and that the people, who since his birth had bowed to him and not dared to cast their eyes upon his godly person, now held him in contempt. What came to him in those words was the end not yet of his life but of his power, and of something worse: his honoured place in the annals of our race. What we feared as we stood looking at him was no less sombre: that here might be an image of ourselves reflected in his shrunken figure.

Itzquauhtzin stepped forward in front of the emperor in a way he would not have ventured to do at other times. "By fighting, you do violence to yourselves," he shouted in the stentorian tone familiar to all who had heard him issue orders over the bustle of the Tlatelolco market. "Your city crumbles, your leaders are detained. Cacama, King of Texcoco, already dwells with the gods."

A great sigh swept through us at the news of Cacama's death for the people of Texcoco were our brothers.

"See how my own head inclines before the foreigner," Itzquauhtzin continued. "Peace is our only hope."

Looking back, I see the old governor leaning unsteadily on a stick and standing close to the roof's edge. How frail he looked! Of his former self, little remained beyond the voice, which resounded in defiance of his declining powers as if it issued not from his mouth but from a memory of the past. Itzquauhtzin we could not despise, for his years commanded respect, and his wisdom went before him and entered the thoughts of all who knew him. Few lived to his great age, and of those who did, we said that they already dwelled half with the gods and passed back and forth through the mist separating this life from the next so that they might bring the thoughts and knowledge of our ancestors to the ears of we who walked the earth.

Although I didn't know Itzquauhtzin well, our family looked upon him with affection because he had given Atza a choice spot in the market after hearing of our father's death. And once, at my brother's invitation, he honoured our house with a visit and dined with us.

As soon as he pleaded with us to stop fighting, my instinct was to obey, and I saw others lower their weapons too. The fight seemed to drain out of us. Without anyone issuing an order to stand down, we broke ranks and drifted away, wretched that we had no victory to repay the sacrifices of those who had lost their lives, and confused by our leaders' calls for peace when war so clearly beckoned. Cuauhtémoc, who might have rallied us, was nowhere to be seen.

Why, you may ask, could we not ignore Itzquauhtzin's entreaty when he had merely echoed the words of our discredited emperor? The answer is simple. From childhood, we learned respect for our elders and for those who ruled over us. We could not change our habit of obedience as if it were a garment. Revolt takes time to ferment in men's souls like *pulque*[46] from the honeyed water of maguey.

Our losses soon came home to us. Most of the emperor's counsellors had fallen during the slaughter. But what of the people? Few families had escaped bereavement. What a wailing was then to be heard. What cries of anguish and despair. Women wept over the husbands they would embrace no more, men over the ravished bodies of their wives. Children lay among the dead, some of them run through as they sought refuge in the arms of butchered parents, others struck down in flight and lying in pools of blood beside severed heads and limbs.

We lost my brother in that massacre. Teudile brought the news. He and Atza had been standing together in the crowd when the attack began, and as they retreated, a Spanish soldier had driven his sword into Atza's breast.

My first thought was to find the body. Teudile and I rushed back to the spot where my brother had fallen, but he had already been carried away. We went in search of him, running from one place of cremation to another hoping that his body had not yet turned to ash – for the law required the immediate disposal of unclaimed corpses. Lord Quetzalcóatl took pity on us that day. We came across Atza at the Temple of Chalchiuhtotolin among a litter of bodies being loaded by slaves onto a funeral pyre. He was laid out on the ground, his gentle eyes staring lifeless at heaven, his lips apart as if he had just spoken, a ragged, blood-soaked hole in his cloak made by Spanish steel on its way into his heart. We bore him home, washed him and dressed him in fine clothes in readiness for his final journey.

My mother never recovered from losing her firstborn. Thereafter, she carried through the motions of living, but the joy had gone out of her. Family and friends came over to pay their

---

46 Traditional fermented drink.

respects and to mourn with us, but my mother scarcely greeted them and left the duties of hospitality to my aunts, Papan and Izel. Only to Tecuichpo did she open her lips, but her words, I heard later, were drowned in sobs and in any case I did not hear them.

I had no opportunity then to speak with Tecuichpo alone, but her eyes spoke of suffering and worry. She too had lost family in the massacre, her father and her uncle Cuitláhuac were prisoners of the Spaniards, and she had seen close up what we were only beginning to glimpse: that the order of our world was overturned and we lacked direction and leadership.

On the fourth day after my brother's death, we carried him to the temple of Quetzalcóatl and laid him on the funeral pyre that already blazed with remains of the fallen.

There we chanted the eternal reminder of our fragility:

Grieving that ever life on earth should end,
We Mexica well know our destiny
Will be to bend before the storm and break,
And Mexico will no more be the flower
Beneath the sun god and his star-lit bower.

In those days, the air was filled with the sounds of mourning, and with the odour of burning flesh that lingered long after the flames had died and the ashes had been swept away.

THIRTY-NINE

MEXICO CITY – 1976

James

On the weekend that we broke up for the vacation, Fernández invited the faculty to a gathering at his home. Each of us received a card with a sketch map showing the house marked by a red cross and the words "Avenida Francisco Sosa, Coyoacán" in bold letters.

The address staggered me. I had expected Fernández – as a refugee – to be living in a modest apartment, but Coyoacán did not lend itself to modesty. It was and remains famous for its colonial architecture, its picturesque plazas, miniature chapels and cobbled streets, heroic survivors of assaults by earthquakes, wars, and the unremitting ambitions of urban planners. Presidents of Mexico, stars of the screen, renowned artists have lived there, their houses often hidden behind impassive walls and guarded by men with paunches and dark glasses.

The village that gave its name to the neighbourhood originally stood on the lakeshore. Cortés built a home there for his mistress

Malinali. Marked by a plaque, the building still stands near the central square. After the imperial authorities drained the lake and the metropolis spread outwards, absorbing everything in its path, Coyoacán became a district at the city's southern edge – a status it retains to this day, even though new neighbourhoods have long since gone beyond like an onrushing tide flowing round an island.

Avenida Francisco Sosa has good claim to be the most exclusive of Coyoacán's graceful streets. It runs between the modern thoroughfare of Avenida Universidad and the old town centre with its twin plazas and grand diocesan church of St John the Baptist. Colonial houses line the street on each side, demotic yet stately, with façades of burnt ochre, terracotta roofs, doors framed in ancient stone and windows inset behind black *rejas*.[47]

Fernández's home turned out to lack any pretence of humility. It stood behind a rampart with inscrutable double doors for an entrance, above which was an old bell suspended from an arch. I rang and presently a cut-out in the door slid open to reveal a pair of eyes behind an iron grill. Their owner checked my identity and verified my name on the guest list before unbolting the door to let me in.

Deferential where seconds before he had been stiff and suspicious, the porter greeted me with a slight bow. "*Muy buenas tardes, Licenciado. Si gusta pasar al jardín de atrás, ahí lo espera el Ing. Fernández con su esposa. Están a punto de servir la comida.*"

"*Y Vd como se llama, si no es indiscreción?*"

"*Gustavo Alvarez Peralta, a sus órdenes.*"[48]

I held out my hand. "*Señor Alvarez, mucho gusto.*"

We shook hands.

---

47 Iron grills.

48 "Good afternoon, Licenciado. Please go through to the back garden, where Professor Fernández and his wife are expecting you. The meal will be served shortly." – "May I ask your name?" – "Gustavo Alvarez Peralta, at your service."

"*Me da mucho gusto, Licenciado, de verdad.*"[49]

He directed me to the rear garden via a footpath that ran across a wide lawn and then alongside the house. Squat, whitewashed and glowing under the early afternoon sun, it looked tiny by comparison with the size of the lawn, like a sugar cube on a green tablecloth.

Behind the house, the lawn stretched for another fifteen metres to a line of shrubs and then a high wall topped with shards of glass. Fifty or so guests stood in scattered groups chatting. Towards the rear wall, beneath the bright lavender canopy of a jacaranda, a long table covered with white cloth was laden with plates, cutlery, napkins, salads, bread, bowls of guacamole, tortilla baskets, freshly made sauces and prepared chillies. Adjacent to the table, a man in chef's regalia with more than a passing resemblance to Pancho Villa attended the barbecue with spatula and tongs. The grill spat and sizzled, sending an aroma of singed beef and spring onion into the air. From a separate table, positioned at a right angle to the first, a uniformed waiter served wine and sweet water flavoured with *jamaica* and tamarind.

I went in search of the host and found him holding forth to a group of exiles. He greeted me as I approached and introduced his wife Gloria who was standing next to him. She was wearing a broad-brimmed sun hat that shaded without concealing a pair of dark, intelligent eyes.

"*Encantado, señora.*"

She smiled. "You are a colleague of my husband?"

"More like a student…"

"A colleague," Fernández said, impatient with this hint of deference.

I exchanged greetings with the other members of the group, all of whom – to judge by their accents – were Chilean but among whom only Mendoza was familiar.

---

49   "Delighted to meet you, Licenciado, truly." Licenciado is used to address those presumed or known to be well educated or to have a university degree.

A call from the chef summoned us to the buffet. With my plate duly laden with steak and salad, I looked about for company. People were sitting on the grass in circles of familiars. Fernández's group was reassembling, exuding self-absorption. Carmen Azcárraga, a little further off, was deep in conversation with R – a famous Mexican economist. Pablo had evidently not received an invitation, nor any of the CENCIAS students with whom I had struck up friendship.

I spotted a familiar face – a young woman sitting in a ring of five or six others. Her appearance threw me for a moment because I remembered her in ill-fitting jeans, her black hair wild like an untended garden. Now she wore a ponytail, toreador pants and matching waistcoat over a white shirt, dark eyes framed in mascara. I watched her lift a morsel of food on a fork and pop it into her mouth with the delicacy of a geisha. How little resemblance to my recollection of her. Four years had passed since we had stood pressed together in a doorway. But there could be no mistake. I had felt the beating of her heart against mine. She had kissed me.

"Maribel," I said. "Maribel Rivera."

She looked up, puzzled.

"May I join you?"

Murmurs of welcome.

I sat down cross-legged opposite her, balancing my plate on my lap. "It's been a long time. How are you?"

"You're mistaken," Maribel said. "We don't know each other."

"We sheltered from the falcons. From the bullets. Remember?"

"You sheltered from the falcons!" one of the circle exclaimed.

A shadow crossed Maribel's face. "It wasn't me. I don't know you."

I looked into her eyes. They were the same eyes, but with stone in their gaze.

"I must be wrong then, forgive me."

"But how did you know her name?" someone asked.

"I'm not the only Maribel Rivera in town. He must have heard my name somewhere. It's just a coincidence."

The remark stunned me, both the denial and the condescending use of the third person.

I remember nothing else of the conversation, only that I kept glancing at Maribel for a sign or gesture, but she made none. After the meal, I wandered around for a time, but if I spoke to anyone else, the recollection has faded. By now, the sun's rays were casting shadows across the lawn, glancing off a tangle of bougainvillea on the garden wall and sending it into a blaze of purple and crimson fire. The waiter pulled a trolley along the path, laden with desserts: fruit, egg flan, a selection of cakes and tarts.

"Now my weaknesses will be exposed," said a stout man eyeing the trolley.

"It already is," said another, eyeing the man's girth.

A burst of laughter.

Citing a need to call my mother on the false pretext that she was recovering from a hip operation, I bade farewell to the hosts and received in return their expressions of understanding and disappointment at my early departure. At the entrance, finding Gustavo still at his post by the door, I again shook his hand and asked him how long he had been working for Fernández.

"About a month, Licenciado."

"And do you like the work?"

"Nowadays a man is lucky to get a job. I'm a carpenter, but times are hard, you understand, and one has responsibilities."

"Does Ingeniero Fernández know you're a carpenter?"

"No, señor. He's a busy man. Always running. He's very distinguished, isn't he?"

"Yes he is. Still, I could tell him you're a carpenter. He might have other work."

"It's kind of you, Licenciado, but I think it would be better to leave things as they are."

I nodded. "Tell me something."

"*A sus órdenes, Licenciado.*"

I recounted my first encounter with Maribel four years before, and her refusal now to acknowledge me. "Do you think she really doesn't remember? Or maybe she just doesn't like me..."

"No, no, Licenciado. That's not it at all. It's simply...Perhaps it was not convenient for her to know you."

"Not convenient?"

"She may have a jealous boyfriend. Some men do not like their women to have experiences, if you see what I mean."

"Not sure I do."

"We Mexicans are a free people. I mean inside, where we are masters of our own thoughts. In public, we are cautious, we hide, we fear freedom because it has so often caused us pain."

230

FORTY

TENOCHTITLAN – 1520

Alva

The rains came hard and fierce that year, turning the streets into rivers and the central square into a shallow lagoon whose waters washed out the stains of war.

We had been doing our best to deprive the Spaniards of food and water, and while the run-off now filled the wells of Axayácatl's palace, not even their powerful god could make food fall from heaven (though they claim that he could if he so desired). Heavily armed groups of Spaniards began to make sorties, forcing their way where they would in an effort to find supplies, but we kept the markets closed and made sure they would find as little food as possible. Sooner or later, hunger would surely weaken them, make them careless and vulnerable. Then we would take our revenge.

Meanwhile, a group of city officials that had survived the massacre organized repairs to the temple precinct. The Spaniards had wrought much damage. Sacred structures stood half-ruined, most notably the skull rack and parts of the surrounding serpent wall, effigies of Xólotl the dog and Xiuhtecuhtli patron of hearth and fire lay in shattered pieces on the ground, and worst of all Christian artefacts defiled the shrines to Huizilopochtli and Tlaloc. Such desecrations traditionally characterized defeat, but despite our terrible losses, our thoughts were filled not with despair but with collective anger and wounded pride. What foreigners had destroyed, we would rebuild.

Soon after restoration work commenced, Cortés reappeared having evidently won the dispute with his fellow countrymen. He arrived with even more soldiers than he took and since they could not all be accommodated in Axayácatl's palace, he resolved the problem by commandeering an adjacent block of houses and ejecting their inhabitants at sword point, an impertinence that infuriated but which, for lack of direction, we were unable to countermand.

At the same time, rumour had it that all was not well with the Spaniards, that Cortés was displeased to learn of the butchery of our people at the Feast of Toxcatl and was sorry for it. Yet he admonished us for fighting back, and blamed Moctezuma for encouraging our subsequent hostility – as if the emperor had any say in the matter! My own view – with the benefit of hindsight – is that the Spaniards were unnerved, unsure how to proceed, and were arguing among themselves. Hunger too must have been gnawing at their self-confidence. They needed the market to reopen, but this wasn't going to happen without imperial direction. Someone in high authority had to be found who was prepared to do the Spaniards' bidding. Candidates for the task were few because those of our senior leaders who hadn't already been murdered were detained in Axayácatl's palace. In the end, Cortés chose Cuitláhuac for the job, and so one morning, unheralded and without an escort, the emperor's brother walked free, armed with instructions to open the market and feed the enemy.

How little the Spaniards understood! No sooner had Cuitláhuac emerged from captivity than he set about planning their expulsion. He placed the city on a war footing, reorganized the army, appointing new commanders to replace those that had been killed, and established a day and night siege of the Spanish quarters. We found ourselves obeying him with scarcely a thought for Moctezuma. When Cuitláhuac went on to proclaim himself as rightful emperor, the change of regime had already occurred in our minds so that no one thought his ascent strange or wondered at the propriety. A quiet inauguration took place out of sight of the enemy.

I myself heard the priest speak words addressed only to those who rule over us: *Do not be easily led, nor punish people for trivial reasons. For the power you wield comes from god... Neither should you belittle anyone, nor shout at them, nor address them with anger nor terrorize them. Although you are our friend and brother, we are no longer your equal, nor do we see you solely as a man, for you have the bearing and speech of god our Father who speaks and teaches us through you...*

So ended Moctezuma's reign. As the ceremony drew to a close, Cuitláhuac took Tecuichpo by the hand, acknowledging formally that she was now his queen as well as his niece. I was standing near the front in the officers' guard of honour when she turned to face the crowd. There was a moment – I am sure of it – when she looked straight at me unblinking, an expression of stillness in her face that forestalled any possibility of acknowledgement or even of observing what lay before her. I was to see that expression again many years later in quite different circumstances.

Though I admired Cuitláhuac, I can't say I liked him. His possession of Tecuichpo was galling certainly, but that was a mere personal detail. More disturbing not just to me but a good many others was his reputation for ruthlessness. We knew him as the equal of his brother in his taste for sacrifice and for the blood of victims. On the other hand, he was by common consent one of the cleverest men in the city. We feared his anger, but we trusted his ability. From the start he had counselled Moctezuma against welcoming the Spaniards, and subsequent events had proven him right. At a time of crisis, no one could think of a better leader.

He lost no time in consolidating his power. On the day of his inauguration, he ordered all Moctezuma's male children to be put to death so that none could plot to usurp him or lay claim to the former emperor's estate. Yes, he murdered his own nephews! Perhaps it is the way of kings to seek out shadows and to eradicate whoever makes them.

Next, he summoned all his key officials and the high priests to a meeting and had them swear allegiance to him one by one. None demurred.

Once he was sure of his authority, he turned his attention once more to war. Gathering his officers around him, of whom I was one, he established a rota of responsibilities for maintaining the siege, guarding the causeways and entrances to the city, protecting food supplies, patrolling the lake, and controlling the armouries. On learning my name, he nodded, for he knew of our family's connection with his niece, but he gave me no special attention thereafter, for which I was grateful. Great men are ever insecure, fearful of challenge to their authority, suspicious of those who shine, quick to seek vengeance for real or imagined slights. Always it is safer to avoid their line of sight. I obeyed orders, led my troops quietly, and kept my head down.

Cuitláhuac's tactics did not take long to bite. If the Spaniards had struggled to get supplies when we were disorganized and lacked leadership, they now found themselves wholly cut off. We figured they must have been surviving on stockpiles of food and livestock kept in the palace, but sooner or later these would run out. In desperation, they sent Moctezuma with an escort back onto the roof of the palace, presumably so that he could plead with us to lay down our arms. This time his appearance moved us to open fury.

By chance, Cuitláhuac was present and it was he who first raised his voice: "Who is that Spanish whore on the roof?" he shouted.

"Does he think we will follow him in his cowardly trade? He is no longer our lord. Call him not my brother for he is a traitor. We must punish him as we punish all those who are wicked."

When Moctezuma tried to speak, a hail of stones greeted his words. I threw one myself. His Spanish keepers dragged him away but not before we had bloodied his forehead and driven his shame like a spear into his heart.

That was the last time any of us saw him alive. A few days later, the Spaniards dumped his body outside the palace gates. How he died, no one truly knows. Perhaps a stone killed him, though it could just as easily have been a Spanish knife since he had surely outlived his usefulness to the invaders as well as to ourselves. Or did he flee to heaven of his own will to escape the contempt of his people? Whatever the truth, the priests chose to cremate him according to custom, though they sent him on his way without the usual rites and public ceremony. Nor did we observe the due period of mourning, but instead pushed him into the background of our thoughts like a shameful memory. He was the first and last emperor in our history to depart in disgrace, pursued by curses.

Our siege settled into a routine. By day, we hurled spears and stones at any foreigner who tried to break out of Axayácatl's palace. As night fell, we stationed men on nearby rooftops from where we beat drums, played flutes, shouted, and sang at the top of our voices so that the intruders would enjoy no rest.

From time to time, a group of Spaniards came forth on horseback, but though we continued to lose men, we unfailingly attacked, meeting their superior weaponry with our superiority in numbers. Mostly they headed in the direction of Tlatelolco. Cuitláhuac had given Cuauhtémoc the job of guarding its approaches and the latter had put Tlaco in charge of the market with orders to keep it open long enough for our own people to obtain supplies but making sure the Spaniards would always find it deserted.

In their frustration, the invaders vented their fury as and where they could, burning houses, smashing idols, looting whatever treasures they came upon. One day an enemy force made its way to the top of the main temple, set fire to the shrines of Huizilopochtli and Tlaloc, and hurled all the priests to their death. On another they set fire to all the buildings bordering the palace that they had not taken for themselves so as to prevent us from hurling rocks at them from the rooftops.

At sundown, they would retire, hoping perhaps that on the morrow we would sue for peace, seeing as how our losses were mounting, but every morning they woke to see us assembled and armed before the palace gates, ready to attack.

How many of my own men died during these skirmishes I can hardly tell. Some fell and were replaced before I even had a chance to know their names. Each evening, an officer's melancholy task was to report the day's losses and request replacements for which there seemed to be no shortage of candidates. Young for the most part, fresh-faced and eager for glory, they could not know – as I did – that few would see their home again. To survive, you needed to get through the first days, to learn the cuts and thrusts of Spanish swords, the timing of blows and how to dodge them, to recognize the ruses and anticipate the feints by which the enemy sought to triumph. Four or five days of learning doubled your chances of survival; another three or four and you could count yourself among the veterans – your life no longer depending solely on luck. Training might have improved the odds, but there was no time; our ranks had to be filled by daybreak so that our troops were ready to fight should the doors of Axayácatl's palace open and the enemy choose to emerge.

My company was positioned alongside the great temple. To my surprise and pleasure, on the eleventh or twelfth day of fighting, Xihuitl showed up to head a platoon in the next street that had lost its commander in battle. I had not seen him since the day when the Spaniards first reached our city. We fell into each other's arms like old friends.

Speech among troops is never delicate, but Xihuitl – a model of courtesy and wit as a guest in our home – had the foulest tongue of anyone I ever knew. When he was on fire, upbraiding the enemy or one of his own soldiers, or even the midday heat, his curses rained down on his target like hail in a storm. With a growl for a voice and fresh scars on each cheek that twisted his natural expression into a rictal scowl, he looked and sounded menacing. I believe the men under his command found him intimidating at first until they discovered that his gruff manner was simply an outer coating beneath which lay the generous humour that had so attracted my mother.

I thought how unlike a Mexica he seemed in his mannerisms. He came from Texcoco – nothing unusual in that for they were our neighbours – but while his father was "one of us" – a distant relative of the king to boot – his mother was Zapotec and had been snatched by his father in a raid.

"Know why I'm a bloody-minded son of a bitch?" he once asked me. "I'm a rape kid, that's why. My mum never got over it. Tears in her eyes whenever she thought back on how I was born."

"You're not a bloody-minded son of a bitch," I objected.

"You don't think so?"

"No."

"Then I need to try harder."

Despite this outward sheen of toughness, he was by nature gentle. He loathed war and violence, and I believe that despite his army language, no officer – not even General Palintzin – was ever more respected by those he commanded. Until the Spaniards came upon us, he had never killed or seriously wounded anyone even in the heat of battle, and he would help prisoners escape rather than deliver them to the gods. Older than me by a good ten years, he had probably been passed over for promotion on account of his "failures" to take enough prisoners.

In those days of street fighting, when Xihuitl and I led our troops side by side, we cemented a friendship that rode over our differences of background, and blossomed independently of his friendship with my mother. My own allegiances to our people and our city were clear and I had no reason to question them. Not so Xihuitl. A part of him, inherited from his mother, could only think of us Mexica as oppressors. He abhorred our domination and exploitation of other nations. Yet he could not but recognize our achievements.

"The city's all very fine and beautiful," he told me. "Only most of it" –he made a sweeping gesture as if to take in our entire world – "was built by slaves."

"Surely we owe what we have to the gods," I argued.

"Fuck the gods. What do they have to do with it?"

"They inspired us to settle and build here. Without their protection and guidance–"

"Protection and guidance? Take my fucking word for it, they couldn't care less. The wealth of this place didn't come from heaven but from war. Mexico did no more than conquer, rape, oppress and bring home the spoils." For a moment he looked angry, but then softened. "Problem is, I've become a bloody Mexica myself. Otherwise, I'd be fighting alongside the Spaniards."

"If Cuitláhuac heard you speak like that about our gods, he'd send you to feed them," I said.

"Yeah. That's why I screw so much. Make sure I leave something behind while I can."

He wasn't boasting. After counting up our lost soldiers together and reporting to headquarters, he'd be off to the whorehouses. Every night. He used to beg me to go with him, but with Tecuichpo ever in my mind, I had no stomach for lesser pleasures, and after a day of fighting, no energy either. Just once, I agreed to accompany him across the lake half hoping to bump into Huehue, who I hadn't seen for a while. There was no sign of the old shit-shoveller, and when I let a young girl take me by the hand and lead me off, I simply lay down beside her and fell asleep.

"Pussy, that's what you need before a battle," Xihuitl said as we paddled back just before sun up. "You're a different man now. Don't deny it."

I let him think I'd passed the night in riotous loving. Next day, he wanted me to go with him again, but this time I told him I had a jealous mistress.

"Ah women," he said. "They're the real gods."

FORTY-ONE

MEXICO CITY – A CAFÉ IN THE COLONIA DEL VALLE

September 2010
James

"My father used to come here before he died," Olivia said. "Only time I ever heard him speak Arabic."

"He didn't teach you?"

"He wanted his children to grow up Mexican. He adored this country. We were peaceful in those days, despite all the poverty. It was a place of music and romance. When he was feeling happy, and always on my mother's birthday, my father would sing to her. Always the same song."

She leaned towards me, her voice barely a whisper:

"Voz de la guitarra mía,
Al despertar la mañana
Quiere cantar su alegría...[50]

---

[50] "Voice of my guitar sings joyfully when the morn awakens..."

240

My mother would smile with a pleasure that perhaps we can no longer feel. She believed in the words and the man who sang them. Nowadays we might be better off but the belief has gone. We've become cynical. A country of drug dealers, kidnappers and corrupt politicians."

"Don't we always see the past as innocent?"

"Life was never perfect, but my parents could dream at night of a better world – a better Mexico – and wake up feeling that both were possible. Our sophistication is not a higher form of knowledge but a descent into ignorance. We no longer know what to do or even what to wish for. The future has fled from us."

She retrieved some magazines from a bag and put them on the table. "I brought you some copies of Proceso."

On top of the pile was the April 2010 issue with a cover photograph of two men, one elderly, white-haired, squinting into the camera, the other mid-to-late fifties, eyes shadowed by the long peak of a baseball cap, an arm protectively thrown across the other's shoulder.

I recognized the older man: Julio Scherer, a renowned journalist. As chief editor of Excelsior, then the country's top daily, he had the distinction in 1976 of being thrown out along with his editorial team in a putsch ordered by President Echeverría, he of the dark glasses and sinister demeanour, the butcher of Tlatelolco. In those days, speech was free in Mexico provided you didn't use it. Scherer had made the mistake of giving his journalists free rein to criticize the government.

In response, Scherer and his colleagues launched Proceso – a monthly aimed at the throat of the Mexican political system. I remember wondering all those years ago, as I devoured the first edition and marvelled at its effrontery, whether the entire editorial team would be found on a country road with a bullet in the head.

Somehow they survived along with the periodical they

founded. Evidently the president didn't think a small-circulation journal, no matter how radical, was worth worrying about. He might have welcomed it as proof of the liberality and openness of the regime. That *Proceso* might become the country's leading independent voice would have struck him as absurd.

But who was the other man on the cover of the April 2010 edition?

"That's Ismael Zambada, one of the leaders of the Sinaloa cartel," Olivia said. "We call him El Mayo. I don't know why."

She drew another number from the pile, turned it towards me and flicked slowly through the pages. "Look."

Shots of corpses slumped in contorted angles on a roadside, vehicles driven into walls and bollards, buildings pock-marked by gunfire, the interior of a car smeared with coagulating blood.

"Gun battles in our streets. Civilians caught in the crossfire. We have a crazy president.[51] Ever since he started the war against drugs, more and more people have died."

"What should he do?"

"Let the Americans deal with them."

"Them?"

"Traffickers. Who cares if they run drugs to the US so long as they leave us in peace?"

"That's just…defeatism."

"It's reality. Why should drugs be illegal because the Americans say so? Did you know they only banned cocaine in 1970? Before then, anyone could buy it and no one got killed."

That evening, in my hotel room, I read through Scherer's article in the magazine Olivia had given me. *If the Devil offered me an interview, I'd travel to hell to meet him* read the headline. El Mayo had invited the veteran journalist for a chat. What fears might have coursed through Scherer's thoughts at such a prospect? Had he offended Zambada? Was this an invitation he

---

51 Felipe Calderón, president of Mexico from 2006 to 2012.

couldn't refuse but from which he wouldn't return – payback maybe for some journalism the gangster didn't like?

Scherer admits to nervousness. He documents his journey to the rendezvous: first, a cab ride, then longer rides in two different cars followed by twenty-four hours in an untenanted house – all in the company of a "minder". Next comes another ride in a pick-up truck across sun-scorched flatlands and through mountain passes until at last he reaches a country cabin hidden from view by vegetation and set in a landscape otherwise devoid of human settlement. Framed in the doorway and waiting to greet him stands one of the most powerful criminals in the western hemisphere, a man with a million-dollar price on his head and a reputation that inspires fear wherever it cannot buy devotion. Mildly overweight but solid, he wears spotless pressed jeans and a sports shirt. A thin moustache and faintly mocking gaze project irony and self-containment.

"Thought we might have a bite together," El Mayo says.

We have travelled via a Hollywood B movie to an encounter with the underworld and we read El Mayo's greeting as if his words carried a dreadful menace beneath the surface courtesy. The two men sit at a table in the open air. Armed guards patrol the compound, scanning the landscape for signs of movement.

We know nothing of who serves the meal, only its constituents: orange juice, steak, beans, melted cheese, sweet coffee.

Scherer asks questions, and El Mayo responds in monosyllables. Their conversation is thin. Journalist and criminal – household names and eager to meet – have little to say to each other, though out of the banality of a dialogue meagre in content and even of mutual understanding comes one strange revelation. El Mayo lives in fear, haunted by the thought of capture, by a horror of the prison cell. Will he kill himself if the police find him? He hopes he has the guts.

That is all we learn. Of the bloodied streets, there is no mention; nothing of warfare between rival cartels, summary executions, intimidation of prosecutors, infiltration of governments, bribery of officials. We are left to wonder about who and how many this man might have murdered with his own hand and with the many hands under his command.

A hitman takes the cover snapshot using the journalist's camera. Scherer is old, stately, with a prominent nose, white hair swept back from his forehead, face wrinkled and heavy with experience; El Mayo, thirty years his junior, stands upright, legs apart, jaunty, unsmiling. The newsman could have stepped off a flight from Europe; the trafficker could only be a child of the earth on which they stand.

Following Scherer's piece are two more also about the narcotics trade.

From the beginning of the year, the Sinaloa cartel – headed by El Mayo and El Chapo – have been at war with the Carrillo Fuentes and Beltran Leyva organizations. Six hundred people have died so far – most of them caught in the crossfire.

On the next page another war, this time between the Sinaloa cartel and another rival gang, the Zetas.

This time we are in a remote village in the state of Durango. Laid out in the Chapel of the Virgin of Guadalupe are the bodies of ten youngsters side by side, each covered by a white or a purple shroud dotted with scarlet blooms.

The Zetas ambushed them. Or maybe it was the Sinaloa gang...

Nobody knows.

Putting the magazine aside, I open the window. My hotel room looks out onto a yard of storerooms and back entrances, and beyond to a side street lined with stores and cafés. Snatches of conversation reach me, the rumble of passing cars, dogs yelping. An odour of sizzling meat and chilli floats over the cloacal undertow of a subterranean drain. Night is falling and street lights flicker into life, throwing the sky into blackness.

A high-pitched whistle pierces the air, hovers, then fades into silence, the unmistakeable, poignant siren call of the *camotero*[52] and, though I can't see him, I know he is there with his little handcart, his brazier and steaming pan of sweet yams, and I go in search of him.

---

52 Sweet-potato seller.

FORTY-TWO

TENOCHTITLAN – 1520

Alva

We had no experience of night fighting. When the sun edged over the horizon, we stood down until the next day. Why fight an enemy you could see imperfectly and might easily mistake for a friend? Moonlight plunged the world into shadow, erasing distinctions of rank and race, so that we became as one until the sun rose again and threw light on our differences. Observing this custom of ours, the Spaniards employed it to advantage, and though I don't believe their eyes pierced the darkness better than ours, they cared less where and on whom their violence fell.

Their night raids took us by surprise, allowing them to uncover sources of supply that we had believed well hidden by darkness. Cuitláhuac responded by closing all the warehouses and organizing secret caches of food in different parts of the city. He also realized that night could favour us if we learned to use its shadows since we knew the city better than the enemy, and so we adopted the Spaniards' way and prepared ourselves to meet them whenever they chose to appear. Thereafter, enemy sorties became ever more fruitless. Sooner or later, lack of food would surely flush them out and when that moment arrived, we would be able to finish them off.

So it happened that one night as the city slumbered, the enemy force – soldiers, horses, cannon, carriages laden with gold – slipped as one out of their quarters and made for the Tacuba Causeway. Despite Cuitláhuac's precautions, no one saw them. Absorbed in their own halo of noise, the musicians on the rooftops noticed nothing. Soldiers stationed round Axayácatl's palace were found the next morning with their throats cut. We never found out how this was done. The Spaniards might well have escaped unobserved but for a woman who by chance had risen to fetch water. As she dipped her jug into the lake, she spotted enemy armour reflected in the moonlight and raised the alarm. I woke to the sound of war drums. Rubbing sleep from my eyes, I grabbed my weapons and ran to the great square which was already boiling with activity. On the temple summit, priests were calling the city to arms and pointing towards the Tacuba Causeway. Cuitláhuac had already taken charge. When I arrived, he was standing halfway up the temple steps giving instructions to his generals. Moments later, he was down in the square helping to marshal the troops, then back up the temple steps again gesticulating and calling out to officers by name.

My orders were to take a company, head for the Tacuba Causeway, and attack the Spanish rearguard as it made for the shore. Others were instructed to race ahead by canoe and to launch assaults on each flank of the enemy from the waterside.

At intervals along all the causeways were wooden bridges constructed to allow passage of the water from one side to the other. These were easily removed or broken in case of attack and Cuitláhuac assigned separate groups of canoeists to this task. By the time we reached the causeway, we could make out, in the half-light, that the enemy rearguard had stalled before the innermost bridge, and we could hear the neighing of horses and voices calling "*socorro*" and "*madre de Dios*" and other things in their Spanish language, and the crashing of bodies into the water. A moment later we were upon them. Oh I remember this time of glory for our people when we showed our true heart. All night and into the morning we fought them, and little by little we pressed forward, each step a small triumph that filled us with courage. Something new and strange was occurring. We were not retreating before the Spaniards but putting them to flight. When my company reached the first breach in the causeway, we found it filled with the bodies of men and horses and had to step on them to reach the other side. Spanish men, Spanish horses. Now we knew for certain they were not gods. I myself killed one of them, and I took wounds for my pains, gashes from enemy steel that have left scars I now bear as marks of honour, though I keep them from view for fear of giving offence. My limp came later from a deeper injury and cannot be concealed so I attribute it instead to the inconvenience of advancing years. Discretion in such matters must ever prevail over truth.

When the sun rose in the morning, he smiled on our victory. Many of the enemy, it is true, succeeded in reaching the shore – Cortés included, for he had travelled at the head of the column. But a like number perished if not at the hands of our soldiers then by falling into the lake and drowning. Horses they lost too, as well as most of their cannon and, as we learned later (for they complained about it ever after), the gold they had stolen from us but which they now considered to be theirs. As for the survivors, they ran off to seek refuge with their friends the Tlaxcalans, who like fools took them in instead of seizing the opportunity to complete what we had begun.

Why didn't we finish them off when they were in flight, you might well ask. Many of us, to be sure, were wounded and all of us were tired, yet our condition could not have been worse than the enemy's. If we had pursued them, I believe we could have destroyed them, though the effort would likely have been in vain because, as we now know, other foreigners would have come after them. In the far-off land of their birth, they are by all accounts as numerous as the stars in heaven, and there would have been no prevailing against their numbers. Think how many have settled here since those days! And still they keep coming as if their children sprout from the earth like blades of grass.

In any case, Cuitláhuac would not hear of pursuit. Maybe he felt we needed first to bury our dead, heal our wounds and repair the damage to our city. Who knows? I always considered him a wayward leader – smarter and better than his brother, but like him lacking in decisiveness.

Nowadays, the Spaniards commemorate the night when we chased them from the city as *Noche Triste*[53], but for us their sorrows were a cause of celebration and so they have remained in my thoughts.

Xihuitl was among those who did not survive that encounter. He had commanded a contingent of canoes and according to reports had led one of the first assaults on the second breach in the causeway, a spot where a great slaughter took place, with many on our side and more than a few on theirs breathing their last. No one saw him die, nor was his body ever found. I take this opportunity to honour his memory and trust that his spirit rests where it belongs, among the gods.

With the enemy's departure, the tension under which we had been living flowed out of our minds like a river. We took our eyes from war, turning our attention to reparation, to the simple routines in daily life, to pleasure and to love. Now that the Spaniards no longer lodged with us like an ulcer in the flesh, we ceased speaking of them. It was as if we had determined to erase them from memory, even from our own history so that we would never again have to think on them, or suffer their contempt.

---

53   Night of Sorrows.

There was much rebuilding to do, for the foreigners had turned whatever they touched to rubble. Temples needed repair; statues of the gods remade and returned to their rightful place. Magnificent gardens in Axayácatl's palace were left ravaged and lifeless – with not a plant remaining. Some of the destruction seemed to have no purpose other than to lay waste as if an evil force had come among us bent on sweeping away all the flowers and fruits of civilized life.

After clearing away the rubble and trash, we set about restoring us to ourselves. We mourned our dead as custom demanded with sadness and due ritual, but we drew comfort from a sense of being masters once more in our own house.

At home, the experience of insecurity had brought the family together. My aunt Papan and her husband, Zolin, came to live with us, their own house having been knocked down by the invaders; Izel and Teudile – they were now a couple – also moved in. With Xochitl and Tlaco a mere street away, we became a close-knit unit, finding needed reassurance in each other, for we'd all been traumatized by what had happened to us, by the shocking discovery that beyond the horizon dwelled aliens as powerful and menacing as the gods and who wielded weapons against which there was scant defence.

I believe even my mother knew some moments of quiet happiness during that time. Atza's name was never far from her lips nor surely his image from her mind, but as the matriarch, with her family around her and her sisters with whom to share the pleasures and labours of caring for an enlarged household, she visibly relaxed.

Sisterly gossip was something else. Once, I eavesdropped on their conversation when they thought themselves alone. Huehue himself might have been shocked. Amid gales of laughter, they spoke of the delights of love, exchanged tips on masturbation technique, wondered what the Spaniards might be like as sexual partners, and so on. We men know nothing about women really, while I suspect they read our thoughts as if we wore them on our face like a painting.

My sister Xochitl spent as much time with us as in her own home. Her belly was beginning to swell and she felt the need – as she put it – to nestle under her mother's wing, not least because Tlaco was often absent on diplomatic missions. During most of the period of fighting with the invaders, he had been with the Purépechas in a vain attempt to persuade them into an alliance. They had imprisoned him for his pains, and earmarked him for sacrifice on one of their holy days. Fortunately, we had a couple of their nobles in the same predicament and Tlaco was released in a prisoner exchange.

"I found out what it felt like to be meat for someone else's larder," Tlaco told me on his return. Thereafter he rejected sacrifice and became a convert to our way – the way of Quetzalcóatl.

At a get-together to celebrate Tlaco's homecoming, Zolin, who was an artist and poet, gave him a painting depicting his escape from the Purépecha and likening it to our collective victory over the Spaniards.

We sang, drank too much for the good of our senses, and bathed in the warmth of mutual affection. Zolin recited poem after poem – his memory was prodigious – and he played the flute too, the music cloaking us in gentle melancholy that made us happy and sad at the same time.

We could not have guessed then that the Spaniards had left behind a curse more terrible even than themselves, nor how close we were to tragedy of another, unsuspected kind.

251

FORTY-THREE

MEXICO CITY – 1976

James

Olivia had been avoiding me, refusing to return my calls. I was missing her, the music of her voice, her caresses, her laughter, the tears in her eyes and in mine when she spoke of something that moved her, the smoothness of her skin, the yielding of her body to my touch. I became prey to fears that she had come to despise me, that she had already replaced me in her affections; anxieties such as might serve only to embellish her beauty, her warmth, her intelligence, make of her a companion and lover beyond any that I could have imagined and whose like I could never hope to meet again. I cursed myself for losing her, tortured myself with images of her lying in the arms of a stranger, aware at the same time with a sense of humiliation that I could not lose what I had never owned, that possession is love's first illusion.

I tried persuading myself that we were engaged in a lover's tiff, but the device lacked credibility and I could see no way of twisting the evidence in my favour. Despair at her absence clashed with self-contempt for my own weakness. How, I asked myself, could I step from worrying about the savage poverty and inequality of this beautiful, violent land to the frivolous agonizing of a wounded heart? Was I not a fraud, a cosseted scion of the so-called First World, a spectator in a country I could leave at any time, on the next flight if need be, leaving the unaccommodated masses to their misery? What right could I have to personal grief in a country where so many lacked the bare amenities of a dignified life? With time I have learned that irreconcilable ideas live side by side within us, but in those days, I believed all things compatible and that nature would in the end obey us.

Two days before my flight home, Olivia called. She sounded cold, disengaged.

"You're leaving."

"A quick visit home."

"Is María Isabel still with you? Tell her I'll come for lunch."

María Isabel was forty-four when she came to work for me, but looked much older. She was small and wiry, with dark features that identified her as a daughter of the soil. Her eyes, though they hovered mostly between weariness and resignation, seemed to me infinitely gentle, and I came to think of her more as a surrogate mother or a kindly aunt than a housekeeper.

Pepe had sent her to me. "You need a maid," he had insisted. I must have looked shocked because he had added, "It is your duty to employ someone. I will find a suitable person."

And so María Isabel knocked on my door early one morning and thereafter came every other day to clean, wash my clothes, shop for food and household supplies, and prepare my meals. In all the years she worked for me, I never once gave her an order. She knew better than I what to do. I fought with her only in the matter of how we stood towards each other. Long before she admitted me into her affections, she came to occupy a place in mine, and when she stepped at last over the barrier of race and class that had stood since the Conquest, it was not with a

253

statement or a tear, but in her sudden decision one day (had I wearied her with my insisting?) to sit with me at table and share the meal she had prepared for me.

Over time, she gave one other signal of our friendship, by telling me something of her circumstances. She had had seven children by different men, none of whom had stayed. For years, the fatherless family had lived in a cardboard house that had to be repaired after every rainfall.

"Now we have a solid roof over our heads even if our home isn't very big. Thanks to you and to others like you who give me work," she told me.

"It's little enough."

"No, *joven*, it is much."

Olivia arrived in a flurry of unruly hair and breathless, unselfconscious beauty. She offered her cheek to my lips as if she were a distant cousin, and then in like fashion to María Isabel.

"I'm starving. Is lunch ready? Oh, María Isabel, I'm so looking forward to your cooking again. Hasn't it been a long time? Is there anything I can do to help?"

"Certainly not," said María Isabel. "You two have things to discuss that are not for me to hear."

"We have nothing special," Olivia replied.

Simple words lightly spoken, razor sharp to my hearing.

"Everything'll be ready in a moment or two," said María Isabel on her way to the kitchen. Moments later, she re-emerged with two steaming bowls from which arose a heady aroma of shrimp, coriander and chilli.

"It smells wonderful," Olivia said. "Will we enjoy your company?"

"No, señorita," said María Isabel. "*El joven* Jaime is going away soon. You have things to talk about. And besides, I'm busy."

I followed María Isabel into the kitchen to insist that she join us. She shook her head.

"You should be with la señorita."

"You need to eat."

"I'll eat afterwards. That's how things should be when you have a guest. You deserve a nice girl, *joven*."

"I don't know if she believes that, María Isabel. Or even if I do."

Emerging from the kitchen, I caught my breath. Olivia was seated at the table in half profile, shaded by window blinds against the blazing sunlight but with threads of face and form bright where beams filtered through the interstices. She had moved her bowl aside and was flicking through the pages of a magazine, leaning forward, her breasts full against her blouse, a patch of light outlining the press of her nipples against the white cloth. Desire seized me, crossed by panic at the idea of losing her. I wanted to rush up to her, to kiss those breasts, to tell her whatever came into my head that might convince her to love me.

Olivia looked up. "Aren't you going to sit down?" She put the magazine aside, replaced the bowl of soup so that it was once more in front of her, and sat upright. "I'm so hungry."

Her voice weightless, unconcerned. She held out a hand as if inviting me to her table. I sat down opposite her.

"I heard Moya Palencia will be the next president," I said.

"Then he won't be."

"You can't know that."

"Moya Palencia is the favourite but that's a good reason to believe it will be someone else. The newspapers have a ball speculating on who will get the nod. Everyone gossips and pretends to know the outcome, but in the end it's up to the president to choose who he wants."

"Very democratic."

"It's controlled democracy. The people are ignorant. Without direction they wouldn't know how to vote and we could end up with a peasant in Los Pinos."

255

"That's the standard defence of dictatorship."

"We have elections."

"Which the party candidate always wins."

"You shouldn't mock our ways until you understand them."

María Isabel reappeared with a dish of chicken in *mole de cacahuates*[54] and a basket of tortillas which she set down on the table. A medley of aromas: maize, peanut, chilli, sesame.

"María Isabel, you're such a wonderful cook," Olivia said. "Why don't you leave this dreadful man and come to our house? We'd promise to eat all your food."

"I make this dish specially for Jaime."

"Does he deserve to be so lucky?"

"Is he not a good man?"

Without waiting for an answer, María Isabel excused herself with a *con permiso*, and returned to the kitchen. We ate in monosyllables, cutting pieces of chicken onto tortillas, ladling sauce on top, folding once and eating with our fingers. For dessert, María Isabel served slices of papaya with honey.

When the meal came to an end, Olivia picked up the thread of our disagreement. "If you were Mexican, you would think as I do. We might wish for change but we're not so foolish as to hope for it."

"But with so much poverty..."

"The poor always ye have with you. Isn't that what it says in the Bible? There's nothing to be done. You have poor people in your country."

"Not so many. Not so poor."

"Of course. Things are always better over there."

"Richer maybe. But colder too. Sometimes I wonder if we've forgotten how to love." The remark came unexpectedly and I wasn't sure what I meant. Reaching across the table, I took Olivia's hand in mine. "Come. I want to show you something."

"Why not show me here?"

---

54 Peanut sauce.

256

María Isabel appeared to ask if she should serve coffee.

"*Gracias*, María Isabel. We'll be back in a moment."

I led Olivia down the corridor to the bedroom, letting go of her hand only to close the door behind us. She glanced at the bed. A single marigold lay on each pillow.

"And the flowers?" Olivia asked.

Stepping quietly behind her, I kissed her on the neck.

"Don't."

"María Isabel must have put them there for the occasion."

I nuzzled her again in a way I knew she liked. She turned to face me.

"What will she think?"

"She'll be happy for us."

"I told myself I wouldn't do this again."

I heard only the concession and through my excitement – as much emotional as sexual – saw what I had to do. My thinking seemed as clear to me then as it seems muddled and hapless in recollection. I had to bind her to me. Make love to her as no other could. Success lay in the control she had once proposed as a challenge, in service to her pleasure, and in suppression of my own for as long as necessary. These thoughts were not cold or calculating but suffused with a sensation close to reverence, for I knew at that moment that I had never loved anyone as I loved her and I resolved to do everything I could think of to make her love me in return.

We undressed and I pulled her towards me as gently as urgency allowed, eager to command yet conscious of an underlying helplessness. My euphoria in that first press of her body against mine came tempered by a sense of being on trial, by knowing that her verdict would be inexorable and that there could be no appeal – for in matters of love, entreaty merely evokes contempt or revulsion. This I understood even in the fever of holding her in my arms.

In my anxiety to please, I fell back on what little I had gleaned of technique from readings. "Do nothing in haste. Linger over your caresses…"

The instructions came fresh to my thoughts as we lay down. I worked hands and lips as if performing a delicate labour, like a sculpture's assistant fearful of misusing his master's tools, alert to her slightest movement, to every escape of her breath, to every frisson. But what was "haste"? How fast was too fast? Wasn't the lover also warned against causing irritation through caresses that were too persistent or fulfilment so delayed that desire dissolved into impatience? "Banish anxiety from your mind," the sages advised, "though be aware, too, that offence is easily given (how close are the sounds of pleasure to those of distaste?)." She dispelled my doubts by a gesture I could not mistake. Cradling her shoulders with my hands, I started out on the journey.

Yes, it felt like a journey, perhaps because the longing seemed beyond distance, a destination at the far edge of the world, and the anxiety beyond time. An unexpected surge of emotion gripped me, a conviction that this was not the end of a search, because searching was all that existed, that I was glimpsing – if only faintly – the distant abode where life and death dwelled, and to where we must all, in the end, find our way.

I had read in an oriental manual – the kind popular with nineteenth-century voluptuaries – that a spiritual bonding takes place between a man and a woman if they repress the urge to move, the instinctual rush to orgasm. As she received me, the text came to mind. I saw the page with the paragraph underlined in red ink with an exclamation mark in the margin.

"Don't move. Listen to the silence."

Minutes slid by. Our breathing fell into step. Olivia's cheeks were flushed, her lips parted, her eyes focused on something distant and inaccessible. The sight inflamed me unexpectedly, and I felt a loss of control welling at the base of my spinal column. Had she stirred at that moment, my effort to win her admiration would have dissolved in a humiliating spasm, but she did not, and I had a precious second to regain my composure. Even so, my little struggle would have ended in defeat had not a palliative popped into mind, an incident unearthed from another place and time.

Paris. I am standing between two parked cars on a city street. In front of me a restaurant. Tables spill out onto the sidewalk as far as the kerb with an aisle between the last and the penultimate row for pedestrians to pass through. Lunchtime. Fine weather, an early summer's day, sunshine cooled by a gentle breeze. The daily menu chalked on a blackboard hanging from the awning over the entrance. Every table occupied; waiters take orders, scurry to and fro with dishes, baskets of bread, carafes of wine; diners chat, lean towards each other to exchange a confidence, laugh from time to time. A medley of mouth-watering odours – fresh baguettes, steak frites, potage au chou-fleur. *Hungry, but too poor to afford a meal at such a place, I must be satisfied with reading the menu and savouring the aromas.*

A young woman enters stage left. She is struggling, pulling at a leash on the other end of which a mongrel resists, half-sitting, paws digging into the pavement. She heaves, both hands on the leash, and the animal skids forward on its hind legs, but the woman is slight, progress arduous. Halfway along the aisle, in the midst of the tables and the diners, the dog tastes a moment of victory: the woman tugs without effect. The dog's hind quarters are pumping as if it had seized upon a bitch. A brief stalemate before another tug on the leash produces the desired effect. Back on all fours, the dog trots obediently behind its mistress as if no conflict of aims had ever occurred. In the place where seconds before it had forced a halt, a coil of excrement squats in a pyramidal heap. The mass is large, commanding attention, like a work of art deposited by an enfant terrible *to mock the sensibilities of the bourgeoisie. Several diners (those with a ringside seat), having glanced at the steaming pile, return to the dish set before them to find their appetite diminished. Fascinated and appalled, their eyes steal back to the place of the offence as if to assure themselves that the heap is truly there or maybe in hope that it is no more than a trick of light which a second glance will dispel. A waiter serving wine at a nearby table pretends not to notice, though he must pass close by en route to the interior. Mistress and dog have rounded a corner and are out of sight.*

That mound steaming on a sidewalk came to my aid. As soon as it erupted in my thoughts, my excitement subsided. All happened in an instant: one moment I stood on the edge of the precipice, the next self-possession returned as the faecal image dulled my senses. Though now a contrary danger threatened – of losing touch with the moment and confronting failure of a different but no less humiliating kind, and I hastily returned to the sight and touch of the woman in my arms. By quick trial and error I learned to summon or banish the image as needed, and so remain balanced between arousal and a muddle of countervailing sensations: repulsion, laughter, fear of failure, cold calculation. When her orgasm rose, my joy in her pleasure came tempered by thoughts of the dog and its deposit: love laced with impurities without which, perhaps, it can't find expression. A second orgasm followed, perhaps a third, until at length I felt licensed to leave the dog alone and release my own. Now surely I had done well and would receive acknowledgement. I was proud of my efforts.

"Of course I enjoyed it," she said as we sipped the tepid coffee that María Isabel had prepared before leaving. "But it doesn't mean anything. What has love to do with pleasure?" She stopped my protest with a finger pressed against my lips. "I need to go home."

FORTY-FOUR

TENOCHTITLAN — 1520

Alva

A curious levity came over me after the fighting stopped, as if Ometochtli, god of pulque and fertility, had me tethered to his will so that I could only follow where he chose to lead. I fell to gambling again, began to drink, gave myself over to the pursuit of pleasure no matter where it might lead. Above all, I lusted after female company. Not that I forgot Tecuichpo, nor ceased longing for her, but these new compulsions had nothing to do with love. Rather they arose, I think, from knowing I had faced death and administered it, something that had not occurred during the Quetzalan war. Life was death's opponent, and life's expression and life's demands burst from me like wild shoots from the earth.

I met a woman, Nenetl. A dancer and occasional courtesan, she had come to the city, like so many of her kind, as a captured slave and had used her beauty and charm to gain her freedom. She was intelligent and well experienced in the art of love. I buried myself in her with an energy I hardly recognized as mine. No peace seemed possible without her, and yet with her I could find no peace, only desire and need. For her part, she asked for nothing more than what I could give her: the satisfactions that were her right as a woman, and the gifts that were my duty to provide, a simple transaction, but also a kind of game in which she took care to avoid the consequences of our activities – allowing full pleasure only at certain times while at others she took me by the mouth or with her hand and so forestalled the impulse that brought me to her.

This interlude of peace and pleasure lasted a couple of moons, and then a calamity assailed the city of a kind that would prove no less fearful and more horrifying in its effect even than the Spanish invasion. My sister, Xochitl, was among the first to be stricken. She complained of unbearable pain in her head and stomach. I remember Tlaco bearing her in his arms to our house, and the desperation in his eyes when he told us that the doctors he had summoned had been unable to help. He thought the illness must be something to do with her pregnancy and that my mother would know what to do. Two days later a rash appeared on her; no more than a few spots at first on her cheeks, but soon they erupted elsewhere, more and more until they could no longer be counted and no part of her remained free of them. Even her feet and the palms of her hands broke out in pustules, and every movement, every touch of another hand caused her pain so that she cried out. Within days, Tlaco went down with the same symptoms, and then Papan and her husband, Zolin. My mother nursed them, bathing their foreheads with sweet water, spreading oil over their boiling skin.

What was occurring in our family was but a reflection of the affliction that visited the whole city. No district remained unaffected, no household immune. Appeals to the gods went unheard; either they were uninterested in our plight or angered at some offence of which we were unaware. We had heard of this illness; we knew that it had followed hard upon the Spanish arrival on the coast and that it had ravaged other nations, but we had scarcely imagined its virulence.

Before long, people began crawling out of their homes in search of succour and, finding none, died in the street. Some dragged themselves to the lake thinking to cool themselves – and sank into its depths from exhaustion or despair. No rank was spared: the sickness attacked slaves and nobles without distinction. Merchants went down with it, administrators, soldiers, artisans, poets, farmers and fishermen and market gardeners on whom the city relied for nourishment.

On the tenth day of her sickness, my sister died as she lay beside her prostrate husband – so sick himself that he barely registered the passing of his beloved and of the child she carried. Two suns later, Papan too went on her way, and then Zolin closed his eyes and departed, the lips that had spoken so much poetry drawn together tight, thin and silent. No sooner had we bidden farewell to Zolin than Izel fell ill, her arms erupting in tiny red volcanoes too numerous to count. Our family seemed to be wilting like flowers under a desert sun. The image of these loved ones in their agony comes back to me as I write, plunging me again into the depths of that terrible nightmare from which only death – or perhaps not even death – could afford relief. Whenever I think of that time, I relive the fear that the disease might return and strike again like the recoil of a snake that seeks out the life it has failed to take before.

No language could describe my mother's distress. She told me she prayed each day to the gods that they might take her too so that she could join her loved ones in the afterworld. I urged her not to provoke them with such prayers, told her how much we who remained would be lost without her knowledge and wisdom. She nodded assent but I sensed that what she heard were not my words but rather the strains of her firstborn, my brother, calling her to join him, for her brief responses came laced with his name and memory. In the end, it was Izel's and Tlaco's misery that kept her going – for they needed care and solace and she would not abandon the responsibility to another.

Apart from my mother, only Teudile and I remained healthy. I don't know why that should be. The gods play with us humans as they wish, choosing who shall die and who shall live according to their whims.

My survival I may owe in part to the fact that the day after Izel went down with the fever, I was sent to take military command of the island of Xaltocan, whose governor had departed for the coast on a government mission. Officers were becoming thin on the ground, and we middle-rankers were routinely reassigned as the authorities wrestled with the task of replacing senior personnel who had passed on. At home, Teudile was left with the job of feeding the household. He wasn't a member of the family, but we had come to trust him, and he was plainly devoted to my aunt. He had lived his life by sniffing out sources of supply; he knew every trader and warehouse in the city and then some. He would manage.

Mother worried me more. When I took my leave, she clung to me with an expression of such anguish on her face that the image has never left me. I had to prise her fingers from my arm so as to get on my way.

"You will come back," she said, "you will come back…", but in a tone of disbelief that revealed too clearly her fear of never seeing me again. She watched me all the way to the end of the street, and each time I turned around, I saw her gazing in my direction, an unfathomable sadness in her posture, her head thrust forward as if to break free, while Teudile stood behind her with a hand on her shoulder guarding her like a sentinel and, I suppose, making sure she would not run after me.

My orders were to make for the Tenayuca Causeway in the north, where a crew would be waiting to take me to Xaltocan by canoe. Never will I forget that walk through the city: the streets devoid of bustle; foul-smelling bodies slumped against walls like bundles of putrescent meat because they had no one well enough to wash them, mourn them or send them on their way; the air pierced by cries of distress that seemed to pursue me like a summons from the underworld. I might have been moving among the spirits of the departed, hearing ancestral voices calling to me from their place in heaven or beneath the earth. What terror in that brief passage! Who, on experiencing such sights and sounds, would not think that they too journeyed towards their last end?

More even than the massacre and the street fighting, the plague that coursed through our city changed our way of life. Custom demanded that we mourn our dead: four days at home with the body, a funeral pyre and eighty days of remembrance. Now, there was no time for leisurely rituals; deaths were too numerous and priests too few. Instead, the bodies were collected as resources allowed and burned in lots with no respect for ceremony. Whole families passed away during the sickness and thus had no one to weep for them or remember that they had ever inhabited the earth. Without anyone saying so, a suspicion crept over us that the old traditions, the religious observances we had believed so vital to our survival, might be redundant and our trust in the gods illusory. Either we had failed to placate their wrath, or they lacked the power to help us. Whatever the case, we were alone and had to learn to survive without them.

FORTY-FIVE

LONDON – 1976

James

On June 16, US Ambassador Francis Meloy Junior, his aide Robert O. Waring and their driver Zuhair Mohammed Moghrabi were kidnapped in Beirut and later shot: the Americans for favouring Christians over Muslims, the driver for acting as their "lackey".

One month later, Christopher Ewart-Biggs, British Ambassador to Ireland, died together with his secretary, Judith Cooke, when their car hit a landmine planted by the Irish Republican Army.

A week later, an earthquake destroyed the Chinese city of Tangshan. Two hundred and fifty thousand perished; ten million lost their homes.

Zhou En-Lai and Mao Tse-Tung died that year.

The year Jimmy Carter beat Gerald Ford to the White House.

And Apple Computers appeared; and Concorde entered service; and the Soviet Press hailed Leonid Brezhnev as *vozhd*

– the supreme leader – an honour previously bestowed only on Lenin and Stalin.

The year "Sunny" Jim Callaghan took up residence in London's 10 Downing Street before leading the country into a wilderness of industrial disputes and stoppages, so demonstrating in a few short months how far the UK had journeyed from a colonial past on which the sun never set to a present on which it seldom shone.

Though the land to which I return in my imagination is not Callaghan's but Orwell's: a golden country of footpaths and rabbit-bitten pasture where dace swim in pools under willow trees and the boughs of English elms sway in the breeze.

A steady drizzle falls into dark mid-morning streets that glisten in the reflected lights of shop windows. Crowded sidewalks. Buses splash through kerbside puddles, sending sprays of grimy water onto pedestrians who pretend not to notice as if resolved to ignore the insult. Streets littered with drink cans, greasy paper, polystyrene burger-boxes smeared with scarlet and yellow residues, cigarette packets, drinking straws, cardboard coffee cups. Overflowing waste bins stand sentinel outside pubs and fast-food joints. On the corner of Pentonville Road, a man with a weather-beaten face and grey matted hair empties the contents of a bin onto the pavement and sifts through the midden. He works slowly, impervious to the rain, examining every bag and box for its contents no matter how torn or broken or obviously empty. Reward comes in the form of some fries in a carton that he consumes with wary glances around him like a hyena come upon a kill.

A strike has reduced rail services to a minimum. King's Cross station is closed. I catch the only available train heading north from St Pancras to Sheffield, a four-hour trip – standing-room only. Passengers address each other as friends; expressions of solidarity intermingle with complaints directed variously at government, unions, the disappearance of principle, the decay of the realm. I am wedged mid-corridor; my near-companions – a couple in jeans and T-shirts, their arms tattooed with androgynous figures draped in petals and blue-red leaves – are pale, undersized, wiry, with gruff, smokers' voices and faces honed by underprivilege, multiple defeats and defiant survival. Each sits astride a rucksack, the frame as saddle horn.

"Don't bother us. We're used to it," the man says in lowland brogue, half to his companion, half to the air. "Best seats on the train."

We burst through London's dreary outer fringe to the gentle velvet of middle England. Trees in full leaf, green meadows dotted with sheep, swathes of startling yellow rapeseed.

"View's the same here as in first class, right?" He turns his head in my direction.

I nod assent.

"I'm Ron. This 'ere's Jennie."

"Hi," Jennie says.

"James."

"Want some coffee?" Jennie brandishes a flask.

"Better than the piss you get on trains and cheaper too," Ron says.

The coffee is strong, grainy, sweet "like in North Africa", from where they have just returned after a year camping in fields and on beaches and roadsides.

I ask how it feels to be back in a country of strikes and summer rain.

"We don't mind, do we, pet," Jennie says. "Some places we've been, nothing works, not even the taps."

"Yeah," says Ron. "In some of 'em, you can't even flush a shit. Way we see things, you don't rely on nothing 'cept yourself. All fucking governments are the same. Bit more 'ere, bit less there. Dunno why people bother to strike. They should just fuck off and do their own thing."

"Like we do," says Jennie.

"Yeah. Like we do."

In Sheffield, we embrace before parting.

"Maybe we'll meet again somewhere," I tell them.

"Don't think so," Ron answers. "We've been on the road for – how long is it now?"

"Nine years, pet," says Jennie.

"Nine years," says Ron. "An' we never met nobody twice. Never. But good luck to you."

They trudge off, rucksacks on their back, bent forward, determined. I take a succession of buses to my mother's front door.

FORTY-SIX

HAWORTH

James

Evening; fading light; clouds hanging dark and sullen. A chill north wind blows unchecked across the moors.

A line of single-storey, red-brick apartments. I knock at the green door, her favourite colour. The other doors are red.

Pause. Two years. We will have grown older.

Knock.

Pause.

The wind howls through the high copse behind the apartments.

Knock.

"Who is it?"

"Who do you think?"

"Go away or I'll call the police."

"It's your son."

"Who?"

"Your SON."

"He's in Mexico."

Rain lashes my cheeks.

"Let me in. Unless you want me to die of chill on your doorstep."

She pushes the door ajar and peers out. "You'll catch your death standing out there in the wet. Look at how you're dressed. Anybody'd think we were in the tropics. Come in and shut that door, it's perishing. Supposed to be summer. Feels like the middle of winter to me."

She turns huffily and shuffles back down the corridor to her sitting room. I follow with my suitcase.

"Been waiting all day without news. Why didn't you tell me you'd be late? What a time to arrive. I'd given up. At this time of the day, you could have been a murderer at the door for all I knew. Never mind. It's lovely to see you. I'll put the kettle on. Your dinner's ready, only needs to be warmed. Don't just stand there. Give your mother a hug. That's better. I miss you. Don't know what the world's coming to when children go all over the world rather than staying near their loved ones. Come and get warm. Shall I put the heating on? Is your hair wet? There's a towel in the airing cupboard. I made roast beef and Yorkshire pudding. Too late for me to eat and anyway I don't need much at my age. Suppose you'll go walking on the moors every day. You don't know how I worry when I know you're out there on your own. Look well if something happened to you and me not knowing a thing while you're lying in a hollow. I know you think I talk rubbish but those moors are full of people up to no good. Newspapers are full of it. Why don't you go walking in the village or up to Oxenhope and back, that would be exercise enough. Look at the time, ten o'clock. Put the television on. You can watch the news while you're having your supper. Isn't lunch any more, is it? The news'll be better than listening to an old woman grumbling."

A BBC stalwart on screen elegant with an impeccable upper-crust accent.

271

"What's her name?"

"Who?"

"The news reader."

Lowering herself into her armchair, she retrieves a bundle of navy-blue knitting from a basket alongside. "Don't ask me. Moira somebody or other, I think. Why?"

"I recognize her. It's like coming home."

"Good thing you recognize something of your own country. Mind you, she looks like a foreigner to me. There's too many of them coming in here. Before you know it, they'll be taking over. Mark my words. Anybody'd think she owned the BBC the way she talks."

"An earthquake," says Moira, "said to be at least eight on the Richter scale has struck the Chinese province of Hebei. Tangshan, the provincial capital, is reported to have been almost completely destroyed. Our correspondent John Burford reports from Beijing."

"Terrible," my mother says, "been on the news all day."

Burford is on screen, bearded, breathless. "The death toll rises as I speak. Chinese authorities remain cautious about allowing Western journalists access to the worst-affected area, but people here are talking about fatalities as high as three hundred thousand mainly in the city of Tangshan, with many more seriously injured. Several million may have been made homeless."

"What's the name of the city?"

"Tangshan."

"Funny name."

"Offers of assistance are pouring in from countries round the world," Burford continues, "but it is not yet clear how much – if any – will be accepted."

"They may be Chinese," my mother says, "but they're still people. Glad we don't have bloomin' earthquakes. Must be ever so frightening. Mind you, they'll take over the world one day, you see if I'm not right."

"Who will?"

"The Chinese. You look at me as if I don't know anything, but I've been alive a lot longer than you. And I know a few things when I see them."

"Mind if I switch off?"

"You used to love the news."

"Tired. It's a long way from Mexico."

Pause.

"Food's delicious, Mum."

"Would have been better if I hadn't had to reheat it."

Pause.

"Your old mother still knows how to cook."

"You bet."

Silence broken only by the rhythmical click of knitting needles.

"Don't know if this sweater will be ready before you go back. Might have to post it."

"If you do, they'll nick it at the Mexican post office."

"Don't know why you say such things."

"Because they're true."

"Such a beautiful country. Can't understand them taking things like that."

"It's nothing beside what the British have taken from others."

"Hate the thought of you flying all that way." She bundles up her knitting and replaces it in the basket. "Just look at the time."

We fetch bed linen from the airing cupboard and make up the sofa bed. The linen smells of lavender.

"If you hear noise in the night, it'll be me. Have to get up four or five times to go to the toilet. When you're my age, the waterworks start letting you down. I'm so happy you're home even if it's only for a few days. You'll be off again no doubt before I can say boo to a goose. Goodnight, my son. I never stop loving you, you know."

She shuffles off to her bedroom and I close the door behind her.

Next day, booted and anoraked, I cross the village park with its immaculate bowling green, gardens laid out to pansies, African violets, crocuses in neat diamond patterns, pathways edged with rhododendrons and azaleas meandering like asphalt rivulets between the vegetation.

These tidy few acres in a hilly corner of a small island, laid out in days when the streets resounded with the clip-clop of shire horses dragging cartloads of raw and finished wool to and from the mills, belong to a dimension of time and space so distant from Mexico's din-filled, sun-lit capital that I can hardly make sense of their juxtaposition in my thoughts.

Emerging from the park, I climb the steep, cobblestone high street with its Victorian-style stores kitted out with Brontë bric-a-brac, sweetmeats, postcards, paperbacks, cafés offering authentic fare direct from the pages of the Brontë recipe book updated for the modern kitchen, copies available within, discount for diners. Like much of the country, Haworth is a shrine to the past, a museum within a museum, as faithful to a fantasy of English quaintness and as enduring in the popular imagination as the holly and puddings of a Dickensian Christmas.

I pass the Fleece Inn, one of two pubs claiming the distinction of supplying Branwell, brother of the famous sisters, with the liquor that clouded his illness and led to an early death. A hundred metres higher and rival for the honour lies the Black Bull, where Branwell's favourite chair remains on display as evidence of the establishment's role in his demise.

Haworth parish church stands hard by where Reverend Patrick Brontë, perpetual curate, preached to the shepherds and mill workers, and buried them in the cemetery whose glowering headstones, grimed by age and climate to reflect the flint-hard lives of those who rest there, are carved with simple words of commendation to the god who took so many in their prime of years. Nor was heaven sparing of the curate's own. Patrick outlived all his gifted children and in his maturity, so they say, walked grimly and with a limp because he had looked the Lord in the eye and the Lord had left His mark.

Grey-haired matrons in Sunday livery climb the steps to the church entrance where a young male guide in suit and tie counts them into the holy precinct.

"This is where Charlotte, Anne and Emily prayed alongside the rude forefathers of the hamlet," he tells them.

From the churchyard, an uphill path at right angle to the high street leads past the Brontë Parsonage Museum (a deferential nod to the mystery of genius) across a field at the edge of the village, and so to the moor. A sharp breeze keens the air, bringing features of the landscape, a derelict barn, a single ancient oak, close enough to touch as if I stood before a painting. From this first high point, beyond the narrow winding road to Ponden Mill, a valley appears, dark green in its depths, then browning and purpling as it rises into heather and heath, the whole divided into folds by slate-coloured, dry-stone walls that wander over the casual contours of the terrain to meet at odd angles like chance encounters on a country walk. On the far side of the valley, a pencil line of cottages, erected a hundred and fifty years before for the workers of a forgotten enterprise, a little mill perhaps or a landowner's estate, and beyond them, cattle and sheep form brown and white smudges against a patch of distant meadow.

An arrow points the way to "Brontë Falls", the trail leading past a solitary manse shadowed by tall oak and birch and into open space where the sounds, entering and leaving a wider silence, are of the wind humming over the heather, the intermittent bleating of sheep, and the scrape and thud of my own footsteps. An hour passes; the trail is longer than expected, more rugged, offering alternative routes – diversions into adjacent pastures, over stiles, through breaches in old walls where rubble has spilled onto the ground and lies half-buried in moss and wild grasses. A ruined shepherd's cottage rises in a green field among grazing sheep, the cavities of vanished doors and windows staring into

275

vacancy like the hollow orifices of a skull. Inside, a dozen sheep have sought refuge either from the wind – there being no roof to offer shelter from rain – or maybe because they enjoy rubbing shoulders with their fellow creatures as we do. Are they hoping (if hope is possible in a sheep's brain) for freedom, to escape the shepherd's notice or the butcher's block?

They scatter in panic at my approach, leaving behind a pungent mélange of mud and excrement. Some mammals seem to do without hygiene of the kind we find essential and yet do not fall prey to diseases from their own evacuations. Are wild animals more punctilious about cleanliness than these domesticated breeds? Could we have so degraded the creatures we keep for food that they no longer care for their own dignity?

At length, the trail turns downhill, narrowing into a gully of loose stones and pebbles through which a trickle of water gurgles for a mile until it joins a stream that rushes through rocks and over a miniature precipice – the Falls – where we are to suppose the sisters came to summon their muses and to dream of rapture in the arms of Heathcliff, Rochester and Gilbert Markham.

No one in sight. A surround of solitude in the libation of the waters. The thought occurs that if I die there, victim of a stumble or a murder (for which the moors have a reputation), all those jumbled concerns, emotions, impressions, memories, convictions that make up an identity, the place where my different lives, the contradictory worlds I inhabit, meet, where the garbage-dump slums of Mexico City co-exist with the windswept vistas of a Yorkshire moor, where Chilean refugees sit beside me as I listen to my mother's chatter, where the murder of Ewart-Biggs jostles with that of General Prats and Orlando Letelier, where I walk hand in hand with the Brontës and with Octavio Paz and Pablo Neruda, all would vanish like raindrops in the sea.

Though contained in a single mind, these disparate patterns dwell apart like strangers in a crowded city whose paths approach from time to time without crossing. They are not there by choice but by chance, and we can no more reconcile them than we can reconcile flotsam that waves fling onto a beach. They are part of the chaotic fabric of an individual life, the sum of what we are that resists understanding.

"You've only just arrived," my mother said when I announced that my departure would be on the following day.

"Work calls. It's been nearly a week."

"Five days. I've been counting. You can't fool me. I know I tire you out with my chatter, but you should be a little tolerant. I haven't long left to live, and you're my only comfort. One day, you'll learn what love is. Then you'll regret not spending a bit more time with your old mother."

"Don't talk like that."

"Let's face it. I've had my time."

"You've plenty of life left in you."

"You can't fool me with your sweet talk. By the time you think of coming this way again, I'll like as not be six feet under. Mark my words."

She sat down on the edge of her armchair, lips pursed, chin thrust forward, eyes narrowed as if she were peering through mist. Neither of us spoke for a while. Then she said, "Don't you want the television on?"

"No."

"Chou En-Lai passed away. Was in the news this morning."

Pause.

"They'll all be gone soon, the old communists."

Pause.

"They were the ones. Cared for the people. Not that I'm a communist. I don't hold with the prole...what do they call it?"

"Proletariat?"

"Funny name. I don't hold with all that nonsense anyway. Mind you, so what if the Chinese did come here and took over. They couldn't do a worse job than our lot."

"Thought you were Labour."

"Don't talk to me about the Labour Party. Bunch of hypocrites. Do as I say not as I do. That's Labour. I'm voting Conservative next time, see if I don't."

"What did the Tories ever do for the working class?"

"Churchill was a Tory. And he won the war. That's good enough for me."

Silence. Tic-toc of the clock on the mantelpiece over the hearth.

"Shall I put on the heating?"

"It's summer."

"Doesn't mean you can't feel the cold. I'm used to it, but you've just come from the tropics. What about another cup of tea?"

"I'll put the kettle on."

"Let me do it. Does me good to get on my feet. Besides, I don't get much chance to do things for you. You look so thin. Don't suppose anyone takes care of you over there."

"I have a maid."

"A maid?" Her voice indignant. "A maid! Never heard of such a thing. Somebody to wait on you hand and foot. What's the world coming to when your own son behaves as if he were an aristocrat? You're forgetting where you come from, my lad. Before we know it, you won't be speaking to your own family."

"It's an obligation to employ someone. There isn't enough work."

"I won't half miss you when you're gone. It gets so lonely here. No one to talk to, that's the problem. Only old dears with sand between their ears."

FORTY-SEVEN

XALTOCAN – 1520

Alva

Xaltocan surprised me. I had expected an austere military outpost but found an orderly town with clean streets, a fine temple in the central square dedicated to Huizilopochtli, and a market well supplied with foodstuffs from local gardens and *chinampas*.

The garrison, modest as one might expect in so small a place, was located on a hill in the centre of the island. It had a complement of ninety-two men and about half that number of slaves, mainly women. From an observation tower on the roof of the main building, you could view the entire island plus a sweep of shoreline embracing the towns of Cuauhtitlan, Tepotzotlán and Citláltepec. No causeways connected Xaltocan to the mainland, so access was by canoe only. Part of my job was to ensure that soldiers were always on watch day and night, and that three manned canoes were ever at the ready on the dock below to convey news to Tenochtitlan of an enemy approach.

On my arrival, a local official at the head of a delegation met me on the shore and led me to my quarters. His name was Uemantzin – "venerable" in our language – and venerable he was, for he had white hair and walked haltingly and with a stoop like a man who had seen many seasons.

Noting that the people looked healthy and contented, I asked him how many on the island had come down with the sickness. He looked at me curiously.

"None," he answered.

"You do know what I'm talking about?"

"We have heard that it is a weapon of the Spaniards or of their god. But they did not come here."

I asked him again if he was sure no one from the island had been inflicted and he confirmed once more that it was so.

That night I thought about the strangeness: a small island less than a day's distance from the capital by canoe with not a single case of the sickness. On the following day, I inspected the garrison, the slaves too, then walked through the island, stopping from time to time to question the people. No one had died unexpectedly; no one had caught a fever or developed a rash. Yes, there were the usual illnesses, stomach upsets and so on, but no plague.

It didn't make sense. Why would the Spaniards – or the gods – have spared Xaltocan, a minor place, easy to conquer and with no defences beyond a stretch of shallow water and a handful of common soldiers? If the island were too insignificant to interest an enemy, surely the same could not be true of a disease which seemed to break out effortlessly and against which there was no defence?

"You are right," I told Uemantzin after I had completed my inspection, "Xaltocan is healthy. But why?"

"Perhaps the disease cannot cross the water alone."

"What do you mean?"

"That the wind does not carry it. Only people."

"Or Xólotl, god of sickness, thinks to spare the people of Xaltocan," I suggested.

Uemantzin bowed his head – as befitted a man formally my junior. His white hair and wise bearing, however, commanded deference of a kind mere rank could not confer. I thanked him for his explanation, told him I thought his wisdom superior to mine, and asked him to think of me as an uncle might think of a nephew. From that moment, we established a partnership in which I made no decision of note without first seeking his views. On his advice, I gave an order that whoever arrived in Xaltocan from the mainland must either return at once or live in isolation for eight days to make sure they had not been contaminated, and we set aside a compound where they could dwell during their confinement. Anyone subsequently found to have the sickness was to be supplied with food and medicine and sent away; a cruel stricture no doubt but one that Uemantzin persuaded me would protect the population.

I do not pretend to understand by what means Uemantzin came to offer this advice, still less why it seems to have worked. Did the gods inspire him as part of a plan to ensure that Xaltocan was not utterly wiped out? Had Patécatl, god of health, intervened on behalf of that little island, to spare it the agonies and suffering inflicted on everyone else? Who can tell? We humans are not privy to celestial motives. All I can say is that no one fell ill during my stay of half a year with the Xaltocan people.

As news continued to reach us of the sickness elsewhere (news that came mainly via fishermen working the lake), the islanders became increasingly conscious of their good fortune. Forgetting that they were free of sickness when I arrived in Xaltocan, they began attributing their well-being to me. Much undeserved praise came my way, while my efforts to set the record straight were interpreted as the false modesty to be expected of a hero. Uemantzin confirmed that my renown as a warrior had preceded my arrival, and when I tried to tell him that it was undeserved, he refused to listen.

"True heroes think little of their deeds," he said. "Only the boastful are unworthy of the praise they receive."

Whether he truly believed this, I can't tell, but I could draw no further comment from him beyond a laconic remark that "we can't do without heroes".

One consequence of the admiration that came my way was that I had the run of the island – not least of the women, who seemed to consider me a kind of trophy, so many were the offers to share my bed. Another was that it enabled me to dispense with the usual conventions of command – the need to give orders and to see that they were followed. Such was the respect my name inspired that the garrison ran itself with no more than an occasional word of guidance from Uemantzin, while the islanders, anxious to win my approval and proud of their ability to do so, cooperated in governing themselves. Thus my lack of experience escaped notice, and my reluctance to issue edicts and to show authority for fear of doing or saying something foolish came to be seen as the self-confidence of a mature leader. Luck and dissembling thus rendered my responsibilities in Xaltocan agreeably easy, though I could never shake off the sense of being a fraud – a hero who lacked heroism, an officer who understood little of command, a seer who knew only his own ignorance.

So much deference gave me a sensation of being wrapped in clothes that belonged to someone else and were much finer than I deserved. More than once – though I dared not mention it even to Uemantzin – I was tempted to throw off the disguise and reveal myself as I was, dressed in the dull vestments of low achievement. In the end I thought it would do more harm than good for me to persuade people of the truth. If they became unruly on account of my loss of prestige, it wouldn't give them any greater contentment, merely irritate my superiors. And I'd doubtless end up a slave as punishment for my stupidity.

Adulation, I admit, can intoxicate no less than a dose of *tlapatl*, and with more lasting effect. Had I stayed longer on the island, who knows if I would not have ended up believing in my fine reputation? As it was, in its defence, I invented past exploits, battles fought, prisoners captured, arduous journeys undertaken full of risk and daring. Falsehoods breed their own children, and if there is no one to refute them, they may crowd out the truth until it can no longer be grasped. By the time orders came for me to return to the capital, I was beginning to confound fact with fiction – uncertain whether some of my most vivid inventions were not, after all, true recollections. Perhaps that is a good way to live – better and easier than with one's own failings, if we could but choose.

The day before my departure, town and garrison together organized a farewell party. Many were the expressions of thanks for my "wise and gentle leadership", and of hope for my speedy return. People spoke of me as the saviour of Xaltocan, begged me not to forget them in my communion with the gods. I played my part, listened, smiled, gave assurances that neither I nor anyone could keep. That final evening, I could have serviced half the island's young women and many of the men too had I but the strength to do so. Parents sent their daughters to me, and several husbands their wives in hope of engendering a hero. I sent all away but one young woman whose beauty I could not resist, though now I remember nothing of her, not even her name.

At dawn, Uemantzin saw me off. "You will be returning to a different place to the one you left," he told me.

I asked him what he meant.

"They say whole neighbourhoods are desolate for no one there is left alive."

"The sickness?"

"Did you not hear?"

"Commanders seem always to be shielded from bad news."

He bowed his head. "May the gods keep you safe."

During my sojourn in Xaltocan, I had put family cares out of mind, assuming without thinking too much on the matter that Teudile would send word if all were not well. Now anxiety seized me. Images flashed through my thoughts of our home layered with dust and silence, and of myself running to the temple in hope of seeing the last end of my loved ones.

Uemantzin and I embraced and bid each other farewell, aware that we would likely not see each other again.

"Don't worry," I said, "we will recover and before long everything will be as it was."

"Let us trust that it will be so," he answered – but with an expression in his eyes suggesting that trust had departed from him, as I suppose it had from me.

FORTY-EIGHT

TENOCHTITLAN – 1521

Alva

A canoe crewed by four young soldiers came from the capital to collect me. As soon as I stepped aboard, the cares I had put away during my absence came fresh to mind. I pestered the crew with questions. They told me the plague had passed on, though numbers beyond counting had succumbed to its anger, Cuitláhuac among them together with the priests and doctors who attended him. His young cousin Cuauhtémoc now wore the mantle of emperor, though whether by right of inheritance or by public acclaim was unclear, which was maybe why his first act had been to condemn all Cuitláhuac's male children to death just as the latter had condemned Moctezuma's.

"It was quickly done," said one of the crew. "The emperor is a good and noble lord."

"What of Moctezuma's daughters," I asked.

"They are well. The emperor has taken Tecuichpotzin to wife."

Discretion overruled my desire to pursue the conversation,

285

but the knowledge that Tecuichpo was alive filled me with joy and I laughed out loud. "Life is not so bad then."

"You may think so," came the reply.

"Lord Tonatiuh does not warm the dead," one of his companions added.

The crew bent to their paddles and would not be drawn again. I understood that my comment had not been well received.

We landed in silence on the Tenayuca Causeway and before I had a chance to thank them, the crew paddled off without a glance in my direction, thereby letting me know that my laughter had offended them and that joy had no place among us in those days of mourning.

Retracing the route across the city that I had taken on the day of my departure, I saw that the bodies had been cleared away, and with them had gone the stench of death and the smoke of funeral pyres. Bustle, however, had not returned to the streets. No echoes of conversation and laughter reverberated across the squares; no drumbeats, no flutes, no voices singing; no priests chanting prayers from the temple heights. One or two strolling merchants offered their wares as I passed by – an avocado, a *zapote*, a few beans, a piece of cloth – but with an air of resignation as if they were following a ritual rather than expecting a sale.

On reaching the corner of our street, I hesitated. Until that moment, I had avoided thinking too deeply about what I might find at home, or not find. Now it came to me that what remained of our family might have perished, the house might be occupied by strangers, it might be our home no longer and what I took to be the present might have shrunk in my absence to a memory. As I took those last few steps to the entrance, my feet felt heavy as if they waded through sludge. Maybe a neighbour would pass by who could tell me whether…who would spare me from discovering the truth for myself. Would that not be easier than marching in to find people I didn't know? The idea that my mother, or

Tlaco, or my dear aunt Izel might have fallen sick after I left for Xaltocan…I could barely allow such fears to enter my thoughts, let alone muster the courage to see if they were justified. I longed to see them, and yet would almost have preferred to walk away and live in doubt than to learn that I would never see them again. What if the neighbours too had gone?

How long I skulked on that corner, I can't say, for the sun was hidden behind clouds. Rain came to my rescue: at first a few drops large enough for me to feel their weight on my shoulders, followed by a crack of thunder, and then a deluge. Almost at once, water began pouring from the rooftops and coursing along the streets into the canals. In an instant, my cloak felt sodden and heavy. I found myself standing in a stream.

How trivial are the reasons that impel us to action! I didn't overcome my hesitation by thought or the use of reason, but to seek shelter from the rain and a change of clothes. Hurrying home, I burst through the entrance, and ran smack into Tlaco.

Still weak from the sickness, he staggered, but I grasped him to stop him from falling and held him in an embrace that lasted until I heard, behind me, my mother's cry of joy as she hurried in from the rain to see us locked together in the doorway. I parted from Tlaco and swept her into my arms.

Later, when the storm had passed, Aunt Izel and Teudile showed up. Like Izel, Teudile too had gone down with the sickness, and though both had recovered, the ordeal had left its scars on their skin. My joy at seeing them came tempered by the sight of their ravaged faces.

Tlaco too had ugly pockmarks on face and arms, though this was not the sole change in him, for he wore an air of sadness that thereafter never left him. I assumed that he was in mourning for my sister and their lost child, and he didn't deny it when I asked him about this later.

"The gods have deserted us," he said. "We will go the way of other nations into poverty and slavery. It is the beginning of the end."

I did my utmost to encourage him not to give way to despair. We were still a great nation, I told him. Throughout our history we had known reverses and had always overcome them. We would do so again. Many had survived the sickness. We still outnumbered the enemy should they choose to return. My words fell helplessly to earth. Nothing seemed to shake his conviction that our nation's glory was withering, "like a flower," he said, "whose very beauty harbours death."

In the end, I suspect Tlaco's melancholy may have reflected the feelings of all of us better than my poor attempts at optimism. The exhilaration of finding each other alive came filtered through the sorrows of our losses, and who could say whether happiness or misery held sway among us, for both seemed present in every word and gesture.

For several days after my arrival, my mother could barely tear herself away from me, and kept on touching me, hanging onto my arm, caressing my cheek, running her hands through my hair as if to reassure herself that I was real.

As soon as he was strong enough, Tlaco returned to his duties at the market in Tlatelolco. During the epidemic, the fields and *chinampas* had been left unattended so that corn, fruits and vegetables were scarce. Trade with other nations had slowed and tribute all but ceased. Fish from the lake remained abundant, but the fishery had dwindled and needed to be revived. We would not easily starve, for so great a city necessarily had many sources of provision. Still, food distribution became – as never before in my lifetime – an issue of concern. Quarrels had been breaking out in the markets over handfuls of corn. Some of our elderly had begun to go hungry. Order was fraying at the edges. Armed with a special authority from the palace, and a commission to resolve the food shortage problem by whatever means, Tlaco took command of the warehouses, instituted a system of rationing of basic foodstuffs, and announced that no one would receive preferential treatment no matter their rank or station. He possessed powers of persuasion like no one else so that even Cuauhtémoc submitted to his orderly administration and doubtless also to his charm.

I was seconded to the Army School, not this time as a trainee but as an instructor of new recruits. Defence was uppermost in our thoughts, since we were uncertain of the Spaniards' intentions. Would their retreat discourage them from returning, or were they preparing a new assault? Reports reached us that more of their floating houses – which they call ships – had arrived on the coast, bringing fresh contingents of men and weapons. Evidently they had no intention of leaving our shores (how we regretted not finishing them off when we had the chance!). Before long, we heard they had taken control of stretches of the coastal plain – areas subject to our rule – and had persuaded the Huastecos who lived there to refuse to send us tribute or even to trade with us. On the other hand, they were not marching inland. At least not yet.

One of my first trainees turned out to be Teudile who, as an able-bodied man (albeit a foreigner), could not escape conscription. A more improbable soldier could scarcely be conceived. He had spent his adult life intriguing, poking his nose into the affairs of others, making profitable enterprise out of gossip and innuendo. That he had a way with the opposite sex can't be denied. My aunt Izel remained besotted with him and since they had been together, she had worn a perpetual satisfied smile that even their sickness had not dispelled.

I could never understand what Izel saw in him, though they say mine is a familiar complaint of envious and less successful lovers. One thing for certain was that he could not have been less suitable for soldiering. The first time he picked up a sword he managed to cut himself, and every time he threw a lance, he seemed more likely to injure his own side than the enemy. After a couple of exercises, I took him aside and suggested he might like to make a different kind of contribution to the state. He fell on me with gratitude and asked how he could repay me for the kindness of throwing him out.

"Surely there's something I can get for you?"

"No need," I told him. "We are better off without you. You're a danger to the army as well as to yourself."

"I know, but still…" He thought for a moment. "What about a slave? A nice young virgin to look after you?"

I shook my head and sent him off to Tlaco. At least he wouldn't do any damage there, and perhaps his trading skills would prove useful.

As soon as I found the time, I went in search of Nenetl. She lived in Azcapotzalco on the mainland, so I canoed over there one afternoon feverish with desire of the kind that strikes the young from time to time. I had not been close to a woman since my return from Xaltocan. On the way, my thoughts filled with images of her charms.

She shared a large house with several girls of the same age. It stood just behind the slave compound – one of seven in a row – all providing similar services. Like most of her companions, Nenetl came from out of town, in her case Tepoztlán, far away enough to keep her lifestyle secret from her family. For although girls like her were highly prized in the city, not least among the military, parents did not enjoy the idea of their daughters living on the proceeds of love.

So filled were my thoughts of delight in Nenetl's arms that I had not considered the possibility she might have caught the sickness. Not, that is, until, at the entrance to the house, I encountered a woman so horribly scarred and scabbed that I could scarcely bring myself to look on her. I introduced myself and asked her name, and she reminded me in a sudden flood of tears that we knew each other. She was one of Nenetl's closest friends. Her name no longer matters, but never will I forget the shock of seeing such terrible disfigurement in a girl whose delicate features and unblemished skin had made her an object of envy to her companions and earned the admiration of every man who saw her. Will we ever know why the gods visit such a fate on those they have created? What can be their purpose?

Nenetl, too, had been stricken – it turned out that none of the girls in the house had escaped the sickness and half had died. Though she had been left with only moderate scars and her face had retained something of its former beauty, the sickness had taken from her the sight of an eye. Her freshness, too, had faded. She moved wearily and with a slight stoop as if exhausted by the burden of survival.

I had anticipated a joyful reunion and she greeted me pleasantly enough, even warmly, but of her old flirtatiousness there was no sign. We talked for a while. She spoke of the sickness, the death of her friends, the poverty into which those who remained were sinking because men no longer sought them. I responded with frivolous anecdotes about my time in Xaltocan, hoping to recapture some of the gaiety of our previous times together, and she rewarded me with an occasional smile. By the time we lay down together, my excitement had long since abated, nor could she rouse herself to a pretence of pleasure. In the end, we abandoned the effort to join in love and simply held each other.

"You will not come again," she told me when the time came for me to leave.

"Of course I'll come."

"No one returns here any more."

I fully intended to keep my word to her, not for reasons of personal gratification, but because I knew life would be hard for all these girls without gifts from their clients and that they would need help. They gathered to see me off with many assurances of Nenetl's love and of their affection. Impossible to miss the undertow of desperation in their voices. Compassion filled my thoughts as I paddled my way home.

But Nenetl was right. I didn't return or even think of her again until the Spaniards invaded Azcapotzalco, after which crossing to the mainland ceased to be a routine matter. Only then – briefly – did I wonder about her fate, and I'm ashamed to admit that the danger of making the trip became my justification for not making the attempt. How easy it is to overlook an inconvenient duty. One of the many regrets of my life is that I failed to keep my promise to Nenetl. She had given me pleasure beyond price – yet I had valued her no more than I might value a basket of fruit from the market, a commodity to purchase and consume.

Knowing that Tecuichpo could never have been my wife, I wonder if I should not after all have asked Nenetl to marry me during the early days when a normal life was still possible. How could I ever erase the memory of her graceful movements, the way she danced for me, the curve of her hips, her breasts whose nipples pointed skyward as if poised for the act of love, her tinkling laughter, her skill in teasing and then satisfying? Such images come to me still like raindrops falling on a desert seed, and I tell myself that if she stood before me now as the woman I first knew, I would hold her and never let her go. Nonsense of course, because no such idea occurred to me in the days of our loving when I might have asked her. Nor can I be sure that she would have accepted me for she liked the independence her profession afforded. Later, subdued by the sickness, she might have considered me, but that is not how she catches fire in my mind. Such are the confused musings of solitude, the thin nourishment of foolish memories and regrets on which we who outlive our usefulness play out our days.

FORTY-NINE

TENOCHTITLAN – 1521

Alva

Gradually, the city returned to life. There was much to do. Restoration work on ruined buildings had stalled during the sickness, not least that of Axayácatl's palace which the Spaniards had left in lamentable disrepair and squalor. Officials, craftsmen and farmers had to be recruited to replace those who had died, links re-established with our neighbours, newly orphaned children placed with foster parents, and care organized for the sick and injured, whose numbers had grown like the stars at dusk.

Though aware of the Spanish presence on the coast, most of us were too busy to think much on them. It was enough that they had departed, that we could breathe our own air again. If a student asked me what had become of them, I would offer a stock answer that they had retreated to the coast and were surely too chastened to risk another encounter with our army. A comforting story and one I made no effort to verify. Tlaco must have been better informed than I of their movements and intentions, but I felt no desire to question him and he didn't raise the topic. Nor, apart from students, did anyone else. Perhaps it was a measure of the fear the Spaniards had inspired in us and the chaos they had left behind that we were unwilling even to contemplate their possible return.

I learned the truth finally from Tecuichpo who had sent word for me to meet her in our special place. When we spoke our first words of greeting, I knew at once that in the period since our last encounter, she had changed. Her voice had darkened, and her eyes – ever expressive – reflected a loss of innocence, an awareness of pain and abandonment. I had forgotten until that moment that the emperor we had jeered and stoned on the palace roof and who had died a despised prisoner of the Spaniards was her father, and that she had also lost her uncle Cuitláhuac to the sickness.

This time we did not rush into love, but lay side by side in our little cave and chatted with the freedom and trust in each other we had always enjoyed.

She told me Cuauhtémoc had not yet lain with her mainly, she thought, because he was too preoccupied with the duties of government. He was already married to one of Tecuichpo's sisters, Xuchimazatl, whose position had to be considered. Such matters required delicate handling. The young emperor had told Tecuichpo that she would become uppermost in his affections as soon as the press of state affairs became less urgent and he had time to find another husband for her sister, for he neither sought to humiliate Xuchimazatl nor leave space for rivalry between them.

Meanwhile, he spent his days supervising the city defences and rebuilding the army, and his evenings in conference with his counsellors. At night, he hardly slept but instead paced the corridors of the palace ruminating on the burdens of office, often with no more company than his own footsteps. He had not confided the reasons for his restlessness, but in the palace where the nation's secrets flowed along corridors like water in a stream, they were not hard to uncover. The Spaniards had gathered an army so large that a day of marching separated the head from the tail. They were on their way towards us with bearers carrying heavy lengths of trees whose purpose no one knew. Among their forces were hosts of Totonacas and Tlaxcalans, old enemies thirsting for our blood.

Cuauhtémoc had done his best to issue calming pronouncements from the palace. He had also sent a force against the invaders in an effort to interrupt their progress. It had vanished without trace.

"The enemy made our soldiers disappear, as only gods can," Tecuichpo said.

"They are not gods," I insisted.

"Then what are they?"

"A different kind of people."

"Why are they so powerful?"

"They are strong, as we are strong. Nations rise and fall, isn't that what we are taught?"

"Have they come to replace us?"

"I don't know."

She shivered and drew closer to me. I felt torn between the excitement of her young body pressed against mine and the obligation to respond gently to her, knowing it was not pleasure she sought in my arms but comfort.

As ever, her thoughts flew ahead of mine. She took me in hand with what I can only describe in hindsight as a woman's wisdom, as if she were performing a delicate duty that history had assigned to her sex out of pity for the undisciplined cravings of men.

"You men are completely useless when you get into a state," she murmured.

Our conversation wandered then in different directions like a bird hopping from tree to tree for reasons of its own that we can never know. Snatches remain: her sobs as she recalled her father's death; how we both missed my beloved brother, Atza; her longing for the family life that she had known in our home; a shared foreboding that an unspeakable fate awaited us. And I remember her last words to me, spoken as the sun began to glow red on the surface of the lake: "My life will be in the hands of powerful men and will go wherever they command as a leaf is carried on the wind. But always I will carry your image with me."

"When will we meet again," I asked.

"I think we will not."

Lacking her knowledge and insight, I didn't understand the finality of these words, or take them seriously. As so often, however, she was right. Though as it happened, we did meet again beneath the rays of a different sun, and in a way neither of us could have foreseen.

FIFTY

TENOCHTITLAN – 1521

Alva

The enemy approach could not remain secret for long. Within days of my last encounter with Tecuichpo, a vanguard of Spanish soldiers had reached the north-east shore of Lake Texcoco. Their first act was to take Xaltocan, the little island of treasured memory. A single canoe escaped to bring news that Xaltocan's males, men and children alike, had been put to the sword, and the women distributed among the invaders. They had set fire to the town.

Texcoco, capital of our closest ally, came next. Alerted to Spanish intentions by the flames engulfing Xaltocan, most of the population sought shelter with us, either crossing the lake by canoe or stealing round the shore at night to the causeway at Ixtapalapa. Despite the additional strain on resources, the city welcomed them as kin. Our cousins Cualli and Mazatl lodged with us, and we erected makeshift shelters in our compound for several other families. Thus it was in every home, even in the great palaces and the temples. With so many more mouths to feed, Tlaco had his hands full rationing supplies, but he carried out his work with such concern for justice that few found cause for complaint. I do believe that the need to share what we had brought a special kind of happiness, a sense of solidarity and comfort, and that it strengthened our resolve to confront the beast that prowled our borders.

When the Spaniards entered Texcoco, they found it emptied of people. Looking back, I am not so sure the Texcocans did well to leave their home exposed to the invader. But after the Spaniards had murdered King Cacama, there had been much squabbling over the succession, and Texcoco was not well governed. In any case, with no one to oppose them, the Spanish gave the Tlaxcalans and the Totonacas licence to run riot.

Within days, many of Texcoco's important buildings had been razed, the potteries, workshops and warehouses ransacked, temples set ablaze – their flames rising high into the sky like a giant funeral pyre. We knew then that what we faced was a fight to the death, and that if we could not defend ourselves against these foreigners, then the Mexican race as we knew it, our way of life, our gardens and beautiful palaces and high temples, our songs and dances, our rituals, everything that made our life what it was and gave it meaning could be washed away in a river of blood and tears.

FIFTY-ONE

LONDON TO MEXICO CITY – 1976

James

I took copies of Time, Newsweek and The Economist to read during the return flight to Mexico. Their opinionated editorials and political correctness would irritate, but they would offer a crib on world events, a cover for ignorance that would otherwise be all too evident to my colleagues at CENCIAS.

The Economist gave the impression of having been written by a coterie of unhinged political obsessives, the two US journals by a middle-brow robot – every item written in a house style superficially vigorous but lacking the quirkiness of individual thought.

Theme of the month: "stagflation", uniformly described as "unprecedented", "a fresh challenge to economists and politicians alike". Theory had defined "inflation" and "stagnation" as opposites, like plus and minus, land and sea, heaven and hell. Inflation happened when demand outstripped supply, creating shortages; stagnation when supply outstripped demand, creating

299

surpluses. To suffer either was to be considered a misfortune, but both together deserved the scandalized judgement of Lady Bracknell that it could not be other than "carelessness".

My reading meandered through the distractions of a ten-hour air trip: a baby crying two rows back, service trolleys patrolling the aisles, dinner, and a movie about aliens and the eternal tussle between good and evil. After the film, a more arresting diversion: two middle-aged men a few rows in front challenging each other over a female companion. One of them, rising unsteadily from his seat, stumbled into a service trolley, sending a carton of juice and another of milk into the lap of an elderly woman seated opposite. Cabin staff converged on the scene. Raised voices of the disputants; the words "made advances", "little shit" and "asshole" resounded over the hum of the engines. A long negotiation ended with the man who had upset the refreshment trolley allowing himself to be escorted to a distant part of the aircraft. Two of the cabin staff applied towels and soothing words to the discomforted passenger.

The incident diverted my thoughts from the crisis of the capitalist system in an erotic direction. I pictured Olivia, flamboyantly beautiful as she waited for me at the airport, falling into my arms as I emerged from customs, talking excitedly as we drove home, her laughter caressing, her voice full of laughter and promise. For a few moments, the dream journeyed as dreams do, towards an end too fugitive to grasp but too enchanting to release, until the aircraft shuddered through low cloud, a steward announced that the captain had switched on the seat belt sign in preparation for landing, and I woke to a painful certainty that she would not be there.

Her absence and the casual thrusting of the three journals into my hand luggage both played a part in what happened next, a part that led me to the edge of an abyss that has ever since remained in view, and which I can't be sure of not stumbling into during some dark excursion of my thoughts or dreams.

FIFTY-TWO

TENOCHTITLAN – 1521

Alva

How it happened is a question whose answer lies deep in the minds of those who bore witness. In my memory, a handful of incidents stand out like promontories on a shoreline, while the rest is a blur of flames and falling masonry, starvation and thirst, the acrid smell of gunpowder and the foul smell of death.

I am not even sure when the real battle began. Fearful of the Spaniards' power and of how to repel them, we tried at first to avoid a direct confrontation, confining ourselves to observing their manoeuvres and seeking opportunities to undermine them by subterfuge. When they marched south from Texcoco to Ixtapalapa, we waited until they had settled down for the night and then opened Nezahualcoyotl's dyke, hoping they might be carried away in the flood. No one considered that the water level was low at that time of year and the flood would be correspondingly weak. We rose in the morning to news that

301

they had all escaped. In retrospect, the ploy looks pathetically inadequate, like trying to drown a jaguar by pissing in its path.

We next spotted them moving north to Tenayuca where our jewellers lived. A few days later they were in Azcapotzalco. They were encircling the lake, overrunning all the towns and villages, persuading some into their ranks and sacking those that dared to resist. Wherever they encountered a farm or a silo, they took possession of the crops and storehouses and forbade any deliveries to us. Their boats roamed the lake, scuttling any of our canoes they happened upon and preventing our fishermen from going about their trade. They placed troops and cannon at the end of the causeways, blocking supplies from the mainland. Most of all from that period of waiting and strangulation, I remember fear stalking every one of us like the shadow of a hostile god. Stories circulated of how they'd destroyed such and such a town that had refused to submit to them, forced another to take arms against us, murdered children at play, men working their fields, grandmothers too old to be worth the rough honour of their bed. Young women alone were guaranteed survival as objects of pleasure for the invaders. One story had it that they would afterwards give birth to monsters who would end up controlling the earth and all its people; another that the Spanish god was jealous, would tolerate no other and killed all those he encountered who failed to acknowledge him. We hardly knew what to think or who to believe.

The city lived in tension, the same unspoken questions churning in every mind: when would they attack? What would become of us? In the military, we were not troubled by the numbers ranged against us (the Spaniards were still relatively few and though the Tlaxcalans and Totonacas swelled the ranks of the opposing army, we had no fear of such lesser races). What caused us anxiety was the Spanish weaponry: the cannon and crossbows that killed at a distance, and the metal swords harder than the hardest rock.

I had spent the night commanding the duty guard on the Tepeyac Causeway. A priest stopped by shortly after dark to offer encouragement and ended up sharing our vigil. White-haired and kindly, with a stately bearing that comes only with advancing years, he impressed with his knowledge of the gods and his willingness to explain their thinking. When I asked about our chances of defeating the invaders, he said that the gods had always singled us out for special protection and would never destroy what they themselves had created – not at any rate until they were ready to do so.

"Maybe they are ready now," I suggested.

"They are not yet ready," he returned. "We will know when our end approaches."

Only later, in the light of experience, did the ambiguity of these words become clear. At the time, I took them as a guarantee that no matter how difficult and painful might be the trial that confronted us, we would in the end prevail.

Relieved just before dawn, I made my way home through quiet streets, happy that nothing untoward had occurred on my watch, pleasantly at peace with myself and with the world. Once there, I sat down to breakfast with the family – a few grains of corn washed down with thin chocolate, not much compared with how things were before the Spaniards, but still enough for our needs. Tlaco was absent on duty, but everyone else was present, anxious as ever to hear the latest from the front. I spoke of my belief in the future, my certainty that the clouds hanging over us would pass, that our nation would survive and our family and friends prosper. There would be losses, of course, but no more than the gods had always demanded of the living.

My mother's entreaties stopped me and, though she remained quiet, I had clearly gone too far.

Izel had tears in her eyes. "Please, little nephew," she said, "the gods have already taken your brother, your aunts, your cousins. Is there no end to their hunger?"

Always she called me "little nephew" even after I grew up and her head barely reached my chin.

Mazatl – the more outspoken of the twins – asked if I knew what the enemy had done in Texcoco.

"Burned the temples, smashed the images of the gods and replaced them with their own," I replied, knowing this to be the Spanish way.

"That's nothing–" Mazatl stopped, emotion choking his voice.

"Say it," Cualli urged. We looked at him, surprised, for he seldom spoke and no one ever heard him issue an order or make a demand.

Mazatl turned towards Teudile. "You saw thick smoke rising from the palace compound, isn't that so?"

No one replied until Mazatl repeated the question, angrily and challenging.

"I saw it," Teudile said. "They burned the library."

Cualli and Mazatl had worked as assistants in the great library of Texcoco ever since childhood. They knew its maze of shelves and passageways better perhaps even than the custodians, for they were the ones who fetched and carried the works for consultation and marked their location. Built by Nezahualcoyotl, the great poet king who had elevated our culture to its finest heights, the library at Texcoco housed archives of all our people, our past, our poetry, the books and paintings, the records of who we were and whence we came. Tenochtitlan itself could not boast a library to compare with Texcoco's. When the Spaniards set fire to it, a part of our selves perished in the flames. No act of vandalism or butchery could have better demonstrated what we were facing.

"These are no ordinary creatures," my mother said.

"They're uncivilized savages. We have to defeat them," I said, conscious of my duty as an army officer to stiffen the morale of nervous civilians.

"We can never bring back what was," said Mazatl.

"No. But we have other libraries here and in Tlatelolco." My attempt at comfort fell into a well of silence.

"Perhaps you are weary after your sleepless night," my mother said to me at length.

Her reprimand carried its usual authority. I excused myself and went to bed, but the thought I carried into sleep was the one we all shared, that if the Spaniards entered our city again, they would burn our libraries too.

FIFTY-THREE

TENOCHTITLAN – 1521

Alva

For a few days more nothing further occurred. Then the enemy began making sorties to test our defences. Detachments would approach via one of the causeways, and when they were within hailing distance one of their number would shout to us that they came in peace and begged us to welcome them into the city as we had before. We would reply by wondering aloud if they thought we were all idiots like Moctezuma.

One morning, Cortés himself rode up on horseback with that woman interpreter of his, Malinali. I happened to be on duty with my company at the entrance to the causeway.

He looked just as impressive as the day he first arrived, dressed in black and silver and astride a silver-grey horse, with Malinali riding alongside him on a smaller beast. Nor did he show any fear even though he wore no armour. To my eyes, he had the bearing one might expect of a king or the emissary of a god and I had to force myself to shake off a submissive impulse.

Riding right up to the city gateway before coming to a halt, he cupped gloved hands to his mouth and bellowed, "Get your leader or one of your lords down here. Someone I can speak to."

Malinali translated the words more or less well (she had picked up their language by then), but the arrogance of tone came directly to us with no need of intermediary. My stomach tightened at that sound. If I'd had one of those Spanish firearms, I would have had no hesitation in shooting Cortés down in defiance of our code of war. Several of my soldiers, those in my line of sight, looked across at me expectantly. I was the only officer present. If there was to be a response, it would have to come from me. My anger was such that I needed no special prompting.

"We're all lords here," I called, injecting as much contempt as I could into my voice. "You can speak to any of us."

On hearing the translation, he shot a furious glance in my direction, but I had darted down beneath a parapet and he saw nothing of me. He shouted something in his own language, then galloped off, leaving his translator to hurry after him. My soldiers encouraged them on their way with jeers and insults.

Back home that evening, with the household present – including Tlaco – I recounted the exchange with Cortés, did my best to describe his awe-inspiring appearance: his flowing hair and beard, his dark costume with its silver highlights, and the great sword he carried by his side. I felt proud of the rebuff I'd given the Spanish leader and pleased with the ensuing response from my troops.

Aunt Izel was less impressed. "Stupid. That foreigner could have killed you with one of those fire weapons."

I pointed out that soldiers needed to hear defiance from their commanders if they were to face the enemy with courage.

"Courage doesn't mean risking your life," she said, turning to Tlaco for confirmation.

He avoided the question and talked instead of the desertions by our allies and by subject peoples, the losses at Chalco,

Cuauhnahuac, Xochimilco and Coyoacán – towns that had all submitted.

"The enemy is massed against us on all sides," he said. "In a matter of days they will begin their attack. Who can foresee the outcome? We should not argue among ourselves but be gentle with each other. King Nezahualcoyotl taught us that life is too short to quarrel with those we love:

As the brightest plumage fades
As jade shatters, and gold fragments
So our stay on earth is brief,
For time turns we who live to shades."

He looked at each of us in turn. "Perhaps I shouldn't speak like this before you."

My mother responded at once to Tlaco's pessimism. Given his status, there was a limit to what she could say directly, so she replied with a song of encouragement to war for those who feared to take up arms, her voice trembling with suppressed anger:

I take my drum and from the temple beat
The rhythm and the heat of war
To rouse our loved ones from their sleep
And summon those who'd wake no more,
Whom cries of victory affright
Who cringe among the shades of night.
Wake to the choruses of dawn
To birdsong falling on the ears like rain
Restoring vigour to the desert plain.

Laurels arrayed upon a shield
The wearing of an eagle's wing
Garlands that glorify the brave and show
The path to manhood that a boy must know

Offering up in war the highest price
His blood to feed the flowers of sacrifice.
So many of our parted friends now dwell
In the hidden citadels of mountain peaks
Hurry soldier to the causeway straight
Where our deadly enemies await,
There lies the glory that our nation seeks.

Tlaco and I joined in at the end for it was one of the songs familiar to every one of us who had trained as a soldier. But still, I was surprised at my mother's zeal, and though as a son I could not upbraid her, my aunt Izel felt no constraint.

"How can you sing in praise of war? Does a mother no longer weep?"

"Let us not die like the Emperor Moctezuma," my mother answered. "I no longer fear the loss of my sons or any of those I love, for I will go with them."

Such became the routine discourse of our table for a time: gloomy defiance from my mother, protests from Izel, tears from the twins Cualli and Mazatl, while Tlaco, Teudile and myself drank *pulque* and held our peace.

None of us were behaving in character. In our hearts, I think we knew what was coming, even if we dared not give it expression, and the knowledge changed us, tempering the unspoken pleasure we found in each other's company, in Tlaco's gentleness, Teudile's tart wit, Izel's chatter, my mother's embracing warmth, with a feeling of helplessness, a sense that meaning and purpose had fled and that no one knew how to bring them back. We were living a low-level panic discernible in the absence of banter at home, the subdued tones in which we mostly conversed, the sisterly squabbles between Izel and my mother over trifles too insignificant to name.

Meanwhile the Spaniards and their allies continued to prowl round the lake and stare at us with a hunger that we never fully understood. During that period of waiting for something to happen, the authorities moved units to different defensive zones from time to time, maybe to relieve us of the tension and the boredom of keeping watch day after day in the same place. An order came for my company to leave the Tlacopan Causeway and to establish an observation post on the tip of the eastern shore from where we could scan a wide area of the lake. We were to report any activity suggestive of an enemy approach over the water.

One morning, as the sun was rising, an ear-splitting roar reached us from the direction of Texcoco. We had already heard stories of Spanish cannon but this was my first experience of their terrifying power. Smoke billowed skyward. Flocks of thrashers, towhees and pigeons soared into the air while ducks scattered in panic, flapping heavy wings over the surface of the lake. Shortly after came another crash, then another.

I despatched a messenger with a report for General Palintzin, then mounted the steps of a nearby temple to get a better look. Out of respect for Xochiquetzal, goddess of love, whose shrine this was, I had posted no guards there despite it being the highest point in the area.

On reaching the top, I spotted Tlaco with Teudile in tow a short distance away and I shouted to them to join me. I remember feeling oddly excited as if conscious that something special was about to happen although there was no sign that it might be the expected invasion.

By now the cannon fire had ceased. I scanned the shoreline in the direction of Texcoco but could see nothing beyond the dark outline of ruined buildings. Something on the water, however, caught my eye: a smudge no bigger than a fingernail that, despite its small size, stood out from the background. I stared at it, trying to figure out whether it was real or a figment of my imagination. Then I saw another, and a third. They seemed to be moving slightly, bobbing.

I greeted Tlaco and Teudile and the three of us searched the lake with our eyes. More smudges appeared. In the end we counted twelve or thirteen. Teudile had no doubt what they were. He had seen the Spanish vessels that had first arrived on our coast.

"They move with the wind," he said, "like the floating houses in which the enemy crossed the sea."

Three of the craft headed towards us, growing in size until we could clearly see their shape. Larger than any of our canoes, with space enough to carry a company of soldiers, each had a cloth raised into the air on a stick, and though these boats were moving, no one was paddling them. How naive we were in those days! We had no word for such things as sails and masts, or for boats that travel swiftly with the breathing of the wind.

Mesmerized, we stood watching their movement, not thinking that the Spaniards might be on their way to attack, until one of my guards hurried up the steps of the temple to warn us that the enemy had been spotted and to ask for orders. Tlaco at once took off for the Tlatelolco armoury, taking Teudile with him, though even as they hurried down the temple steps, the vessels began to diminish in size again as they floated back towards the far shore. For the moment, we were safe, but the cannon and the sails were a reminder – if one were needed – that the invaders possessed knowledge of many things unknown to us. A worm of fear nested in my thoughts that the Spanish god had favoured them with secrets hidden from other mortals and that perhaps they could not be defeated.

FIFTY-FOUR

MEXICO CITY – 1976

James

Ahead of me as we exited the customs hall was one of the protagonists of the in-flight quarrel, the older of the two, pot-bellied, florid, with puffy, off-centre features like those of an ageing pugilist. He was holding hands with the woman. She was in her mid-thirties, immaculate in white pants and jacket. She leaned against him as they walked. A porter preceded them, wheeling a pyramid of luggage with which he opened a passage through the waiting crowd. Still faintly hopeful of seeing Olivia yet certain she would not be there, I felt a pang of envy.

Excited cries drew my attention as parents and two teenage sisters celebrated the safe arrival of a young man. The latter kissed his mother, then embraced his father while the sisters hung onto their hero's arms and gazed at him through tears of admiration. Love was physical, played out on the surface of feeling, and the young man was master of a little universe whose every inhabitant wanted and needed him and gloried in his return.

No sign of Olivia. I called her home. A maid answered and passed the telephone to Olivia's mother who said Olivia was in Acapulco with friends. I wondered if she was with another man but the thought would be as shocking to her mother as it was already painful to me and I could not ask. I told the *señora* how wonderful it was to speak with her, that I hoped the family was well and asked her to convey my best regards to her husband. Once they are learned, the rituals of courtesy come to seem beautiful not least because the emotion must be transparent (insincerity is readily spotted). Language precedes meaning at such moments, producing the delight it expresses and leaving speaker and listener savouring moments of shared humanity. I heard the pleasure in her tone.

"You must come to dinner. I will tell Olivia as soon as she returns."

"You are very kind, señora."

"*Que te vaya bien, Jaime.*"

I replaced the receiver and at once the warmth gave way to desolation, bewilderment. The Mexico of my dreams was evading my grasp, refusing me her secrets.

FIFTY-FIVE

TENOCHTITLAN – 1521

Alva

Another night on watch, a brooding night heavy with cloud and foreboding, a night devoid of moon and stars, and the comforting glimmer of beacons on the mainland all extinguished since the Spaniards' reappearance. We had strained our eyes and ears into blackness but seen only figures of our imagination while flinching at every rustle of a leaf in a breath of air.

At dawn, I returned home exhausted and went straight to bed. Teudile woke me at around midday, an instant it seemed after I had closed my eyes. I knew at once, before he told me, that the invasion had begun.

We had prepared for this moment. Every man of fighting age knew where to assemble and to which force he belonged. The four of us – Teudile, Mazatl, Cualli and myself – took leave of the household and walked together to the main square. There we embraced and went our separate ways, Teudile to Tlatelolco to join Tlaco, Mazatl to the Tenayuca Causeway, Cualli to the canoes. My orders were to join up with my men and lead them to the city gates on the Ixtapalapa Causeway. From now on, we would be on call until the war ended.

Nothing happened in our section on that day, and little for the next 12 or 16 days (I don't really remember how many; it could have been twice that number, or maybe less). Battles were being fought elsewhere – so much we knew, and though we didn't receive much detail about them, it wasn't hard to figure out that the lack of news could only signify the absence of victory.

During our enforced idleness, I organized a roster of leave so that each of my men had a chance to spend half a day or half a night at home. When my own turn came, I found the women of the house – my mother, Aunt Izel and three elderly Texcocan refugees – in a state that I can only describe as near panic. They turned out to have more news of the war than those of us who were stationed in a quiet section of the front line. They spoke of heavy defeats, losses of fine young men, ever dwindling supplies of food. Of the latter they certainly had evidence, for all they could find to welcome me was a tortilla and a bowl of water flies.

Our canoes suffered acutely since they were no match for the sailing boats of the enemy in open water. In the canals it was a different matter, though the Spaniards seldom ventured into our inland waterways, preferring to stand off and fire cannon mounted on the bows of their vessels. Their ammunition – the metal balls especially – caused only modest damage to our defences, but they possessed power enough to topple several men with a single shot. We learned to fear those cannon, and to scatter whenever we saw them to avoid offering an easy target.

I returned to the Ixtapalapa road just as my men were coming under attack for the first time. A handful of Spaniards leading what looked like a full army of Tlaxcalans was marching down the causeway towards us. We withdrew inside the city defences and took up position on the rooftops of the houses on each side where we had stockpiles of rocks at the ready. I told my men to keep out of sight and wait for my signal. Once the invaders had entered the street, I stood up and aimed a rock at the head of the column. A shower of rocks followed, and the enemy, taken by surprise, beat a quick retreat. Had we left things at that, we might have ended our first day of battle with a victory. Flushed with success, I stupidly ordered my men to reassemble on the causeway and chase the enemy away. I should have foreseen that the Spanish soldiers would reform and return to the attack. They did so by sending a flurry of arrows from their crossbows in our direction, downing several of my men; then they rushed at us with their swords, and we felt the horrible, desperate inequality of our weaponry. I think, in the end, we might have been overwhelmed had not reinforcements arrived by canoe. With their help, we managed to sustain a three-sided defence and in such numbers that even the Spanish were forced to retreat – though they did so in good order and shaking their weapons at us in a way that made clear they were in no way defeated.

As a unit we survived the encounter, but there was no rejoicing. The roll call told its own tale. Half my company lay dead or badly injured, gone from our ranks so swiftly that I found the loss hard to digest, and it was with a feeling of shame that, after a single battle, I found myself sending a request to high command for more troops. Only later did I learn that our experience was the common one. Against men whose weapons resembled our own, our losses were minimal, but when we faced the Spaniards, we fell like ears of corn at harvest.

A pattern set in. At night, while we soldiers rested, teams of women and teenagers ventured out onto the causeways to break up bridges and open breaches so as to hamper the enemy's advance towards the city. The Spaniards had ceased their night attacks, perhaps realizing that their knowledge of the city could not match ours and that darkness gave us the advantage. Each morning, the invaders replaced what we had removed, but the labour required afforded us plenty of time to prepare for the next assault.

For many days, we held them off. After our early losses, I trained my men to hit and run, and instructed them at all costs to avoid direct clashes with the enemy. When the latter came at us, we would withdraw to the rooftops or behind buildings, hurl lances and rocks at them from a distance and then melt away through streets familiar to us but unknown to them.

But I'm getting ahead of myself. The tactic wasn't mine, but came from someone I'd forgotten about in the anxiety of war and privation. He was among the replacements sent to replenish our manpower: Huehue.

As soon as we had left off embracing and I had given him an account of the Spanish assault, he drew me aside and suggested we take a walk. We headed towards the lake through back streets, and when we were alone and out of earshot, he fixed me with an expression of mingled challenge and gentle mockery.

"You want to hear an old shit's opinion or you want to pull rank on me?"

I waited.

"Tell me something," he said, "do I stink or not? Can you smell shit on me?"

"You smell okay."

"I smell okay?"

By now we had reached the water's edge and were standing behind a row of old houses. Huehue addressed the lake as if it were a crowd of onlookers.

"He's so spooked he's even lost his sense of smell." He turned back to me. "They're making fun of you, those Spaniards. Even they can smell a Mexican shit-shoveller."

"What are you talking about?"

"What am I talking about?" He shook his head in the direction of the lakeside audience. "I'm trying to tell him to use his nose."

We looked at each other, he expectantly, me quizzically.

"You still don't get it?"

"No."

"We have no chance against Spanish weapons."

"I know that."

"Then we shouldn't try."

"You mean surrender?"

"Why would we do that? We haven't lost."

"Then what?"

In the days when Tlaco and I worked for him as students, he might have allowed himself a few jests at my expense. My status now shielded me from direct barbs, but his kindly, exasperated eyes spoke for him.

"We just have to fight in a different way. Come at them from the rooftops, the side streets, the rear, never face to face. Get it?"

"Isn't that what cowards do?"

"You want to survive?"

"I guess so."

"Trouble with being at the bottom of the pile is that nobody listens."

But I did listen, and that's how we drove off attacks day after day with one of the lowest fatality rates in the army.

I wanted to make Huehue my lieutenant but he wasn't a trained soldier and I knew the men would not take kindly to obeying a man of his background. Instead, he became my aide-de-camp which meant I could have him by my side in battle. Like Teudile, he never did learn to wield a sword, but I trusted his opinion and when we differed, invariably preferred it to my own. Even if his wisdom made no difference to the final outcome, in my eyes that crusty shit-shoveller was made of the same clay as Palintzin. If low birth and impetuosity had not betrayed him, he might have become a senior official, a counsellor at the palace. I once asked him why he hadn't achieved a little more.

"Achieved? Let me tell you something. Nobody bothers with me. That's an achievement. I'm one of the few free men around." He knew this wasn't the answer I was seeking and after a moment's thought, he offered a fuller account. "I'll tell you something, but don't repeat it until after I'm dead."

I gave him my word

"Got into trouble as a teenager – caught trying to stoop the daughter of a senior officer. I'm talking about one of Emperor Axayácatl's cousins. Serious stuff. To make matters worse, I'm a Tlacopan – wrong side of the lake. Couldn't be worse. They arrested me, and the father – he's dead now so I won't name him – the good, kind, understanding father demanded the ultimate sacrifice. Since I wasn't a war captive, I could choose: either an honourable death on the block or life as a slave. Were they kidding? I was only a youngster. Hadn't yet had a decent fuck. I wanted life. Don't look shocked, my dear friend. You're a follower of Quetzalcóatl. Wouldn't the god agree? Sacrifice is for animals not men. So they sent me to work in the *chinampas* as a shit-spreader. 'Make the plants grow,' they told me. Well, I thought, no way I'm going to live like this. Soon as I could, I slipped into the emperor's palace and demanded my freedom. I escaped at night and the owner didn't see me go."

He held up his hands in mock protest. "Don't tell me. I know that's also dishonourable. A slave is supposed to give his owner a chance to catch him. Wonder who made up that rule? Couldn't have been a slave, that's for sure. Anyway I got my freedom back. Problem was, after that, nobody would give me any work. I was in disgrace for refusing death, something no one was supposed to do, and then for outsmarting tradition. Ended up in the excrement business as the only option. There's life in shit. Maybe not an elegant life, but life all the same."

FIFTY-SIX

TENOCHTITLAN – 1521

Alva

S talemate for the best part of a moon. Each morning the invaders repaired the breaches in the causeways, each afternoon they marched into the city firing their weapons at everything that moved, searching every building on their way and putting whoever they found to the sword. On our side, we did our best to evacuate the houses most exposed to danger before launching quick defensive assaults on the enemy from our hiding places. Sometimes, they made hardly any progress before retiring; at others, especially when Spanish officers led the troops on horseback, they would penetrate further. From time to time, they made it to the main square, but always as evening approached, they withdrew.

Though our army was just about holding them at bay, losses mounted – including those of my company, despite the tactic we adopted to avoid face-to-face confrontations. Replacements became ever more youthful as men of regular fighting age dwindled, and I found myself spending more and more time training novices and pleading with the authorities for a few seasoned troops.

Senior officers seldom came to see what was going on. Few had survived the Toxcatl massacre, and those that did were overstretched. Cuauhtémoc made one brief appearance, but he asked no questions and after we had spread ourselves before him and kissed the dirt to signal our obedience, he offered a few bare words of encouragement before hurrying away. When my lips touched the ground in front of him, I felt a mad urge – repressed of course – to ask him about Tecuichpo. That night my dreams were haunted by thoughts of him entering her in a place I had briefly called my own, and I tasted – as I suppose I have done all my life – the bitter flavour of powerlessness.

Tecuichpo bore no children during her time as the young emperor's wife, and I now believe he continued to act more as protector than husband. My jealousy in the passage of time looks unforgivably frivolous and selfish, and yet in the moments when it ruled my thoughts, the fate of my troops and my country seemed less important. Not that I ever thought of abandoning either or of ceasing to fight for them, but I would not have wept if the emperor had fallen to the enemy and been replaced by another (the confession shocks me even as I write it down; perhaps my punishment is that I have outlived all those who then occupied the horizon of my little world).

Practical matters prevented me at the time from sinking too far into such foolishness. Almost as much as our losses (every one of which pained me, no matter that ours were among the lowest), the growing problem of provisions preoccupied me. As a military unit, we were supposed to have privileged access to food, but the amounts dwindled day by day. No one grumbled, for we all knew the score; though we did our best to spur ourselves on with shows of bravado and mutual encouragement, the inadequate diet gnawed at our energy. Worse even than the lack of victuals was the quality of drinking water. Our main supply, which came via an aqueduct from the mainland, had been cut off by the Spaniards. We had wells, but they could never meet the demands of the whole city, and besides, the water tasted brackish and made people ill. Lake water, too salty to drink, served only for cooking.

Despite the difficulty of our position and our grievous losses, the struggle in which we were all engaged drew us closer together, creating a solidarity of feeling and a trust in each other I never experienced before nor since. I remember one evening, after one of our frugal meals, we began speculating about how soon it would be before the Spaniards tired of this stalemate, realized they weren't winning, and retired from the field. The idea made us forget our hunger and thirst for a while. We laughed, cracked jokes at the enemy's expense. Huehue, whose mordant wit had finally earned him general acceptance, got everyone to agree that he smelled much better than any Spaniard, then feigned indignation that he had lost his reputation. Someone produced a flagon of *yolixpa*, someone else a handful of strong mushrooms, and we spent that night bathed in the perfumes and colours of the heavens.

Our heady fantasies of Spanish weariness proved illusory. Rather than retiring, they changed tactic. We sensed the difference before we understood its significance: black clouds billowing skyward, smoke in our nostrils followed shortly thereafter by terrified people – women, children, the elderly – fleeing towards the city centre. A group of frightened teenagers ran into us and from them we learned that enemy soldiers were penetrating residential areas bordering the causeways and were setting fire to everything in their path: houses, temples, storerooms, monuments. In the days that followed, fire consumed wide strips bordering the main thoroughfares. Structures that would not burn, the invaders knocked down and so advanced step by step into a blackened wasteland where there were no more rooftops from which to hurl rocks and barely a wall behind which to hide. The city was crumbling before our eyes.

On the ninth or tenth day after the burning started, one of the Spaniards – it might have been Cortés himself, although I could not swear as much – came to the front line and shouted through an interpreter, "Do you Mexicans not yet understand that we can destroy you? Do you want to lose your whole city?"

Huehue, as usual, was standing beside me. "You must answer."

"What shall I say?"

"Tell them if they burn our city, we'll make them rebuild it before feeding them to the gods."

I took his advice and received a roar of approval from my men. A moment to savour among the many that were sour.

Yes, there were moments during the war when we dared to proclaim our future victory. I feel this was not a childish fantasy, but rather an inability to imagine defeat. True, we might suffer reverses, our great buildings might fall and our houses turn to rubble, many of us might die in defence of our families and our way of life, but in the end the gods would chase our enemies away and we would rebuild. Perhaps struggle is not possible without such faith.

Regardless of our faith, however, it soon became clear that the enemy's new tactic was working. As street after street dissolved into ruin and ash, so the invaders advanced. They had nullified our defensive cover by destroying it. Though we continued to launch counterattacks whenever and wherever possible, casualties rose without mercy, especially among recruits who had had no experience of warfare. Of the old hands – among whom I could count myself – not one was without wounds. When a Spanish sword sliced into my thigh, I escaped death only because the soldier who wielded it stumbled as he prepared to finish me off. Several of my men rushed to attack him before he could recover, while Huehue dragged me away to a shelter behind the front line.

The cut was deep and bleeding heavily and I asked Huehue to wrap a cloth tightly round it.

"Have to clean it first," he said.

"There's no clean water."

"We'll use what we have. Brace yourself. This will sting." He took out his member and pissed over the wound.

I gasped as the hot stream hit its mark. "May Iztli[55] give you grief for this," I told him.

"Patécatl[56] will absolve me. Nothing's cleaner than piss."

"You've probably poisoned me."

"If I have, you won't know much about it."

By the time the nurses got to me in the evening, the bleeding had stopped.

"Where did you learn this stuff," I asked Huehue.

"Nowhere. I just guessed. We had no fresh water. Thought I'd give it a try."

"What if—"

"What if? You'd be dead that's what. Thank the gods you're alive and that you'll be out of action for a few days." He turned to leave, took a few paces, and paused to glance back at me. "Enjoy yourself."

His meaning became clear that night. Somehow he had persuaded a nurse to watch over me "in case I injured myself". After bathing and redressing my wound, she caressed me, took me in her mouth, and afterwards covered me with a blanket and stroked my head and cheeks until I drifted into sleep, smitten and ready to become her slave.

For several days I was unable to fight. Huehue made me a walking stick so I could hobble around and keep command. Not that there was much we could do any longer to stop the enemy advance. Destruction of the buildings that still stood in their path detained them more than our resistance. We were reduced

---

55   God of justice and punishment.
56   God of health and healing.

to harassing them as we could and to retreating step by agonizing step.

Every seven days, the Spaniards withdrew from the field and commanded their allies to do likewise. We know now that their day of inaction is called "Sunday" and that in resting they were obeying the orders of their god. Once we had worked out when Sunday occurred, we were glad of the respite. As soon as my injury allowed me to walk more or less freely, I took the rest day off to visit the family. At least that was my intention. Since the burning began, I had been concerned for their safety of course, though not too concerned because the house stood in a quiet part of the city distant from any of the causeways. There wasn't even a temple nearby, nor a barracks or public building, just a modest shrine to Quetzalcóatl, a school and a care centre for the elderly; no reason, in other words, for the Spaniards to attack such an area. What would be the purpose? To terrorize? What is the use of that? Of what possible value could it be to slaughter the elderly, or children and their mothers?

Soon after I set out, however, the assurances I had given myself looked less secure. My direct way home led through a district of workshops and depots that I had expected to find intact. They had turned to cinder and scattered masonry. Retracing my steps, I tried an alternative route via the rear of Axayácatl's palace. From there, I walked east for a few blocks and then turned south towards the Cuauhnahuac road. That I saw no one en route barely struck me as strange, so intent was I on my purpose. Before long, I again found myself among ruins. I altered course again, only to come across another scene of destruction. And so I went turning first one way and then another, until I ran out of options and ended up stealing from one pile of rubble or charred wall to another like a rat in search of carrion. Well before I came upon the still-smouldering remains of the family home, I knew that it would be gone.

My first thoughts were not for the house, but for my beloved mother, my aunt, and our guests from Texcoco. Trembling with anxiety, I searched the compound for evidence of struggle or that people had died there, anything, a body, blood, clothing. I found shards of pottery, broken household bric-a-brac, a cooking pot badly chipped, a broken stool, all blackened by fire, heaps of ash. Our neighbour's house had suffered a similar fate. From its debris, a wisp of blue smoke coiled towards heaven.

Half blinded with tears and despair, I hurried away as fast as my wound allowed, scarcely conscious this time of my route or of whether I might run into Spaniards. Soon the light began to fade, and when I came across a structure with half the roof still intact, I opted to spend the night there under the cover of a blanket that had somehow escaped the flames. Next morning, I arrived at the great square to find no one on guard at the entrance to the imperial palace. Nor was there any activity discernible within. It dawned on me that I had walked back and forth through some of the busiest and most crowded areas without seeing a soul. In place of the familiar noise and bustle, a strange calm had descended over the city like that of a battlefield from which the clash of weapons and the cries of men had gone. Only at the great temple did I see any sign of life. On high, some priests were petitioning Tlaloc for rain, their chant carrying into the open space below, and seated on a lower step a beggar waited with stoic patience for casual mercy.

"Where is everyone," I asked.

He looked up at me with sightless eyes. "Who?"

"The government."

"Gone to Tlatelolco."

"Everyone?"

"I'm still here. A few crazy priests are still up there chanting. We're not worth killing." He stopped me as I turned to go. "You couldn't spare a little something?"

"I have nothing to give."

"You have eyes."

"I can't give you those."

"What about some water?"

I was carrying a water bag, still half full, and I handed it to him with a warning that the water was brackish.

He drank deeply in big ravenous gulps as if he were surfacing for air. "Tastes good enough to me."

I asked him if he would like me to take him to Tlatelolco but he shook his head.

"I know my way around here. I'd be lost anywhere else."

"When the Spaniards come…"

"Let them."

FIFTY-SEVEN

TENOCHTITLAN – 1521

Alva

My unit greeted me with the news that all remaining troops stationed in Tenochtitlan had received an order to retreat to Tlatelolco.

"They make out it's temporary while we prepare the counterattack," Huehue said. "They're trying to preserve morale."

"Morale?"

"Nobody willingly gives up their home."

As soon as we reached Tlatelolco, I stationed my unit a couple of blocks from the market and went in search of Tlaco. He, if anyone, would know the whereabouts of my mother. I found him at the armoury. Tears appeared in his eyes when he spotted me limping towards him. For days he had heard nothing of me or my unit and had feared the worst. We folded our arms round each other.

"Thought we were finally rid of you," he said.

"What about—"

"They're safe."

He led me to the temple precinct where my mother and Izel were living in an encampment – two among a multitude so numerous that no one could count them. Many whose homes had been destroyed had sought refuge there in the hope that the Spaniards would leave Tlatelolco in peace.

"It's pretty chaotic. No one's keeping order. There's hardly any food," Tlaco said.

The entire temple area and several adjacent alleys were given over to accommodation. Particoloured swathes of cloth hung from every wall or parapet to provide shade and shelter. Beneath this canopy separated by aisles were rows of bedding and little bundles of personal possessions, mainly clothing, but here and there a cooking pot, utensils, an effigy. Women, children and elderly men predominated, the men of fighting age having been conscripted. Groups of adults stood or sat together chatting. Children played among the aisles, excited by the novelty of encampment, their shouts and laughter a contrast to the subdued voices of their parents. Babies cried, one or two unconsolably as they do when unsatisfied hunger pierces them with a cruel awareness that the world does not conform to their wishes. Stretched out here and there were wounded soldiers, some silent and staring as if the life had already gone from them, others restless, groaning, feverish. Sweat, bile and incontinence saturated the air like vapour from a swamp. My stomach heaved as we entered the compound, though I saw at once that those who were quartered there showed no discomfort, nor seemed aware of the stench, and within a short time I too accommodated to it.

Tlaco threaded us through the human thicket, though with frequent stops to offer encouragement to the fearful and especially to the wounded, several of whom – spotting his insignia – called out to him as we passed. His tenderness towards everyone with whom he spoke moved me and I told him so.

"I try to give people some heart," he said, "though I have little enough of my own."

My mother and Izel were safe and well as Tlaco had promised. Teudile too was alive but he had lost the fingers of his left hand to a Spanish sword, and though he embraced me warmly, his injury seemed to have dampened his spirits and he barely spoke.

"He thinks his manhood went with his fingers," Aunt Izel told me. "I keep telling him it isn't so."

Of Cualli and Mazatl, there had been no news. Enemy ships had decimated our canoe fleet and we understood, without saying so, that we might not see either of our cousins again.

My mother's greeting was less emotional than I had expected. She reached up to embrace me with a soft look in her eyes, subdued yet serene. I had seen the expression before, in Macuiltzin's gaze after we had mounted the temple steps together and he had turned to me to say farewell before beginning his journey to the gods.

She drew me aside. "You are limping, my son."

"Just a scratch."

"May I see?"

"I'm fine."

"You do not welcome my concern."

"There is no need."

"I want you to know how proud I am..." She faltered. "I tell you now in case I do not find you again." She held up a hand to forestall the protest forming on my lips. "See how far we have fallen. We have become fugitives like our ancestors who wandered the earth in search of a home." She stole a glance at Izel. "Your aunt and I will not outlive this war."

"Don't say that."

"Women of our age are of no use to the foreigner, neither for his pleasure nor his service. He will discard us like a shell emptied of its fruit. As the last of our family, you must live for us. Become a slave of the foreigner if the gods so will. Only do not die before your time."

"And what will be my time?"

"You will know when it comes, for you will go willingly and at peace."

Before she could say more, Tlaco interrupted to remind me that we both had military duties to attend.

That night, he explained, we were to return to the capital under cover of darkness ready for an early-morning enemy attack. We were to take up defensive positions round the main square, the temple and the palaces.

This was news to me, and I asked him why our company had not been informed. Turned out to have been a muddle. Messages were supposed to have gone out to all units with detailed instructions about when and where to assemble. Ours didn't arrive. Nor – as it transpired – were we the only troops left in ignorance.

"We're not so well organized," Tlaco admitted. "Half the general staff has been killed. No one is getting enough to eat. We're even running out of messengers."

If we were to return to the capital that very night, I had to see that my troops were fed and rested. Tlaco too needed to be back at the armoury. We said our farewells with the usual expressions of confidence in our eventual victory and swift return home, words that surely rang as hollow in our listeners' ears as they did in mine.

"Perhaps I should not have been so open about our situation in front of your family," Tlaco remarked as soon as we were out of earshot. "But what is the use of pretending?" He drew my attention to a trickle of blood running down my leg. "You're bleeding."

"A little wound. Must have reopened."

"I promised your mother I would have it seen to."

"My mother?"

"She pointed it out to me when you were saying goodbye to Izel and Teudile. Said you wouldn't let her deal with it."

"My mother?"

"Yes. Think yourself lucky that she is alive and loves you."

Back at the armoury, Tlaco summoned a nurse who bathed my wound in precious clean water, covered it in a green ointment and wrapped it in a cloth.

"Bet not everybody gets this kind of treatment," I said to Tlaco.

"Life is unfair. Enjoy your fortune."

I asked him what he thought of our chances of winning the war. He told me Cuauhtémoc had recently held a top-level meeting on the same question. The answer was "Fight on."

"But does he think we can win?"

The nurse was knotting my bandage. Tlaco waited for her to finish and gave her an avocado before dismissing her. She was touchingly pleased with the gift.

He waited until she had left before remarking, "An avocado is a day's ration for a nurse."

"Can we win?" I repeated.

He looked at me wearily, his eyes bloodshot, his face creased with the anxieties and burdens of office. "The emperor wondered if we should make peace with the foreigners, but the Tlatelolcans wouldn't hear of it. We are their guests now and we must listen to them."

"Are they right?"

"Only the gods know for sure."

We talked for a while more. He spoke of his love for my sister, of how he missed her, and that he would never meet her like again. Thinking to inject a little cheerfulness into our thoughts, I told him how Huehue had pissed on my wound, but Tlaco offered only a perfunctory grin. We drifted, our words less important than the sound of our voices, which were familiar and comforting. For my part, I couldn't help feeling – absurdly – that the more we chatted, the longer we could postpone the next bitter clash with the invaders, and the longer, too, our way of life would survive, that all we needed to do was go on as before, pretend that nothing terrible was happening, and so it would be.

Sunset came to remind me that I had to rejoin my unit, but still I lingered, loath to break out of the cocoon of our conversation, until Tlaco put on the authoritative voice of high command and ordered me back to my troops. If we were to be in position in the capital before dawn, there would be little time for rest.

As it turned out, no one in my unit managed to get much sleep. With his usual ingenuity, Huehue had secured sufficient rations to go round, but by the time we had prepared and consumed a meal, and everyone had taken turns to wash and answer calls of nature, the moon had reached its zenith which was our signal to set out.

FIFTY-EIGHT

TENOCHTITLAN – 1521

Alva

As the first glimmer of light appeared in the sky, what remained of the army assembled in the main square. Cuauhtémoc addressed us. I don't remember exactly what he said, something about the glory of Mexico and the fate of the nation. His words hardly mattered, for the truth confronted each one of us with no room for mercy: our professional army had not only shrunk in size, but it now consisted largely of untrained recruits led in the main by junior officers. In any case, he had to break off his speech when look-outs posted on the upper temple platform blew the alarm. Moments later, the clatter of horses' hooves reached our ears. We barely had time to take up position before the invaders descended on us, plunging what remained of our world into chaos.

All that day we fought. Nor did the invaders retire at nightfall as in the past but stood their ground and continued fighting under moonlight, forcing us to do likewise. There seemed to be many more of them too, and they seemed tireless. Under the onslaught of their weapons, our men fell like leaves in the wind. Young women took their place in our ranks and fought alongside us as bravely as any man. Street by street we gave ground, as the buildings in front of us erupted in flames. On the second day, we lost the main square. On day three, the temple precinct. Food became a handful of flies or grubs if we were lucky enough to find any. Water became more precious than the finest jewel.

How long did the battle last? I don't know. The days stretched out and seemed beyond counting. My own unit fell apart, dispersed either by the chaos or by death. Even Huehue disappeared from sight. So engaged was I in the struggle that I only saw one of my men fall: a youngster of maybe twenty years, who had recently joined up. In action, he liked to stick close by me and I had noticed that whenever I gave an order, he would be watching me with admiring eyes as if I represented something to which he might aspire. Perhaps he had listened to the nonsense about my first prisoner and the bravery I was reputed to have shown at his age. He was a good kid, sweet-natured, but with a strong arm too and skilled with a sling. We were still in the main square, and he was not more than ten paces away from me, reloading his sling with a rock. A cannon took his head off. It happened so suddenly that I had a glimpse of him standing upright, headless and spurting blood before his body toppled over. That sight still haunts my dreams. I have never ceased to wonder how men can do such things to each other. Perhaps the gods know, for I think no one here on earth can tell.

At length, those of us still able to fight found ourselves back in Tlatelolco. There, the misery knew no bounds, nor have I words to describe it. Men and women alike were weeping, imploring the gods to save them, crying out for food and water that no one could supply, mumbling to themselves in gibberish, wandering back and forth on errands devoid of purpose. Babies lay dying for lack of nourishment. Children wandered about with swollen bellies, their arms and legs no thicker than their bones.

The air stank of excrement, rotting flesh, filth. Heaps of trash and bodies of the sick and dying lay piled in corners, on patches of waste ground, at the water's edge, at the rear of buildings.

My mother, Teudile and Izel were no longer at the temple. Tlaco, however, was still at the armoury. He had run out of weapons to distribute and was sitting on the steps at the entrance. I asked him stupidly what he was doing and he said that he was waiting for the enemy. He didn't know what had become of the family. Many civilians were fleeing along the causeways – in vain, because the enemy had blocked all the exits. Cuauhtémoc too was reportedly trying to escape by canoe in the hope of gaining the mainland and perhaps mounting another army.

"It's hopeless," Tlaco said. "We've lost our country."

I suggested that if the emperor was trying to escape, then perhaps we should do likewise.

"He won't make it. We're surrounded. There's no way out."

For lack of alternative, we spent the night in the armoury half expecting the Spaniards to arrive and kill us but too weary and discouraged to do more than lie down and wait.

FIFTY-NINE
MEXICO CITY – 1976

James

On my first day back at CENCIAS, Mendoza passed by my office. He shook my hand before dropping a typescript on my desk.

"Make sure you read it for the editorial meeting tomorrow."

"Right."

"It's superb by the way."

"What is?"

"Fernández's paper."

"Right."

I flicked through the pages.

"He's a brilliant scholar."

"Yes."

Back in my apartment that evening, I reheated the dish of *mole poblano* and rice that María Isabel had left for me and browsed through Fernández's paper while I ate. No blemishes, no hand corrections, the language elegant, the tone mildly feverish as if the writer were pressing down on an eruption of excitement. Stagflation, that word again, as thrilling and mysterious as the discovery of a comet. What more could an economist wish for than a chance to pursue a new phenomenon and maybe propose an explanation that might secure their place in history, be it no more than a footnote? Though I was struck as I turned the pages by a feeling that the analysis, the language, even the cadences were familiar, followed by a growing awareness that I had read the text before. Clearing away the dishes, I retrieved the magazines I had brought with me from the flight, opened them at their lead articles and spread them over the table. Stagflation in bold type, drama, foreboding, an incontinent scattering of exclamation marks. Casting my eyes eye back and forth between them and Fernández's typescript, I noted the similarities, the histrionic expressions of bewilderment, the assertions that the world economy had crossed into an uncharted region of space. Fernández understood the subject, so much was clear, but the thought that hammered at me was that the ideas he expressed with such eloquence were not his, that he had nothing to offer beyond what anyone could find at the newsstand: not a Latin American perspective but a *gringo* one! How could this brilliant refugee, this advocate of social and political justice, this seeker after truth – for that is how many of us saw those who had escaped the clutches of murderous regimes – have offered a slavish reproduction of received opinion from the Anglo-Saxon world, the same world that had celebrated the fall of Allende and was now applauding the policies of his jack-booted successor? Was this a case of intellectual laziness, it being too laborious to search for a homegrown view? Or did the author bend to the force of argument in those middle-brow texts, convinced that no other interpretation of events was possible?

I look back on this moment not without shame. For I have since learned how much we lean on others for what we are and pretend to be, that originality of thought is rare and precious, and that we should not expect brilliance from our fellows simply because circumstance has glamourized them. Yes, I decorated these strange, gifted men – who did not? – with the noble badge of resistance to tyranny and defence of the poor. I was young, idealistic, and thought myself in the presence of heroes, people who lived according to the noblest principles that I must not fail to make my own.

I missed the luncheon service on the following day, having allowed my morning class to run on too long, so I nipped round the corner to a little café, taking Fernández's paper with me. All the tables were taken but at one I spotted a couple of young graduate students, roughly the same age as myself. Could I join them?

"*Claro que sí, Licenciado. Con gusto.*"

I remember asking them not to think me rude if I studied Fernández's paper.

"He's a kind of genius, isn't he," said one.

"I believe so."

They wanted to know what the paper was about.

"Stagflation."

They both nodded to show their familiarity with the term.

"I can't show you his paper without his permission," I said, "but if you read English, last week's Economist has a good discussion on the subject."

"How does Fernández see things?"

"Much the same as The Economist."

They looked disappointed.

"Maybe there's not much else to say," I suggested.

"There's always something else, *Licenciado*. We must believe that. Otherwise the world won't change."

They excused themselves; both had a class to attend. I had an hour before the editorial meeting to run through Fernández's paper again, and to make a few last-minute corrections to my own.

SIXTY

TLATELOLCO – 1521

Alva

Next morning at dawn, we shared a couple of overripe avocados washed down with a mouthful of water.

"There's nothing else?" I asked.

Tlaco showed the palms of his hands. "Of what use is hunger to the dying?"

"There's no hope then."

"Why should our fate be different from that of others who have fallen?"

Though our chance of survival seemed remote, we nonetheless drifted into rehearsing the options. They boiled down to three: we could either continue to fight, attempt to escape, or surrender in the hope of obtaining mercy. None appeared palatable. We thought the first two doomed to failure and the third unlikely to evoke a sympathetic response in those who worshipped such a vengeful god.

Should we then kill ourselves before the Spaniards got to us? The question came out of nowhere, and we began discussing how we might go about it as calmly as if we were planning a hunting trip. We had one weapon between us: a double-edged obsidian sword we called *macahuitl*. One of us could give the other a fatal blow – no problem. But what then? How could the other guarantee himself a swift end? And which one of us would perform the double deed? We both volunteered but since I was wearing the sword, the decision fell to me. I would be the one.

Tlaco made no attempt to pull rank but accepted the choice and the proximity of death with the show of good cheer we had learned in the Calmecac. Unflinching bravery in the face of death, readiness to meet one's fate no matter what it might be, these were the qualities demanded of an officer. Not that any of us had ever expected to murder our own, but we knew well enough that any battle – even a minor skirmish – might end with our capture and sacrifice. Death at the hands of an enemy we looked upon as a blessing for it bestowed right of entry to the realm of Tonatiuh, the sun and god of light. Surely the end we now planned for ourselves would deserve the same reward for we were acting not to please ourselves but in defiance of the Spaniards, to deny them the pleasure of killing us. Such was our thinking.

By now, the sun was casting his first rays across the armoury entrance. Tlaco stood for a few moments in the glow, bathing himself in a warmth that he said not even the Spaniards could extinguish. Head bowed, he murmured a few words of prayer before rejoining me in the shadow of the interior. "Clouds are forming over Texcoco. It will rain," he said. We embraced and, despite my training, I felt tears coursing down my cheeks.

"I pray that we might be reunited in the next world," he murmured as he prised himself free from my grasp. "Now strike directly at my neck and for god's sake don't waver."

He stood stiff and upright in front of me, his eyes fixed on mine, unwavering. I raised the sword and drew back my arm. As I did so, a voice that might have been Tlaco's or mine or merely a noise in my head urged me on. "Do it. Do it now. If you hesitate you will fail. Think of the shame."

I thought of the shame, but hesitated regardless, and the voice proved to be right. I couldn't do it – not to Tlaco nor to anyone I loved or of my race. And in that faltering moment, I seemed to hear a different message, that our task on earth should never be to seek death, but to find a way to live until the gods themselves called us.

My fingers loosened their grip on the weapon and it dropped on the floor between us. Tlaco made no attempt to pick it up. We hugged each other, then went outside, leaving the instrument of death lying where it had fallen.

SIXTY-ONE

TLATELOLCO – 1521

Alva

Our steps led us towards the market square – slow, distressing steps because the streets were congested with civilians, most of them sitting on the ground or leaning against walls. They looked resigned, defeated. Some spotted Tlaco's insignia of office or my soldier's uniform and reached up as we brushed past, imploring us to help them. We offered soothing words, but there was nothing we could do.

Conditions at the market were, if anything, even worse. Civilians were packed so tightly together that they seemed at first glance indistinguishable one from the other, like heads of corn in a field. How long had they been waiting there? Fetid and barely breathable, the air resounded with cries of anguish and the chanting of desolate prayers. Many were shivering, their faces masked in fear. Overhead, dark clouds cast the square into shadow as if seeking to hide the wretchedness. Out of the question to search for our loved ones among such a crowd.

Having barely penetrated the periphery, we came to a halt, two among countless others and, like them, bewildered and without resource.

I pressed my lips to Tlaco's ear so that he could hear me over the noise. "What do we do?"

Tlaco responded with a gesture of mingled rebuke and despair. How in the name of all the gods would he know?

A series of sharp cracks made the question irrelevant. I had heard such noises on the battlefield: Spanish arquebuses. A hush descended over the square as it used to do when the emperor appeared to his people or a high priest raised his knife for the sacrifice of a noble captive. It lasted for a few breaths and then screams rang out, terrible, piercing screams of pain and terror. From somewhere close to our left came another volley, then another and another from different quarters. People ran into each other in blind panic, trampling the fallen underfoot, advancing and recoiling in response to the direction of fire, while Spanish soldiers stood guard at all the entrances and hacked down whoever tried to escape the encirclement. I assumed with cold resignation such as I had never before felt that the final massacre had begun, and what remained of our nation would soon be lying in pools of blood.

Tlaco and I had now melted into the throng which carried us along in a continuous and aimless momentum. A thrust to one side drew my attention: a contingent of Spanish soldiers with drawn swords were pushing their way into the market square. Fanning out, they slashed left and right as if they were clearing undergrowth. I cried out to Quetzalcóatl and braced myself for the blow that would end my life. I saw a flash, the blade in its descent, and a patch of sky, white, brilliant, so dazzling that it could be nothing other than the opening to the underworld along which I must be travelling already; but then a crash rang out louder by far than any of the Spanish guns, and straight away I felt a torrent on my head, and knew that what I had heard was thunder, and that I was not en route to the gods but still standing among the frailties of human kind, beneath the fury of heaven.

Long and hard the rain fell that day, as if Tlaloc had taken pity on the earth and come to wash it clean of blood. It fell on all the misery of our world, on our own and on our enemies alike, fell on the still-burning embers of our homes and on the rubble and cinders and ashes of our temples, fell as if the living and the dead and all the future generations of our race were pouring out their grief.

Yet the rain saved us, for as the clouds poured out their tears, the firing stopped, and the Spanish soldiers who had been slashing into us with their swords ceased their bloody work and retreated back along the causeway to the shelter of the palaces. When they were out of sight, we who had been packed together awaiting our fate surged out in every direction like an exhalation of breath. An irresistible human tide carried me out of the market precinct down several side streets and along the causeway as far as the ruined outskirts of the capital. When I was at last able to stand still, Tlaco was no longer with me. Sodden and shivering with exhaustion and fear, I found shelter in a half-ruined building and waited for the sun's return.

It rained for many days thereafter until the canals overflowed their banks and even the causeways became partially swamped. Some low-lying neighbourhoods flooded, and trampling feet churned open spaces into mud. Once the rains had ceased, our people began making their way along the causeways into exile or, more likely, into slavery, for most were rounded up and delivered into the hands of Spanish officers. Our great city was emptying like water draining from a broken urn.

For my part, I opted to stay, hoping that the family wouldn't try to leave without me and that sooner or later we would come upon each other. Besides, if I did try to depart and managed to evade the Spaniards, where would I go? To what purpose? Wasn't it better to die among the ruins of home than to live as an outcast among aliens?

I hooked up with a group of fellow survivors who had also opted to remain behind. We found shelter in a half-destroyed mansion and lived on whatever we could find: minnows caught in the shallows, grubs, flies, the rotting discards of Spanish feasts. Once, on a forage, we uncovered a hoard of corn concealed behind a pile of rubble. Most of it was damp and mouldy, but we salvaged what we could and cooked it over a raw flame. I can still taste that corn. No meal was ever more welcome nor better flavoured, for we were starved to wretchedness.

Who were my companions? They changed from day to day. Each time we went out on sorties, one or two of us would not return, while other survivors would crawl out of hiding and beg to join us.

During this strange interval, we occupied ourselves in the evenings by stitching together a poem drawn from what we remembered of other poems, with words and phrases of our own added as they came to us. We never considered the work complete, but we were quietly and sadly proud of our efforts and each of us learned it by heart.

All this happened
While we watched and trembled
and the skies
echoed with our cries

Broken swords lay scattered in the streets
Our houses burned, their walls were stained with red
Heaps of stones stand where temples stood
Worms and vultures feasted on the dead

A price was on our head
Two fingers of corn, a bowl of flies
Became our daily bread.

Strangers rooted in the blackened ruins
For gold and slaves the precious spoils of war
Cries of loss and mourning rent the air
An alien god had occupied our shore.

Suddenly the sun stood still
Noon became our night
Jaguars devoured every
Mexica in sight

Giants strode the earth that day
Greeted each in turn
Do not fall down, for he who falls
In Spanish flames will burn.

In time, the Spaniards rounded up survivors who were still in the
city, and I, like my companions, began a new life as a slave.

SIXTY-TWO

MEXICO CITY – 1976

James

We convened in one of the little classrooms in the garden: Fernández, Ayala, Balcedo, Mendoza, myself. Mendoza presided.

"Our discussion will centre on Fernández's paper. The lead for the first edition of our journal," Mendoza said in a tone that precluded alternatives. "A superb analysis if I may say so. Anyone wish to comment?"

Long pause.

I heard myself cough. Fernández stared at the floor.

My thoughts wander. I am crossing the Hidalgo garden in Coyoacán. Elderly strollers make their measured way through the open space. At the fountain of the two coyotes, a couple sit on the low surround nuzzling; dogs bark at each other in the distance; birdsong chirrups from high branches and rooftops. Outside the church of St John the Baptist, an organ-grinder reels a tune from the days of revolution: "si me han de matar mañana que me maten de una vez."[57] *Background harmonies as defining as the contours of a landscape. But the dogs have fallen silent; the birds too have stopped singing; and the tinkling notes of the street-organ have faded. A hush descends as if the neighbourhood has melted away unobserved like a person's life. My footsteps echo on the cobblestones. The ground shakes beneath them. Branches clatter to the ground. Shards of stonework tumble from the church façade, clattering on the cobblestones. A feeling of helplessness grips me, of being pinned by forces too powerful to resist and too encompassing to evade. Minutes later, the ground resettles, the harmonies resume their round, the barking of dogs, birdsong, and everything is almost as before with only tree litter and a scattering of grit and rubble beneath the church wall to show that the earth has stirred.*

Mendoza was smiling. Ayala sat in his familiar pose, fingers touching. Balcedo, thin-lipped, fixed his gaze on Fernández.

I cleared my throat. "May I...?" No one looked at me. I regretted breaking the silence, but now had to continue. "With. Fernández's permission..." My voice trembled. "I wonder if I may ask a question and I beg in advance to excuse me if I sound naive because my knowledge is sketchy and my aim is only to learn."

Too prolix, I told myself. My humility rings false. A fly buzzed, collided repeatedly with the window pane. Balcedo opened the window to let it out.

At last Fernández raised his head. He looked at the ceiling, then at the garden, then at the wall behind where I sat. "A group like ours," he said, "depends for its existence on trust in each other, and on the protection of this institution from political interference. Lamentably, it has come to my notice that a rat has entered the premises. A spy. Some might call him a Judas, for he is ready to betray everything we stand for. Instead of keeping what we do confidential, he has talked about our work to outsiders,

---

57 "If they're going to kill me tomorrow, let them kill me right now."

criticized and mocked us. Who knows if his purpose is not more sinister…"

Animated now, his locks shaking with every phrase, Fernández went on, finding new phrases for the same thoughts, as if seeking a more perfect expression of his anger, while we listeners sat mute, heads bowed like lackeys before a dread autocrat. When at length he fell silent, Mendoza told us that the meeting was over. As we broke up, I asked Fernández if his fury was directed at me. He left without answering.

"We will continue the discussion later," Mendoza said, his voice barely audible above the scraping of chairs.

Six weeks went by before we met again. Carmen had persuaded the government to acquire the old International University, whch stood on the western edge of the city, and we spent most of the intervening period moving into sixty-four thousand square metres of space, with offices, classrooms and lecture halls laid out among trees, grasses and flower beds.

Sandwiched between the new and the old Toluca highways, the campus peered over the latter into the same garbage dump upon which I had stumbled years before. Within the perimeter fence, a seat of learning staffed by intellectuals, theorists, earnest thinkers about the future of the continent and its inconceivable inequalities, specialists in the complex equations and contorted syntax of academia; beyond it, the objects of so much thinking, the poor and downtrodden, Pablo Neruda's *innumerable y castigada familia de los pobres…*[58]

Our working life mutated. So many were the buildings that it became possible to divide different disciplines geographically: the economists in one area, the political scientists in another, the sociologists in yet a third. Where before we had rubbed shoulders daily and were ever drifting in and out of each other's rooms, we now found ourselves working in isolated pockets.

---

58 "The innumerable, chastised family of the poor…"

Because the cavernous cafeteria was furnished with small square tables that could accommodate no more than half a dozen, we no longer gathered for lunch around a big table but dined in unannounced hierarchies: Bustamante and Carmen invariably together, usually with Fernández and one or two others of distinguished bearing, then Mendoza and Ayala, and so on down the ranks. For my part, I never sat again with the luminaries, but ate as often as not alone or with one or two students, or occasionally with Pablo until, a few short weeks after the move, he told me he had tendered his resignation and would be taking up a position with the Organization of American States.

He came to account for his departure armed, as usual, with coffee and doughnuts. I asked him if he and his colleagues really were revolutionaries. Even to my own ears, the question sounded naive, something a child might ask, less a question than a plea for confirmation that the house would not tumble when the wolf puffed at the walls.

"What is a revolutionary?" he asked morosely. Heaving himself to his feet, he asked me to join him at the window. "Did you see the slum on the other side?"

We stood for a few moments gazing down at the rough-painted hoardings that at street level hid the *inferno* from public view.

"In the end," he continued, "we must decide for ourselves who we are. Labels aren't so important." He turned towards me. "We probably won't meet again. Bureaucracy will swallow me at the OAS. You are young and with luck will avoid our fate."

"I won't forget you, Pablo."

We embraced, both of us moved.

"Did you find Neruda's *España en el Corazón*?" he asked.

I shook my head.

"It ends like this." He lowered his head, fixing his eyes on the floor.

"Preguntaréis por qué su poesía
no nos habla del sueño, de las hojas,
de los grandes volcanes de su país natal?
Venid a ver la sangre por las calles,
venid a ver
la sangre por las calles,
venid a ver la sangre
por las calles!"[59]

Twenty years passed before I came across a copy of the book – it was never easy to find in those days – and was able to understand that he hadn't been asking me for information but was trying to convey something to me of his own experience. It was the only time he ever touched on what had happened to him and his people.

Those lines from the great poet were Pablo's parting words. From time to time over the years, I have searched for him, but he was right about disappearing. I have found no trace of him, no evidence even that he lived, still less of our brief friendship. "Man melts away," Donne tells us, "as if he were a statue not of earth but of snow."

---

59   "You will ask why doesn't your poetry speak of dreams, of leaves, of the great volcanoes of your native land? Come and see the blood in the streets, come and see, the blood in the streets, come and see the blood, in the streets!"

SIXTY-THREE

TENOCHTITLAN – 1522

Alva

Those who wish to know what happened need do no more than trust in what they see. Their eyes will show them rubble, building sites, white-skinned captains armed and full of anger, the people labouring, submissive.

After my capture, I joined a demolition squad working on the temple of Mixcoatl. Our task: to smash all the idols and stack the building materials for future use. Learning that I had been an army officer, the Spanish overseer promoted me to deputy foreman, an honour for which the sole reward was the lash if I was seen to allow any slackening of effort.

Once we had levelled the temple, we carried most of the stones to the site earmarked for the Church of Santa María de Tlacopan. There I was stripped of my new rank and reduced to a common slave – construction being a more noble calling than demolition and therefore requiring Spanish supervisors at every level. They in turn received orders from a priest who took overall charge. In any case, none of us had a clue how to build these structures, so we just followed orders – lifting here, laying there according to what we were told. The priest had everything written down in drawings and he'd start the working day by staring at them and then taking distances and heights, translating what he saw on the parchments into the shape of what we built.

I say "we", but we were a shifting crew. Sometimes we were many, not just from Tenochtitlan, but Tlaxcala, Texiutlan, Cuauhnahuac, Amecameca, even further afield; then from one day to the next we would shrink to a handful because some had been called to a more urgent job elsewhere. Our little church probably didn't seem too important compared with all the other clearing and building that was going on.

Each time our numbers changed, Father Hernández would reorganize. When we were much reduced in number, he brought in other kinds of Spaniards to compensate: novice priests and monks, junior administrators, foot soldiers. Once or twice a dignitary would arrive to inspect the works. I learned to distinguish the status of all these various Spaniards from their mode of dress. Important citizens wear fine clothes, rich in colour and ample in cloth, except for their leg stockings and doublets, which fit tightly and must surely feel uncomfortable in the heat of day. Attached to a sash round their hip or shoulder, they carry swords with decorated handles and scabbards inlaid with gold and silver. Common soldiers dress more simply in coarse cloth of few colours, and their weapons and scabbards are likewise unadorned. Holy men, too, differ in rank. Most noble of those I have seen was a bishop who visited our building site arrayed as a prince with jewelled cloak and a cross on his breast set with precious stones on a silver necklace. How Father Hernández fawned over him, bowed to him, attended his every whim! They say bishops wield a king's power so that even the greatest warriors must kneel before them and kiss their hands, though I believe this is not because they are gods themselves but only that they stand for god. Theirs is a complicated system that I don't pretend to understand. Different layers and kinds of power seem to exist side by side. An almighty emperor lives across the ocean and rules the whole earth. All people work for him and obey him. At the same time, a great god who dwells in the sky commands the emperor through the bishops and priests who are his servants. While the emperor must bow to these servants, he in turn receives their homage because he rules by the grace of god. Confusing to say the least. I wouldn't be surprised if the emperor and god's servants ended up fighting each other from time to time over who has more power.

SIXTY-FOUR

TENOCHTITLAN – 1522

Alva

When my turn came for secondment, they sent me by a trick of fate to my own district. Fire, as I already knew, had swept through the area. Roofs had collapsed; walls that once rang with the voices and music of my neighbours stood open to the air, scorched, blackened, as lifeless as the discarded chrysalis of a butterfly. Shards of pottery were the only signs of domestic life. I searched our family compound as I had done briefly before in hope of finding a keepsake beneath the rubble, but without success. Gone were the beautiful blankets, the sculpture of Quetzalcóatl my brother had brought from his travels and that had graced the entrance to our home, the gift of quetzal feathers the emperor had bestowed on my mother, the avocado tree my grandfather had planted and that furnished half the neighbourhood with fruits, the zinnias, marigolds and dahlias my mother and aunt grew in a patch of earth behind our house. All had vanished along with the laughter, the smell and touch of those who lived there. Love itself had fled, leaving behind a chill the midday sun could not warm. With nothing left to retrieve beyond sad reminders of loss, I felt only a desire to finish things off, to erase any sign that my family had dwelled there and so remove any further opportunity for our conquerors to tread on their memory. I set about knocking down the walls and clearing the detritus with an energy that surprised my fellow workers, that is until I told them we were clearing away my past, and then they understood.

Fate denied me even the small satisfaction of completing the task. Before the work was complete, Father Hernández arrived to fetch me back. He'd told someone high up that he couldn't manage without me. I think he had to beg forgiveness from his god for stretching the truth because he could have found a replacement easily enough. He needed me because he'd heard me repeat bits and pieces of Spanish I'd picked up from guards while we were demolishing Mixcoatl's temple and decided I was the one to teach him our language.

From then on, each morning, before building work started, I had to sit with him. He would point to things or make gestures, and as soon as I understood his meaning, I would tell him the word or expression in our tongue. Then he would transcribe it into a book. That's how I learned Spanish too, and how to write. We would make up phrases using the words in his book and others I might suggest and then we would search for equivalents. Not that we always found them. We had such different ways of being and of seeing the world that even the simplest expressions seemed to pass by each other in translation, like strangers on a dark night.

A good man Father Hernández. We've watched each other grow old and, although I wouldn't say we're friends, we've come to an understanding of our differences. I believe he thinks of me as no less human than himself, something not all his co-religionists are willing to concede. Apart from status, religion is what separates us most. He thinks our gods barbaric and refers to them as the Devil's henchmen, while I find his god – well, the truth is, I don't find him. The reverence on Father Hernández's face when he speaks of his faith reminds me of Huehue's pose of solemnity when about to let fly with a joke. Whenever the good Father refers to his lord, as like as not he'll look towards heaven with an expression of suffering as if someone had stamped on his toe or kicked him in the avocados, and he's constantly saying we are all sinners – including himself – and that we have to repent. His voice changes too, especially when he's giving a sermon or reading a scripture during a service. It becomes a little inhuman, maybe the effect of the echo inside the building, or the fact that priests don't conduct their ceremonies in Spanish but in a language called Latin that few can understand. I suppose it could be the language of his god who speaks through him, but somehow I doubt it, and anyway he makes no such claim himself. After so many years as his servant, I still have to stifle an impulse to laugh when the penitent mood overtakes him, he raises his eyes, clasps his hands together and starts chanting.

We had barely completed the church foundations when I ran into my aunt Izel. I had been sent with a gang to fetch a consignment of stones for the building, and while loading one of the handcarts, I spotted her walking nearby with her hand held out, begging. So altered was she in appearance that I took a moment to be sure it was her. Her hair had lost most of its colour and all of its lustre, her clothes were ragged, and in place of her upright bearing, quickness of step and brisk sensuality, she moved haltingly with a stoop, and as if disengaged from the life around her. I called her by name and she turned towards me, head bowed, hand still held out in supplication, but with no sign that she had recognized my voice. A group of Spanish soldiers strode past talking loudly. One of them brushed against her, knocking her backwards into a pile of rubble. To my surprise, he apologized and after helping her back to her feet took a mamey from his shoulder bag and offered it to her. She savaged it with an intensity familiar to those who have known true hunger. I waited until she had finished eating before calling her name again. This time she knew me and fell into my arms.

SIXTY-FIVE

TOLUCA HIGHWAY – 1976

James

We had been assigned a seminar room of our own: oblong with a blackboard on one wall facing a semi-circle of upright metal chairs. Opposite the blackboard, a row of windows looked out onto a patch of lawn and a cluster of squat, whitewashed classrooms.

I arrived early feeling nervous, hoping the tension of the previous meeting would have dissipated in the excitement of the move and the passing of time, but conscious (how could I forget?) that Fernández's furious outburst had followed my question to him. I could find no reason for his anger, nor grasp why I might be its cause. Yet who, other than myself, could have so provoked him?

As I sat down, an image flashed through my mind that we were somewhere else, a kindlier place, that the blackboard was a broad lintel over a hearth and we were seated *en famille* before a log fire.

Night is falling. A gentle glow from the flames illuminates our faces and turns the windows behind us into mirrors reflecting wayward shadows of ourselves, melding us together into a single body bound by light and community of feeling. Fernández is speaking, not about stagflation or the conspiracies of fifth columnists, but about empty quadrants and black boxes. A pile of papers sits on a table beside him, but he is not referring to them. He gazes alternately at the ceiling and out of the windows at the sky as if verifying with heaven the truth of what he has to say. His language pours out like a particoloured streamer, so intricately patterned that it might be God's own invention, a complex fugue whose form we might admire without knowing whether or not it is beautiful. Our countries, he is saying, either have poverty with a little growth or poverty with no growth. They cannot advance into the modern world without know-how. We need to seize the black box of technology which alone contains the key to unlocking the gates of Eden, and to life. Yes: our challenge in this little room is to seize the key to life and bring it to our Americas.

How long he spoke in my thoughts I can't say – perhaps no more than a few minutes in my mind – but I knew the ideas were his and somewhere I must have heard something of them, even if he may have voiced them as no more than simple sketches or interrogations for the body of work that would later make him famous. He spoke with an implacable conviction, like a potentate dictating terms of submission to a conquered people, or a pontiff delivering messages from the deity. He would suffer no contradiction, but whoever bowed to his wisdom would thereafter know the truth and live in peace. I found myself wanting to believe that he knew best.

My reverie ended with his arrival. We shook hands formally but did not embrace. Balcedo and Mendoza followed close behind, the latter breathless. He had been on the telephone to Washington from where he had recently returned. Ayala, last to arrive, offered a limp hand and a diplomatic smile to each of us in turn. He was a stranger in the room, perhaps more so than I.

A waitress from the cafeteria appeared with a tray of coffee which she poured into small cups and handed round. She was small, dark, her hair braided into twin pigtails at the back. No one acknowledged her presence; we heard her voice when she asked permission to withdraw, "*con permiso*", as soft as a whisper.

"We will continue from where we left off last time," Mendoza said. He glanced at Balcedo. I felt myself trembling. Balcedo stood up, changed his mind, resumed his seat. Fernández said "let's go" in a tone of brisk encouragement.

"Something is amiss," Balcedo began. "We can't carry on in this way."

Several sentences followed that echoed Fernández's intervention at our previous gathering: a fifth columnist had come among us, a rat, whose motives could only be sinister.

Fernández, impatient, interrupted. "We must extirpate the poisonous element in our midst."

I told myself not to react, to remain silent, but the admonishment came too late. A mist clouded my senses.

Ignoring Balcedo, I turned on Fernández. "Clearly, I am the rat and it is I who needs to be removed. Why am I a traitor? You don't know. You have no evidence, because there is none."

Mendoza stood up, angry. "This is a powder keg."

"A little calm, my dear friend," Ayala said, addressing me as if he were offering consolation for the death of a pet.

"I thought you were revolutionaries." I sneered. "Extirpate... Is that what revolutionaries get up to in their spare time? Good fascist word, extirpate. No doubt one of Pinochet's favourites."

In my rage, I had fallen on a nasty insult.

Mendoza, furious, tore off his spectacles. "If you don't shut up, we'll have to use other methods."

"Just like Pinochet," I shot back. "You talk of freedom but you know only violence and repression."

"One moment," Fernández said, his voice calm. "Let's try to be rational."

"Rational! I've just been threatened by your friend here. What's rational about that?"

"Listen for a moment."

"No, Fernández. You don't deserve to be heard."

Blind with fury, I stormed out, banging the door behind me, and walked into a pine tree that stood beside the classroom door, gashing my head on the bark. Holding a handkerchief against the wound, I made my way to Carmen's office and tendered my resignation.

She looked nonplussed.

"They think I'm a CIA agent," I said. "They threatened me."

"Threatened?"

I repeated Mendoza's words.

She gestured at the blood-soaked handkerchief I still held in place on my forehead. "He didn't do that to you?"

"I ran into a tree."

She chuckled. "You must forgive them. They are under strain. It's not easy to be a refugee. They live on their nerves. Always on the alert for danger. Pinochet's tentacles reach a long way."

"As far as Mexico?"

"They say he has spies everywhere. The United States, Europe."

I had cause to remember this remark at the time of Orlando Letelier's murder in Washington DC six months later. A senior minister in Allende's government, Letelier had spent a year in Pinochet's dungeons before international pressure had forced his release. He ended up in the US capital where he worked for the Institute for Policy Studies and lobbied against the Pinochet regime. Chilean agents planted the bomb that killed both him and a young colleague, Ronni Moffat, with whom he was travelling to work. A small plaque at Sheridan Circle, 23rd Street NW and Massachusetts Avenue, commemorates the event.

"You will find other work," Carmen said. "If you need a reference…"

"Thanks."

"Shame this didn't work out for you." She stood up, shook my hand, and offered her cheek. "Why don't you have the nurse patch you up before you leave?"

SIXTY-SIX

TENOCHTITLAN – 1524

Alva

How could I begin to describe my joy at finding my aunt Izel alive? Holding onto each other as if to reassure ourselves that we were not dreaming, we whispered like guilty creatures fearful of discovery, and she spoke words that have remained carved into my heart as a pattern into stone.

"The cruellest casualty of war, my little nephew, is not destruction or death but love."

So many questions to ask of each other. News of the family. What had become of my mother? Izel confirmed she and my mother had been together in Tlatelolco at the moment when the Spaniards started firing and Lord Tlaloc had poured out his anger, but then they had lost sight of each other in the ensuing chaos. She wept as she recalled the hellish scene of terror and flight. I asked her if she had any idea of where my mother might be, but she just bowed her head. I think she knew more but preferred to keep to herself details that could only cause me pain.

Of my cousins Cualli and Mazatl, she had heard nothing. She knew only the fate of her beloved Teudile: a Spanish officer had beaten him to death.

"No one knows why, little nephew. Perhaps he had refused an order. He was working in the *chinampas* in Xochimilco. They say he cracked a joke that made the others laugh, and the Spanish overseer, who didn't speak our language, took offence and whipped him. You know what Teudile was like. Always a rebel. Never afraid of anything. I used to beg him to be obedient and respectful to the conquerors, but it was like asking him to be someone else. They say he refused to cry out or show that he was hurting, so the Spaniard carried on whipping and whipping until he died."

All this Izel told me in those first breathless moments of our finding each other, and I in turn gave her an account of my own journey into slavery. We could not, however, tarry long. All the handcarts were loaded and the other members of the work gang were already on their way back to the building site. If they arrived without me, my absence would be noticed. I asked my aunt where she was living.

"I have nothing," she said. "I sleep wherever tiredness overcomes me."

Her words conveyed such helplessness that I could see no way of leaving her alone. So I asked her to accompany me to our little community. Servants and slaves lived in separate encampments for men and women. There was surely room enough for another.

Izel shook her head. "No, little nephew. Your master will not take me in. I am old and broken and of no use."

We argued – gently, of course, so as not to bruise the happiness of finding each other. I told her that my master was a good man who would surely not turn her away from his door, though I was less certain of this than I pretended. He was a priest of a religion that he suspected I still did not share, and I had no leverage with him other than that of part-time language teacher. But I hid my doubts and assured my aunt that we would be well received.

"You don't understand," my aunt insisted. "My only wish is to join Teudile and your mother – my dear sister – wherever they might be."

I told her I wouldn't leave her and that if we stood much longer arguing, I would be in trouble myself with Father Hernández – the man of god who would otherwise be only too willing to receive her and give her dignified work. That argument won the day. She would not see me punished on her account.

As I had hoped, the good Father took her in and gave her work as a washerwoman and domestic. "A valuable addition to our household," he told me, in a tone so earnest that he might have been praying, and he smiled as he smiles at worshippers when he greets them on holy days so that I might understand he was but observing the will of his god.

So Izel joined the female team. There were eight or ten of them. They cooked and served meals, fetched water, washed our clothes. Some provided other services as well. The prettiest, a Texcoco girl called Cozcatl, was Father Hernández's favourite and could often be seen to-ing and fro-ing his dwelling. She had a way of walking that made her dress swing from side to side and fired the imagination of every man who saw her, myself included. A jealous soldier, whom Cozcatl had rebuffed, was foolish enough to congratulate Father Hernández on his success with the ladies. The good Father blushed, lost his temper, and started talking about god and protesting that he wasn't a sinner. For a few days, Cozcatl kept away from Father Hernández, but she was soon visiting him again just as before.

During one of our early-morning language lessons, I asked the Father why he had so taken offence and he explained that priests weren't allowed to touch women and that the head of the Church – the Pope they call him – chastised any priest who succumbed to temptations of the flesh. That's how he described the joys of love: "temptations of the flesh". Seems Christians believe sexual congress is wicked. Priests set the example by

367

not making children, while the rest are not supposed to enjoy it (though I believe they go to it in secret with the same pleasure as we do). I wonder if we will ever come to grips with the culture of our conquerors.

Having Izel nearby proved a mixed blessing. Knowing that a member of our family had survived and being able to see each other from time to time gave comfort, but it also served as a constant reminder of all we had lost. By the time we stumbled upon each other, I had already resigned myself to solitude and to closing out the past. I had figured the only way to carry on was to avoid thinking on family and friends, to inure myself to feelings that could only cause pain. Izel's reappearance reopened wounds that had barely stopped bleeding, and I know I had the same effect on her because she told me.

"I love you, little nephew," she said one day. "But I see your mother in your eyes, and your brother and sister."

Opportunities to talk at length occurred rarely, since our work kept us busy. Usually we could do little more than exchange a few phrases at mealtimes or when – as sometimes happened – it would fall to her to bring water to the men on the building site. Our discourse scarcely varied from one meeting to the next. I would try to sound cheerful, extolling our good fortune at being reunited and under Father Hernández's protection, and she would mumble a few words in reply in a tone shorn of her old energy and bubble.

"This is no life, little nephew. You are young and must live. I wish only to join the departed and to wait for you there."

I'd urge her not to be pessimistic because the future couldn't be worse than what we had already suffered. In reply, she would purse her lips and stare at the ground, which was her way of telling me that the discussion served no purpose.

Nothing I said could draw her from her sadness but I had no inkling of the darker thoughts that must have been occupying her mind. I had made my own decision to take what I could from life no matter what, even if it meant slavery. I spoke to her of survival as a kind of revenge, a refusal to be conquered. My words sounded so convincing in my own ears that I felt sure she would come to think likewise. That she might truly differ in her view of things did not occur to me until the day I saw her washing linen. I had been sent on an errand that took me past the washhouse, and there she was, one of three, on their knees, pounding sheets against flat stones. Beside each of the women stood a pile of dirty linen, and behind them rows of washing hanging on lines. My aunt was kneeling over her stone, eyes on her task, arms working, body moving rhythmically. She laboured back and forth along the length of the cloth, paused to examine her work, pounded some more. When she was satisfied, she plunged it into a tub of fresh water, then retrieved it little by little, wringing out the excess water with her hands. For a moment, as she engaged in this last task, she raised her head and looked in my direction. I waved, but she gave no sign of having seen me and I repressed an impulse to call out to her. The expression on her face was vacant, exhausted, lifeless. I sensed she didn't want to be recognized.

Shortly afterwards, she disappeared. Father Hernández ordered a search through the compound and then in neighbouring streets, but there was no sign of her. She had spoken to no one about leaving, nor had anyone seen her go. A few days later, they found her body floating among the *chinampas* of Xochimilco. I knew that this was no accident: she had gone in pursuit of her beloved.

Father Hernández brought me the news. Ill at ease in expressing sadness at the misfortune of a servant, he gave a garbled account, starting in my language and, when his vocabulary failed him, ending in his own with much gesturing and shaking of the head. I worked out the message well before he got round to delivering it, but then had to listen while he lectured me about god's mercy and kindness. His nonsense only worsened my grief. What mercy had his lord bestowed on us? What kindness? No comfort could

369

come my way from that source, only bitterness and despair. I wanted to tell him so, but the courage failed me. Besides, he so clearly believed what he was saying that I reckoned he wouldn't grasp what we knew only too well, namely that gods show mercy only to their own.

I took time to recover from Izel's death. In truth, her loss continues to haunt me: the manner of her going, my inability to penetrate her despair. I ask myself why she didn't confide in me. Did she think I was too young to understand or to carry the burden? Or that I would try to dissuade her from her purpose? What, finally, pushed her to the edge? I picture her as she was when I last saw her, bent over the washing and looking up at me without reaction. Had she really not seen me? Or had the sight of me watching her proved unbearable, the awareness that we had both fallen down the ranks of humanity and now ate the dirt that fate fed to slaves?

Sometimes I wonder why I didn't follow Aunt Izel to Xochimilco. I admit to thinking on it more than once. The answer, I suppose, is that I can't find it in me to die by my own hand. Quetzalcóatl teaches that we should live as long and well as we can, and that no matter how deep our humiliations, we should ride with them until he sends for us. Yes, I do believe that, and I pray he will pardon Izel for her disobedience.

SIXTY-SEVEN

MEXICO CITY – 1976

James

Olivia left me, of course. I won't rehearse the details, except to say that she cemented the separation by having an affair with a junior official at the German embassy. The pain – that of a wounded ego (for it is little more) – seems hardly worth speaking of. You may know the story. Sleepless nights, mornings when you can't get out of bed, days that drift by in a turmoil of longing when every movement or gesture seems futile; tears, surges of impotent rage, dreams of revenge and of reconciliation, hatred, self-loathing.

Rejection, unemployment, the contempt of my colleagues at CENCIAS, even Margarita's refusal to acknowledge me at Fernández's party, all brought me face to face with failure. Defeat is a condition of life and comes to most of us sooner or later, but perhaps we do not truly digest it until we are confronted with the frustration of an intense desire, the exposing of some treasured illusion about ourselves and our place in the world. And then our little structure breaks like an eggshell against the sharp flint of reality.

Days passed during which I lay in bed or padded round the walls of my apartment as if it were a prison cell. María Isabel came twice but I sent her away to prevent her catching my illness which I told her was contagious. The telephone rang from time to time but I did not answer it.

Midway in the second week of my funk, I chose a psychiatrist from the *páginas amarillas*[60] and dialled the number.

A secretary put me through.

"*Doctor Herzog a sus órdenes,*" the voice slow, elderly.

"*Buenos días, Doctor.*"

"What can I do for you?"

"I'm depressed."

He gave me an appointment for the afternoon. I took a shower and dressed for the first time in a week.

---

60 Yellow pages

SIXTY-EIGHT

TENOCHTITLAN – 1525

Alva

We had been working on the church for a good while when Huehue showed up with an important-looking Spaniard. I was high on the scaffold when I saw them enter the compound. In my excitement, I kicked a piece of carved stone ready to be fitted and it fell over the side of the platform onto the ground, fortunately without damage. Sebastián, the master for whom I was working, slapped me hard in the face.

"Watch what you're doing, you fucking little idiot. You could have killed someone."

My nose started to bleed and when I tried to wipe it with my sleeve, he knocked my arm away.

"Never mind your nose. Do something like that again and it'll be you over the side. Understand?"

Compact, with bulging biceps and rough hands large enough for a man twice his size, Maestro Sebastián had more than one side to him. A clever craftsman, he could carve patterns and

373

reliefs from raw stone so that they looked and fitted perfectly, and I never saw him err with knife or chisel. Judging by his demeanour, however, his skill gave him scant pleasure. He could scarcely open his mouth without unleashing a curse, and never lost an opportunity to vent his humour on those who worked under him. He would fly into a rage on the slightest pretext, and then look around for someone to punish. None of us escaped a beating at his hands. Though Father Hernández didn't approve of brutality, he never intervened when he saw Sebastián wielding a whip or using a fist, but walked away as if nothing untoward was happening. Only a special kind of Spaniard ever defended a Mexica, no matter how unjust our treatment; I guess that's still so.

This time, as soon as Sebastián had calmed down, I sought permission to answer a call of nature.

"Clean your filthy nose while you're at it," Sebastián said. "The sight of blood makes me puke. Just as well Father Hernández likes you. Otherwise you'd be dead meat."

I ran off to the latrines, and it was there that I found Huehue.

He looked much older than when I had last seen him, hunched, face criss-crossed with wrinkles, the skin of his neck ragged like an old cloth.

Shy as ever of displaying affection, he made a pretence of gruff displeasure. "What in the name of all the gods are you doing alive," he said.

I gave him the outline of my route to slavery, but of his own survival he said little beyond showing me an ugly scar on his leg.

"A Spanish sword saved me. Couldn't walk so couldn't fight. Spent the end of the war lying down."

I asked the purpose of his visit and in reply, he led me by the arm to the cesspit.

"Remember what I always told you? There's always work for a shit-shoveller. I'm back at the old job. Nobody knows more about shit than me. That's why I'm here: to make sure the community has a proper service. My master, Don Diego, gives the orders and I carry them out. He says it's all about preventing disease. At least, that's what I think he means."

"You're an important figure," I teased.

"Spaniards don't like to get their hands dirty. We have to make the best of it." He looked at my nose. "Who did that to you?"

We walked over to the water jars which were stored between the kitchen and the laundry. Huehue took a piece of cloth, wetted it, and gently cleaned away the blood.

"Remember the girls across the lake?" he said.

"Couldn't forget."

"Those days will never come back. Not for me anyhow. Can't get it up any more. Stop laughing and hold still, otherwise your nose will start bleeding again." He dipped the cloth again into the water, squeezed it, and gave my face a final wipe. "Don't know whether it's age or defeat. When you don't own yourself any more. Know what I mean?"

"Uh huh."

"You're young. Don't waste time. Fuck as many girls as you can. Make babies. That's the true poetry of life."

Don Diego called and Huehue hurried off. I followed discreetly, staying close enough to overhear their conversation.

"What do you think?" Don Diego asked.

Huehue inclined his head. "You are right, Don Diego."

"Right, am I?"

"Yes, Don Diego."

"But I'm not sure if we can run a water course here or if it's better to remove the waste manually. Is there enough height for a tunnel?"

By the few words Huehue had already spoken, I could tell his Spanish was halting and that he hadn't fully understood the question. He lacked the benefit of daily sessions with Father Hernández.

"As Don Diego wishes, we will do it."

The Spaniard sighed and looked skywards. "Will no one teach these people to give a straight answer?" He turned back to Huehue. "You're supposed to be an expert."

"Waste is good," said Huehue. "Make plants grow."

Don Diego made a fist of his right hand and brought it down on the hilt of his sword. "Let's get out of here."

Turning on his heels, he marched off with Huehue trotting obediently a few paces behind.

I had tarried too long for Sebastián's liking. When I remounted the scaffolding, he glared at me malevolently. "Where the fuck have you been?"

I told him a lie: that I had run an errand for Father Hernández.

"Don't know what the holy Father sees in you. Know what a *pinche indio* is?"

"No, Don Sebastián."

He laughed. "A lousy Indian. Whenever anyone asks what you are, that's what you tell them. Say it after me. *Pinche indio.*"

"*Pinche indio.*"

"So what are you?"

"A lousy Indian, Don Sebastián."

He laughed and I laughed too – because I figured that's what he wanted.

SIXTY-NINE

MEXICO CITY – 1976

James

Hours to kill before my appointment. I stepped into the street, the traffic, the mid-morning sun unsteadily, as if I had just emerged from a hospital bed and were venturing abroad for the first time. I bought a newspaper from a street vendor before sinking into a chair under the awning at the *Soledad* café. *Soledad*, solitude, sun and age. My stomach heaved at the thought of food but I ordered orange juice, eggs and coffee.

When the juice arrived, I raised the glass, touched it to my lips, then replaced it on the table without drinking. For the last ten days, I had consumed only water and dry tortillas. Without knowing how, I had erected a barrier against flavour and nourishment. Food seemed faintly self-indulgent. A choice confronted me: I could either drink the orange juice or flee before the arrival of the eggs. I felt for my wallet. Thirty pesos would cover the bill including tip. I could leave the money before the waitress returned with my order. No explanation would be needed. Maybe she could eat the food herself or offer it to a beggar. My hands were shaking. I took two twenty-peso notes and placed them on the table. The extra ten would atone for my cowardice. I stared at them, blue, the colour of depression, freedom, the sky. Freedom to leave. Who needed it? I wanted to be told, ordered, so that the choice would not be mine. But I knew the order would be "Drink, idiot, drink!" Why not? If it didn't work, I could put the glass down again as I did before. I picked it up and this time put it to my lips and swallowed. The taste on my tongue was sweet and sharp, a sensation of surprise and pleasure. Pleasure? Were we so simple that something as trivial as a mouthful of juice could penetrate doubt and make light of hopelessness?

I glanced at the headline in the newspaper.

DESTAPADO – LOPEZ PORTILLO
RECIBE DEDAZO[61]
Mexico's finance minister last night received the news
that he will be our next president…

There would be an election, of course, but no matter how the electorate voted, ninety percent of the ballots would go to the candidate of the governing party – the PRI. That's how it worked: the outgoing president chose the incoming one.

Interior minister Mario Moya Palencia – long-time favourite for the top job – will now have to find something else to do with his time…He will be despondent, but the bookies will be quietly thanking President Echeverría for not choosing him.

On the inside pages, a sycophantic biography praised Lopez Portillo for his brilliance, modesty, and life-long defence of Mexico's democracy.

The waitress arrived with my order. What did she think of the new candidate?

---

61   Revealed – Lopez Portillo gets the nod.

"They're all the same as far I can see. So long as he's Mexican..."

"Of course he's Mexican."

"You never know nowadays."

"But the Constitution–"

"Ay, señor! Before they get to rule, they send our presidents to America for a *lavado de cerebro*."

"A brainwash?"

"*Sí, señor*. The *gringos* have to approve our leaders. Everybody knows that." She hesitated. "You're not American?"

"No."

"Thank goodness. I wouldn't like to offend."

I drank the orange juice and the coffee but could only stare at the eggs.

Dr Herzog's office was located in the *Portal de Mercaderes* (the Merchant's Gate) on the *Zócalo*, directly opposite the national palace and roughly where the palace of Axayácatl once stood. While staying there as Moctezuma's guests, Cortés and his men broke into a sealed room to find a hoard of gold and jewels.

Downtown Mexico City once qualified as the nation's most exclusive neighbourhood. This must have been so in the days of Tenochtitlan, and when the great square functioned as the administrative hub of New Spain, and yet again in 1821 when the flag of independence flew from the national palace. But these periods of elegance have been punctuated by longer ones, not so much of decline as of people's occupation, when the side streets, the periphery and the *Zócalo* itself bustled with market stalls, pedlars, musicians, fortune-tellers, scribes, typists, plumbers and brick-layers touting for work, shoe-shine men with little stools, pickpockets too, and pimps, and merchants of stolen goods. From time to time, the authorities have cleared away the commerce and restored the area to sterile vacancy, but the people have always worked their way back to take possession of a space traditionally

Aquí estuvieron las casas viejas de Moctezuma hasta 1521.

theirs. Lawyers, doctors and executives – the professionals – on the other hand, having escaped the hoi polloi by fleeing west to the Juárez and Cuauhtémoc districts and later to the art nouveau and art deco splendours of the Colonias Roma and Condesa, neglected to return. Gradually, the *Zócalo* lost its status as the engine-room of national life. The largest cathedral in the Americas still dominates the north side, but the middle classes seldom go there, and though the palace – where Moctezuma's own house once stood – remains the official headquarters of the administration, the president lives and works elsewhere, in his official residence of Los Pinos. He appears on the famous balcony solely for histrionic purposes, to cry *Viva Mexico*, to celebrate the revolution, and from time to time to shake hands in public with a foreign dignitary.

Not until I reached the Merchant's Gate did Dr Herzog's address strike me as improbable. The *Zócalo* was then under people's occupation. Stalls selling cigarettes, magazines, chewing gum and cheap trinkets ran the length of the building under the shadow of the arcade. Could serious psychiatrists set up their practice in such a place?

A heavy wooden entrance door gave onto a dark, narrow corridor at the end of which was a flight of stairs. On the wall by the staircase, a noticeboard lit by a bare bulb listed the occupants of various offices: Aureliano Gómez P. Accountant, Lic. Felix Grimaldi Soriano, Scribe…a dozen in all. Dr Álvaro Herzog's office was on the second floor. The stairs creaked. Paint was flaking from the walls, and in several places pieces of underlying stonework had fallen away, leaving jagged cracks and holes.

Dr Herzog's door bore a brass number and below it a plate with the doctor's name followed by a trail of letters testifying to his credentials and distinctions, among which was a doctor *honoris causa* from a university in North Dakota.

A secretary ushered me into a small waiting room. "*Si gusta sentarse.*" She pointed to a chesterfield from one of whose arms the stuffing protruded like an eruption of soap suds from a drain. "*Ahorita lo atiende el doctor.*"[62]

Ahorita, a word no supplicant can hear with equanimity. A derivative of *ahora* meaning now or soon, or presently, it works by accretion of diminutives *ahora, ahorita, ahoritita*, each intended to squeeze time – waiting time – into an ever smaller dimension as if it were a sponge. By a reversal of sense, however, additional diminutives serve only to reduce expectation by a like amount, thereby becoming not so much requests for patience as entreaties for the person waiting not to lose hope. Power lurks at the heart of *ahorita*. Used by an employee to a superior, the word stiffens to mean "straight away", "at once". Transmitted in the reverse direction from power-holder to supplicant, more often than not via a secretary or receptionist, it loses precision, moves into a paradigm where time becomes elastic and renders ineffectual the poor reassurances of language. So we receive the word not as a source of anticipation or comfort, but with a faint sinking of the heart, a mild resignation – mild at first, that is, for our feelings can transmute into frustration, and then anguish if the wait proves intolerable – or mortifying. How quickly we are frustrated or demeaned depends on the social relationship. A bureaucrat will

---

62 "The doctor will be with you shortly."

not keep a lawyer still less a politician long in attendance, but will feel no urgency about receiving a labourer or a carpenter, while a rich businessman may keep his gardener waiting for days or weeks for the favour of an interview – or for his wages.

Then there is a level at which even humiliation is inconceivable, when the relation of power is such that waiting becomes a badge of suffering to be born patiently and without protest. The sweep, the taco vendor, the chauffeur know this, and the peasant too, all *los de abajo* (the poor and the powerless) who, for want of a permit or a little leverage, find themselves at the mercy of an official or a boss.

I asked if Dr Herzog was attending another patient.

The secretary, neat in a scarlet nylon blouse and white pants, smiled confidentially. "The doctor is always busy."

She was seated behind a small reception desk on top of which lay a phial of red nail varnish and an open magazine. On the wall behind her, a framed photograph of President Echeverría wearing his sash of office – the sole adornment of a room that otherwise bore the same signs of dilapidation as the corridor.

In front of me, an old wooden coffee table listing in one corner from a leg wound bore a small pot containing a single parched cactus and a copy of Newsweek from the previous year, the cover of which showed an elderly forest dweller wearing a headdress and a bone through his nose. I flicked through to the lead article. Elder of an obscure "tribe" that lived remote from "civilization", the man's name and opinions escaped mention. He had achieved the glory of a front cover solely as an anthropological curiosity. No one had thought to interview him.

Half an hour passed. The secretary was painting her nails with studied concentration.

"Señorita."

She looked up, startled.

"Señorita, do you think I should come back some other time?"

"Ay sí! You've been waiting a while."

"Yes."

"Let me see what I can do." Replacing her brush inside the phial, she picked up the telephone. "Forgive me for interrupting you, Doctor. Your patient has been here for some time. *Sí, Doctor. Sí, como no, Doctor.* I will tell him." She replaced the receiver. "Between you and me, the doctor can become a little distracted."

A buzzer sounded. Evidently pleased at the effectiveness of her intervention, the secretary ushered me into Dr Herzog's presence and closed the door softly behind me.

Small, elderly, with bloodshot eyes, Dr Herzog was seated behind an ornately carved desk, so low down that he might have been peering over a rampart. White shirt, pale-green tie; an old linen jacket on a hanger suspended from a coat rack in the corner. Behind him, a large window, encrusted with dirt. He motioned me to a chair.

"What can I do for you?"

"I'm depressed, Doctor."

"How do you know you're depressed?"

"This is the first time I've been out of the house for a week. Can hardly bring myself to get out of bed."

He thought for a moment. "Did you break up with your wife? Your girlfriend?"

"Lost my job, too."

"Ah!" He looked pleased.

"There's something else. I don't understand what's going on. I mean in this…your country. Nothing is what it seems. People say one thing and then it turns out they mean something else."

"Disoriented?"

"I guess so."

"That's how things are in Mexico. We swim in confusion like fish in the sea." He scribbled a note on a block of paper, tore off the leaf and passed it to me across the desk. "Take one of these three times a day."

"Will that cure me?"

"There's no cure. But you'll feel better."

"Thank you, Doctor."

I shook his hand.

"It'll be two hundred pesos."

"Ah yes." I fished two hundred-peso notes from my wallet.

He waved me off with a flick of his hand. "My secretary will take the money."

"Right."

"Come back if the pills don't work and we'll try something else. We don't want to lose you, do we?"

On my right as I emerged from the arcade was a taco stall in full flow. The cook, a stout woman in a dirty apron, spotted me and called out in the high-pitched sing-song of the *Chilango*.

"*Cuantos va a querer, joven?*"

"*Dos de bistec,*"[63] I answered without thinking.

With rapid movements she placed two warm tortillas on a plastic plate, piled chopped meat on top of them, and handed the dish to me. To each *taco*, I added onion, coriander and chilli sauce from bowls lined up on a shelf in front of the stand. Folding each taco in turn, I ate hungrily without pausing.

"*Para tomar,*" the woman asked.

"*Tiene Manzanita?*"

She passed a bottle of apple soda over the counter.

The meal took no more than five minutes and at the end, as I wiped my lips on a tiny paper napkin, I began to smile and then to laugh. A man wearing a battered Stetson, a plate of tacos in hand, turned towards me.

"*Muy buenos estos tacos.*"

"*Buenísimos.*"[64]

I threw the napkin into the garbage, and then on an impulse

---

63 "How many would you like, young man?"
    "Two beef."
64 "Very good these tacos."
    "First rate."

retrieved the doctor's prescription from my pocket and threw that in too.

Customers were arriving in twos and threes, crowding round the *taquería* and shouting their orders.

"*Ahorita, ahorita,*" cried the cook, cheerfully in command of her métier.

"*Uno mas de bistec,*" I called.

As the plastic plate came my way, a young woman slipped between the man in the Stetson and myself. Neat in a simple trouser suit, dark hair swept into a ponytail.

"*Hay quesadillas, señorita? Soy vegetariana.*"

"*De flor, de huitlacoche, de queso.*"[65]

"*Dos de huitlacoche y uno de queso, por favor.*"

"*Qué cosas,*" said the man in the Stetson, addressing me but eyeing the girl appreciatively. "Who can complain about life when such beauty comes to us? Like a gift from heaven."

Hearing the compliment, the young woman flashed a smile at each of us in turn before moving off with her plate.

"You see," said the man. "A gift."

We finished eating, shook hands and bade each other farewell. Melting into the crowd, I made my way, via its streams and eddies, out of the *Zócalo* as one of their number.

---

65 "Pumpkin flower, corn truffle, cheese."

SEVENTY

TENOCHTITLAN – 1525–1526

Alva

Huehue and his master returned three times to assess how to deal with our waste, though other projects intervened and in the end nothing was done. To this day, we have our waste removed by hand. Still, the visits gave Huehue and I a chance to talk. He told me he had seen Tlaco, news that moved and thrilled me for I had given him up for lost.

Where was he? Did they set him free? Was he well? My questions tumbled into each other like stones down a mountain.

"I saw him only once," Huehue said.

"Did you speak with him? Did he see you? How is he?"

"Did he see me? I don't know. He gave no sign. He was marching like a common soldier. Limping badly, too. A group of Spaniards rode at the head of the column led by Cortés himself, at least I think it was he, and beside him Cuauhtémoc."

"The emperor!"

"He looked more like a slave, a man with no thought for

this world, for he stared straight ahead as if he were seeking a different one."

"Where were they going?"

"Who knows? They were leaving the city. Some said they were off to fight another war."

"Mexica fighting for the Spaniards?"

"Better than being fed to their god."

"If Tlaco was limping, how could he fight?"

"They say the Spaniards torture all the important people. It pleases their god to hear the victims' screams."

Neither our emperor nor Tlaco returned, nor were heard of again. For a while I tried to find out what had happened to them, but no one seemed to know, or maybe those who knew – the Spaniards – kept the knowledge to themselves. I appealed to Father Hernández, but he refused to make inquiries, telling me that some things were best left for god's attention alone.

Later a rumour did the rounds that Cortés had tired of Cuauhtémoc and had him executed. No such gossip attached to Tlaco, but my friend would surely not have suffered the emperor to make his last journey alone. It consoles me to think they reached the realm of heaven together, and that Quetzalcóatl received them kindly.

Army discipline taught us to accept our fate with grace no matter how painful or unexpected. Even so, I grieve for Tlaco more than for my own kin. Relatives are given, they come with birth, but friendship forms like a living sculpture under the hands of those who make it, and when a friend dies, he takes with him a part of who we are. Oh Tlaco, I have no words for your absence. Nothing I write can circumscribe the vacancy you left behind, which is like an ache that swells each time your memory enters my thoughts. You do not grow old, as I have done, but come always fresh with the loveliness and strength of youth and with that ungainliness that made you unfit for war but seemed to radiate your suppleness of mind and generosity of heart.

387

SEVENTY-ONE

MEXICO CITY – 1976

James

The presidential campaign was in full swing: Lopez Portillo's photograph on the front pages of the dailies, his speeches reported at length, his energy admired, his patriotism applauded. He had become a man apart. Though he stood unopposed (the opposition being resigned to defeat), he travelled the country as if the outcome depended on every vote, lecturing the people, proclaiming his devotion to them and to the glorious ideals of the revolution. Wherever he arrived – town halls, theatres, village squares – amid a cavalcade of black limousines and with a regiment of party hacks in dark sunglasses and guayaberas, it was to address an audience bussed in to hear and cheer him, often the same audience that had listened to the same speech fifty kilometres away the day before. Cameras and microphones recorded the proceedings, journalists fawned, flags fluttered from trees and balconies. Appeals to national unity resounded through the streets and the airwaves: *Mexico is not a collection of opposing forces, but an alliance in which all sectors of society join in the march towards progress, justice and prosperity…*

Everywhere the party's favourite strapline: *el respeto al derecho ajeno es la paz*,[66] words known to every school kid, and carved into thousands of effigies and sculptures of the man who spoke them over a century before, the nation's first and only native president, Benito Juárez.

Despite efforts to whip up enthusiasm, the public paid little attention to the campaign. The outcome was assured, and the party had so draped itself in the nation's colours that opposition looked unpatriotic, even traitorous. Voters were fearful of fracturing the stability of a nation that within living memory had suffered a bloody revolution and a religious war of Church against State. If the Party was corrupt and its workings opaque, such was the price of peace.

I write with the perspective of years. At the time, still treading water after my expulsion from CENCIAS and from Olivia's affections, I felt as mystified by the political process as by the social dynamics, puzzled by the purpose of so elaborate a campaign, by a revolutionary rhetoric if not meaningless then impenetrable, by the absence of dissent. I could not square the ubiquitous poverty – shanty towns, ramshackle dwellings lacking every amenity of modern life, beggars with twisted limbs, child street vendors – with the islands of elegance whose inhabitants overlooked the surrounding ocean of misery. Who among the poor ended up voting? How many of those impoverished millions even figured on the lists of the living?

A few weeks before election day, Pepe called me. We hadn't seen or spoken to each other since our chance meeting at the bookstore.

He sounded happy. I told him I was fine.

"You don't sound fine," he said.

---

66   Peace is respect for the rights of others.

"What?"

"Everybody has good days and bad days. In Mexico we tell the truth. If we are miserable, we say so."

"I'm not miserable."

"I think you are."

"Okay, I'm miserable."

"Olivia dumped you, right?"

"How did you know?"

"News travels."

"Did you know I lost my job too?"

"Shit! You okay?"

"I'll survive."

"Listen, I've got something for you. A ticket to the *Cierre de la Campaña*."

"The what?"

"Closing ceremony of the campaign."

"Why the hell…?"

"You'll never have seen anything like it. You can't buy tickets for the *Cierre*. You have to be a Party member. That's what you'll be for the day. We'll have badges, T-shirts, the whole nine yards as the Americans say. You'll meet my new friend. Yes, I'm in love at last. His name's Agustín. You'll adore him."

On the day of the event, we met for breakfast in a little café on Insurgentes. Agustín – small, wiry, with piercing eyes – tested me with a show of camp.

"Pepe didn't tell me he had such an attractive friend. Keeping him a secret, were you, Pepe, just in case we have a row and you need consoling? Wouldn't mind being consoled myself from time to time." His eyes sparkled as he turned to me. "You wouldn't fancy a little consolation from time to time? No? What a shame. If you change your mind, Pepe will always give you my number, won't you, Pepe?"

"Agus is putting on a show for you," said Pepe.

"I can see our interests may not coincide," said Agustín. "You can always change yours, of course. You might come to like it. Meanwhile, Pepe has something for you."

"I should have told you," said Pepe. "But didn't know how you'd react."

"?"

"Olivia asked if she could come. And I couldn't refuse."

"Jesus."

"You don't mind?"

My heart was pounding. "I guess not."

"Are you being English again?"

"Oh god, Pepe, I don't know."

"You still love her?" said Agustín gently.

I nodded.

"We'll look after you, don't worry."

We pulled up in front of Olivia's house. She came out at once, radiant, faded jeans, white blouse, an untidy cascade of dark hair.

She offered her cheek to each of us in turn.

"How have you been," she asked me.

"He's always *bien*," said Pepe. "Even when he isn't."

"It' so exciting. I've never been to a Party gathering," Olivia said. "Where does it take place?"

"They rented the Blue Stadium," Pepe said. "Over thirty thousand seats."

Olivia clapped her hands together. "It's so exciting," she said again.

The stadium was packed. A forest of national flags – red, white and green with the eagle and the serpent in the centre. Streamers draped round the perimeter. At one end a giant blow-up of the candidate. At the other, the largest flag of all suspended above a stage.

Pepe led us up a long concrete stairway. Our seats were about halfway back. He sent me first along the row, then gestured to Olivia to follow. She hesitated, a stab of pain, then acquiesced with a slight toss of the head. We squeezed past a line of adults and children wearing identical baseball caps with "JLP", the candidate's initials, on the peak.

I sat down with Olivia on my right followed by Pepe and Agustín. To my left, an elderly couple – the man in a grey polyester suit and tie, his companion wearing a flower in snow-white hair. They smiled, shook my hand.

"Good to see young people here," the man said. "Where would we be without the Party?"

On stage – distant and tiny in the vastness of the stadium – a mariachi band was belting out a familiar tune from days of old, trumpets blaring, the singer's voice powerful, melodious.

Mexico lindo y querido, si muero lejos de ti...[67]

At the end of the song, the singer cried *Viva Mexico* into the microphones and the response came slow and loud from the spectators: *Viva!* As the band hurried off with their instruments, a lone figure mounted the stage.

"*Señoras y señores...*" He waited for attention before repeating, "*Señoras y señores, señoras y señores, good afternoon, members of the Partido Revolucionario Institucional...*" There was a pause for cheers. "*We are here to celebrate the closure of the campaign for the next president of the Mexican Republic.*"

A smattering of applause, the crowd reserving its enthusiasm for the main event.

"Who is this," I asked Olivia.

She passed the question to Pepe who shared it with Agustín before answering.

"Nobody. He doesn't matter."

Olivia was sitting calmly, rocking back slightly, hands clasped round her left knee.

"*My task,*" said the speaker, "*is not to hold your attention, but to direct it to the man who for the next six years will be your and the nation's leader. I give you Don José Lopez Portillo...*"

_____

67 Beautiful, beloved Mexico, if I die far from thee...

He stood back from the microphone, clapping. At this signal, a group of men in guayaberas and women in country dress, white with red sashes, marched on stage, sat on a row of chairs at the rear and then immediately stood up as the future president, sober in a dark suit but arms outstretched towards his audience, strode into view.

A roar round the stadium.

The candidate walked to one side, then the other to acknowledge and milk the reception, before taking up position before the microphones. From where we were sitting, he was far distant, dwarfed by the backdrop of the terraces and by the gigantic flag above him. He held up a hand, and though it was barely visible, we observed and fell silent.

"*Mexicanas, Mexicanos, ciudadanos, partidarios de la Revolución, members of a Party whose glorious history and whose very name reminds us of our origin and our mission…*"

The voice boomed through the stadium amplified by the speakers but distorted by their volume, by differences of timing that gave to the sound a curious contrapuntal quality like sequences of notes repeated by discordant instruments. My attention began almost at once to drift, lulled partly by the candidate's remoteness and the midday heat, but mostly distracted by Olivia's presence. She was sitting upright, hands clasped no longer round her knee but across her navel – where I had once enjoyed the right to place my lips. I tried to catch her eye, but she was staring down at the tiny figure of the candidate.

"*The people are not interested in empty words and vacuous promises. They want consonance between our duty as revolutionaries and our observance of that duty, between their aspirations and our commitment to meeting them, between our words and our deeds…*"

Fifty young men in identical T-shirts and baseball caps rose as one to their feet, raised their fists to the air, and chanted a slogan ending in the letters of the candidate's name: J…L…P.

Applause echoed round the stadium. Olivia, on the edge of her seat, clapped.

"*Sisters, brothers*," continued the candidate, and the stadium once more fell silent.

"It's fantastic," said Olivia, turning to Pepe and kissing him on the cheek. Pepe whispered something in her ear, and she nodded. Her shirt was open at the neck, and as she settled back in her seat, I caught sight of her breasts and the outline of lace in which they rested. Lust and loss intermingled. I must have gasped because, for the first time since we had entered the stadium, she turned to me.

"What's the matter?"

"Nothing. I mean you look sensational, you smell wonderful, I can see your breasts and they're driving me crazy, I want to take you in my arms and…"

"*Sisters, brothers, Mexicanas, Mexicanos…*"

Olivia mouthed reproof but a smile played on her lips and the reprieve – for so I judged it – calmed me.

"*…If you do me the honour of allowing me to serve you…*"

On the far side of the stadium, another group rose to chant a slogan of their own. This time, the candidate responded.

"*Gracias, gracias, compañeros. Gracias.*"

As the applause faded, I leaned forward to one of the T-shirted young men in front of us.

"Hola."

"Hola."

"Where are you guys from?"

"*Miacatlán.*"

"Where?"

"*Miacatlán, Morelos.* We're farmers, *campesinos.*"

"So what brings you here?"

"The Party drove us in buses. Gave us T-shirts, blue jeans, caps. And some beer money too."

"Good deal?"

"You bet."

"How do you know when to stand up and cheer?"

He grinned. "Our chief gives us a signal. He's at the front."

The candidate's voice was rising in volume again. I fired a last question.

"How does he know whose turn it is to cheer?"

"Search me."

"*Bueno, gracias.*"

We shook hands.

Olivia leaned over and put her lips to my ear.

"They're divine, aren't they? Divine."

"*Our movement is not about allowing some to win and others to lose, nor about fomenting exploitation of the weak, nor standing by while a few benefit and the many sink into poverty. Our aim is to stand together, to work together, to grow together, to prosper together…*"

Applause.

The sweet scent of Olivia's breath settled in my nostrils. I had been fighting the urge to take her hand in mine for fear I might be refused, but my senses were alive and would not be denied. Though she balked for an instant, I held my course, carrying her hand to my lips before returning it to her possession. No admonishment came. A pulse of happiness surged through me at this success, and I felt myself suddenly alive not just to her but to what was happening around me, to Pepe and Agustín who at that moment were gazing into each other's eyes, to the elderly couple on my left who were hanging on the candidate's words with an expression close to rapture, to the speech which now struck me as gripping, moving even. My cherished political passions resurfaced, my indignation at the dispossessed, my sympathy – so akin to love – with this couple whose parched skin and rough, swollen hands betokened a lifetime of struggle with the earth.

"…*We will not accomplish our mission unless we recognize and embrace our shared humanity and our common destiny as citizens. No revolutionary government could ever propose injustice and inequality as aims of public policy. But circumstances have not always favoured our ambitions and our dreams. Population growth, the ups and downs of the world economy, the onward drift of people from the countryside to the cities have conspired to impair progress and expose deficiencies. Such are the all-too-familiar problems of underdevelopment in countries such as ours. We must work to overcome them...*"

Applause.

"*...But we can never overcome them unless we work together, unless we acknowledge our shared humanity and embrace our common destiny as citizens, unless we forget our differences and instead bear in the forefront of our minds that we are all Mexican and that the future of the country is our future and our children's future.*"

Three or four groups were on their feet in different parts of the stadium and in a moment the whole stadium rose to applaud the sentiments and the man who expressed them. Nor could I sit apart from the fervour but lent my voice to it and pumped my fist in the air.

"*...Should the citizens in their wisdom choose me as their president, I promise to place the full shoulder of the state to the task of improving their condition. To those who live in comfort, I say we need your solidarity, your understanding, your contribution to the welfare of the country. To the workers and peasant farmers – backbone of our nation – whose labour puts food on our table and tools in our hands, I ask only for honest work and commitment, and in return I promise to maintain the value of your wages and to keep staple foods – beans, rice, tortillas – at prices everyone can afford. So that no one will go hungry...*"

Applause.

"*To the dispossessed and the impoverished, those of our people who live on the margins, I ask only for their pardon that the Party and the country have not yet succeeded in improving your lives.*

Your condition is an open wound on the conscience of the nation – a wound that all of us must try to heal. And so, dear friends, I express the hope that we will, in this election, come together and with one voice express our faith in our revolution and in the Party. Let us continue to build together, let us meet the challenges of the future with joy and full commitment, let us send out from this stadium the cry first heard from the church of Dolores Hidalgo one hundred and sixty-six years ago: Mexicanos, Viva Mexico!"

And from every voice in the stadium came the reply *Viva*! The cry of independence, the birth-cry of the nation.

"*Viva Mexico!*"

"*Viva!*"

"*Viva Mexico!*"

"*Viva!*"

Now we were all cheering. The elderly man on my left was struggling to stand. I put my arm round him and eased him upright.

"Thank you, young man. Thank you." His wife had remained seated and he now offered his arm to her as a signal that she, too, should rise. Then he turned to me again, straining his voice above the din. "How good to see young people as members of the Party. Is that your girlfriend?"

"Yes."

He looked across at her, his expression full of kindness. "You are both very lucky. May you also be happy."

He went on speaking for a moment or two more but the mariachi band had reappeared and his words melted like those of the song in a joyous blast of trumpets:

Negrita de mis pesares ojos de papel volando
A todos diles que sí,
Pero no les digas cuando
Así me dijiste a mí,
Por eso vivo penando…

Dark one of my sorrows
Eyes that flutter in the wind
Say yes to all of them
But tell no one when
Just as you said to me
Which is why I live in sadness...

The melancholy of the words – belied by the exuberance of the music.

"Well?" Pepe asked afterwards, as we sat in a little café near the stadium.

"I'm impressed."

"By the show?"

"I wasn't expecting him to speak about inequality, to regret the lack of progress. He apologized for the Party's failure to deal with the poverty. I know that's easy to do, but he sounded convincing. Didn't talk down to his audience."

"You haven't heard it all before like we have," Agustín said. "They've taken all the vocabulary: revolution, reform, equality, education. You name it, they have it. None of it means a thing."

"It may have done, once," said Pepe. "A long time ago. When Cárdenas was president."

"I think it was wonderful," Olivia said. "Of course it means something. He'll do his best as president. That's all we can ask."

We looked at her, startled.

"Why should we expect miracles? Nothing will ever be perfect," she said.

After we had thanked Pepe and Agustín and bid them goodbye, Olivia and I repaired to my apartment. We made love and afterwards, as we showered together and I was soaping her back, she said in a matter-of-fact tone, "I'm going to marry Nacho."

"What?"

"I didn't intend to make love today. You wanted us to be together so much that you made me want it too. But it's the last time."

We towelled off and dressed in silence. I drove her home, and as she was getting out of the car, she said, "Nacho and I have known each other since primary school. I don't love him more than you, but I will in time."

"I don't get it."

"We must do what's best for us. *La vida es sueño y los sueños sueños son.*"[68]

In his inaugural speech as president, José Lopez Portillo apologized once again to the millions of impoverished Mexicans whom the revolution had failed and the state ignored. He promised to remedy their plight. Later, deep into his period of office, he made another promise – this time to defend the Mexican peso "like a dog".

He kept neither commitment. The discovery of new oil fields off the Mexican coast allied to an increase in prices brought on by troubles in the Middle East gave his government an unexpected bonanza. Once he understood the fabulous wealth at his disposal, he began, with the frenzy of a fly in a cesspit, to gorge on it, building grandiose schemes on flimsy foundations, and lavishing inconceivable sums on himself, his family and his friends. When the oil price fell, so did the peso; and thereafter, whenever he appeared in public, he would hear mocking yelps in imitation of his canine defence of the currency. The hill overlooking the city, on which he built four mansions for himself and his children, became known as *La Colina del Perro* – Dog Hill – the people's humour, an age-old response to oppression and betrayal. In the line of Mexican presidents, none succeeded better than Lopez Portillo in playing fast and loose with the public purse, and none left office more deeply unlamented.

---

68 "Life is a dream and dreams are just dreams."

SEVENTY-TWO

TENOCHTITLAN – 1528

Alva

Huehue and I went on seeing each other from time to time. Fortune had smiled on him in his mature years. Though he never gave up the rubric of shit-shoveller in which he took self-deprecatory pride, his boss Don Diego favoured him if not with friendship then with respect, ever seeking his advice on waste disposal, and even assigning him a piece of land for a house.

"Don Diego thinks I have useful knowledge," Huehue told me with his familiar crooked grin. "On the other hand, he thinks I'm not too smart, which is how I like it. Take my advice, never be smart in front of the powerful and never speak your mind. Most of the time, I have to guess what he wants. Never could get my head round their language, too old to learn I guess, or too stupid. Anyway, I just say 'yes, Don Diego', and if he sees I haven't understood, he curses, shakes his head and gets somebody to translate. 'Tell him this, ask him that,' he says. Back and forth

I go with the translator until I find out Don Diego's own view of the matter. Then I give it back to him."

"Even if it's not right?"

"Right? Who knows what's right?"

"Maybe you do, Huehue."

"Better to be alive than right I say. Doesn't do to disagree with your master."

"So nothing's changed?"

"All masters are the same at heart. And I'm still at the bottom. But enough about me. I'm old and don't matter; you still have your life before you. How are you, my dear young friend?"

That was my signal to tell him an anecdote or two about my life as a servant; how Father Hernández treated me well enough even if, unlike Huehue, I would never have a house of my own; how the priest considered me his own property, a bit like his horse, except that he seemed to love the horse more – for he always spoke gently to it, whereas with me he could be impatient because he sensed, despite my protestations, that I didn't worship his god; how he scolded me for my lack of fervour and made me recite prayers and kneel in front of a cross and sometimes to sing, which everyone had to do, including the women, with only the horse spared the ordeal because it wasn't human, though Father Hernández talked to it as if it were a person, and said "god bless you for you are a fine beast and with god's help will bear me safely to and fro".

"Life moves on," Huehue would mutter, "and we must move with it." Whenever our conversation took a melancholy turn, as it often did when we talked of old times, he would ask me if I was enjoying a woman because if not he knew of some pretty ones who would be only too happy to know me, and then laughter would break into the gloom like the sun appearing through a bank of cloud.

So ran our conversations, never reaching anything new, nor dwelling too long on the past, but keeping each other warm and in touch with who we were. Each time we parted, we would embrace, and he would tell me to keep my privates in working order because the nation still needed them.

So the years went by. Work on the church came to an end and I became Father Hernández's gardener and handyman. And Huehue advanced into old age, his sharpness of mind and humour gradually fading until one day, bent over, leaning on a stick, his gait reduced to a shuffle, he told me that death had called him and that this would be our last encounter.

I asked him not to be foolish, assured him he had many years still to live and that he couldn't die until he had confessed to Tlaelquani, goddess of unlawful love, for his womanizing and whoring, which for sure he hadn't done.

"Where would I find one of her priests to hear me," he asked. "If any remain alive, they will have fled."

I begged him not to go without me, not to leave me alone as the last of our little group. It struck me that perhaps this would be a good time for me also to begin my last journey and that we could go together.

Huehue would hear none of it. "From now," he said, "we will walk different paths. I will descend to the last region, to Mictlan, the cold underworld. You have been a warrior and with luck Huizilopochtli will take you in glory to his realm. For me, I ask only that you see to my cremation and that you send a dog to keep me company."

Such was the custom for whoever expected little of the afterlife: to sacrifice a dog so that it would walk beside the deceased on the long journey to the underworld, these faithful creatures having ever been a source of comfort to the bereft.

That was the last I saw of Huehue. How and where he died I cannot say. When he did not reappear in our usual meeting place near the ruined temple of Tezcatlipoca, I inquired after his boss who I thought could surely tell me of Huehue's fate. Many Spaniards went by the name Don Diego, however, and I had no other name to give, nor knew where Huehue's master lived or might be found. After a while I let it go. My strength of mind had begun to waver, exhaustion took hold of me, and then a fever that left me scarcely able to move. For days, so they tell me, I lay as if Micantlecuhtli had called me after all to follow Huehue's footsteps to the underworld. Father Hernández sent nurses to care for me, bathe me and give me to drink. A doctor came, listened to my heart, then shook his head and walked away. Of so much, at least, I was aware, though of little else because my eyes were mostly filled with visions. I relived – as terrified as the first time – my summons into Moctezuma's presence, the sharp questions in his reedy voice that were like a sword held to my throat so that I trembled lest my answers might displease him. Then I was making love to Tecuichpo except that it was not Tecuichpo but Nenetl, no not her either but my aunt Izel stricken with the pox, and I could hear her cries of pain. Moctezuma became angry. He stretched his hand towards me – though I dared not look at it – and fury darted from his fingertips. Next I was lying on the sacrificial stone with a priest standing over me holding the knife above my heart, and I was struggling because this was not a noble end but one full of shame and disgrace and I was crying out to Tlazolteotl, mother of all the gods, to have pity on me.

Later, as I began to recover, the figures around me took shape. They were the nurses who tended me and Father Hernández who visited often and prayed to his god for me. Though as soon as I was back on my feet and working, he lost no time in upbraiding me for calling on false deities and evil spirits during my illness.

"You must forget these creatures of the Devil."

"Yes, Father. I have forgotten them already."

"We must both pray to god that it is so."

Praying to his god never caused me the slightest difficulty. What has always seemed strange is the Christian insistence that theirs is the only one. Do they have no respect for others? Do they not understand that a people and their gods are one? I bow to the Christian god and respect his power, but I give reverence to the gods of our fathers too, at times and places hidden from Christian view.

As soon as I had recovered sufficiently, I sacrificed a dog for Huehue since I was sure by then that he must have passed on, and as the smoke rose from the little fire, I chanted the customary refrain:

When the gods call
We all must take our leave
Now is the time for mourning,
Four long years
Of knowing nothing
Of wandering fleshless
Among the unnumbered dead
Beneath the forgetful earth.

SEVENTY-THREE

MEXICO CITY – 1994

James

On my way home from a writing assignment in South America, I stopped for a few days in Mexico City. Eighteen years had passed since I had fled, vowing never to return; though as time healed the wounds of rejection, I had long since started to think once more of walking the streets, of rediscovering the landmarks and the people where and with whom I felt I had left a portion of my self.

My expenses were generous enough for me to book into a quality hotel, so I chose a famous old one – the Geneve. Built in 1907, it had played host to such people as Winston Churchill, Julio Cortázar and Gabriel García Márquez, and had enjoyed a reputation as the most elegant place in town. Eighteen years before, I could not have afforded the room rate, but I had occasionally sat at the bar, or wandered with a beer through the curlicued columns of one of the restaurants with its glass ceiling and tiled windows bordered with red, green and ochre highlights,

or sat in the ornate "library" decorated with solemn oil paintings and floor-to-ceiling bookshelves.

Always the Geneve had struck me as unattainable, a place where, on the few occasions when I dared approach its portals, I would wonder whether the doorman would bar my way on account of having observed – with the penetration of a duty guard at the gates of heaven – that I might not possess the wherewithal to deserve the honour. He never did, but greeted me with the same enthusiasm he offered those who entered as if by right: "*Muy buenas tardes, señor. Welcome to Hotel Geneve.*" Then, having passed muster and entered the lobby, I would experience an aftertaste of guilt that I might have snubbed him by hurrying past without acknowledging his welcome and thereby inflicted yet another of the slights young men of his complexion have carried as a birthright since the Conquest, and I would make a mental note to slip him a banknote should he still be on duty when I left.

Once inside, confronted by the stately interior and the elegant attire of the patrons – for these were the days before rich travellers turned up in jeans – I found it hard not to feel an intruder, and so could easily find myself spending more than I could afford on food and drink in an effort to prove otherwise.

Fame and prestige are transitory. By 1994, unable to stand toe to toe with the newer and grander hotels of Reforma and Chapultepec, the Geneve had shed a star or two and was offering itself as a refuge for business executives on a budget.

Olivia joined me for breakfast – the only time she could spare, when the children were at school, her husband at work, and the maids assigned their duties for the day. She was dressed exactly as I remembered her, in jeans and a white blouse with the gold pendant nestled between her breasts.

She told me about her children, about her marriage – as happy as she had imagined it would be. She said that her parents and sister were well. Pepe had died of AIDS in New York.

"Agustín left him for a university professor in Los Angeles and Pepe went to pieces. He ran away to New York and buried himself in sex. Must have slept with half the gay men in Manhattan. I went to see him before he died. He was so wasted and thin. Covered in ugly blotches. I couldn't leave him all alone, so I stayed with him until the end. Six weeks of horror and pain watching him die, and all the time trying to comfort him and keep my own spirits up. Had a bit of a breakdown afterwards. Ate and ate until I blew up like a balloon. You wouldn't have recognized me. Or loved me." She produced a handkerchief and dabbed her eyes. "I'm so happy to see you. I told Hernando you were coming."

"Hernando?"

"My therapist. You don't remember him? Why should you? But he remembers you because I talked about you so often to him. Hernando knows more about me than Nacho."

"Nacho?"

"My husband. You've forgotten his name too! It doesn't matter. Anyway, Hernando said real love doesn't die and that it was natural for me to want to see you. As soon as you sent news that you were coming, I began dreaming about the past, day-dreaming really. And I got so excited. Last week I was alone in the house – apart from the maids – sitting, trying to read a book. You came into my thoughts and I had a little orgasm just like that. Please stop me talking. I want you to take me by the hand like you used to."

When, an hour later, I saw her to her car, I tried to draw us together for a parting caress but she pushed me away.

"You forget I'm a married woman. Someone might see."

"But…"

"Just accept, enjoy, and think well of me."

I took a cab downtown to the Café La Habana on Morelos and Bucarelli, half expecting it to have vanished. But there it was, the same off-pink façade, dirty neon sign, and within, the same 1950s interior of burnished wood and lemon-cream tabletops, whirring ceiling fans, energetic waiters of indeterminate age, an air of timelessness and stout resistance to the frenetic world outside from which it offered a refuge and a quiet welcome, a place where no one minded if you sat over a coffee for half a day with a newspaper or a book of poetry or plotted with a group of friends to change the world. Rumour has it that in this unfashionable haven of the old metropolis, the Castro brothers and Che Guevara planned the Cuban revolution. Juan Rulfo and Augusto Monterroso were said to be regulars. Roberto Bolaño made it the headquarters of his visceral realists.

A knot of people had gathered at the entrance.

"What's going on?"

"We're watching the news."

"Is there no room inside?"

"*Pase, pase.*"

I pushed through to a crowded interior. Someone had placed a television on the counter and all eyes were turned towards

it. Waiters threaded through the congestion, deftly balancing trays above their heads on outstretched fingers. I found a patch of wall to lean against from where I had a view of the screen. Shots of a milling crowd, people crying, thickets of uniformed police. A reporter was delivering a rapid-fire commentary over a background wail of sirens and a clamour of other voices.

"What's going on," I asked in a loud whisper.

A woman seated at a table in front of me turned round and beckoned to me to lower my head. "The candidate."

"What about him?"

"Shot."

On screen, a reporter, microphone in hand: "*This comes to you live from Calle La Punta, Tijuana, on a black day in the history of our nation. For those of you who have not yet heard the news, the presidential candidate, Licenciado Luis Donaldo Colosio, has been shot. He has been rushed to Tijuana General Hospital in the company of police and bodyguards but we have no information on whether he has survived the attack. I have with me a witness to what happened.*"

The screen pans out to show a thin, middle-aged man in a red nylon shirt and jeans.

"*Could you tell us your name, señor?*"

"*Abelardo Rodriguez Lopez, a sus órdenes.*"

"*Well, Señor Rodriguez, let me thank you for agreeing to speak to our audience. The whole nation is shocked and saddened by this terrible event. What can you tell us about it?*"

The man lowers his head. "*Forgive me…it's difficult.*"

"*Take your time.*"

"*I didn't really see anything. The candidate had already stepped down from the platform where he had given his speech. There were people all round him.*"

The reporter changes tack. "*Are you from this part of town?*"

"*Yes, señor. From Lomas Taurinas. You can see we are poor here. Many of the houses are squatters' homes. For the president to visit such a humble neighbourhood…*"

"*You mean the candidate…*"

"*Licenciado Colosio yes. It's the same thing, isn't it?*"

"*Nearly.*"

"*For him to come to see us…it's special. No one else ever bothered.*"

A woman, tears streaming from her eyes, snatches the microphone. "*And then they come to kill him,*" she screams. "*Because they don't want anyone who supports the poor. They want to keep us down, trample on us as if we're worthless. They're the worthless ones. May they rot in hell.*"

A hand takes the microphone and returns it to the reporter while the woman is ushered away.

"*Sr Rodriguez, you were saying?*"

"*I saw nothing. Licenciado Colosio stepped into the crowd so that I couldn't see him any more. And then I heard shots.*"

"*How many?*"

"*Two or three, I think. The crowd swayed first one way and then the other and I was swept up in it.*"

"*We'll be back in a few moments after these messages.*"

The screen flashes to a young blonde woman in a short dress and thigh-length boots sashaying through the furniture department of a fashionable store. Another flash and a cartoon figure of a child is eating a slice of white bread: *Pan Bimbo*. Cut to a Volkswagen Beetle drawing smoothly to a halt from which a couple and three teenagers emerge, smiling and impeccable. "*Everyone fits into a Volkswagen*," says a voice, "*and so can your family.*" Back to the furniture department. The young woman has found a three-piece suite on sale for five thousand pesos. She drapes herself fetchingly on the sofa, thighs on display, breasts peeking from a tight décolleté.

"*I have the furniture. Now all I need is a man to go with it...*"

Cut to the reporter. "*While we await further news of this terrible incident, here is what the candidate had to tell us in his great speech of March 6th. Licenciado Colosio generously recorded the speech for us in our studios on the following day.*"

Colosio's figure appears on screen. He looks straight into the camera, confident, vigorous, sure of himself. "*I see a country of poor who can wait no longer for the dignity of progress; I see native communities that, with the strength of their culture and their natural cohesion, are ready to seek new horizons. I see a Mexico hungry for justice, a Mexico deeply injured by the contempt for law of those whose job it is to uphold it; a Mexico of women and men afflicted by the abuses of officialdom and the arrogance of government...*"

The young blonde reappears, this time in the kitchenware department. A waiter turns off the television.

"They killed him for that speech," someone shouted.

"He was a man of the people," said another.

Several voices joined in.

"We don't know if he's dead..."

"If he's still alive, they'll find a way to finish the job."

"Salinas de Gortari is behind this."

411

"*Ese hijo de la chingada.*"[69]
"Or the Americans."
"What's the difference?"
"Salinas chose Colosio."
"And Colosio turned round and bit him with the truth."
"Truth? In this fucking country, there is no truth."
"*Pobre Mexico, tan lejos de Dios.*"[70]

Carlos Salinas de Gortari was president between 1988 and 1994. He'd been budget and planning minister in the previous administration and knew where the money was and how to use it. One of his first moves was to award himself a US$850 million piggy bank to spend as he wished. Some believe that a good chunk of the cash was stashed in a Swiss vault.

A child of the free market, President Salinas signed a Free Trade Agreement with the United States and Canada on terms that put two million peasants out of work and hundreds of thousands of small firms out of business. He sold off state enterprises to friends and colleagues at fire-sale prices – including the national telephone company, jewel in the crown of the man who was later to become one of the world's wealthiest: Carlos Slim Helú. As I write these lines, Slim – a portly caricature of his name – is making seventy million dollars a day, ten thousand times the country's annual per capita income. The telephone company charges the highest rates in the western hemisphere – maybe even the highest in the world give or take a few isolated enclaves. Slim and Salinas are said to be partners.

Leaving the economy in ruins and his own reputation in shreds, Salinas slunk away at the end of his term, out of town and out of the country.

---

69 "That mother-fucking son of a bitch."
70 "Poor Mexico, so far from God."

SEVENTY-FOUR

TENOCHTITLAN – 1537–1538

Alva

Nothing could have prepared us for life as underdogs. We had grown used to power, to pride in our nation and our achievements. Our superiority over others seemed as natural as Tlaloc's gift of rain and Tonatiuh's of sunlight, subject to fluctuations but always in the end confirmed if not by persuasion then by war.

After the conquest, we survivors took time to grasp how far we had sunk in the esteem of heaven. No one told us we had become slaves, only that we belonged to our conquerors and must work for them. Nor did our traditional enemies, the Tlaxcalans and the Purépecha, fare differently – or any of those over whom we once held sway. Spaniards do not distinguish between us, and judge us only by our defeated condition and the darker colour of our skin.

Father Hernández, for all his goodness of heart, never saw me except as a possession, a servant to be ordered hither and

413

thither according to his will. Still, I thank the good fortune that placed me in the hands of so gentle a priest and allowed me to win his confidence.

Early on in my servitude, he began using me as an errand boy to deliver messages across what remained of the city. On seeing how well I accomplished that task, added to "my success as a language teacher" and my disinclination to run away (where would I run to?), he started sending me to the market to buy supplies for our community. I had often accompanied him on shopping expeditions, but my role had been limited to loading goods into the handcart and pushing them home. He took many moons before he thought to introduce me to their money, and then several years before he ventured to send me to the market alone. Imagine his astonishment when he saw, on my return from my first shopping trip, not that I returned with all the goods he had ordered but that I had spent less than half the money he had given me.

"How come you took so long? I nearly sent a soldier to seek you out," he scolded. "And what's this money? Did you steal some of the goods? You can't have bought so much with so little."

"The merchant's first price is never the real one," I told him. "But to bargain requires time. You must show yourself to be a friend. You must speak of your poverty. You must entertain with stories so that your company becomes delightful. You must convey the impression that you are enjoying the conversation and have no pressing need to buy anything. Above all you must not be anxious but ever ready to walk away with an air of confidence knowing, if there has been no deal, that you will likely receive an entreaty to return. That is the way to spend little and to leave the merchant well content with the trade."

On the next buying trip, I suggested he might like to watch me so that he could verify for himself what I had told him.

So it was that on the next trip, Father Hernández observed from a distance while I bargained for a basket of corn, parted with less than half the asking price and left the merchant smiling.

The good Father shook his head. "Bargaining takes a long time."

"My time is cheap, is it not, Father, while money is costly."

Thereafter, he was content to let me do the shopping, and thus I won a measure of freedom, with a licence to wander at will among the stalls, engage in conversation as I wished, and sometimes to speak my own language. How I enjoyed seeing the Spanish merchants adopt our ways, bargaining as we do! They alone treated us from the start almost as equals, knowing that the value of a coin in my hand is the same as in the hand of the king of Spain.

So I settled to a routine. Once every seven days, which the Spaniards call a week, I went to market, sometimes with a helper if there was much to buy, but usually alone. With some of the traders I struck up an acquaintance, and with one especially a true friendship despite his being a Spaniard. I never knew a fatter human being than Martín nor a more cheerful one. He sold fresh meat and fowl, and pieces of cooked or preserved flesh called *embutidos*.[71] Father Hernández always ordered *embutidos*, so no matter what else I had to buy, a visit to Martín's stall was essential. A passionate trader, Martín loved his own produce, exemplified its benefits, and pressed his enthusiasm on whoever came within hailing distance. Whenever I approached, he would make a show of not wanting to see me on account of my slight frame – so much the opposite of his own.

"You'll frighten away my customers. I tell them my produce will make them big, strong and healthy, and here you are buying every week and still thinner than a starving dog."

I would grin and ask politely if he knew of any other meat trader whose produce might be more effective, at which he would shake his head and ask god to spare him any more customers so anxious, like me, to destroy his reputation.

As soon as I gave him my order, the bargaining would begin

---

71 Cured sausages.

and often continue until the sun had begun to grow weary, with Martín breaking off to serve others usually at prices much higher than those I was disputing.

"Given all the free food I send him, it's me your Father Hernández should be thanking, not you," he would say when at last we reached an agreement. "You might at least tell him about my generosity so he can put in a word for me in his prayers."

Whether or not Martín truly made bad business with me I couldn't say, but I believe he valued our friendship as something unusual to which few of his compatriots could aspire. In his eyes, I seemed to acquire the status of a mascot or a prized possession. He took every chance to show me off to fellow compatriots, introducing me to them as his little "Mexican" and "my friend Salvador" – my Spanish name – and boasting about my command of Spanish, which he considered "remarkable for an Indian".

I might have found such comments humiliating but for his transparent goodwill and kindness. If he repeated the prejudices of the conqueror, he did so thoughtlessly. Once, when he saw me in danger, he gave proof of friendship by throwing a protective arm round me against a fellow countryman and so spared me a terrible punishment.

Not that he made concessions to me when it came to sealing a deal. I had to negotiate as hard in the fifth year of our acquaintance as the first, even though we had long since grown used to the banter that would lead us to agreement. If I let slip my guard, shook his hand at the wrong moment or signalled a premature assent, he would pounce on my carelessness, insist that a deal is a deal, and claim the higher price.

"Bad luck, my little Mexican," he would cry. "It's about time I won a round with you." Though on the few occasions when he could claim a victory, remorse would seize him and he would slip some extras into the handcart, "so you won't get into trouble with the boss."

"If you were my only customer, little Mexican, I'd have gone out of business years ago," he'd tell me in a tone of exasperated weariness. Deep down, I believe the inequality of our status – he being a free man and I a peon – fired his generosity. All he demanded in return for "losing" our negotiations was the pleasure of the tussle.

Our friendship thus played out in negotiation and banter, its foundation taken for granted, its solidity unquestioned until, one day, it was put to the test. We were disputing the price of a couple of turkeys – a bird the Spaniards had never seen before they came to our country – when a sudden hush came over the market. People stopped what they were doing, Martín and myself included, without at first knowing why. We did not have long to wait. From the far end of the passage between the stalls, two uniformed soldiers were approaching. As they drew closer, we saw behind them a man with a woman, followed by another soldier and several servants.

"Must be damned aristocrats with that body guard," Martín muttered.

The group moved slowly, stopping first at one stall and then at another. We looked on curiously as they made their way towards us, wondering who they might be and perhaps a little relieved to see that they bore no aggressive purpose. As they drew closer, however, I became uneasy. Something in the woman drew my attention, the way she carried herself, upright and proud yet gentle, and though she wore a long gown in the manner of Spanish women, her dark hair and skin betrayed her as one of us. Surely I knew her, and yet I hardly dared to believe what my heart told until she came fully into view and then there could be no doubt. Tecuichpo.

Her name escaped my lips while the group was still several stalls distant. Those standing close by – mostly of my own kind – pretended not to have heard. Martín hissed at me to keep quiet and to take my eyes off the strangers if I wanted to keep a head on my shoulders.

417

One of the soldiers stared in my direction and then turned with a bow to address Tecuichpo's companion. Clearly a Spaniard of distinction, he was dressed in a fine white doublet with gold trimmings, dark-red hose, and a black hat with a green feather. On his belt he carried a long sword with bright stones glinting on the handle. The soldier explained something to him and then both glanced in my direction.

"Looks like you've put your foot in it, my little one," Martín said.

"It's Emperor Moctezuma's daughter," I whispered.

"You know her?"

"My mother suckled her."

"Well keep quiet about it."

"I will."

"Don't even look at her."

What confusion of feelings: love, need, fear of authority and of betraying myself and her too! How should I react? Part of me wanted to steal away unobserved so as to avoid risk to my life and her tranquillity, but a mad desire also tugged at me to throw myself at her feet, to clasp her in my arms, knowing that I would be cut down but happy to leave this world in the joy of her touch.

Before these wild thoughts could find expression, the visitors were upon us. I lowered my gaze as Martín had instructed, but I could hear their approach, the rhythmic tread of the two soldiers, the uneven footsteps behind. I listened. They halted. The Spaniard asked Martín a question, something about the quality of his *embutidos* and were they fit for a princess, and I knew she was standing there, in front of me. I told myself not to look up, not to tempt fate with emotions that were difficult to hide and dangerous to display. But my mind goaded me with a question that had no answer: how could I let someone so cherished pass by as if she were a stranger, she who carried in her person the living record of who and what we were?

418

Martín launched into his familiar patter, assuring his visitors that no butcher in the whole of New Spain offered finer *embutidos* than were to be found on his modest stall. No expense was spared in their preparation. All the ingredients were of the highest quality. How fortunate that they had stumbled on the greatest sausage-maker west of Madrid.

The Spaniard laughed. "Enough already…"

"Here, sir, are two of my most popular products, a string of *chorizos* and a fine piece of *serrano* ham. No money, sir, no. A gift, sir, to celebrate the honour of your visit, sir, and that of the noble lady of course. Once you have tasted them, sir…"

As he said "noble lady", I raised my eyes, and there she stood, her arm balanced lightly on that of her companion, older to be sure, a little fuller as befitted a mature woman, but more beautiful even than the image of her I carried in memory.

"Tecuichpo," I muttered, my voice sounding loud in my ears.

Martín, startled, broke off in mid-sentence and both he and the Spaniard looked in my direction. Only Tecuichpo seemed not to have heard.

"Tecuichpo," I said again and this time she glanced at me but with no sign of recognition. For an instant our eyes met, but I saw nothing in them except, perhaps, a barely perceptible flicker (I have always told myself so) before she looked away again.

"Who is this man?" the Spaniard asked Martín.

"Servant of one of my customers, sir. Comes to buy meat."

"Is he not aware of the insult to my wife?"

I have no words to describe the hurt of that little sentence. Nor can I count the times those words have resounded in my thoughts, like a scar that will not heal. Later I learned that Tecuichpo, renamed Doña Isabel, had been received into the Christian faith and so had departed the world we once shared and been reborn to a new one.

The Spaniard's question demanded no reply and Martín offered none. Instead, he meekly handed a string of chorizos and a leg of ham to one of the servants and bowed his head as the Spaniard, after a nod to one of the soldiers, walked on with his princess. I stared after them, hoping that Tecuichpo might risk a parting glance, but she did not.

As soon as the retinue had disappeared from sight, the soldier, who had lingered behind, seized me, put an arm round my throat, and began to force-march me in the opposite direction. We had travelled no more than a few paces, however, when Martín appeared. Somehow, despite his bulk, he had managed to get ahead of us. "Wait a minute, soldier," he ordered in a tone of command I had never heard before. "Mind telling me where you're taking this Indian?"

"He's due for a thrashing at the very least," the soldier replied. "They'll hang him as like as not."

"Not this one," Martín said.

"What do you mean?"

"Let him go."

Sensing a conflict, people were already gathering to watch.

I felt the soldier's grip tighten so that I could barely breathe.

Martín repeated his order: jaws clenched, lips pressed together, his huge form blocking the passageway.

"If you don't move out of the way, butcher–" The soldier broke off in mid-sentence, pushed me hard to one side and reached for his sword. But in the instant it took for his hand to reach the hilt, a long, heavy blade settled against his neck, held there by Martín's enormous hand.

"I use this to cut the heads off beasts," Martín said, "and it'll do yours just as well."

"What do you want of me," the soldier muttered. He was breathing heavily. "I'm just doing my duty. And this is a native you're protecting."

"Tell your superiors the little Mexican tried to run away and you had to finish him off. They won't mind."

"They won't believe me."

"You've plenty of witnesses." He had raised his voice, appealing to those who stood closest to the scene, many of them fellow traders. Martín was a popular figure.

A chorus of voices – some Spanish, some Mexican – responded with cries of "let him go", "do as Martín says".

The argument continued for a while, but the soldier could make no headway and in the end he capitulated.

"A dead Indian, a live Indian. I suppose it makes no odds," he conceded.

Martín lowered his knife. "We must not part in anger," he said, beaming with sudden good humour. He insisted on shaking the soldier's hand, "because after all they were compatriots", leaving the latter no alternative but to acknowledge his defeat with good grace and to accept the generous gift of sausages that Martín pressed on him as a token of their friendship.

When he had gone, Martín pulled me to my feet and folded me into a monstrous embrace, holding me so tightly that I had to beg him – with failing breath for I was in danger of suffocating – to release me.

Later, when the crowd had dispersed, I did my best to offer him a formal thanks, but he would here none of it.

"You've cost me a fortune today, little Mexican. Now about those turkeys…" It was not until we had struck a deal and I had loaded the birds onto the handcart that he allowed himself another reference to what had taken place. "Friends are hard to come by," he said. "We have to take care of them. Just do me one favour – forget about that woman. If you see her again, move out of range."

I think those words helped me to see that, like Tecuichpo, I too had entered a different world and had a place there if I would but take it.

As it happened, that incident was the last I ever saw of Tecuichpo – Doña Isabel. I heard that she died a few years ago, though I cannot vouch for it. Looking back on that encounter in the market, I still can't say for sure if she knew who I was. Maybe she could not acknowledge me even had she wanted to because she had shut off the old life and could no longer access the past with its memories of pain and loss. They say she owned much land, and made slaves of her own people by whose work she and her husband lived as the wealthy Spaniards do. The woman I encountered in the market looked and dressed and carried herself as if she belonged to the conquering race and not, as we do, to the vanquished. Could it be that we are separated less by race and history than by our station, and that survival demands different sacrifices, sometimes of others, sometimes of ourselves, according to time and place and the will of the gods?

Of Martín I can say more because we continue to meet every week in the market. A boy attends his stall nowadays, while Martín sits by in a huge rocking chair chatting to customers and smoking tobacco, which he has taken to with much relish. He has a second chair reserved for me that he will allow no one else to use. Out of habit, he still calls me his "little Mexican" but I know that he values our friendship as much as any for he has told me so, and he has let it be known among the Spanish traders, too, all of whom treat me as Martín's friend. It is something.

SEVENTY-FIVE

MEXICO CITY – SEPTEMBER 2010

James

On the day of my departure, Olivia invited me to lunch at her home.

"Nacho will be there," she said on the telephone. "He's looking forward to seeing you. He says you met once before."

"Does he know about us?"

Olivia laughed. "Of course not. He probably guesses that something happened but as long as it's not confirmed, he won't worry. He's a man of the world."

They lived in a middle-class neighbourhood of neat houses nestling behind tall iron railings. Nacho greeted me with a handshake. He looked older than I expected, slightly stooped, salt and pepper hair with a drooping moustache of the same colour.

"At last we meet. Olivia has told me so much about you," he said.

I braced myself for an inference but he picked up my suitcase, put his other arm round my shoulder, and led me into the house with a warmth that left no room for nervousness.

At the door, Olivia embraced me as an old friend before leading me inside, while her husband called "the boys".

We entered a spacious rectangular room with a dining area dominated by a long wooden table laid for seven. Occupying the remainder of the room were three cushioned sofas set at angles in front of an open hearth. Wide leaded windows gave onto the front and rear gardens. The interior walls – of white-painted concrete roughly finished to resemble stonework – were hung floor to ceiling with oil paintings and bas-relief sculptures. Two paintings caught my eye: one of a couple in profile against a background of fired earthenware, the other of a bright red face, round like the sun with eyes and mouth childlike in their simplicity and yet oddly discomforting.

"They look like Tamayo's," I said. "Aren't they worth a fortune?"

"We bought them twenty years ago in a little art gallery," Nacho said. "They were cheap in those days. Nobody thought a Zapotec artist could be important. They aren't so highly prized even now."

"They're wonderful."

"Come," said Olivia, "I want you to meet someone."

In one of the sofas, engulfed by its size and the softness of the cushions, sat a frail, elderly woman in a printed floral dress, and by her side, a young woman wearing a crisp beige trouser suit over a white blouse. The young woman stood up as we approached and shook my hand.

"Sonia Morales, delighted to meet you."

"*Encantado, señorita.*"

Morales? I looked at her and then at the old woman who was gazing up at me with dark eyes and the hint of a smile.

"María Isabel?"

"*Sí, joven. Soy yo.*"

I leaned towards her and her thin arms grasped me and drew me down until my face lay against hers.

"María Isabel," I whispered.

"*Sí, joven.*"

"My mother doesn't see too well any more," Sonia said.

"You've met my daughter, Sonia?" María Isabel asked.

"Just."

"She's the clever one of the family."

"She's also very beautiful."

A rumble of heavy feet on a staircase interrupted us. Two young men in their twenties erupted into the room followed by their father. Nacho introduced them as Alberto and Davíd. After shaking my hand, they excused themselves, Olivia begging them in vain to stay for lunch. Before leaving, they kissed their mother and embraced their father.

"I can't do anything with them," Olivia said happily.

"Exactly as it should be," said Nacho.

This domestic scene reminded me of the physicality of emotion in this country, the ease with which love expressed itself through touch and caress, without any of the associations of guilty inappropriateness and sinister predation that weigh so heavily on the Anglo-Saxon world. And I saw, too, that in such a setting, Nacho had no need to know more of whatever his wife had shared with me, for the past was mere incident and lacked the power to impose itself on the intervening years of family life. In every sense that mattered, time and distance were as interchangeable on the map of human experience as in Einstein's universe.

Over lunch, Sonia told us that she had recently finished her exams and had started work as an assistant to Professor Delgado. She glanced at Nacho.

"One of my brightest students," said Nacho.

I asked María Isabel where the family was living.

425

Sonia answered for her mother. "We have an apartment in the Colonia Nápoles – a little crowded because we are many but the area is good."

"When I met your mother, you were all living…less well."

María Isabel smiled, her head nodding from side to side, unsteady on its pin. "*Sí, joven*. In those days, our house was of cardboard. What a game we had when it rained. Water pouring in. It's better now for us thanks be to God. Not everyone has been so lucky."

"That's true, señora," Nacho agreed. "We still have too many poor in this country. Too much injustice."

We fell quietly to our plates, subdued by Nacho's remark and by the images of inequality invading our thoughts.

Alberto interrupted our reverie by bursting into the room. He had hurried back to join us for coffee and dessert. After kissing his mother and acknowledging his father, he walked round the table to shake everyone's hand before taking a seat beside Sonia – for whom he had evidently returned. As soon as the two had finished their coffee, he made an excuse for both of them to withdraw so that he could show her the house. An image of Olivia flashed into my mind as I knew her thirty years before, naked and beautiful.

"They get on well," María Isabel said.

"I believe we met once before," said Nacho, changing the subject and addressing me directly. "I think it was at a seminar with Tomás Segovia the poet. You were the only foreigner. Perhaps you don't remember."

"I remember it well. Segovia gave a lecture on a poem by Gilberto Owen."

Nacho nodded.

"Jacob and the Sea," I continued. "The poem gripped me with its contrasts of love and cruelty, so much so that I learned it by heart. '*How beautiful you are, Devil, like an angel with sex, only much more ruthless, When you are the dawn and my night is more night because I await you. When your silken skin tramples my abstinence like a cloven hoof…'* Then suddenly the last line: *'Tomorrow another sailor will limp along the shoreline.'*[72] And I would have had no idea what it meant if Segovia hadn't explained the reference to the Bible and Jacob's fight with the angel, and that anyone who struggles with meaning, with the spirit of life and death, anyone who has touched the underworld or the heavens is maimed by the experience and that disability runs through all of western culture as sacred, a sign that those who limp have been touched by god."

"We have great writers," Olivia murmured.

Lunch at an end, Nacho embraced me before leaving to give an evening class at the university. Time, too, for me to catch my flight. Alberto and Sonia appeared, looking dishevelled and happy, to bid me farewell. I bent down to María Isabel. She in turn drew me towards her and kissed me.

"You will always be in my heart, *joven*," she said, "even when I'm in heaven."

"And you have never left mine," I told her.

Olivia drove me to the airport. We said farewell just as we had greeted each other a few days before, the same angle of her cheek to my lips. She handed me a silver bookmark engraved with my name. "A little memento of your visit."

I dropped it into my shoulder bag, proceeded through passport control and waited in line for my bags to be searched. When my turn came, I found myself at the intrusive mercy of an overweight official in his fifties wearing an ill-fitting uniform and an expression of terminal boredom. He rummaged first in my suitcase and then in my shoulder bag. From the latter, he drew out the silver bookmark and held it up.

---

72 *Qué hermosa eres, Diablo, como un ángel con sexo pero mucho más despiadada,*
cuando te llamas alba y mi noche es más noche de esperarte,
cuando tu piel de seda se clava de caprina pezuña en mi abstiencia…
Mañana habrá en la playa otro marino cojo.

"Is this a knife? Knives are not permitted on aircraft."

"It's not a knife, *señor*, merely a bookmark. A gift from an old girlfriend."

"It could be used as a knife. I'll have to confiscate it."

"Surely you don't think…? I'm an ordinary citizen. Do I look like a terrorist?"

"Of course not, *señor*. I'm not saying…"

I took a twenty-dollar note from my wallet and using the open lid of the suitcase as concealment, slid it into his hand.

"*Muy bien, señor.*"

He released the bookmark and with a gesture ordered me, unsmiling, to pickup my bags and move on.

As the aircraft reached cruising altitude, I accepted a glass of wine from one of the cabin crew and eased back the seat rest. I had a book ready to read on the flight, one that I have carried with me over the years, keeping its dog-eared pages together with tape and glue: Poetry in Motion – Mexico 1915–1966. I sought out some lines by Tomás Segovia that I remembered reading aloud to Olivia one afternoon in the aftermath of love:

…I never want to remove my eyes from you…

Let me never lose sight of your mysterious presence

Your gaze of wings and silk and black lake…

Your body infinitely more yours than mine could ever be for me…[73]

I reached into my bag again for the bookmark, as if for the image of her as she was when Segovia wrote those lines. It wasn't there; the official had taken it after all. Maybe that was how it should be.

---

73 *…quiero no apartarme nunca de tí los ojos…*
déjame siempre ver tu misteriosa presencia
tu mirada de ala y de seda y de lago negro…
tu cuerpo infinitamente más tuyo que para mí el mío…

SEVENTY-SIX

TENOCHTITLAN – 1563

Alva

"We've grown old together, you and I," Father Hernández said to me the other day.

He must have noticed my astonishment because after hearing my stock response, "*Sí, Padre*" (in all my years in his service, I have never once ventured to disagree with him), he shuffled off muttering to himself about whether or not the Lord would think me fit for heaven.

What surprised me about his remark was the idea that we had been "together", as if our bond were not that of master and servant but a comradeship of equals. To be sure, we have spent the best part of our lives in this church compound, seen each other daily, learned the rudiments of each other's language. Still, I hesitate to look him in the eye, and try as I will, I can't reconcile myself to his god, though I tell him otherwise so as to spare myself his lectures on the subject – and his threats that without faith, I will spend the afterlife burning in the fires of hell.

His intentions are worthy. He believes he must do his best to save me from a terrible fate. He does not see that his is the god whose army turned our city into rubble, murdered the finest flowers of our race, burned our libraries, smashed our idols, raped our women, tortured our leaders, sent plagues among us for which there is no cure, destroyed our way of life. I can't deny the power of such a god, but how can he be mine or of my people? We have grown old, certainly, Father Hernández and I, but not together. Masters do not travel in the same carriage as their slaves.

Why would he say such a thing? I have noticed that priests such as he live without family. They do not lie with women and therefore have no children. Could loneliness have caused him to look for someone with whom to share his closing years? He knows that I too am alone, though he has never sought the reasons – so different from his own. What he doesn't know is that I would rather pass to the underworld with Martín, who treats me as a free man, than with a priest who, if he could see into my thoughts, would condemn me as an unbeliever to an eternity of pain.

Still, when my life comes to an end, I will die with more hope in my heart than seemed possible a few years ago. After the war, surrounded by loss and ruin, I thought we survivors would drown among the countless foreigners who flooded in from across the sea. Most who have come, however, are men and, for want of choice, they have taken our women for their pleasure and sometimes, like Tecuichpo, even for their companions. And so children are born who carry our life within them. We must see to it that they also carry our language and our way of being.

I like to think that Mexico cannot be truly conquered. Strangers may take possession of the land and call it their own. But land is not a people. To conquer the Mexica, we would have to disappear from the world with only rubble and broken idols left to show that we ever in flesh and blood walked upon the earth. While we live, we may suffer defeat in war, but no one is conquered while their thoughts remain their own, and what are triumph and loss but illusions in the larger flow of time? So let it be.

In the end, joy in life has little to do with what befalls us. Whether the world is kind or cruel as we pass through cannot alter the way we see it. Ask me if Huehue or Moctezuma died happier and I will tell you it was the shit-shoveller. Those like Tlaco who knew the emperor said he lived like a statue, his features as immobile and sullen as stone; that he never knew contentment; that he was vindictive, cruel, lived in fear of betrayal and of losing face. But I can still hear the sound of Huehue's laughter and see the crinkled lines of his face wreathed in kindness and good humour. And I remember how he recited the poet's song:

Ha tamonahuiyazque,
ha tahuellamatizque, tocnihuan?
Ca niccuiz in yectla xochitli,
In yectli yan cuicatl.

Should we not enjoy our days?
Are we not to seek pleasure, my friends?
For my part, I will bear flowers in my arms,
And songs in my heart.

Acknowledgment

I wish to express my gratitude to two great scholars of pre-conquest Mexican culture: Ángel María Garibay (1892-1967) and Miguel León-Portilla (1926-2019) in whose works – listed below – I found material and inspiration for creating the Nahua songs and poems included in this book.

Veinte Himnos Sacros de los Nahuas – recogidos por Fray Bernadino de Sahagún, ed. Ángel María Garibay, UNAM, Mexico 1958

Poesía Indígena de la Altiplanicie, ed. Ángel María Garibay, UNAM, México 1940

Quince poetas del mundo náhuatl, ed. Miguel León-Portilla, Editorial Diana, Mexico 1994

Los Antiguos Mexicanos, Miguel León-Portilla, Fondo de Cultura Económica, Mexico 1961

Visión de los vencidos (Crónicas Indígenas), ed. Miguel León-Portilla – with versions of Nahua texts by Ángel María Garibay, Historia 16, Madrid 1985.

 Matador